Clash of Eagles

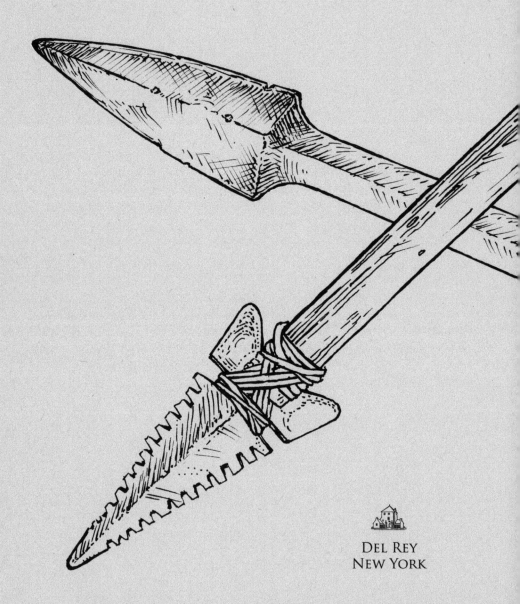

DEL REY
NEW YORK

Clash
of
Eagles

Book One of The Hesperian Trilogy

Alan
Smale

Published in the United States by Del Rey, an imprint of Random House, a division of Random House LLC, a Penguin Random House Company, New York.

DEL REY and the HOUSE colophon are registered trademarks of Random House LLC.

Library of Congress Cataloging-in-Publication Data
Smale, Alan (Astronomer)
Clash of eagles Book one of the Hesperian Trilogy / Alan Smale.
p. cm.—(Hesperidan Trilogy; Book one)
ISBN 978-0-8041-7722-1 (hardback)—ISBN 978-0-8041-7723-8 (ebook)
1. Rome—History—Fiction. I. Title.
PS3619.M33C53 2015
813'.6—dc23
2014034654

Printed in the United States of America on acid-free paper

www.delreybooks.com

2 4 6 8 9 7 5 3 1

First Edition

Book design by Elizabeth A. D. Eno

For Karen

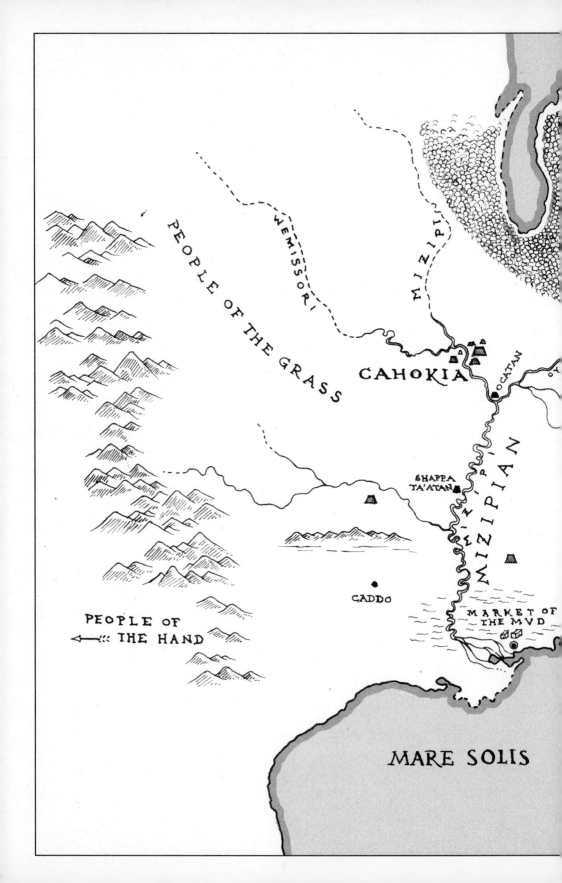

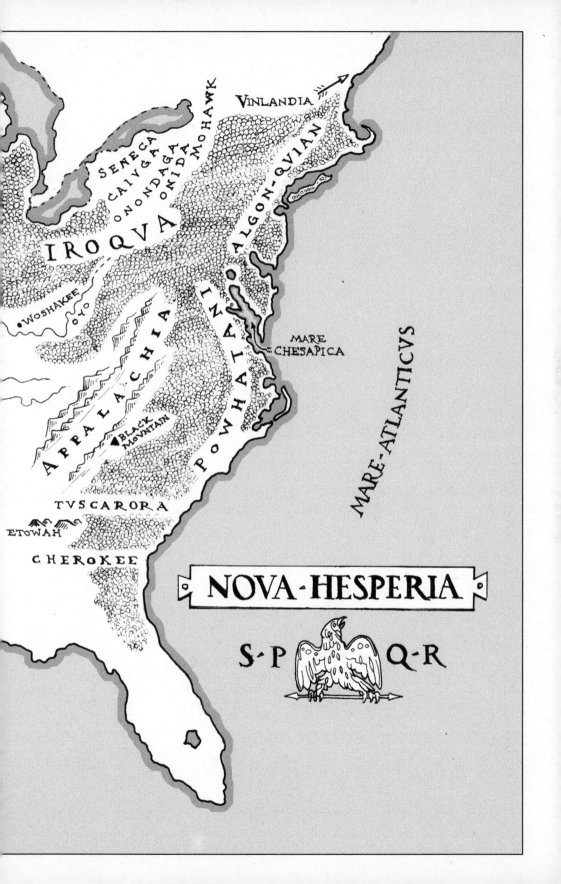

VINLANDIA

SENECA
CAIVGA
ONONDAGA
ONIDA
MOHAWK

IROQVA

ALGON-QVIAN

WOSHAKEE

APPALACHIA

POWHATAN

MARE
CHESAPICA

BLACK
MOVNTAIN

MARE-ATLANTICVS

TVSCARORA

ETOWAH

CHEROKEE

NOVA·HESPERIA

S·P   Q·R

CONTENTS

PART 1

NOVA HESPERIA

CHAPTER I

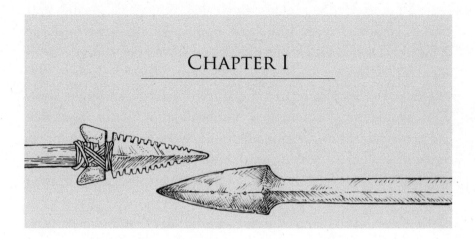

Gaius Publius Marcellinus galloped his horse along the marching line of his Sixth Cohort, racing toward the site where two of his men had been slain by skulking Iroqua warriors.

Trumpets blared, steel armor clanked, and leather creaked, but the footfalls of his legionaries made little sound in the torn-up soil. The corps of engineers that went ahead of the 33rd Legion carved a road through the Hesperian forest barely wide enough for ten men to march abreast. The skies were heavy with cloud, and this late in the afternoon there was no singing and little talking in the ranks. In front of Marcellinus stretched a column of men three miles long. Behind him, the Seventh and Eighth Cohorts would extend back at least another two miles, guarding the two hundred supply wagons that groaned in the Legion's wake.

First Centurion Pollius Scapax awaited Marcellinus on the path, pointing into the trees. Marcellinus slid off his horse and peered into the undergrowth. "In there?"

"Two men dead," Scapax said tersely. "Half a dozen grieving. Thirty or so standing guard."

"Tullius?" The Tribune of the Sixth.

Scapax shrugged. "Not here yet."

Marcellinus barely hesitated. His adjutants were far forward with the

First Cohort, but if he couldn't trust Pollius Scapax, he couldn't trust anyone. He strode off the path, between the oaks, and into a small gap in the trees hardly wide enough to be honored with the name of a clearing.

One of the dead legionaries rested against an oak, an Iroqua arrow in his shoulder and a short spear buried deep in his gut. The other had been clubbed to the ground, arms broken and legs splayed, his throat slashed open. Both men had been scalped, their foreheads and hair hacked away roughly, leaving shocking bloody gashes in their place.

Torn bushes and trampled grass gave evidence of a short, sharp struggle. The soldiers' weapons and armor were gone, presumably stolen by their murderers.

The dead men were both fresh-faced and callow; neither could have been more than eighteen years old.

At least it was obvious how they had died. Other legionaries had been found with ferocious wounds ripped into their flesh or—maybe even more terrifying—barely a mark on them at all.

Six men knelt in grief by the corpses, bare-headed, presumably the tent mates of the dead. "Helmets on, soldiers," said Marcellinus. "Let's not lose anyone else here."

They gaped up at him, incredulous. One man thrust his helmet back onto his head with bad grace. The rest ignored the command, their faces a mixture of pain and insolence. Marcellinus chose not to notice. The days of unquestioning obedience were far behind them now.

Three contubernia—twenty-four men in all—faced outward to secure the clearing, heavy spears at the ready. Their eyes scoured the thickets. The men looked nervous, and with good reason. The dead legionaries' wounds were fresh, and the alarm had been sounded recently. Whoever had done this could still be hiding in the brush nearby.

Not twenty feet behind them the behemoth of the 33rd Legion still marched grimly through the eternal forest.

Marcellinus looked again at the mourning soldiers. He was intruding on their pain, and nothing he could say or do would ease it. "Just a few moments longer," he said to Scapax. "Then everyone goes back to the column." The men on guard looked relieved.

Scapax cleared his throat. "Burial detail, sir?"

Marcellinus looked again into the underbrush that surrounded them. Pale light filtered through the trees. The last thing he wanted was to have his men exposed any longer than they had to be. But the Seventh Cohort, with the baggage train, must be only minutes away.

"Their choice," he said. "They can wait by the column, put the bodies onto one of the wagons, and bury them tonight, or say their goodbyes now and be done."

The centurion saluted. As Marcellinus turned to leave the glade, the trumpets sounded again, one far to the west followed by another just a few hundred feet away, a complicated sequence of notes.

It was a message from Corbulo, his First Tribune. Marcellinus was needed at the head of his Legion. Another obstacle, and clearly something their engineers could not tackle easily.

Marcellinus's shoulders and back ached from riding. Worse was the low throb of tiredness behind his eyes. Pulling himself wearily back into the saddle, he drummed his heels against his horse's flanks.

As he rode forward, the Legion was already slowing to a halt.

Pollius Scapax's voice boomed out across the sloping hillside. "First Cohort, stand to! Eyes up, spears out!"

The men of the First fell into battle formation, three ranks in close order. Tired soldiers set the hafts of their heavy pila in the ground and held them angled outward. Archers stood with bows strung and quivers of arrows at their feet, blinking owlishly at the shallow valley. The evening breeze ruffled the crests on their steel helmets.

No enemy was in sight, but men had died today, and this was hostile territory. The First was mustered to repel any potential attacks while the slaves and the soldiers of the other cohorts made camp.

The castra was a roving town that re-created itself daily in its own image. They rebuilt it identically every afternoon, occupied it for one night only, then abandoned it the next morning: civilization on the march through Nova Hesperia.

The engineers had chosen a site only a couple of miles past the Legion's sudden stop. As usual it was a large open area near a river, on rising ground, with little nearby cover that could be exploited by attackers. Even before the First and Second had arrived, the engineer corps had measured and marked with a knotted rope where the streets would be laid out. Now, the meadow became a hive of activity. Up went the ramparts, earthworks six feet high around the perimeter surrounded by a deep defensive ditch. Down came any trees unfortunate enough to be within the square, their wood pressed into use to construct the raised guard platforms at each corner and above the four gates. Up went the tents, down went the latrines. Finally, up would go the five temples obligatory for feeding the Legion's faiths: the Mithraic temple, the shrines to Cybele and Sol Invictus, the open-air altar and prayer rail of the Christ-Risen, and the small but rather forbidding statue of Jupiter Imperator, which had more presence than any of the real-life Imperators Marcellinus had served.

The camp was square, with streets constructed on a grid. Its alignment was as constant as its arrangement, with the wide main street called the Cardo aligned north-south so that the evening and morning light shone down the long cross streets named for the cohorts and centuries that lived on them. The rank and file lived eight men to a tent, and Marcellinus's own Praetorium tent formed the center of the camp. Latrines, the field hospital, stables, the smithy, and the armory were arrayed around the rim with open areas at the corners for the slaves.

As always, Marcellinus walked the streets as the camp took shape, receiving reports from his tribunes and centurions. The air reeked of stale sweat and fresh wood and rang with shouted orders, banging and sawing, and curses in a broad range of dialects.

"Two more soldiers down," said First Tribune Lucius Domitius Corbulo moodily, joining him at the Eastgate.

Beside them legionaries and auxiliaries shoveled earth with resolve, digging the deep ditch and throwing the soil up to where their colleagues were shaping the ramparts. The soldiers knew they were being watched by their commanding officers as well as their centurion, and their faces gleamed with sweat. At the crest of the ridge of earth, other men set and bound the sharpened stakes that formed the palisade.

Marcellinus stepped aside to let a line of a dozen slaves pass, sweating and weighted down by the bags of grain they carried in from the wagons. "Two more."

"Were they good men?"

"They're all good men," said Marcellinus. "Legionaries, not auxiliaries, if that's what you're asking. Young."

"Do we know what happened?"

"Saw a deer and went after it, most likely. Fresh meat is hard to come by."

Corbulo nodded, acknowledging the convenient lie. "Of course."

Deer rarely approached a marching column. Much more likely that one of them had been caught short by his stomach and had left the column to relieve himself, guarded by his friend, and both had died for it.

Better for a soldier to die in battle, or hunting, than squatting behind a bush.

"Either way, it has to stop," said Corbulo. "Stupid deaths like these?"

Marcellinus glanced sideways. His First Tribune was veering perilously close to insubordination. "The centurions have their orders. We can't be more clear. Nobody leaves the column, ever. Nobody lets down their guard for a moment." He shook his head in frustration and set off to walk north along the intervallum inside the still-growing rampart. After a pause, Corbulo followed in his wake.

The 33rd Legion had begun to leak men as if from a slow wound soon after they'd broken camp and marched away from the Mare Chesapica. Now, four weeks inland, they were down fifty-eight soldiers, this out of a legion in which their so-called centuries had been only seventy men strong to begin with.

They had cleared villages and taken slaves but had yet to be engaged by the enemy in a real fight. Their losses were due solely to harassing actions: the lone arrow flying out of the trees, the blade from behind, and more often than not, the unexplained disappearance. It was hard enough to march into an empty continent on the wrong side of a giant ocean, blaze a trail, tramp twenty miles along it each day, and then build a marching camp the size of a small town every night without having to risk being picked off by cowardly savages whenever a few twigs' worth of cover separated you from your comrades.

And, since Marcellinus's cohorts were rounded out with the superstitious denizens of Roman provinces from Aethiopia to Scythia, Magyar to Hispania, and back around, the night camp was always alive with rumors. Man-bears were hiding behind trees; huge hawks were swooping in from the air to pick off the valiant Roman infantry one by one. Giant rodents burrowed up from beneath them. It seemed that in the wilderness of a foot soldier's imagination no animal was allowed to be normally proportioned. Superstition was strong at the best of times in a rabble like that, and the farther away from Urbs Roma he took them, the worse they got.

Marcellinus shook his head. Nobody in his right mind could feel comfortable with two months of ocean separating him from the Imperium. But however far afield his duties took him, he wasn't about to start believing in giant hawks.

That left the natives. They were everywhere; on the fleet's arrival the shores of the bay had been crowded with villages of cringing fishermen. Many had fled. Others were now roped to the heavy carts that made up the Legion's supply train.

Now, though, they'd left behind the fisherfolk and the berry pickers. The villages they passed might be empty, but the woods around them were not. Hiding behind the tree trunks of inland Nova Hesperia was a different breed of native altogether.

Marcellinus turned. "Where have you put our prisoner?"

"Should be in your tent by now." Corbulo cocked an eye at him. "I thought you might want her undamaged."

"Very considerate of you," said Marcellinus, straight-faced. "You have a heart after all."

"If I do, this country will be the destruction of it."

"Aren't we supposed to march over all obstacles in our path?" If Corbulo could needle him about the deaths, the least Marcellinus could do in return was chide his tribune for letting the whole Legion come to an ignominious halt.

"I was at the rear of the First at the time, consulting with Gnaeus Fabius," said Corbulo, and then, seeing Marcellinus's frown, grudgingly drew himself up a little straighter. "Yes, sir . . . It shouldn't have happened. I take responsibility. And I'll talk to Scapax about it."

"Scapax was back with me, at the . . . with the Sixth."

"That would be part of the problem, then." Corbulo grinned wryly. "But stopping like that? The First Cohort? I'm surprised they didn't break into a run, straight at her."

"So am I," said Marcellinus. "So am I."

Corbulo glanced past Marcellinus, grimacing. "Ah. Here comes our Britannic ray of sunshine."

Aelfric, Tribune of the Fourth and Fifth Cohorts, gruff and mustachioed, was walking down a lane toward them. He had shed his armor, but retained the padded jerkin that went between that armor and his tunic, and the scarf that prevented chafing at the neck. Unlike the other legionaries he wore braccae, the woolen breeches of his countrymen. The overall effect was unflattering. Corbulo sniffed.

Aelfric eyed Corbulo with trepidation but addressed Marcellinus directly. "West rampart is up and ready for your inspection, sir. And most of my lot are tents up and set for the evening." He looked leftward at the northern ramparts, where the Second and Third were still toiling, and grinned at Corbulo. "Your fellows need a hand, do they?"

"Hardly," said Corbulo, frost in his tone. "They just do a proper job."

"Oooh," said Aelfric. "Is that a fact? And what do mine do, then?"

"Gentlemen," said Marcellinus.

Corbulo raised a sardonic eyebrow. Certainly he himself was a patrician, a Roman citizen of the Imperium. The Briton could never be.

Dropping the matter, Aelfric looked at the skies. The wind was picking up, the tents flapping behind him. "Might rain in a bit." To Marcellinus he said, "Want me to stop by the Sixth? See if Tully needs anything?

He's probably got his hands full, what with the burials and morale and all."

"I'm sure he can't wait to see you," said Corbulo. "Well, sir, my centurions will be expecting me. Enjoy your interrogation."

"Interrogation?" said Aelfric.

"Up with the news as always," said Corbulo, and with a curt nod to Marcellinus he strode forward to heap invective on a soldier of the Second who had stopped to lollygag with his shovel mate.

Aelfric watched Corbulo go. "He seems out of sorts. What did you do to him?"

"Two more dead," said Marcellinus.

"I hadn't forgotten," said the Briton. "But they weren't *his* men."

"Shouldn't matter. Either way, it's my fault." Marcellinus was their Praetor. As Corbulo had just made very clear, it was his job to stop things like this from happening.

"If you say so. But at least it's a slow bloodletting. At this rate we'll have time to walk twice around the world before they get us all."

Marcellinus grunted. Corbulo was right; Britons had a dark sense of humor.

The blacksmiths' forge was already up and running, sending a wave of heat across the intervallum area. Two of the smiths were shoeing horses, a third hammered out the rim of a wagon wheel that had gotten bent on the road, and a fourth man made nails. Marcellinus looked longingly at the flurry of activity, the flying sparks, and the hiss of the quenching. Back in Campania his family had owned a small horse farm with stables and a forge, and on calmer evenings on the march Marcellinus liked nothing better than to banter with the Legion's smiths and sometimes even take a turn at the anvil. Shaping iron was a simpler art than leading soldiers.

He turned his back. Tonight he had other duties.

"Aelfric. With me, if you please."

It was time to face their captive.

———

"I am supposed to ravish you now," said Marcellinus, "but I shall not."

The young Powhatani brave gaped, shaking so hard that the necklace of seashells on his chest rattled and the crow feathers nearly fell out of his hair.

"Not *you*," said Marcellinus, exasperated. "You're here to translate. Tell *her* that."

The Powhatani word slave—they called him Fuscus because he was brown—only now saw the woman sitting on the blanket on the floor of the Praetor's tent headquarters. Fuscus eyed her warily but didn't seem upset on her behalf. Why would he be? She wasn't of his tribe.

He babbled at her, and she replied rather haughtily for one of her smallness and unpromising situation. Compared with the mellifluous flow of patrician Latin, their primitive Algon-Quian tongue sounded like baby talk and twigs snapping. Fuscus gestured as he spoke, and the gestures were not hard to interpret.

Her eyes narrowed. The expression she turned on Marcellinus was contemptuous.

Perhaps she had misunderstood. Algon-Quian had an ungodly wide range of dialects. Marcellinus turned to the word slave. "She understands? She is my prisoner. I should brutalize—use?—use her, then give her to my men. Custom demands it. But I shall not do that. I show her mercy. Yes?" Here he knew he was on safe ground; "mercy" was one of the first words Fuscus had learned. He repeated it often.

The woman spit out a couple of words, steel in her sneer. Marcellinus sighed. "Now you're supposed to tell me what she said."

Fuscus cleared his throat nervously. "She say, 'Disgust.' And that Roman are like wild dog." Alert to Marcellinus's irritation, he took a step back. "*She* say it, sir. Not me."

"Ask her what she was doing in the road in front of my army," the Praetor said.

Such was the height of the 33rd Legion's superstition that it had taken just one lone woman to bring them to a halt. Faced with twenty braves, or a thousand, his soldiers would have charged and hacked them into bloody meat. But at the sight of a solitary woman standing calmly in their path with flames leaping up from a fire behind her, they'd slowed to a ragged stand-easy and looked back over their shoulders for orders. Marcellinus would have to thicken their spines somehow before they reached the lands of the mound builders and their—Norse-alleged—city of gold.

"She from west farther, sir. Over hills-and-hills. Hear tell of Roman, come to see. She chieftain, daughter of chieftain. She ask you, go home where you come."

"I see," said Marcellinus.

The woman struggled to her feet. The two guards who stood in the doorway of the Praetorium tent looked at Marcellinus hopefully, but he shook his head at them, allowing her impertinence.

The woman gestured.

"She ask what you want."

Marcellinus looked at her. "We want your land. Your country. Your gold and spices. Whatever you have is now ours."

She glanced blankly at Fuscus and spoke. Fuscus translated, "She say you cannot take the ground. Cannot take sky. It here always."

Marcellinus stepped closer. Well nourished compared with these people, he towered over her. The woman's eyes widened, but she stood as tall as she could. Given that the Romans in their metal armor and red-plumed helmets must have appeared utterly alien to her, her courage was considerable.

Her forehead was flat and her hair muddy, but her cheekbones were set higher than those of the coastal tribes and her bronze skin seemed better cared for. Most telling of all, she stood straight and calm, with a dignity their local captives lacked. She was the dusk, the evening star; she was Nova Hesperia, the giant unopened continent of it. And he, Marcellinus, was a bully and past his prime. Worse, he knew it.

He made his decision. "What is her name?"

"She calls her Sisika," said the brave.

"Well, if Sisika really is 'daughter of chieftain,' the tribes to the west will know her. Yes?"

"Yes," Fuscus said.

"Then say this to her: 'Sisika, I set you free. You will run ahead of my army and tell all the tribes of the Iroqua, tell whoever else might lie in our path that the Romans are coming.'" He struck his steel chest plate with his fist, making an impressive clang. "She will tell the tribes we are mighty and shall not be stopped. We will pass through their lands and onward to the west."

The Powhatani quacked and popped at Sisika, relaying Marcellinus's message. He continued: "If the tribes allow us passage, we will spare them. But if they resist, if any more of my men die in these cowardly sneak attacks, we will kill every man, woman, and child, every deer and bird, and the land will be silent and broken after our passing. She must tell them this or their blood will be on her head." Marcellinus jabbed a finger toward her, and she flinched. "On *you*, Sisika. We will wipe them from the earth because of *you*."

As Fuscus finished his translation, Marcellinus held the woman's gaze, stern and unblinking. She stared back. Her deep brown eyes were very disconcerting.

She babbled while Marcellinus waited. One of his soldiers languidly drew his pugio, a short dagger, and poked the Powhatani from behind. The word slave yelped and said, "Sisika will do this, tell tribes Praetor words."

She had certainly said more than that. "And . . . ?"

"And, but, land of Iroqua, very savage, very hurt. Men of harsh."

"And?"

"And once past Iroqua, west, is then great city, people of Hawk and Thunderbird. These will fall on you and . . . burn, cut off your hair, laugh."

The city the Norsemen had told them of, perhaps. Marcellinus's interest quickened. Now he was getting somewhere. "This Great City has gold?" He showed Sisika the ring on his finger, the plate on his table, the small statues of his lares, his household gods. "Gold?"

Sisika reached for one of the statues, and Marcellinus had to slap her hand away. Her eyes flared, and for a frozen moment he thought she might actually hit him back, guaranteeing her instant execution. Instead she turned to Fuscus and spoke.

"She ask who these toy persons are."

"They are not toys. Ask her about the gold."

Fuscus tried again, pointing anew to the various objects, but the answer was clear in her demeanor. She didn't understand gold's significance. She had never seen it before.

Fuscus looked nervous. "She say no gold."

"And how far to the city?"

"Far and far. She not know."

Of course she didn't. How could she?

"All right," said Marcellinus. "Enough. Get them out of here. Wait outside with them until I come."

He turned as his guards manhandled the captives out of his tent. "Well, so much for that. What d'you think?"

"That your soft heart will be the death of you." Aelfric stood comfortably at the rear of the Praetorium tent, arms folded.

"Likely enough," said Marcellinus.

Aelfric shrugged. "Not bad, to send the woman on ahead, though the Iroqua will probably cut her down before she gets twenty miles."

"She made it here. She can make it back."

"Perhaps."

Marcellinus walked to the tent door. "Did Sigurdsson return yet?"

"None of the scouts did. I'll bring 'em to you right away when they do."

"Hmm."

"Don't fret," said his tribune dismissively, walking past him out of the tent. "Our Norsemen can rip the arse out of any 'men of harsh' *this* sorry land might throw at 'em."

Strictly speaking, they weren't yet Roma's Norsemen. The Imperator Titus Augustus had shut down the Viking raids on the coasts of Britannia thirty years ago, gobbling up Scand for the Imperium and acquiring every Dane and Geat and Sami clear up to Ultima Thule. But these days a nation had to live loyally within the Pax Romana for two hundred years before its people were granted full citizenship.

By the calendar of the Christ-Risen that Aelfric's people and most of the Norse used, it was A.D. 1218. It was a full 1,971 years since the founding of Roma, *Ab Urbe Condita*, and it would be the year 2100 by the Roman reckoning before every new Scand child would enter the world a Roman citizen.

The Norse didn't care a fig about the delay, though. A pragmatic race, they had already carved themselves out a critical role. Roma needed its navy now as never before, and the well-traveled Norsemen were just the people to help them run it.

After a decade of stagnation and even retreat under the rulers who had followed Titus, the new Imperator Hadrianus III had grasped the nettle. Right out of the gate the man had thought big. He had vowed at his coronation that under his leadership the power of Roma would encircle the globe. Only twenty-nine years of age at his accession, he had figured that if he set the wheels moving quickly enough and remained popular enough to die of old age, he might leave as his legacy a world where the sun never set on the Roman Imperium.

Candidly, Marcellinus thought the man was cracked. Roma had reined in its expansion in the first place because of the high cost of defeating the Khazars and the eastern sultanates. And now Hadrianus was trying to expand the Imperium even farther into the east at precisely the moment when the Mongols and Turkic tribes were swooping westward into Kara Khitai and southward toward the Chin Dynasty. Leave the buggers to it; that was what Marcellinus thought. Let the nomadic Mongol Khan swallow all that and try to administer it. Roma should hold its current line in the sultanates around the Ganges, which Temujinus—or Chinggis, or however he wanted to be addressed these days—had shown no ambitions toward. Eventually the Mongol Khanate would overreach itself and crumble, and that would be Roma's moment to march eastward again. In the meantime, the real estate from Hispania to the Himalaya and from the barren northern ice to the fetid jungles of Aethiopia Interior should surely be enough Imperium for anyone.

But of course it wasn't, and so here they were, pushing on beyond the sunset into Nova Hesperia, New Land of the Evening. Because clearly if your territorial ambitions were stalled in one direction, it was only logical to spearhead an attack in the other. As if controlling two frontiers at the same time hadn't been a nightmare for the Imperium ever since the first Nero had tried to conquer the barbarians beyond the Danube while simultaneously holding the Parthians at bay.

"Imperators," as Marcellinus might say over dinner, "have no sense of history."

And "Soldiers," as First Tribune Corbulo would regularly chide him in response, "have no grasp of economics."

Corbulo would remind Marcellinus that if popularity cost money, keeping your army loyal cost even more. Bread, circuses, and bribes: big money. And if you were an Imperator spending coin faster than you were collecting it in taxes, you needed somewhere to invade so you could steal more.

Which brought Marcellinus full circle, back to the Norse.

His officers awaited him in the open air outside his Praetorium, armor off and cloaks on against the growing breeze of dusk: Corbulo, sitting off to one side looking bored; Aelfric, tapping his foot; Tribune Marcus Tullius, solid, earnest, sunburned, and blond, still brooding over his lost men; Gnaeus Fabius, the magistrate and junior tribune Hadrianus had assigned to the 33rd Legion at the last minute either to get him out from underfoot or to spy on Marcellinus (most likely both); and Leogild, his Visigoth quartermaster. Nearby, Marcellinus's guards stood bunched around Sisika and Fuscus.

Sisika's eyes were wide. When they had frog-marched her into the Praetorium the castra had been little more than an outline, a large square ditch and embankment surrounding virgin meadowland. In the intervening hours the camp had sprung up all around them to become a living community of wooden buildings and goatskin tents as familiar to Marcellinus as his hometown and as foreign to Sisika as the surface of the moon.

Fuscus, who witnessed this transformation every night, had adopted an even more noticeable air of condescension toward her. It was a dynamic Marcellinus often saw among slaves and captives, this petty jockeying among the have-nothings for small scraps of perceived status. He smacked the word slave over the head and pointed down the lane toward the slave quarters, and Fuscus cringed obsequiously and set off at a trot.

To his guards, the Praetor said: "Safe conduct for this one, out of the camp. No interference. Understood?"

Leogild assessed her up and down. Sisika's hair was still matted and her knees skinned, but her light brown skin was clear and uncreased, almost glowing in the evening light. She was easily the most attractive native they'd come across since landing on the shores of Nova Hesperia. He cleared his throat. "Couldn't the men have a go with her first? Send her on her way proper like?"

"That is hardly what 'safe conduct' means," said Marcellinus.

"They'll be disappointed," the Visigoth said.

"They can have the next hundred women we snare. This one has a job to do. I'm sending her out with an ultimatum to the villages ahead: get out of our way or perish." He turned back to his guards. "Two of you, escort her to the Northgate. Nobody meddles with her."

Sisika looked back at him with those disconcerting brown eyes. His soldiers unhappily watched her go.

Corbulo eyed her legs as she walked by. "We make agreements with barbarians now?"

"This is a new land," said the Praetor. "We try things, and we see what works. Worst case, we've only lost one woman."

"Whatever will get us to the gold more quickly," said Gnaeus Fabius.

Too many expectations of gold. "And home more quickly," said Marcellinus.

It was quite the walk Sisika had to make down the Cardo, hemmed in close by a long silent gauntlet of leering soldiers, but Marcellinus noted that she walked with her chin up and showed little fear. Maybe she really was "daughter of chieftain."

"Cut off your hair, eh?" murmured Aelfric, referring to the woman's earlier statement. "A dire threat. I'll wager you didn't see that one coming."

Marcellinus swallowed. Aelfric had not seen the dead soldiers scalped by the Iroqua just hours earlier. "Perhaps they could arrange me a manicure as well," he said.

Fifty yards shy of the Northgate, Sisika came level with the wooden shrine housing the golden eagle standard of the Legion. Her mouth dropped open, and she turned to stare at it. The Aquila, wings upraised, lightning bolts around its feet, glowered back at her with its beady raptor gaze. The aquiliferi honor guard stepped forward instantly, hands on sword hilts; orders or no orders, if Sisika had disrespected the Aquila, its guards would have cut her down where she stood. But Sisika knelt, bowing so deeply that her forehead touched the road.

Tribune Corbulo stood to watch. "She's left it a little late to curry favor."

Marcellinus had seen real eagles here, wheeling high in the dusk skies. And Sisika had mentioned them. "Maybe the Aquila is sacred to her, too. She honors the bird, not us."

Sisika stood and walked on through the Northgate. If she ran, she waited until she was out of sight.

Marcellinus wished he hadn't asked her name.

Corbulo tutted. "A wasted opportunity to raise morale, Gaius. It'll be trouble, and we need no more of that."

"One woman," said the Praetor.

"Still bad tactics with the troops as fractious as they are."

"Discipline's a problem," added Gnaeus Fabius, who rarely passed up an opportunity to state the obvious, or suck up to Corbulo.

"An even worse problem if the redskins keep picking us off." Marcellinus looked around him. "I did not request a discussion on this topic, gentlemen."

"God knows what we'd all have caught off her," Aelfric said loudly, glancing around at the other tribunes. "I doubt these people ever bathe. A good commander safeguards his men's health as well as his own."

"And the men bless you for it, sir," Leogild said to Marcellinus, straight-faced.

Marcellinus grimaced. "Don't we have a convenient festival coming up? Where do we stand on wine?"

"We'll be out of corn and cheese first," said the quartermaster. "Wine's not yet an issue."

The other officers looked at one another. None of them had any clearer idea of the date than Marcellinus did. His adjutants would be keeping track, but they weren't here. And Marcellinus had raised the issue of supplies again, and that was something none of them wanted to think about.

"Let's call it Easter," said Aelfric. "That's a movable feast anyway."

"Tomorrow, not today," warned Corbulo. "Let them walk off this disappointment first."

"Of course," said Marcellinus, who'd had no intention of inciting his legionaries with extra liquor this night. "All right. Get out there and make it known that she was a chieftain's daughter whom I sent out to calm the way ahead and that I'm not setting any new precedents with this. And then remind them that tomorrow's Easter."

"Most of them won't know what that is," said Fabius.

"Or care," said Marcus Tullius, scratching under his helmet.

"Tell 'em it's the Christ-Risen feast of double wine rations," said Aelfric. "They'll understand *that*."

"Dismissed," said Marcellinus, and Leogild and most of his tribunes—Corbulo, Fabius, Tullius—saluted and set off through the camp in various directions to brief their centurions.

Naturally, Aelfric dallied. "So, Praetor. Even when you were younger. Would you have spoiled her?" He raised his hands. "Nothing implied. I'm just making conversation."

Marcellinus looked at him. It was an impertinent question, but that was Aelfric's way. Britons were very direct. "You don't have daughters, do you, Aelfric?"

"No."

"Ask me again when you do."

Much like the Britons, the Norse were a smart people who understood the advantages of being important to the Imperium and the
terrible costs of being an irritant. But every race contained its bad
apples, and so the Imperator Hadrianus had issued an edict allowing
no quarter to Norse pirates, those renegade few who refused to come
to heel.

Two years earlier, a Roman navy warship had intercepted a Norse
longship approaching the north coast of Hibernia. An innocent Norse
vessel sailing home from the recently discovered Vinlandia had naught
to fear from a Roman inspection; this longship had tried to use its
greater maneuverability to escape and, when that failed, had tried to
bluff the Roman captain, badly.

After a brief but fierce engagement the Romans boarded the vessel to
find it stuffed with gold plate, jewelry, and bizarre statues from an as yet
unknown culture, along with large quantities of turquoise and lapis la-
zuli and a few bags of spice. Alas, Roman efficiency had slammed into
Viking berserker battle ardor with such completeness that there was
nobody left alive on the longship capable of testifying about where they
had acquired such a lucrative cargo.

Despite this inconvenience, Hadrianus was badly in need of revenue
and not one to pass up such an opportunity. It was at that point that he
had raised the priority of the conquest of the continent beyond Vinlandia.

There was no reason to suspect that the equatorial regions of the
Evening Continent should be any richer than those of famine-stricken
Aethiopia. Logically, then, the gold must have originated around the
same latitude as Roma.

Hadrianus sent scouting parties into Nova Hesperia. Those who returned brought back tales of a large city of mounds, longhouses, and at
least ten thousand people in the plains far beyond the mountains. Ad-
mittedly they hadn't brought any gold back with them, but then again,
the locals hadn't allowed them within the boundaries of the city.

Very well; Hadrianus could spare a legion to throw at a high-risk, high-return venture. All he needed was the right Praetor to lead it.

By dawn the next day the legionaries had folded tents and were on the trail again, heading west in as straight a line as they could manage. Which, being Romans, was pretty damned straight.

For a while, Marcellinus's tactic seemed to be working. The harassing actions the Iroqua had been running against the Legion's advanced corps of engineers and its flanks and stragglers stopped. Freeing one woman had apparently earned the Fighting 33rd a clear path all the way to the mountains. Even the grumpy Domitius Corbulo had to agree it was well done. The miles fell away under the military sandals of the Legion. Day by day they left the sea farther behind, and the interior of the giant land opened up around them. They covered two hundred miles without a single death, and the march became so routine that the centurions grumbled that the men were getting soft and added daily weapons drills.

True to his word, Marcellinus left the villages unscathed. Usually the inhabitants deserted them and hid out in the wilds till the army had passed; sometimes they sat sullenly outside their scrappy, insect-ridden hovels with their heads bowed. *Good enough*, thought Marcellinus. *They may be untouched by civilization, but at least they comprehend a threat when they hear it.*

Truth be told, Marcellinus felt sorry for them. He hadn't asked to be sent here, and these folks hadn't asked to have a Roman legion trampling their pastoral quiet. The Hesperians had so little to begin with. Roma's ancient ancestors might have been painted men very much like these, long before all the marble buildings and the metalsmithing and the lawmaking. They were less than farmers, and their tiny patches of sickly corn were so pitiful that even Leogild didn't think them worth requisitioning; as far as Marcellinus could tell, the inland peoples survived by trapping coneys and picking berries. Marcellinus could be ruthless when necessary, but there was no glory in waging war against beggars. The true enemy lay ahead, in the Great City that the Norse scouts had reported and Sisika had confirmed.

Soon enough, the terrain creased around them and rose up into a series of rolling ridges and craggy mountains that Fuscus, in his broken tongue, called Appalachia. The peaks were neither as classically sculpted as the Alps of Europa nor as grand as the ranges of the Himalaya, but they had a hazy comeliness to them that reminded Marcellinus of parts of northern Italia. Despite the rigors of getting the Legion through such a trackless wilderness, Marcellinus thought it a land of some charm. Then again, he got to ride a horse up the interminable hills.

They had only a couple of dozen horses, and only the Praetor and his tribunes, scouts, and dispatch riders rode them. They were much too valuable to put to work hauling the supply wagons, and besides, they had slaves for that; to their surprise the Hesperian shores had proved to be devoid of beasts of burden. Aside from the Powhatani themselves, that is.

Marcellinus felt the odd twinge of guilt about resting easy in the saddle, but he genuinely needed to conserve his strength. At night in castra his men might drink their watered wine and gossip over games of knucklebones with no further cares, but Marcellinus spent those hours meeting with his quartermaster about the ever-present question of supplies, his tribunes and armorers about their battle readiness, his centurions on matters of discipline, and doing a hundred and one other things. There was never a lazy evening for a Praetor. Technically he might have left some of these details to others, but with his authority over the Legion as precarious as it now seemed, it behooved him to stay involved with all aspects of legionary logistics. If Marcellinus could be everywhere at once, no one could talk about him behind his back.

The men noted his diligence and didn't seem to begrudge him the ride. Their job was the hike; his was to look after his men and keep them as comfortable as possible, not waste the sweat they were donating to the enterprise, and be trusted not to squander their lives when the crunch came.

Around noon one day Marcellinus found himself riding near Marcus Tullius, who hailed from Etruria. "What d'you think, Tully? Long views and enough land for anyone once we get rid of some of these damned trees."

Tullius made a sour face. "Over that whore of an ocean? It's too far from Roma. Nobody is going to want to come and farm this crap."

It was true enough. Romans were not natural sailors, and the trans-Atlanticus voyage had been a puking nightmare the way the big troop transports rolled on a heavy swell.

"Some men might prize a bit of separation from the capital. Independent sorts, regulation-weary?"

"Ex-convicts, maybe. But they won't be growing olives or grapes on these slopes. Bad soil, worse sun. You've seen what passes for corn here? Even the Norse can't make a go of it, and they can farm Graenlandia."

"Well, only with sheep and a few cattle," said Marcellinus. "They don't grow crops there."

"Either way. No, if the redskins have gold, we want it; if not, we just kill the bastards off. Hack ourselves a bloody road right across the continent and use it to go and stab the slant eyes in the back."

Marcellinus winced. "That might be quite a distance," he murmured, and didn't raise the issue of natural beauty again.

Whatever their scenic glory, the Legion found the high ridges heavy going, and their average daily march dropped from twenty-two miles to nearer twelve. On one frustrating day when they had to ford several streams and backtrack twice in search of a route the baggage carts could negotiate, they advanced only seven. Finding areas broad and flat enough to host a full castra added to the challenge, and Marcellinus sorely missed the guidance of Thorkell Sigurdsson and his other Norse scouts, still conspicuous by their absence.

His men grumbled, and even Leogild's sunny Visigoth humor began to cloud over. Each day took them farther from the coast and stretched their provisions even thinner. Battle was ahead, a city to be sacked, spoils to be had—but how far? It was the conversation on every tongue, the thought in everyone's mind.

Arguments broke out over the Legion's campfires on a nightly basis. Best to go on to death or glory, risk everything on a single throw of the dice? Or eventually beat a prudent retreat to the coast, winter up, and next spring surge back along the path they had already carved?

They could go on, but once winter came, the march would be over. The Legion would have to build a fortress and hunker down within it, unable to travel again until the thaw. And then what would they eat?

Marcellinus heard the discontent and shared it, but all he could do was show a resolute face and push on.

Then came the ambush, and everything changed.

CHAPTER 2

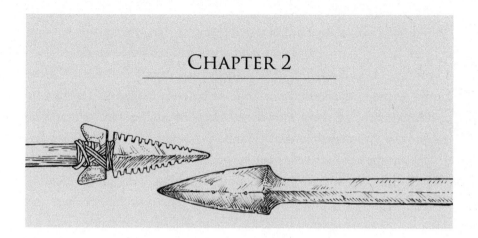

The Legion marched down a long valley that was narrow and high-sided. Below them the plains opened up; they had conquered the Appalachia, and an enemy might suppose that high spirits would make them careless. But the Fighting 33rd were career soldiers to a man, and this was such an obvious site for an ambush that there really had to be one.

They had been sighting Iroqua all day: a fleeting glimpse of a warrior behind a tree here, a feather seen over a rock there. Once the trend was clear, Marcellinus passed the order down through his tribunes and centurions that the men were to ignore the natives until actively engaged. That way, the natives might assume they'd gone unnoticed. Even as the Iroqua tried to lull the Romans into a false sense of security, Marcellinus was sanguine that he had instead tricked them into overconfidence.

As his cohorts tromped downhill, eagerly awaiting the onslaught and whistling like longshoremen, Marcellinus felt that surge of energy he loved, the spark that ran like lightning through well-trained men on the verge of combat. Today, at least, his Legion was behind him to the last man.

Sure enough, where the way was narrow and the crags around them tall, the Iroqua attacked.

Predictable. And yet not.

Suddenly the air was full of darting shapes that whirled above them as if the laws of nature and common sense had ceased to apply.

Briefly, Marcellinus feared he had lost his mind. A swarm of giant moths seemed to assault him, and for several dangerous seconds he couldn't even bring them into focus. Then the shapes resolved, and he realized they were farther away than he'd thought.

The moths were actually men harnessed to rigid triangular wings.

Each pilot was spread-eagled beneath his wing, lying prone, steering left and right by tugging at a stiff cord that passed under his chest and extended from wingtip to wingtip. Yet control of these crude aerial vehicles required only part of their energy; each also held a bow and could reach across himself to pull arrows from a streamlined quiver strapped to his thigh to rain down death on Marcellinus's troops. Each aviator wore a mask bearing the powerful hooked beak of a falcon.

His thoughts raced. Men in flight! Had this been a circus display, he might have laughed for joy. But these wings were not for sport; their intent was deadly serious. Marcellinus had been caught flat-footed. Behind the beat of the battle, he mentally lunged to catch up.

He was not the only one. Legionaries shouted, turning around and around, flinching from this strange aerial threat but finding nowhere to retreat to. Centurions barked, fighting to regain control. Close to Marcellinus a soldier lifted his shield over his head in defense, knocking the helmet off the man next to him. Soldiers slipped and fell.

The archers of his First Cohort, the cream of his military crop, capable of recognizing an enemy no matter what direction it came from, laconically pumped arrows into the air. But they were below the thrust of the attack and so were forced to fire back over the mass of the Legion. If they weren't careful, there was a real risk that their arrows would fall among their own fellows.

As the Iroqua swooped over the densely packed line of the Legion, their deadly projectiles rarely failed to find a mark. These arrows needed only to wound, poison-tipped for sure; legionary after legionary toppled to the ground like a cut-string puppet moments after suffering no more than the shallowest nick. Fortunately, most of the arrows plinked off armor.

The trumpeters looked to Marcellinus for commands. A pair of flying Iroqua buzzed them, an arrow thwacked into the ground by his side, and Marcellinus found his tongue. Over the pandemonium he shouted, "First, Second, Third: split line! Fire outward! All other cohorts, orbis!"

The signalmen nodded, and the trumpets brayed.

As always, the 33rd Legion spread over several miles. The Iroqua attack was concentrated on his first three cohorts, bottling up the men behind. Expecting a ground assault from both sides, Marcellinus had planned a split line anyway, and it was also the best formation to resist an attack from the air. The cohorts in the rear were overextended, and for them the hollow-square orbis formation would form the best defense even if hordes of barbarians flooded down the ravine behind them, given the advantages of discipline and steel armor.

More Iroqua swooped and soared; more legionaries fell. Up the hill the cohorts of Tullius and Aelfric were breaking into sections and forming ragged squares. Beyond them, in the distance, the slaves were crawling under the supply wagons. From somewhere came the unmistakable scream of a horse.

On either side of Marcellinus, the First and Second fell into close-order parallel lines, facing out to the left and right. Behind the First, the honor guard clustered around the Aquila.

From the sky came stones as well as arrows. Some of the flying warriors were armed with slings rather than bows. More arrows came from Iroqua archers standing on the crags above, shooting from much greater range.

One of his signiferi took an arrow in the neck and went down, screaming. Carrying no shields, the standard-bearers made easy targets from above. Next to Marcellinus an adjutant received an arrow to the arm; calmly, the man knelt and used his pugio to slice into his skin to yank out the arrowhead and then sucked the poison from his wound.

Then the Third Cohort broke in panic. Legionaries milled and shouted, unable to evade the soaring enemies without trampling their comrades. Such a loss of discipline was unacceptable. Where was Corbulo? Marcellinus recovered himself, left the First under the control of his senior centurion, Pollius Scapax, and ran uphill into the ranks of the Third.

Marcellinus thought Corbulo was down and wounded until he reached his tribune's side. Instead, Corbulo was watching the wings whirl over his head with something like terror, his hand thrown up as if to ward off a curse.

Marcellinus applied his foot to Corbulo's ribs. "Up, man! Must your men see you trembling and afraid?"

"What?" Corbulo's eyes searched for him as if the tribune were drunk or in darkness.

"Men in kites! You're not so daunted by that?"

"Kites?" said Corbulo in a daze.

"Aye, kites," the Praetor said. "And aboard them, just men."

"Men!" said Corbulo. "Of course, I see it now," and rose to his feet. Rushing into a group of his archers, he marshaled them to shoot long at the Iroqua who stood on the crag tops waiting to launch. A fusillade of arrows knocked a good half dozen of the attackers off their perches, and several more leaped off the crags, consigning themselves to the air. At least one crashed to earth immediately, a victim of the treacherous winds swirling up the valley.

Marcellinus leaned back to study the flying braves. It was the Praetor's job to think strategically, but he was hard-pressed to devise a strategy against an enemy that soared out of reach.

Now, up the hill, he saw smoke. A flaming arrow had embedded itself in the canvas of one of the supply train carts and was setting a merry blaze. Critical provisions were at risk.

Marcellinus grabbed a pilum from a fallen soldier and ran to launch it upward at the nearest Iroqua. The javelin drifted lazily behind the wing and dropped back to earth; Marcellinus had badly underestimated the flying brave's height and speed.

"Lead with your bows!" he shouted. "Fire ahead of them! *Well* ahead!"

Across the Legion the wave of terror had passed. The cohorts were getting back under control, shields arrayed in defense and bows at the ready. The men had found themselves an enemy they could fight. It became a game now, though a deadly one; the more practiced Iroqua slew three Romans for every wing the legionaries sent tumbling into the rocks.

Marcellinus took a bow from a man of the Third who had fallen to his knees, cradling his arm. Nocking an arrow, he swung it upward and let fly. And then he did it again. His second arrow pierced an Iroqua's stomach, and he savored the man's scream as he plummeted into the ground.

The bow was not Marcellinus's favored weapon. Let no man say the Praetor was not flexible in a pinch.

When the final tally came in, the Legion had lost two hundred fifty men in the skirmish. In return the Romans had shot down several dozen of the wings. Perhaps a couple of dozen more of the Iroqua had fallen out of the sky from overzealousness, or had misjudged the canyon walls, forging their own disasters.

Marcellinus loathed the loss of even a single legionary out here beyond the edge of the world, where they could not be replaced. Yet the deaths of their comrades brought such fire and fury to his men that considered as a whole, his Legion might well be the stronger for it.

"Cowards and skulkers, shooting their poison arrows from on high! We can hardly clamber into the air and meet them blade to blade!"

Side by side they rode at the head of the Legion, Praetor Gaius Publius Marcellinus and First Tribune Lucius Domitius Corbulo, as they had in happier times out east.

"Aye," said Marcellinus tactfully. Corbulo was obviously not taking his momentary lapse of reason on the battlefield well.

Corbulo skewered him with a glance, and Marcellinus added, "As cowardly as picking off our legionaries when they step out of their marching line or go to fetch firewood."

"Worse. What kind of man hides in the air?"

"The flying itself is not without risk," Marcellinus pointed out.

"Merely learning the skill must present its hazards. Plenty of opportunities to tumble out of the sky onto your head."

"The basic trick looked simple enough," Corbulo grumbled. "Those men were not warriors."

Marcellinus doubted the simplicity of it. He had ordered his adjutants to ensure that one of the crashed wings was packed into his cart for later study. The wing appeared to be constructed of deerskin scraped thin as parchment and stretched over pine and cedar spars and adorned with feathers. Certainly Marcellinus would never jump off a cliff under such a flimsy frame and knew of no other sane Roman who would. And once the Romans had organized and begun to get their enemies' range, the Iroqua had retreated by flying back up to land on the crags once more, also hardly an easy task.

The skills of these aerial warriors must have taken a lifetime's learning. More ominously, the fliers must be supported by their community while honing their talents. On the shores of the Mare Chesapica it had been every Hesperian's chore to trap his own fish. Here, though, they were no longer scrabbling farmers and part-time warriors, but specialists. It implied civilization and a level of organization previously unthinkable for barbarian tribes such as these.

"But there'll be no next time," said Corbulo, shaking Marcellinus out of his reverie. "It's a trick that only works once. You know how the wind rises on meeting a steep slope? Their kites ride on that. But the mountains are behind us now, and I see no terrain ahead where they'd have that advantage."

Marcellinus glanced sidelong at his First Tribune. "No more element of surprise."

"No more surprises," Corbulo agreed.

And yet a small part of Marcellinus regretted that he would never see such a thing again. If the aerial Iroqua had not been deadly enemies, he could have watched them all day. Idly, he imagined himself jumping off the Palatine Hill and circling over the glitter and marble of the Roman Forum before alighting in front of the new Curia building where the Senate met. Now *that* would be a triumph!

He wished he'd opened his eyes even wider to take it all in.

Domitius Corbulo checked back over his shoulder. "And speaking of savages . . . a word in your ear about Aelfric."

"Aelfric?" Marcellinus said, startled.

"He presumes too much. And you allow too much."

"Is that so?"

"Yes. Have a care, Marcellinus. Your friends should be patrician Romans, not Norse, Britons, or any other bloody outlanders. You'll be chumming it up with Fuscus next."

"Last I heard, Britannia was still solidly part of the Imperium."

Corbulo gave a laugh so short that it was almost a cough. "Then you've never been there. Did you know I was stationed up in Caledonia, at the Wall of Antoninus? For three years."

"That's a long time," Marcellinus said.

"Dismal bloody weather and a complete mess politically. You wouldn't believe so many client kings and bizarre religions would fit onto such a small pair of islands. I could write you a list of the odd things they believe. It's one of the few regions left in the Imperium where they still have genuine shamans, you know. The Hibernians are the worst: mystics and moaners. They'd wail as soon as talk."

"Somehow Aelfric never struck me as the wailing type," Marcellinus said.

Corbulo would not be distracted from his theme. "Britons are all natural plotters and counterplotters; it's in their blood. And they mask it with congeniality. They'll worm their way inside your thoughts, get you talking, though they're quiet ones themselves. Before you know it, you've told 'em secrets they can use against you."

That brought Marcellinus up short. He had certainly discussed many things with Aelfric that it would never have occurred to him to tell Corbulo. About his long-lost wife and daughter, his doubts that they'd find gold, and probably a dozen other topics that he probably shouldn't have confided to a tribune. All because he felt comfortable with the man. What did he really know about Aelfric's motivations?

"I see I'm not wrong," Corbulo said. "And what do you know of him in return? Do you even know where he was born? I do. Eboracum. He's a Brigante."

The Brigantes were a Celtic gens with an ancient heritage in the north of Britannia, one of the last tribes to fall to Roma during the conquest. But that was a thousand years ago.

Marcellinus frowned. "He's really a Celt? Isn't Aelfric a Saxon name?"

"Celt, Saxon, they're all mixed up together now. But either way, Aelfric is too familiar by far. Ponder on it; that's all I ask."

"I'll take care," said Marcellinus. He paused. "Thank you."

Corbulo smiled.

Imperators come and go. In Marcellinus's time he'd seen six and served four, and he would not have donned the Imperial purple himself for a million sesterces. He would sooner have lived as a beggar in a shack than be Imperator of Roma, and everyone knew it, so he had survived many a bloody Imperial transition to become one of the most senior legates in the army. His problem with Hadrianus III was the Imperator's ambition, not his own.

Gaius Publius Marcellinus was that rare thing, a Roman who was actually born in Urbs Roma. His family had been military for four generations, and his gens was not well to do. His father had retired from the army a senior centurion and legionary camp prefect with the characteristic streak of the martinet in him, a man who wanted his boy to make his own way in life. Thus, despite his obvious pedigree, Marcellinus had entered the military with no letters of recommendation and had gone through boot camp with the conscripted men rather than beginning his career with a commission. It had taken him four years of hard work as an optio and then five further years as a centurion in a dangerous campaign against the Ayyubid Sultanate before he was promoted to tribune by acclamation.

By contrast, Lucius Domitius Corbulo was a member of an old patrician family and a distant descendant of that Gnaeus Domitius Corbulo who had served as a Consul under Caligula, commanded the armies of Germania Inferior under Claudius, and been appointed Governor of Asia under Nero. One day he would make the leap from army to politics and perhaps end up a Consul himself. Perhaps it was predictable, then, that Corbulo was the most alert to their place in history. More than any other Roman present he felt the full sweep of Roman power. But Corbulo was also alert to money and sought riches as well as glory. His star was rising within the Imperium.

But as Marcellinus and everyone around him knew, at forty-one years of age, twenty-five of them in the army, this would be his last campaign and his last chance for a military triumph to provide him with a comfortable retirement. Marcellinus would do his utmost to succeed. The Imperator knew his man.

When Hadrianus had picked Marcellinus to lead the 33rd into the new land across the Atlanticus, Marcellinus had chosen Corbulo to be his First Tribune. Corbulo had served under him in his Sindh campaign, and Marcellinus knew him as a man of breeding, spotless record, and endless anecdote. If Marcellinus had to dine with someone for months on end, he wanted him by all means not to be tedious.

So what did it say about Marcellinus that he now spent more time with Aelfric the Briton and Sigurdsson the Norse scout than he did with the Romans among his tribunes? The truth was that his Roman compatriots reminded him too much of the corruption and casual nepotism that had increased again under Roma's most recent Imperators. At least Corbulo had overcome his silver spoon to become a tribune of considerable quality, but Tully and Fabius, each barely twenty-five years of age, had gained their tribuneships through patronage and cronyism. In contrast, Marcellinus and Aelfric had scaled the ranks through skill and bravery and sheer bloody-minded hard work. Not for the first time, Marcellinus was blazing his own social trail. A practice, he recalled, that was not without risks.

"You didn't tell me about the wings," said Marcellinus.

Fuscus gulped. The Praetor's pugio was at his throat, and the word slave was rammed back against the wooden walls of the cart he'd spent the day helping to haul across his own country.

"Not know," Fuscus whimpered.

"Oh? 'People of Hawk and Thunderbird will drop on you'? Words chosen carefully. Aren't you a clever rascal, Fuscus. 'Man of smart,' no?" He pushed the blade a little harder.

"No! I stupid man!"

"That's right," said the Praetor. "So, what next? How soon comes the next surprise from your people?"

"Mercy!" said the word slave, his eyes full of tears. "Mercy!"

Aelfric ambled over. "Sir, not to stand up for the little weasel, but Fuscus is quite likely farther from his birthplace now than he's ever been before. I doubt he knows much more about this place than we do."

Marcellinus glared at the interruption, but he recognized the truth when he heard it. Anything Fuscus knew would be hearsay, tales told over a campfire. He'd established long ago that the little runt knew nothing substantive about the Great City. But it had been worth a try.

The Praetor dropped his word slave on the ground, giving him a kick for good measure. "All right, Fuscus. One more chance. One!"

"You do know there's no gold ahead, right?" Aelfric said quietly as they walked away. "Fool's gold, maybe. A coppery mirage or two."

"Hush," said Marcellinus, though the men nearby were hard at work getting the castra situated. "Such talk is treasonous."

He was only half joking. Few of his common legionaries cared much for the lofty ideals of global conquest and would be indefinitely content to molest and slaughter barbarians. Their battle with the flying men had been a novelty. But by now they were marching on half rations across a largely uninteresting and seemingly endless plain interspersed with forestland that would be equally boring if not for the danger of being picked off and slaughtered by hidden braves.

Aelfric tutted. "You still cling to the hope that these simpletons are hiding cities of gold? You know better. You had to show that woman what gold was. She'd never seen it before."

"The gold is just over the horizon," Marcellinus said with a straight face.

"It always is."

"Maybe we'll find them something else worth the effort," said Marcellinus.

"'Course you will," Aelfric said. "That's your job. But you might want to plan ahead for what that'll be."

At the rate their supply wagons were lightening, his men might just be glad enough of a good meal. "You're a real bearer of good cheer tonight."

"One more word," said Aelfric. "Corbulo."

Marcellinus sighed.

"The centurions are reporting rumors of him freezing up during the ambush. Panicking. Not giving timely orders in the heat of battle."

"I hear rumors about giant rodents, too," Marcellinus said carefully.

"Oh, I didn't say I gave them any credence," said Aelfric. "I mean, a veteran like Corbulo? It's surely nonsense. But I thought you should know."

"Right."

Up the Cardo they saw Leogild and Corbulo step out of their respective side streets and head toward the Praetorium tent. "Speak of the devil," said Aelfric.

"He feels the same way about you," Marcellinus said.

"Does he, now?" Aelfric said thoughtfully, and Marcellinus kicked himself. Once again he'd spoken too freely.

He nodded to Aelfric and walked on, vowing it would be the last time he'd make that mistake.

Once his meetings with his quartermaster and tribunes were over, Gaius Marcellinus liked to walk the camp. A Praetor should never be a stranger to his men, not if he wanted to keep his command and his neck intact.

At dusk the castra was alive with sound, movement, and purpose as the men set their campfires to cook their fry bread and soup and corn hash.

Marcellinus strolled among the tents, past the cook pots and the knucklebone games. Around him, men were sharpening blades, polishing armor, tightening a strap, hammering a new sole onto a sandal, lancing a boil or a blister, and trying to rinse stiff sweat stains out of their tunics. Some were writing letters that they would not be able to send for months to sweethearts who probably had already forgotten them. The Praetor smiled wryly. How many heartfelt letters must the younger Marcellinus have written to Julia from the scorching deserts of the Ayyubid Sultanate while she was disporting in Roma with wealthy businessmen?

Even more men than usual were paying their respects at the temples. Soldiers had died today, and perhaps their piety was useful in calming their unease. Marcellinus envied them their ability to believe. Life on the road could be lonely for a man without a personal god.

As he wandered, Marcellinus was generally greeted with a nod, a joke, or a comment on the weather. He spared some words for the syco-phants and operators, little as he enjoyed the company of either; broke up a couple of squabbles before they turned into brawls; and reminded himself of the names of some of his more seasoned centurions. He did not, however, intrude on two men fistfighting over the attentions of one of the signiferi of the Seventh Cohort, a duplicitous lad with smooth skin and improbably long eyelashes. Nobody would thank Marcellinus for getting in the middle of *that*.

He took particular care to compliment tonight's sentries of the watch, who would get only a few hours' sleep. He also spent a while gossiping with the aquiliferi honor guard, which was easy enough to do. Not only were they veterans of a similar age to his, with similar memo-ries of old campaigns and bygone Imperators, but these were men who would give their lives for the Aquila. Their loyalty to the Legion was absolute: they *were* the Fighting 33rd.

All in an evening's rounds.

Marcellinus had begun his army days sleeping in a contubernium tent just like those he now walked by. Unlike many of his men, he did not miss Roma and rarely yearned for its comforts. However, deep within the pitiless interior of Nova Hesperia, he found that he did miss the Mare Chesapica, a bay so wide that it almost counted as a sea. He had enjoyed the slightly ridiculous sight of the immense Roman troop transports wallowing in the deep waters of the bay as the square-rigged Viking longships danced around them, tiny by comparison. The longships had guided the mighty vessels of Roma down the chilly coastline of the new continent like sprightly mice leading a lion on a leash. He had liked watching the gulls floating on the breeze and the herons wading in the marshlands, liked walking the small sandy beaches that had proved quite pleasant once they'd cleared the savages away and cleaned up the sand. It was not at all like the Campania coast in southern Italia where he had furloughed between campaigns—the land around the Chesapica was too flat for true beauty—but it had its appeal nonetheless.

More particularly, their time in the bay had marked the optimistic beginnings of their expedition, before their energy was sapped by the endless marching and their numbers were depleted by cowardly foes. Back then they had been able to hope that this whole campaign might be easy.

And back then Marcellinus had still felt the authority of Roma on his shoulders, guiding his actions.

Roma had never lost its savagery: a bit of muscle and the willingness to shed blood were crucial in keeping an Imperium strong. Kindness to your own, brutality to those who opposed you; those were the ways of Roma. The Imperium was the greatest civilizing force in the world and must remain so even if it had to hack off a few heads from time to time. But here in the heartland of Nova Hesperia they were far away from all that, so far from the Forum in Urbs Roma that they might as well have been at the bottom of the sea or—why not?—high in the air.

The farther they marched, the less Marcellinus felt Roma's power. Nova Hesperia owned a different power, something forceful and primal. The natives might be weak, but the land itself was strong, and Marcellinus had not come to terms with it. In his heart of hearts, it daunted him.

Here, for the first time in his life, Praetor Gaius Marcellinus felt like he might be the only law.

And with this thought, his sixth sense for danger suddenly came alive.

He was strolling down a lane occupied by auxiliaries. Around him a blur of provincial languages filled the air: German, Magyar, Nubian. But despite the comfortable low babble of conversation, the men nearest him were too alert by far. These were men on the verge of action, maybe about to rush him.

Suddenly Marcellinus was in the lion's den.

Was he sure?

He did not look around him again. The men might interpret that as weakness, seeking help. Marcellinus did not need help. He stopped walking and placed his hand on the hilt of his gladius.

Auxiliaries glanced about, estimating spaces and angles, checking for their centurion, who was conspicuously absent. Yes, his instincts were correct.

Marcellinus said: "The punishment for laying a hand on your commanding officer is death. I'm sure I don't need to remind you."

All heads turned toward him.

"However, that death need not be immediate. I could have you whipped till your limbs fall off and the skin peels from your bones."

He knew they were listening intently. They all understood Latin. It was a condition of service. How many of them were in on this? Who might they crown as the Legion's new legate once he was dead?

He pushed the thoughts aside. "If you have a grievance, make it known now. Otherwise—"

To his left, someone moved. Marcellinus spun and stamped down hard on him, and the man howled in Magyar. Leaving his gladius sheathed, Marcellinus grabbed the man's wrist and twisted his arm up and around in a full circle behind his back; the Magyar came up halfway off the ground and hung there, helpless.

Marcellinus looked not at his potential assailant but at the other men who surrounded him. He did not blink. This was the moment of truth. It was time for them to decide.

The auxiliaries showed their decision by shuffling back, dropping their gazes, keeping their hands clearly visible. All right, then. To the soldier whose arm he still held in an iron grip Marcellinus said, "When

I release you, fall and stay down or I'll kill you." He let go, and the man immediately toppled to a supine position, clutching his arm.

"I meant you no harm, sir," said the auxiliary. "I swear!"

Marcellinus doubted it, but any further action against the man would be pointless and would stir up even more resentment. "Then up you come, soldier," he said, and lent the Magyar an arm, pulling him to his feet. "In the future, be more careful." He looked around at the others. "Without discipline, we'll never get out of this country alive. Think on that."

He turned and walked away without looking back.

Rounding the lane's end, he glanced casually up at the signum. Third Century, Fifth Auxiliaries. Aelfric's cohort. A minor incident, but potentially a harbinger of worse to come.

Apparently, his men also felt the waning power of Roma. The farther west they went with no visible gain or reward, the more his Legion threatened to degenerate into a mob. Marcellinus could imagine another thousand miles ahead of them. And another. How far could they march before all order would be lost?

Of course, they'd probably starve first.

A week later they found the remains of one of their Norse scouts tied to a tree, carefully positioned in the path of their relentless advance.

Thorkell Sigurdsson would march no more. His thighs were blackened stumps, his legs burned off completely to just above the knee. His face was intact but hideously distorted. He had received a haircut clear through to the bone; his scalp had been hacked away, revealing the gray-white of his skull. His chest was a bloody hole where his tormentors had torn out his heart.

The wreckage of the scout was an essay in torture and barbarism. It was an act of appalling atrocity, and judging by the decaying state of the body, it had happened several days earlier. The Romans might not know exactly the route they would take, but the Iroqua did.

Once more the Legion had come to a halt. The standard-bearer looked like he might throw up at any moment, his eyes darting about nervously.

Marcellinus did not fear an ambush. They stood in a meadow with the trees well separated and little undergrowth, and they could see for hundreds of yards in each direction. The Iroqua had arranged their violent tableau with care and would allow time for the lesson to sink in.

Very well. But the lesson his men learned might not be the one the Iroqua had intended.

"Bring me my tribunes," said Marcellinus. "Then have the cohorts march past this spot. Parade order, half speed, no chatter."

Pollius Scapax nodded. "Helmets?"

Helmets off would have been the standard mark of respect, but this was enemy territory. "On. Sigurdsson would understand."

Flanked by an honor guard of tribunes and holding the Legion's golden eagle standard in his own hands, Marcellinus stood to attention by Thorkell Sigurdsson's side for the two hours it took the Legion to march past. On each of the three thousand faces, legionaries and auxiliaries alike, he saw the same expression: neither fear nor revulsion but respect tinged with a steely determination.

Toward the rear of the army came the baggage carts, hauled by their slaves. Marcellinus stared hard-faced as the Hesperians trudged by with their shoulders to the wheel, but none of them showed disrespect to the dead man. Most, in fact, looked quite sickened at the spectacle.

"That man," said Marcellinus. "Fuscus. Fetch him."

Pollius Scapax strode into the baggage train, cuffing men aside until he reached the word slave. He hacked through the cord that bound Fuscus to the cart and hauled him out unceremoniously. The five braves that remained tethered to the vehicle leaned into their task even more grimly.

Marcellinus drew his gladius and whacked Fuscus on the back of his thighs with the flat of the blade, driving the word slave to his knees. Fuscus bit off a scream as he found himself face-to-face with Sigurdsson but cried out in earnest when Marcellinus struck his bare shoulders another blow.

"This is what your people do? The cowardly maiming of captives!"

Fuscus gaped at the ruined Norseman. "Is not!"

"We don't need you anymore, verpa. Know why? Because there will be no more *talking* to your people. Only killing."

"Marcellinus, man, let him be. His kind didn't do this."

Marcellinus whirled, and the point of his gladius stopped inches from Aelfric's throat. "What?"

Aelfric took a slow step back from the blade. "Sir, Fuscus here, he's coastal. His Powhatani are crab eaters and berry pickers. The savages hereabouts are of a different stripe."

"Iroqua," said Fuscus. "Men of hurt. Many take—"

"More warlike," Aelfric interrupted. "The savages we're seeing around here are painted odd, and they move different. They're real hunters and killers." He gestured at Sigurdsson's body. "If the Iroqua got their hands on Fuscus, they'd probably do this to *him*."

The Praetor looked down. Fuscus was groveling so hard that he was practically tunneling into the ground. He seized Fuscus by his topknot and dragged the man up onto his knees.

"Look, spare him," said Aelfric. "God knows we might need—"

Marcellinus slit the word slave's throat. He died quickly, gurgling, his eyes bulging almost out of his head as he drowned in his own blood.

"Never mind," said Aelfric.

Marcellinus swayed. Had he really just slain a defenseless man in anger? Would he have done such a thing anywhere other than this despicable, gigantic, savage land?

He pulled himself together. His legionaries had died more barbarically in the trees and from the air. And here was Sigurdsson, scalped, burned, maimed. Marcellinus let go of Fuscus, and the word slave's body tumbled forward onto the ground.

Aelfric was staring. "Something you wanted to say?" Marcellinus said coldly, his sword still unsheathed.

The Briton shrugged. "Me? No. We don't need him. There'll be no more talking to his kind."

"That's right."

The atmosphere over the glade remained icy as the last echelons of the Legion straggled past. At the end, Corbulo cleared his throat, stood easy, and broke the silence. "Good. The men are fired up now. I pity the poor red bastards we encounter next."

Marcellinus nodded tautly. Corbulo and his other tribunes saluted him and the hideous remains of Sigurdsson once more and rode forward to rejoin their cohorts.

The Praetor looked down again at the mutilated body of his Norseman and for the first time on this campaign felt genuinely exhausted. Not just in his body, because physical weariness was a constant aspect of commanding a legion, but also in his soul.

All his life he had fought for Roma, struggled for rank and authority, just to be sent westward into a brutal wilderness on a fool's errand. To see his men killed slowly, one by one.

Yet again, Aelfric had presumed to stay behind. "They knew the path we'd take," said the Briton. "They arranged him here, right in our way. You bloody Romans and your straight lines."

"For gods' sakes, we *want* to be predictable," said Marcellinus. "We know where we're going. So do they. We *want* to fight them. Let the scum try to stop us. And in case you've forgotten, you're a Roman, too."

"I wonder what became of the other scouts," Aelfric said moodily.

Enslaved, perhaps. Or cooked and eaten for all they knew.

"March on, Tribune," Marcellinus responded gruffly.

He felt dazed. Could the Hesperians really not distinguish between soldiers and scouts? Did they intuit nothing of civilized conduct? How could a war even take place without scouts to guide the armies together?

"Cowards," he said. "An entire landmass of bloody cowards." Corbulo was right, after all.

Marcellinus and his tribune were off the back of the Legion now, guarded only by First Centurion Scapax and four contubernia of trusted soldiers. Normally it would be untenable for a legion commander to be this exposed, but the undergrowth was sparse and the sight lines long. A quarter mile away, and despite the recent passage of his army, he saw a pair of white-tailed deer meandering through the trees. This was very different terrain from the dense woods that lined the coast of the Chesapica.

The sandals of thousands of marching Romans and the wheels of dozens of baggage carts had beaten quite a furrow into the meadow floor. Marcellinus looked down thoughtfully, then stepped onto undisturbed ground.

"Praetor," said Scapax. "We must advance and rejoin the Legion."

Scapax might well worry. By law he faced summary execution if his Praetor came to harm while under his protection. Marcellinus didn't think it too likely to happen today. Squatting, he slipped his fingers into the rough grass and probed the loam beneath. His hand came up streaked with charcoal and ash.

"They make this," he said. "D'you see?"

"Let's go, sir," Scapax said.

"The redskins. They burn away the undergrowth with care so the deer and elk can graze and they can see clear to shoot them from afar with bow and arrow. And the trees here: chestnuts, hickory nuts. It's . . ." Words suddenly failed him at the magnitude of what he was saying. "This is a park, not a forest. It only *looks* natural. They *tend* this. Our dusky savages practice land husbandry."

The centurion came to Marcellinus's side. "Now, sir, if you please."

Behind the trees, Marcellinus saw something gliding high and straight on the breeze. He squinted at it, pretty sure it was a hawk and not a man.

"Don't make me order the good centurion to carry you," Aelfric said mildly.

Marcellinus turned on him. "You forget yourself. Why didn't you leave with the other tribunes?"

At his tone, Aelfric quickly stood to attention. "Sorry, sir."

"You and I, Tribune, we're not friends."

"No, Praetor."

"Your place is with your cohorts."

"Yes, Praetor."

"Then get back to them!"

"Yes, sir." Aelfric made haste to depart.

Straightening, Marcellinus walked back and placed his hand on the shoulder of his maimed scout, looking at Sigurdsson's eyes rather than his injuries. "Thank you, my friend. Watch the road for us till we return."

Only then did Marcellinus allow his guards to pace him back into the protection of the Legion.

"I heard the speech you made for Sigurdsson earlier this evening," said Isleifur Bjarnason. "A pretty thing it was. Excellent and rousing. You'll really take the time to grind the redskins' bones?"

Marcellinus whirled. He had dismissed his guards for the night and had believed himself alone in his Praetorium. But there sat another of his long-missing Norse scouts, on the same blanket Sisika had occupied. His flaxen hair was filthy and pulled back into a long braid, and his clothes were darkened with dirt and green smears, indicating a great deal of time spent concealed in foliage.

The Praetor recovered his composure quickly, as if men crept up on him every day. "I've done it before."

"I thank you for the tribute on his behalf," said Bjarnason. "Thorkell was a good man. But much as it pains me to say it, the loss of one good Norseman doesn't justify a massacre."

Marcellinus held the man's gaze for several moments, then turned and poured wine and water for them both. If Bjarnason had intended to kill him, he'd be dead already. "I'm surprised no one told me you'd returned to camp."

"I haven't. Leastways, not officially." He grinned. "A poor scout I'd be if I couldn't find a path through a castra unseen."

"Such undue stealthiness could get you killed."

"Perhaps. But I'm no use to you here. If I'm to be of service, I need to be out feeling the lay of the land. Learning to think as the redskins do."

Marcellinus eyed him. "This territory appeals? Perhaps you're thinking you've served Roma long enough?"

"The scenery's to my taste, I'll admit. I sojourned in Vinlandia awhile; did you know? And Graenlandia before that. I like the spaces empty and the skies big."

"Then why are you here in my tent?"

"Because I still work for you, Praetor. I wouldn't want you to imagine I'd deserted. And to advise you." Marcellinus raised his eyebrows. "To tell you my impressions, rather," the Norseman amended quickly.

"You have the floor," Marcellinus said ironically, and sat in his chair.

Bjarnason sipped his wine. He must have grown unused to it during his weeks in the woods; it was the first time Marcellinus had seen a Viking sip anything. "Very well, then. They're a powerful people, the Iroqua. Warriors the like of which I've not seen before in Europa or beyond. Bloodier than we Norse. We generally leave people alive, but they kill for sport. I'm keeping my wits about me, I don't mind telling you. I don't sleep much."

"And these are the people I shouldn't massacre?"

"Nay," said Bjarnason. "I don't give a hoot about the Iroqua. Vile folk, but you'll be out of their territory in a few more days, anyway. The people you shouldn't kill are the next lot, the Cahokiani. Great builders, they are: longhouses, thatched roofs. Not the equals of the Norse great halls, but they could be with a tad more practice. And they build mounds of earth, too, wide and tall. And riverine harbors and irrigation canals. They're like no people you've seen yet."

"Do they have gold?" Marcellinus asked automatically, and almost laughed at himself for the question.

The Norseman shook his head. "We'll not make our fortunes there. Furs and pretty shells. Aside from that it's mostly stone and bone, wood and feathers. Especially feathers. For they're fliers as well as runners and swimmers, you see."

"We saw what their wings could do in Appalachia. It's a fancy trick, but not one that leaves much of a dent on Roman steel."

"You've not seen the best of what they can throw into the air," said Bjarnason. "You haven't seen anything yet."

"But we can beat them," Marcellinus said, and it wasn't a question.

"Oh, aye, handily, should you choose to. But maybe you should consider the advantages of trade over pillage." Bjarnason smiled ruefully. "And when a Norseman says that, you should probably listen."

"We don't need any shells. How much farther, Bjarnason?"

"To the city of mounds? As the crow flies and the legion marches? Six weeks." The Norseman waggled his hand to show that his estimate was rough.

"Six?" Marcellinus said, appalled.

As the year wore on, Marcellinus was becoming uncomfortably aware of just how long this march was taking. He worked the dates in his head. The Ides of Julius had just passed. Six weeks further would take them well past the limit of how far west they could travel and still have any hope of making it back to the Chesapica before winter closed in. For a moment, his heart already felt the chill.

The mounted Norse scouts had made it to the city of mounds and back again in a couple of months. It had always been obvious that the Legion would take much longer. No one had expected it to take *this* long.

"You're worried about supplies?"

"Of course."

"Don't be. They have better corn than you've seen so far, and soon ready for the harvest."

Marcellinus looked wry. "Enough to feed the 33rd over a winter?"

"Enough to feed a city," Bjarnason assured him. "Take the city and you take the food, too."

He put the wine cup down and stretched. "I haven't been into that city, mind. Can't even get close. There's no cover in the last stages, and I'll not get far trying to disguise myself as one of them. But ten thousand people's my guess."

"If you're wrong—" Marcellinus caught himself.

On their arrival at the Chesapica the weather had been surprisingly blustery and fierce for the latitude. If Marcellinus had to build a fortress and overwinter the 33rd out here in the desolate backcountry of Nova Hesperia, he would really have problems. The decimation of his troops from starvation and infighting would make their losses at the hands of the natives look paltry. Marcellinus could hardly expect the locals to feed his legion out of the goodness of their hearts.

Of course, if he had to turn around and slink back to the Chesapica without having found gold or achieved substantial military success conquering new territory for the Imperium, Marcellinus would have wasted the year. Hadrianus would not view that favorably.

He really had no choice. None at all.

They had to go on.

"I'm not wrong," the scout said.

Hating himself, Marcellinus clutched at a further straw. "If you've not been in, how can you be sure there's no gold?"

"I suppose they might have a bit, if it was well hidden." The Norseman leaned forward. "But these people have more than that, Praetor. They know this land, and they know the air above it. The air! Gods' sakes! And they don't think the way we do. I can't really explain it, because I only speak a few words of their lingo. But there are virtues to them. There are virtues.

"You've seen it yourself, I know; I heard you trying to persuade your tribune back there by Thorkell's corpse. The Cahokiani husband the land even more so than the Iroqua; they live almost *inside* the land. And that's how they fly, you know. They've tamed the air because they have an understanding of it that we lack."

Marcellinus drained his cup. "Tell me something I can use, Isleifur Bjarnason."

"You've only seen the small wings," said the Viking. "Wait till you see the larger. In their language, they call them Thunderbirds. If the little birds are like sparrows, the Thunderbirds are like . . . well, eagles."

"Eagles."

"Flying through the air, quick as ballista bolts."

Larger wings. Marcellinus's pulse quickened, but he remained resolute. "The bigger they are, the larger the hole they'll make in the ground when we shoot them down. They're a gimmick. There's little strategic value to them."

"Well," said the Norseman. "That may be so, and it may be not."

"You do realize that I should arrest you?" Marcellinus said bluntly. "Fraternizing with the enemy, pleading their case with me, breaking in here by night."

Bjarnason grinned. "I'm at my Praetor's disposal."

"Yes, till you turn renegade on me. I haven't forgotten what good pirates you people make."

Bjarnason looked pained. "Damn it, now . . . sir. That's the Danes. The Danes were never anything but trouble, just like the Britons. I'm a Geat, one of the true Scands. We're just like you, always were."

"Just like us?" Marcellinus murmured.

"Aye. Romans and Norse, we're solid stock, hard dreamers with a vision and the guts to make it stick. Both out to claim the world for ourselves. Oh, the Norse bow to the stronger," he said, ducking his head in deference, "but if it wasn't you Romans, it'd be us out there, carving an empire."

"You're something of a freethinker," Marcellinus said drily.

"It's true. If Roma had fallen to the Visigoths and Vandals and all— and that was a closer-run thing than people like to suppose—you can wager it'd have been we Norse sweeping up and building an Imperium now. Who'd have gainsaid us? The bloody Mongols, eventually. But certainly not the Gauls or the Parthians or the Britons. Stay-at-homes with mud on their faces, the lot of 'em, no soldiers. No sailors, either."

Marcellinus grinned. Despite Bjarnason's impertinence, he liked the man. "Very well. I withdraw the accusation of piracy."

"Right, then." The Norseman shuffled backward, wriggled through a tiny gap between the tent canvas and the ground, and was gone.

"Anyone else like to put in an appearance?" Marcellinus said to the goatskin walls of his Praetorium, but if any further spies were present, they remained mute.

Marcellinus went to bed then, but he did not sleep well.

CHAPTER 3

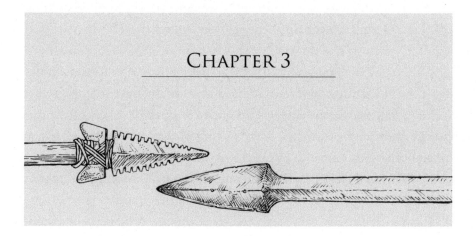

The Iroqua war party hit them two days later in the early afternoon, rising like ghosts from the long grasses to fling their spears and fire their arrows into the side of Fabius's Seventh Cohort, howling like banshees all the while. Though they had been on the march for six hours without a break, the Seventh responded instantly, bursting out of its marching line to hammer the braves with Roman steel. The assault turned into a running battle amid the trees of hickory and beech, and if the Iroqua were surprised at the turn of speed a fully armored legionary could attain, their surprise generally did not last long.

Throughout the Legion, Roman discipline prevailed. The cohorts behind and in front of the Seventh came to order, the nearer groups dashing into the fray while the centuries farther out hunkered down in defense. Sure enough, two more Iroqua bands burst out from behind the trees, one assaulting Marcellinus and the Roman standards at the head of the Legion and the other aiming to destroy the baggage train and perhaps capture the Romans' slaves for their own use.

Neither attempt succeeded. The elite troops of Pollius Scapax mowed down the forward band of Iroqua with surgical skill and utter ruthlessness, and Marcellinus bloodied his gladius in combat for the first time on this campaign, cutting down four braves and crippling another. Meanwhile, in the rear the terrified Powhatani and other Algon-Quian slaves circled the wagons and aided the stragglers of the Sixth in holding off the ululating Iroqua until the massed line of the Fourth slammed into the warriors, slaughtering them to a man.

Other smaller bands of painted Hesperians appeared helter-skelter amid the trees, and the Fifth and Second were the next to engage in a running fight in the meadows. This ended with the remains of the war parties encircled by Romans. Some twenty of the Iroqua tried to escape by climbing into a tree; the Romans set the tree ablaze and made them choose between death by fire and death by steel. Dozens of others, trapped on the ground, threw aside their slings and bows.

If by surrendering they expected to be spared to join their eastern brethren in the slave line, the Iroqua were sorely disappointed. The Legion needed no more slaves, and Marcellinus would not have trusted a warrior in the role as readily as a fisherman. Slavery was an economic contract between thinking beings, but Marcellinus knew these Iroqua to be feral creatures who would never knuckle under.

After mourning Thorkell Sigurdsson so recently, the men were not inclined to award their captives easy deaths, and Marcellinus would hardly insist on such a thing. Several more of his legionaries were dead and others still thrashed on the ground with poisoned flesh wounds, and he had no sympathy for an enemy that adopted such foul tactics as the Iroqua. He withdrew to secure the front of the legionary line and left his troops to their revenge. The screams of the braves troubled him little enough. He hoped the gruesome sounds would travel far enough to deter any further Hesperian foolishness.

They had marched sixteen miles that day, and it would have to be enough. Marcellinus sent in his tribunes and Scapax to declare a halt to the festivities, and his men cheerfully yielded and threw up the castra then and there in the clearing. Camp had never been set up so quickly.

"I see you've put the Briton in his place," Corbulo said, dismounting to walk beside him. "A worthy decision."

Gaius Publius Marcellinus was leading his horse, allowing it to walk unencumbered for a while. For his own part, it felt good to shake the stiffness out of his legs, and the brisk exercise was helping to shift the fog from his thoughts.

He missed Aelfric's easy companionship but was not about to confess it. "You were right," he said shortly. "It's easy for a man to grow careless."

The views in Appalachia had often been stunning. Here in the lowlands, often surrounded once more by forest, the tedium of marching had taken over again. By now Marcellinus heartily endorsed Tully's conviction that no Roman would want to farm here. The land had become ungodly flat. His eyes ached for want of a hill or even a hummock. He had never seen such a terrain. Like all learned men, Marcellinus knew that the earth was round like a ball, but even for him it was easy to imagine the world petering off into an increasingly featureless desert as they marched out of reality altogether.

"Killing Fuscus," said his tribune. "Another worthy simplification. Easier not to hear his lying tongue at all than risk being misled by it."

With uncanny precision Corbulo had just congratulated Marcellinus on the second matter that was troubling him. He could not dispel the knowledge that cutting down the word slave in cold blood had been shameful, despite the provocation, and was possibly as bad an error as that of the Roman captain who had slaughtered the Norse pirates. Information was always valuable. And in the Praetor's personal experience, his acting in anger had rarely produced laudable results.

They hiked in silence. Marcellinus recognized that an olive branch was being offered, a bid to return to their former camaraderie, but could not find the words to respond. Corbulo's moment of failure still hung in the air, surely the cause of the remaining awkwardness between them. *Everything's all right, Lucius*, he wanted to say, *and I think no worse of you*. But that would admit the possibility that another man might have. Corbulo had ambition, and a persistent rumor about him panicking on the battlefield could be deadly to his career, sinking his chances of one day getting his own legion or advancing in politics. Somehow the thing must be dealt with without being acknowledged.

Unexpectedly, Corbulo raised the topic. He turned to Marcellinus and said: "I apologize for my dithering back at the ambush. Thank you for plucking me upright. It was well done."

Marcellinus recovered quickly from his surprise and waved his hand dismissively. "We were all startled." He leaned over. "I hope my sandal print in your ribs is not causing you too much anguish."

Corbulo laughed. "Always better to be beaten up by a friend."

"I would never mention it to another soul, you know."

"And I thank you for that," was all Corbulo said, but Marcellinus felt the man's spirits lift.

If only Marcellinus's mood could be elevated so easily.

"I responded to murder with murder," he said abruptly.

"What?"

Marcellinus bit his tongue and walked on, facing straight ahead.

"What choice did you have?" Corbulo asked. "You did what you had to. I'd have done the same."

"Would you?"

"Of course."

Marcellinus looked at him for a long moment, then nodded. "Very well, then. I should ride again."

"We each have times when we doubt," said his First Tribune quietly. "But we just need to stick together and get the job done. Whether or not there's gold here, we can make this work for Hadrianus, you and I. In the conquest and annexation of such a vast area we can cover ourselves in glory. You can retire in comfort. I can move on to higher things. Let us not be enemies, Gaius. And let us not forget who rules this world."

"I never shall," said Marcellinus. "Count on it."

As the month of Julius gave way to Augustus, the heat soared. The sky became white with humidity, and the air felt like a damp sponge against their skin. The shade of the few remaining stands of trees offered little relief. The moisture invaded the fabric of the tents and wouldn't come out; by night the castra stank like a barnyard.

The occasional downpours just made it worse. The rain came down in giant sheets of water that did not freshen the air but merely sat rancid overnight and then boiled off the soil in the morning sun in great mists.

Marcellinus had not known the air could hold so much liquid. Beneath his armor his tunic was permanently wet and would not dry out at night. His crotch felt like a fouled bird's nest.

Bengal had sometimes been like this. But at least they'd had a cooling monsoon every afternoon and drier air by night. Here in Nova Hesperia, so far from the sea, the wind had forgotten how to blow. The soldiers were surly, and the horses spooked at nothing, their ears flat back against their heads.

The Hesperians were still out there. Another nine of his legionaries died, picked off and mutilated gruesomely while collecting firewood or stalking the white-tailed deer. With supplies this short, forbidding the men to hunt was futile, yet all too often they themselves became the prey.

By now everyone knew that they were going on, that there could be no return to the Chesapica before winter, that once the weather turned cold they would be building a fortress and staying put out here in the wilderness.

The heat and damp and uncertainty played with men's tempers. Marcellinus lost an additional seven soldiers to violence when a brawl turned murderous and he had to execute the culprits. Once more he cursed the ill mix of the men given him to command: raw Nubians, Magyar mercenaries, veteran Teutons, and even some patrician Romans, a mixed bag of races and languages that turned his centurions into diplomats who spent as much time coaxing their men not to kill one another as they did in maintaining their battle readiness.

His feelings of isolation grew. Urbs Roma became a marbled dream. And just as his legion eroded further into squalor and ill temper, the barbarians around them seemed to grow ever more civilized.

Though they saw few natives, they passed plenty of evidence of their activities. The tents and lean-tos of the east had given way to firmer structures of wood and wattle and daub. In some areas the remains of broad tree stumps showed that the locals had torn down the forests for farmland. Though Marcellinus was no lover of trees for trees' sake, he was surprised at how much of an effect this had on him.

The Romans became the beneficiaries of the increased cultivation of the land; they swarmed the corn like locusts, leaving only stalks behind them. Deer would still appear startlingly close to the Legion's path and die quickly in a hail of arrows. The soldiers often had to pull fifteen or twenty arrows out of a downed buck before they could skin and dress it for the fire.

Despite their living off the land as much as they were able, the Hesperian corn still provided a paltry yield compared with the robust crops of Europa. Leogild's baggage carts continued to grow lighter as the victuals dwindled. A few thousand men on the march ate a great deal.

As long damp day followed long damp day, Marcellinus saw more and more evidence of how the local tribes were taming the land. And more than once he could have sworn he saw an aviator fly by, banking and swooping behind the trees.

In his dreams they wheeled over him in a giant flock, and he awoke with his ears still full of the beating of their wings.

Now the Legion started coming across the mounds: small conical earthworks in the clearings by the abandoned villages. In the days that followed, the number of villages and the size of the mounds both showed a marked increase.

"This is more like it," said Marcellinus as they rode past a mound fifteen feet tall.

"Piles of earth?" Corbulo said.

"Yes, just piles of earth, patted down nice and neat. We could put one up in an hour that would put this one to shame. But these people aren't Romans. For them to build a mound like this is a triumph of effort and organization. And these are just the beginning. Ahead, there are cities of these things."

"Ah, *big* piles of earth," said Corbulo. "You should have said so sooner."

"Support me, Lucius," Marcellinus said quietly. "Your sarcasm grows wearying."

"Of course. Sorry."

Leogild cleared his throat. "Sir, we should talk again about supplies."

"Supplies, always supplies." Corbulo put his hand up to his temple as if deafened by the Visigoth.

Leogild eyed him. "Fine. You don't want to eat, that's more for everyone else."

Until now they had scavenged from the fields and forests as they'd gone by. Now the tended forests were giving way to plains, and—at long last—Bjarnason's promised fields of tall, odd-looking, but well-tended corn were replacing the earlier sickly patches. The cornfields were separated by stands of nut trees; by this time nobody doubted that the Hesperians had transformed the landscape around them. But reaping the new bounty would take time.

"We march on," Marcellinus said. "Let's travel light and get this done. Their crops aren't quite ready yet, anyway. Once we've taken their city, an organized harvest from these fields will feed us to bursting."

Corbulo looked relieved; he obviously had feared a delay in reaching their goal. As for Marcellinus, now suddenly freed from constant worry about running out of food, he felt positively giddy.

The gamble was going to pay off. Once they'd harvested the corn, the Legion could overwinter here in relative comfort. He would even have time before winter to send an exploratory cohort or two to march on farther or lead it himself, maximizing their westward expansion. Even without gold, Hadrianus might be pleased at their annexation of so much land.

All they had to do was take the city.

"Give the orders that any redskin farmers who don't flee are not to be harassed. From now on the corn is to be left undisturbed. We can come back for it at need."

"Four days I'll give you," said Leogild. "After that I'll counsel a day or two to restock the wagons before going farther."

"Agreed," the Praetor said.

On they went. The stillness of the air was uncanny, and the utter absence of any breeze was stifling. Marcellinus rarely saw a face that was not dripping with sweat or passed a soldier who did not reek. Much more of this and the leather and wool would rot on their bodies.

In Europa such an epic trek could have taken them from Urbs Roma almost as far as Parisi in Gaul, but in Europa the way would be well signed and the rivers already bridged. Nova Hesperia was a giant land with no roads at all aside from the one they were creating. This was going to be one hell of a province for a Roman legate to administer one day.

To Marcellinus it felt as if the past weeks had carried the Legion on a long march through time. First, the poverty-racked fisher-gatherers of the Powhatani by the giant bay of the Chesapica, at the mercy of the tide and the berry plant. Next, the woodland husbandry of the Iroqua, savage to invaders but gentle to the land, cultivating their meadows, burning their undergrowth, shooting their deer. Now, here in the alluvial bottomlands of deepest Nova Hesperia, the Cahokiani farmed their fields and lived in stout wooden huts that represented a giant leap forward from the animal-skin tents and lean-to shacks on the coast. Such settled and well-ordered agriculture was essential to support the Great City they sought, and judging by the increasing size of the Cahokiani settlements they passed, that city must now be very close.

Soon it would be time to fight.

CHAPTER 4

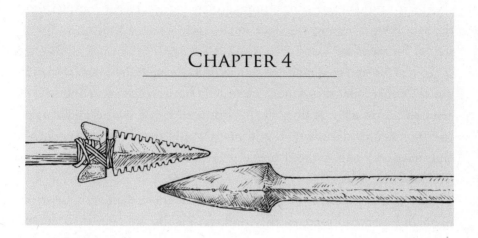

"Damn it, man," said the centurion Pollius Scapax. "If you're not sure you're within bow range, hold your fire."

"Yes, sir," said the soldier thus chastened. "Thought I had him, sir."

"Arrows don't grow on trees, you know." An old Legion joke.

"No, sir. Sorry, sir."

Their enemy was no longer invisible, yet the armed braves in the road ahead did not engage them; instead, they withdrew before the approaching Roman army. From a distance Marcellinus could see they were warriors in full regalia, feathers in their hair and javelins and bows in their hands. They looked very different from the earlier peoples. No one could confuse the Cahokiani with the fishing tribes of the shore, the flying tribes of the mountains, or the warrior bands of the woodlands. These were men of much grander aspect than the previous collections of natives.

Never had Marcellinus seen men so practiced in running backward. Yet their appearance of retreat was obviously a ruse; they were luring the Romans toward a place where they would stand and do battle. Fair enough. Since Marcellinus could no longer safely send his scouts forward to locate the enemy for himself, he welcomed the assistance. Let the Cahokiani choose the battlefield; this land was all flat, anyway. Aside from the mounds there was no high ground for the savages to launch their wings from and few natural features aside from the stands of trees and the occasional creek. Little opportunity for a trap or an ambush.

Unless the braves planned to retreat right through their own city and out the other side, they would eventually have to stop dancing backward and form a battle line. Then, with their metal swords and armor and professional discipline, the Romans would march right over them and massacre them without breaking step, and irrigate the Cahokiani fields with their blood.

Marcellinus checked the sun. It was a little more than an hour after noon and mercy of mercies, the wind was picking up after their many days of marching through stagnant air. A wise general might call a halt now to build a formidable castra for the night, stepping up to battle fresh in the dawn. But the rank and file would never stand for that. He could feel their turbulent energy, pent up over these long weeks of marching. Calming it would be impossible.

So be it. They'd marched only twelve miles today. Still enough freshness in those hard Roman legs to carry them up and over a half-naked foe armed with sticks. They might even sleep in the Great City tonight.

Another stand of tall hickory trees stood in their path, and Tribune Corbulo, riding ahead of him in the vanguard, steered the Legion around it in a broad rightward curve. A series of long huts with thatched roofs now bordered the Hesperian road; the troops stayed wary, shields at the ready in case of a sudden fusillade of arrows, but none came. Corbulo sent in his incendiary-men to fire the huts, which went up in a fast popping blaze.

Now a corresponding crackle of excitement flooded the Legion, the men in the lead raising a ruckus, shouting "Roma!" and fanning out efficiently into battle formation. Marcellinus spurred his mount forward and was soon by Corbulo's side, where he took in the scene with a broad sweeping glance.

He looked out across a plain studded with hundreds of sculpted earthworks: cones, ridge mounds, and square-sided platform mounds arranged in well-ordered lines. Set around them in a more haphazard pattern was a swarm of long huts with walls of reed matting and thatched roofs, along with larger wooden structures that must be granaries and lodges. The Cahokiani obviously did not believe in urban planning or a grid pattern or even in streets. But a mile or more away, across what looked like a giant plaza, Marcellinus saw a stockade fifteen feet tall, built of giant logs, extending hundreds of yards in each direction. And within the stockade . . .

"Juno!" Marcellinus swore. "Hold! Hold!"

Within the stockade sat an immense two-level platform mound constructed entirely of earth. Its four sides angled up steeply like a pyramid to a first plateau with a thatched hut on one corner and then up again to a final flat crest. The mound was topped with a huge wooden structure that must have been eighty feet long and two or three stories high.

"What?" Corbulo paused, contemptuous. "It's a lump. We'll slaughter 'em, then kick it down."

"It's farther away than you think," Marcellinus said. "*Look* at it. It must be over a hundred feet high and a thousand feet across the base of it."

How long must it have taken to construct such a massive pyramid, even using slave labor? The legion dug a six-foot earthen ridge around the castra each night, but that was the work of thousands of tough men at the peak of fitness. This thing had to be fifteen acres in area and as tall as the Palatine Hill in Roma. They must have spent lifetimes building it up to its current height and girth. And on wet foundations such an earthwork had to be hell's own job to stabilize. How could one even engineer it?

This was no scaled-up version of a fishing camp or nomads' village. This truly was a Great City, complete with suburbs, urbs, and citadel. From the sheer number of houses and mounds and the expanse of corn that stretched beyond and behind them as far as he could see, Marcellinus reckoned it must hold well over the ten thousand people Bjarnason had estimated, perhaps twice that number. After their trek across the most desolate and unpromising territory he had ever seen, the Great City had a grandeur for which he was not prepared.

In that moment Marcellinus radically revised his assessment of their enemy. Savage, yes, but in the scope of their organization as civilized as many a Roman province.

And here they came, row upon row of Cahokiani pouring out from the palisade and hurrying in like ants from the outer regions of their city. Around Marcellinus his legionaries were similarly arraying themselves for battle, as they had to, since their enemy could charge at any time. He became aware that near him Corbulo was shouting the order to advance. The trumpeters raised their instruments to their lips.

"Wait," Marcellinus said. "Deploy and hold. We don't advance yet."

Corbulo turned, stiff-necked. "What?"

"There's more here than meets the eye. Look at the terrain. The braves can use the huts and mounds to good effect. Advancing, we'll take attacks from the flanks as well as the front."

Twenty-five years of soldiering had lent Marcellinus a powerful intuition. He had not become a Praetor for nothing, and his gut told him now to keep his distance from that Master Mound.

"We wait?" said Corbulo in contempt just as Aelfric rode up from behind and cursed in his own tongue at the stupendous sight before them. "No, we must charge immediately while they're still forming up. Frontal assault. We've come a thousand miles for this."

"Yes, and so we can wait ten minutes more." In the ranks his centurions were in the thick of preparations, running back and forth bellowing at their men. Despite never having received a command from Marcellinus, his Legion already was deployed in an admirably straight north-south triple line. The banners of the cohorts flapped in the growing breeze, the signa of individual centuries were displayed proudly, and at the line's center he saw the golden Aquila raised high.

Despite the stress of the moment a lump came to Marcellinus's throat. They'd endured a grueling trek with hunger, discomfort, and danger. Dissent and discord had never been far away, but his men had risen to the occasion in double-quick time. The Legio XXXIII Hesperia was ready for battle. And yet, and yet . . .

"Wings ho!" someone cried. And so there were, a dozen or more, leaping off the top of the Master Mound and circling out over the assembling barbarian horde like moths before gliding back to land behind the palisade.

"They can't reach us," Fabius said. "That mound isn't so high, and they have no updrafts to sustain them. Showy enough but no threat."

Corbulo nodded. "These red bastards don't like to fight unless they hold the advantage of stealth, darkness, or altitude. There's no honor in 'em. Burn a captive, drop a rock, poison a scratch, hack at a soldier squatting under a tree—that's their game. We kill them all now."

"Tribune. Attend me."

Corbulo turned on him. "*You* told the men the redskins are cowards! They cower in defeat. Look at Fuscus!"

"The Powhatani, yes. Even the Iroqua. Perhaps not these Cahokiani." Marcellinus strode forward and clamped his hand onto Corbulo's arm. "I gave you an order, Tribune. Obey me."

Corbulo's hand dropped to the hilt of his gladius. "Not today, I think."

Their eyes met. Looking deep into Corbulo's soul, Marcellinus saw many things: fear, resentment, and above all Corbulo's desperate and enduring need to redeem himself.

It was the same wild look he had seen in Corbulo's eye during the ambush in Appalachia. Corbulo was suffering from that same panic now. His nerve was cracking.

Corbulo broke eye contact but dropped his voice. "I know you, Gaius. You're looking for an excuse to avoid slaughter. But it's too late. The men will revolt and kill us both if we don't attack *now*."

"The men will do as I order. They respect prudence."

"Prudence?" said Corbulo, reverting to a voice loud enough to carry to the nearest troops. "Prudence says we wipe out the savages, take their corn and their gold and their women, and, yes, grind the bones of the men to pave the temple to Jupiter Imperator that we'll build on that sand castle of theirs. As *you* said yourself just the other night. Did you lose your stomach for the fight, Gaius Marcellinus? Forget so soon how these savages mutilated your Norse catamite? Or have you made deals by night and now favor the red men?"

"What?" Marcellinus shook his head, overwhelmed at this knot of bizarre accusations. But Corbulo's gladius was now unsheathed, and *that* was something Marcellinus could understand.

Legionaries might take advantage of the chaos on the battlefield to rough up an unpopular centurion. It happened often enough. But for a tribune to challenge a legate's authority a few hundred yards from the enemy's gate was unthinkable.

"I'm relieving you of your command," Marcellinus said.

Corbulo grinned. "I think not."

Suddenly, all around Marcellinus was movement; Gnaeus Fabius seized a pilum and stepped up to stand with Corbulo, and flanking the two mutineers came four swarthy auxiliaries, mercenaries from east of the Danube, Magyars, perhaps, or Bulgars. Too late, Marcellinus saw that this little scene was not as impromptu as it had first appeared. He dropped back several paces to open up space around him, his adrenaline surging.

The pilum of Fabius was the first danger, with its reach so much longer than a sword's. The javelin was capable of ending a fight in a single well-aimed throw but could be cumbersome as a hand-to-hand weapon. A better fighter than Fabius might have charged in and pinned Marcellinus to ready him for the dispatch, but apparently Fabius's magistracy had not primed him for such martial boldness; instead he launched the pilum at Marcellinus from fifteen feet away. The Praetor took a single step to the right as it flew by, and remained on balance.

Hands free, no shield within reach, Marcellinus unsheathed his gladius with his right hand and his pugio with his left and stood fast as the six men charged him.

With a strange howl that was neither a berserker yell nor a cry of abandon, Aelfric hurled himself into the fray at his commander's side. So nimble was his charge that if the Briton had been a party to the treachery, Marcellinus would have been on his knees with a blade through his kidney before he could have parried.

Marcellinus cut down the first two mercenaries with swift slices to the gut. They were hardly the first young hotheads to fatally misjudge his speed. The paid help from Roma's provinces were generally not skilled gladiatorial fighters; on the battlefield they relied on ferocity rather than virtuosity, and Marcellinus had been training daily in sword-play since he'd been a child.

Once they saw the fight was not as simple as they'd hoped the third and fourth auxiliaries backed away rapidly and stepped apart to encircle him.

Meanwhile, Aelfric's gladius clashed with Corbulo's; the two men slashed and parried, swung and ducked, and Aelfric staggered back. Faced with the choice between two opponents, Marcellinus chose the third, darting between the two Magyars to lunge at Domitius Corbulo's flank. Corbulo spun to face him, startled, and Marcellinus drove the pugio up under his breastplate and deep into his ribs, leaning back to slice his gladius across his former tribune's gut. As Corbulo reeled like a drunkard, swinging his blade wildly, Marcellinus dropped to one knee, allowing Aelfric to leap over his sword arm and slam bodily into the nearest of the mercenaries, bowling him over.

The unexpected trade in opponents made short work of the insur-rection. Corbulo screamed like a banshee as his entrails tumbled out into the dirt, a cry that turned into a guttural bubbling as Marcellinus tugged his dagger free and severed the man's windpipe.

The mutineer fell to the ground with an audible thump.

Beside him Aelfric had handily slain the third mercenary. The fourth raised his sword over them with a yell and was almost casually decapi-tated by Pollius Scapax, arriving better late than not at all.

Left alone in his mutiny in a matter of seconds, Gnaeus Fabius stood stupidly before them, his gladius pointing at the ground. He looked around for reinforcements, but the men near him stood mute. Praetor Gaius Marcellinus calmly cleaned his two blades on Corbulo's tunic at his feet while holding his Second Tribune's gaze.

Pollius Scapax strode the ten paces that separated them. Fabius raised his sword but didn't have the courage to swing it at the centurion.

Gently, almost kindly, Scapax reached forward and seized the tribune's gladius at the hilt, turned it toward Fabius's belly, and kicked his knees from behind. As Gnaeus Fabius fell onto his own sword, Scapax ripped off the man's cape and plumed helmet and threw them aside, demoting him from the rank of tribune and the ranks of the living in the same moment.

Marcellinus sheathed his pugio. The closest legionaries swiveled their heads almost comically back and forth between Marcellinus, Scapax, and the assembled swath of the Cahokiani nation behind them. Marcellinus realized that two entire armies had come to a halt, waiting for the leadership battle to be decided.

Aelfric had stood by him, after all. But Marcellinus was not surprised that no one else had come to his aid. To most of the men Marcellinus and Corbulo were of a common stripe: patricians, Roma's natural masters, representatives of the ruling class. Their lot would be much the same whichever man wore the Praetor's crest. Unless they were paid or coerced, they had naught to gain and all to lose by picking a side.

Scapax approached, his gladius still unsheathed but reversed so that the point pushed up against his breast. "I was not close by when I might have served you, Praetor," he said gruffly. "And so I offer you my life. But I'd rather expend it killing some barbarians for you than follow Fabius to hell right away if you'll give me leave."

"Of course," Marcellinus said calmly. "Think nothing of it. I relished the chance to clean house."

His First Centurion's relief was palpable. "My thanks."

"In addition, I find myself short of field lieutenants. I will take the Second and Third. Assume the tribuneship of the First if you please."

Scapax's eyes glinted. "Very good, sir."

He saluted, and Marcellinus returned the salute. His new officer marched to his command.

Likewise, Aelfric turned to hurry back to the Fifth.

"Tribune?" said Marcellinus. "My thanks."

Aelfric looked back, and their eyes met.

"And my apologies. I was perhaps . . . harsh."

The Briton grinned. "Not at all, sir."

"We'll drink wine tonight."

"As my Praetor requests." Aelfric bowed and set off toward his co-horts at a trot.

Considering that there were thousands of men present, the stillness of the afternoon was impressive. If not for the tension in the air, Marcellinus could have closed his eyes and thought himself alone in the sunshine. As it was, he felt his army extending out from him in all directions like a drawn bow, arrow nocked and at the ready, bowstring tight, arm muscles aquiver.

The Praetor slowed his breathing and studied the battlefield. His Legion was deployed uniformly, presenting an even front a thousand yards long. The Cahokiani horde was by no means so well distributed; the northern end of their line was thicker, holding thousands more than the southern end that stood between him and the Master Mound. Would they deliberately expend more troops defending their population center than their sacred hill? Was it just an accident of formation? Or was the nearer end of their line guarded by something he couldn't see?

Not the wings, certainly. Though impressive, their Master Mound did not approximate to a mountain. Pilots who leaped from its top barely had time to loop back around before they were on the ground again.

A hidden pit? All the soil that went into the mounds had to come from somewhere. Had the Cahokiani concealed their borrow pits in the hope of enticing their enemies to charge headlong into them?

Perhaps. But in that case all Marcellinus had to do to minimize his losses was have the Legion walk rather than run. And Marcellinus still didn't like the looks of the mounds and houses that stood between his army and the palisade; he wasn't about to rush pell-mell into them in any case.

He turned his attention to the enemy line. At last Marcellinus could see the Cahokiani clearly. In their garb they were a mixed bunch, some wearing only breechcloths and swirling tattoos, others decked out in what might be tunics with wooden mats hanging down over their chests and stomachs as the simplest armor. Here and there men wore a woven sash, a kilt bearing geometric patterns, moccasins of deerskin, or a collar of what might have been rabbit. Hanging from many ears he saw pendulous adornments of antler and bone.

The Cahokiani had no flags, standards, or symbols and little organization. Nowhere was this more apparent than in their array of weaponry: wooden bows probably crafted of hickory, spears of wood much shorter and lighter than the Roman pila, and clubs and axes, too, but also a variety of tools hurriedly pressed into service: hafted hoes, mattocks. Some of the men clutched nothing more deadly than a rock or a knife.

He faced a mass of nobles and commoners, farmers and traders, warriors and weavers all mixed together, and a style of fighting the Romans had outgrown a millennium and a half earlier. The Romans were heavily outnumbered, but they had metal blades and armor and intense discipline on their side. Marcellinus's sympathies lay with his foes.

Yet he still felt an instinctive unease at these people with their almost intimate stares, waiting as calmly as if they went toe-to-toe with a Roman army once a week. In the mountains, people not so different from these had assaulted them from above. What was about to happen here?

Isleifur Bjarnason's voice echoed in his head. "They have more . . . You haven't seen anything yet . . ."

Corbulo had been quite right; now that Marcellinus had seen the Great City for himself, he would have given anything to avoid this battle. But such a thing was impossible.

They already knew the Hesperians did not understand the civilized conduct of war. Their sneak attacks, their use of poison arrows, the torture and murder of his scout, and their use of the flying machines all provided adequate testimony to that. Marcellinus could easily ride out between the armies under a flag of truce to try to parley only to perish in a hail of arrows for his pains. No leader or chieftain was evident in the massed line of Cahokiani that faced him. He saw no one to negotiate with even if he'd still had a word slave at his disposal.

Besides, they had literally passed the point of no return. The Legion needed the city's food. And for that Marcellinus needed to conquer the city.

It was a testament to the steadiness of his centurions that none of his cohorts had yet erupted into a charge. Marcellinus could not halt this battle any more than he could hold back the tide.

Very well, then.

Praetor Gaius Publius Marcellinus raised his gladius high and gave the signals to his aquilifer and signiferi while shouting: "Advance in steps, covering! Burn all buildings; secure high ground! Arrows in rotation once in range; maintain formation till melee. Forward the Legion, for Roma, the Imperator, and the Fighting 33rd!"

Marcellinus dropped his arm. His sword rent the air. Trumpets sounded. With a roar the Legion surged forward, but tightly, masterfully, and in control.

Across the plaza the amassed braves raised their bows, their axes, their hoes. Marcellinus was sure they roared just as loudly as his own men, but thankfully he could not hear them.

The Legion had methodically advanced a quarter of the distance separating them from the Cahokiani when the nearest houses burst into flame. Marcellinus had given the order to fire them in passing so that the enemy could not use them as cover, but these ignitions were not Roman doing. The thatched houses went up in a series of giant *whumphs*, burning with an intense red-white flare. What had the savages put in them to make them blaze so fiercely?

Yet no real explosion came, no scattering of burning debris. Not a single Roman was harmed by the incendiaries. Nor were they accompanied by an ambush: no Hesperians tumbled out from behind a mound or inside a hut. The Legion marched forward steadily, its front line replenishing itself, inexorably closing the distance to the foe that waited on the other side of the Cahokiani plaza.

The locals adopted no formation except the simple line, and still Marcellinus saw no leaders, no orders given. They seemed content to watch the Romans closing in.

Up the Roman line to the north, Marcellinus saw the front ranks of the Fourth drop to one knee. Auxiliaries less encumbered by shields and armor and with fewer huts and mounds to navigate around, the Fourth had advanced more swiftly than the other cohorts and was now within arrow range.

His attention was pulled back by cries of surprise from the men close by him. He followed their gaze and pointing fingers, and his eyes widened.

From the summit of the Master Mound, the Cahokiani were shooting bodies into the air.

Clearly a ballista or onager of considerable power ran up the far side of the giant mound. Marcellinus's first thought—that they were lobbing diseased cattle carcasses as one might heft over a city wall to break a siege—was wrong; these were living humans that were being catapulted aloft with incredible heft and force. At the greatest altitude of their arc they unfurled broad wings in a sudden stroke to become the now familiar fixed-wing flying craft. In minutes, the air was alive with them.

They dived low and fast over the cohorts like winged demons, each pilot feathered and bird masked and with an arrow nocked. They flew barely thirty feet above the Roman helmets but were so swift and agile that it would take a lucky pilum indeed to bring one down. Legionaries flung themselves right and left, breaking formation to avoid the flight paths of the wings, but even as Marcellinus drew breath to bellow a harsh command, he heard his centurions' voices booming across the battlefield: "Raise up your shields!" "Maintain formation!" "Stand firm, damn you!"

Discipline reestablished, the Legion lunged forward again. The front lines of the Fourth and Sixth Auxiliaries discharged a volley of arrows into the enemy line, advanced a dozen paces, and dropped to one knee; the men behind marched through to become the new front rank, firing their own swath of arrows into the massed bodies of the savages. A wave of Cahokiani stumbled and fell, the Roman arrows scraping off the whole front layer of the opposing army.

Now Marcellinus saw the real purpose of the brightly burning huts. As the wings flew overhead, loosing many an arrow into a Roman breastplate, their paths inevitably took them over the burning houses, where their pilots expertly rode the hot, rising air up into the skies to recover their altitude. Again and again Marcellinus watched the human moths pass above the white fire and arc up into the sky, their skill even more dazzling than the flames. Three of the wings crossed paths a thousand feet above him, an incredible height with no strategic value, surely just an exhilarating distraction. But as Marcellinus watched them, he experienced another dizzying mental leap: the pilots were using their very patterns of flight to signal to their comrades. From their aerial vantage point the battle was laid out beneath them like a map. The wings were the ultimate surveillance tools: scouts in the sky.

Something had become abundantly clear to Praetor Gaius Marcellinus: these people were not neophytes at war. The Cahokiani were a tribe—a nation—that had faced large-scale armed assault before, from the savage Iroqua, perhaps, or from even fiercer tribes that the Romans had not yet encountered.

The aviators were not all men. Here came a woman, circling over him. She was alone and unarmed, ribbons streaming out behind her in the air; her job was surely to find the Praetor and loop over his position, perhaps marking him out for attack.

A flaming arrow hit a hut that so far had remained unexploded, and it lit up like a torch. Greek fire, thought Marcellinus; these people had independently discovered Greek fire hundreds of years after the secret was lost on the Roman side of the Atlanticus. He made a note to keep some of their apothecaries and armorers—or perhaps their priests— alive at the end of this day, in addition to a handful of the pilots.

The infantry at Marcellinus's end of the line was now within bow range of the enemy. This time the Cahokians loosed a salvo of arrows first, a ragged torrent of sticks that scattered harmlessly off the tall Roman shields. The men of the First and Third cohorts jeered, drew, and sent a focused wave of metal-tipped death into the midst of the Cahokiani . . .

But then, with a titanic roar the world changed again.

Marcellinus's gaze was wrenched skyward once more, and all of a sudden he became aware of his own labored breathing and the sweat that trickled down his forehead, the smell of thousands of men in armor, the screams of the wounded, the strong breeze from the west. And the massive, incredible shape that soared unsupported through the low skies toward them, spreading the broadest of shadows across the Roman army.

"Jove!" he shouted, though he was a man who seldom cursed, and then, more reverently: "Thunderbird." Because now everything made sense.

Above them loomed a startling creation of sticks and skins, as if the longest of the Cahokiani longhouses had unfurled itself and taken flight. It did not flap like a bird but rocked on the breeze like a gull hovering over a cliff top. Mesmerized, Marcellinus noted how the Thunderbird swung steadily on the very air, how the dozen fliers who hung beneath it steered it with concerted leans and pulls and heavy shoves against the rudder bars they clutched, steering the giant craft in a smooth arc. The aerial leviathan flew south of him and then turned, the flying men using the warm air from the farthest of the burning huts to raise the craft's nose.

And here came a second Thunderbird, rising from behind the Master Mound in a thrumming *whoosh* that surely was caused by the passage of the air over the giant wing and the vibrating of the skins stretched between the wooden poles.

Bitter laughter bubbled in Marcellinus's throat at the audacity of it. This was why the Cahokiani had built their giant mounds. It was not merely a conceit to put themselves closer to their gods or for their privileged classes to look down upon their people from on high. It was to train their pilots. Why go to the trouble of building a mound in the featureless flatness of the bottomlands if not to throw yourself off it? Lining the far side of the mound must be the ballista to end all ballistas, used both to fling the insanely courageous braves in their tiny single-man wings to suicidal heights and to launch these behemoths of the air.

These beasts had not been fabricated purely for the joy of riding the winds. Marcellinus saw the row of sacks hanging beneath the wings of the first Thunderbird even as the braves began releasing them to fall into the infantry of his First and Second Cohorts.

A burning thunderclap rippled toward the Praetor, blowing him backward. The screams of his men merged into a single agonized wail as the liquid fire of Nova Hesperia rained down across entire centuries of his men. Those not directly smitten by the deadly flaring liquid fell to the ground once they trod in it with their sandaled feet, there to roll in torment. Through the bright afterimages that dazzled his eyes, Marcellinus saw the red flaming weals on his soldiers' bodies as they frantically tugged their armor away, smelled their seared flesh. Men who splashed water from their canteens onto their burning skin howled anew, as the water did not quench the fire but only spread it further.

The second Thunderbird lumbered over them, directed and shepherded by the smaller wings, sparrows looping around eagles. Marcellinus viewed its trajectory carefully, but the crew of this bird was saving its firebombs for cohorts farther up the line; as he watched, it shed Greek fire into the square formations of the Fourth and Fifth Cohorts. By then his centurions had called their infantry into the defensive testudo formation, their solid metal shields interlocked above them in the tortoiselike structure that gave the formation its name. But huge and terrifying gouts of liquid poured over them, the fire splashed and dripped between the shields, and the shell of the tortoise splintered quickly as the soldiers flung their bodies back and forth in the same terrible dance as their comrades in the First and Second.

In a single pass the two Thunderbirds had rendered a thousand Romans ineffective.

All the formations Marcellinus could see had fallen apart. And clearly audible above the screams of the Romans came the battle cries of the

Cahokiani as they sprinted across the hundred short yards that separated the armies, their clubs and hoes raised high above their heads.

Marcellinus bellowed, ripping his voice hoarse with commands to
the troops around him to fall in and regain fighting formation. He ordered his Romans to set pila and march forward and his Teutons and
Scythians to ready axes and gladii for the melee, but his words were
swept away in the din.

The two armies crashed together. Marcellinus felt the visceral shock
as Roman met Hesperian. The exultation of combat filled him, and the
surge of simple ecstasy threatened to explode his heart. With battle
joined, no doubts remained, no fears of fiery torture or flint-tipped
death, no visions of his lost family or regrets at the man he had become;
even the memory of his tribunes' treachery was swept aside. Marcellinus
had dedicated his life to moments like these. It was time to fight.

In his nose was the smell of battle, the blood and mud and dust; in
his ears, the warrior roars, the din of steel on wood, flint on steel, the
screams of the wounded, and the pounding of his pulse. The frenzy
around him became a series of sharp images: a Cahokiani brave bay-
ing as he held aloft a curly-haired Roman scalp, the sickening crunch
as a pilum cleaved a path between ribs into a living heart, a Roman
sandal skidding in blood, a plumed helmet banged aside by an ax
head, the skull beneath smashed open in the backswing. The people
of the Great City of Nova Hesperia showed themselves no simple
brawlers after all but true warriors, less armored and drilled than the
soldiers of the Imperium but with a berserker strength equal to that
of any Roman.

Marcellinus dispatched a tattooed dervish armed only with a hoe
who seemed nonetheless to be moving with preternatural speed. He
took a fearful blow to his shield and at the same time planted his gladius
into the man's face and saw him fall, cheek and throat gashed to the
bone. With a fluid motion Marcellinus tugged the sword free and spun
to meet the next threat, then froze in midswing. For it was a woman
who attacked him now, fierce and howling yet large-breasted and unar-
mored, ridiculously vulnerable. As he paused, her club struck him full

on the helmet; he dropped to a knee to absorb the pain, his ears ringing, and sliced through the woman's thigh. As she fell, he threw himself forward, his shield grinding her head into the muck.

She stopped moving. Marcellinus spared himself not a moment to wonder whether she was dead or merely unconscious but hurled himself at the next of them. Knowing that that one short moment of hesitation could have been his last added even more vigor to his arm.

For a while it seemed that Marcellinus fought alone, a single man against the ferocious horde. Then soldiers bearing the signum of the Fourth Century of the First Cohort found him and began to group around him in a rough phalanx. Pollius Scapax was there, dispatching barbarians with ruthless and narrow-eyed efficiency while still finding the breath to bark orders to the other Roman troops nearby, gathering them around their Praetor.

A Thunderbird roared over them, and Marcellinus leaped up, gladius outstretched, as if he could actually have slashed it from the sky.

They had to stop this. They had to destroy the launching system that threw the giant wings aloft. If it wasn't already too late.

Whirling, Marcellinus got his bearings.

"Scapax! The mound!"

His First Centurion nodded and bellowed orders. His soldiers closed up and surged forward, crashing once more into the thinned battle line, fifty men with swords and shields in a wedge-shaped cuneus formation with Marcellinus and Scapax fighting side by side at its tip.

Fury and pain drenched the air, and for a while it all became a blur again. Then, miraculously, the Roman squad was running unassailed through corpses. Beside and behind them the melee still raged, yet only a short stretch of mud separated them from the palisade of the Cahokiani. They had punched their way through the barbarian army and out the other side.

A quarter mile north, the new Thunderbird disgorged its bellyful of fire. Close by, yet another bird creaked in the air, flying in the opposite direction.

Marcellinus cast his shield aside and ran, the thud of each sandal fall sending a bang of pain up his spine and into his head. Beside him ran Scapax, and behind them the remains of the First Cohort.

The Master Mound grew before their eyes. The gates of the palisade were open. The Cahokiani guards at the gates backed up and made no move to prevent them from running on through. Marcellinus heard a new cacophony in his ears and realized it was his own voice screaming out the names of Roma and Titus Augustus; in addition to his country, he was invoking the name of an Imperator long dead.

Now Marcellinus was on the mound, and he pounded up it with all the energy and determination he could muster. It wasn't enough. The earthwork was enormous, and after the travails of battle, a sprint to the top of it was beyond him.

At the first plateau, where the steep incline leveled out, Marcellinus bent over, panting. Sweat poured into his eyes, and the hot fire of combat had drained from his blood. Far above at the mound's crest he could see the top of the giant unmarked wooden building. A palace? Temple? Marshaling yard for the wings? Below them was the palisade, and beyond that the battlefield they had left behind.

Beside him Scapax roared orders at the tattered remnants of the cuneus, bringing them together and back into close order for the last stand. From the top of the mound and around its sides came the Cahokiani, long spears at the ready.

The end was brief and bloody. The braves overwhelmed them, bowling the Romans over and back down the side of the mound and then leaping after them to rain blows upon them. Marcellinus saw Scapax go down, three of the Cahokiani beating him with clubs and finishing him with a spear thrust, just before his own gladius was knocked out of his hand and he was barged off his feet and onto his back. Two Cahokiani sat on Marcellinus's legs and arms, and another pulled off his plumed helmet, leaving him bareheaded and unprotected, almost steaming.

He was pinned ignominiously, trapped against the soil of the Master Mound. He struggled, desisting only when his own pugio was jabbed at his face, perilously close to his eye. Around him Cahokians screeched, gleeful.

It was over. Marcellinus panted, staring at the sky, waiting to be speared or bludgeoned or scalped, waiting for the end.

It did not come.

He heard no command, but his captors got off him, rising to their feet and looking around them and down to the plaza below. Cautiously, Marcellinus sat up to see where they were looking. The savages did not stop him, but the two who flanked him kept a watchful eye on him.

Down in the plaza some areas of fighting still raged, a last desperate effort by the few remaining Roman centuries to take as many barbarians to hell with them as they could. One of the fiercest pockets of resistance marked the distant area where the Fourth Cohort had been; Marcellinus hoped Aelfric was still fighting and would die well. Such pockets aside, the battlefield was a morass of downed Romans, charred leather, and blackened steel doused in blood. From this elevation it was clear beyond doubt that Marcellinus's army was no more.

The 33rd Hesperian Legion had been utterly destroyed in a matter of minutes.

From the fringes of the killing ground, some Romans fled eastward. Marcellinus did not begrudge them their escape. For him there could be no future that way. Even if he could escape from the mound and catch up with the fragments of his Legion, they'd probably kill him. And then on the terrible march back to the Chesapica, the Iroqua would kill *them*.

Two Thunderbirds had landed, one in a cornfield far distant and the other at the northern edge of the Urbs Cahokiani. The nearer bird was being carried back into the palisade by its pilots; from Marcellinus's vantage point it looked like an enormous crawling insect. In the distant sky two other aerial bombers turned in formation and flew back toward the mound, their giant wings flexing in the invisible air currents. And in the air far above him, fliers wearing the individual wings still danced like dragonflies, wheeling and swooping in victory.

One of the small wings separated itself from the throng and spiraled down. It shot over his head at speed and looped around. Its pilot pushed up her craft's nose to spill air and landed running along the plateau toward Marcellinus. Ribbons fluttered behind the wing.

The pilot shrugged out of her wing harness and laid the wing carefully against the slope of the mound. Marcellinus's captors drew back to let her pass.

Sisika wore a light leather tunic that was haphazardly cut. Her falcon mask hung around her neck. In her hair she wore a band studded with eagle feathers. Her face was painted with swirling marks, a forked pattern around her eyes making her look even more hawklike. Back east she had not worn such marks, perhaps adapting to local customs. That had been bravery, he now realized: to come all that way just to see the Romans for herself.

"Chieftain, daughter of chieftain," Fuscus had called her. Once again, understanding had eluded Marcellinus. Here on her home territory, Sisika's poise and authority were clear.

Sisika squatted on her heels just a few feet away, staring into his face. Marcellinus tried to imagine how rough and uncanny he must seem to her.

"Sisika," he said, and, feeling ridiculous even as he did it, he pointed at himself and said, "Gaius."

She put her head on one side, birdlike, but seeing the harsh disdain in her eyes, Marcellinus did not smile.

Marcellinus was battle-torn and filthy. He had cuts on his head and burns on his arm from splashes of Greek fire. His leg was gouged bloody, and he had lost a chunk of skin from his shoulder, wounds he did not remember getting. But of all his men he had survived and was here, now, on the mound.

Soon he would be the only Roman left alive within the city. He was the farthest west any Roman had gone, buried deep in a whole new world completely independent of the Imperium.

Below, three braves walked in through the palisade gates carrying the Legion's golden Aquila. It looked unharmed, down to the two plaques mounted on the pole beneath the eagle, the "S.P.Q.R." of the Imperium and "XXXIII Hesperia" under that. Chattering excitedly, the braves began the long walk up the mound with their trophy.

Well, they'd won it fair and square; nobody could deny that.

As the braves stepped over the shattered bodies of Pollius Scapax and the nameless Romans who had fought alongside him at the last, the reaction hit him. Deep pain plunged through his heart and stomach at the loss of his Legion. And if these people chose to burn him and tear out his heart, that would be his just deserts.

Sisika stood, and with a final contemptuous glance she turned and walked away. As if it were a signal, the Cahokians pounced upon Marcellinus and dragged him to his feet.

Marcellinus did not fight back. He had rarely shown mercy. Let none be shown to him in return.

PART 2

CAHOKIA

CHAPTER 5

YEAR ONE, THUNDER MOON

Still, they did not kill him.

Marcellinus knelt at the top of the Master Mound of the Cahokiani, his head bowed. Sweat, blood, and dirt caked him, and the late afternoon sun burned his neck. Above him glowed the golden Aquila of the lost 33rd Hesperian, the shaft that held it buried deep in the soil of an alien land. Around him stood silent braves dressed in breechcloths and feathers. Tattoos, war paint, and scarifications adorned their brown skin. Like Marcellinus, some of the warriors still clutched battle-fresh wounds that dripped blood into the clay of the mound.

The warrior standing behind him held his gladius and pugio. At any moment Marcellinus expected to feel the steel of one of his own weapons pierce his neck. He had no objections. His will to live had drained away with the last of his adrenaline.

The hubbub from the plaza faded, leaving only the sound of the breeze that had helped the Cahokians soar high above his army and destroy it.

Not far away, a man began to speak. His words were incomprehensible to Marcellinus, but the man's tone was that of an orator, and his powers of projection would have been the envy of any in the Roman Senate. Marcellinus raised his head.

Sisika stood close by, still clad in her leather flying tunic. Her falcon mask dangled from her fingers, and her face was impassive. Perspiration lined her temples and the hawklike forked design painted around her eyes had smeared, but her chin was held high. Despite her obvious weariness, her stance breathed power and strength.

Beyond her stood the much taller figure of the man who was addressing the crowd. He wore a headdress adorned with eagle feathers and a woven kilt in blocky patterns. His chest was bare and muscular, and around his shoulders was a short feather cape. From his earlobes hung pendulous copper ear spools crudely fashioned into the shape of a human head. He carried a mace of chert and stood so still that if it were not for the movement of his mouth as he spoke, he could have been fashioned out of rock himself.

The man stood at the very edge of the plateau, proclaiming in a sonorous baritone that seemed to roll down the face of the mound and wash over his people. Even so, it was miraculous that such a large assembly could hear him. The Great Plaza had to be fifty acres in area, but the sea of Hesperians all appeared to be following his words. Marcellinus glanced to the right and left and only now saw braves on the lower plateau of the Great Mound gesturing in big sweeping movements, eloquent motions of a sign language that conveyed this chieftain's meaning farther than his voice could reach. Along the sides of the plaza and far beyond, other braves took the gestures and repeated them, spreading the words so that all could share them.

The crowd was enthralled. Every face was upturned. The chieftain of the Cahokians commanded absolute attention from his people.

Marcellinus wished he could understand what they were hearing. Clearly, he himself was the object of much of it; the chieftain would occasionally lift an arm and point at him.

He also wished he could stand, but only because of the pain in his knees and legs. It should have been ignominious for a Roman Praetor to be kneeling at the beck and call of a foreign army, but Marcellinus was beyond that. Stoically, he took the shame as his due. He was, after all, defeated.

The chief's voice built to a crescendo, then stopped abruptly. He made another sweeping gesture toward Marcellinus while still facing out over the mass of his people.

From behind Marcellinus came the familiar ring of steel. Above him, he saw the glint of a blade. The warrior had raised Marcellinus's sword over his head.

An expectant silence fell. Sisika turned slowly to gaze at him.

Unable to meet her eyes, Marcellinus looked out beyond the crowd to where the sun sank over a great brown river and wide fields of Hesperian corn. Plumes of smoke rose from the thousands of huts that made up the Great City. Mounds, some truncated pyramids of earth topped with a house and palisade and others conical and unadorned, dotted the landscape as far as he could see. Away to the east, the golden rays of the sunset illuminated the pale face of the low landlocked river bluffs that marked the edge of the immense Cahokian floodplain five or more miles distant.

If Marcellinus did not look down into the fields of death beyond the plaza, he might have imagined that nothing in particular had happened this day, that this was just another glorious evening deep in the heart of a new continent.

If these were his last moments on earth, he wanted above all to feel at peace.

The killing stroke did not come. The silence extended. The chief held his position, his hand pointed toward the Roman. Nobody else spoke. No ritual was being conducted here. Marcellinus was still breathing.

A broad shadow swept the plaza as the sun set, and as if they had been freed from bondage, a mighty howl burst forth from the crowd accompanied by the rattle of wood against wood, wood against steel, steel against steel. Thousands of Cahokiani were beating captured Roman weapons against Roman armor in a deafening cacophony.

"Holy gods," Marcellinus said aloud, awed at the din. He looked up.

Above him, the Roman standard still gleamed. It wounded Marcellinus to see the Legion's eagle captured. But the loss of a golden bird was nothing to the loss of three thousand men, his command, and his world.

It was as if the Cahokiani had been waiting for him to move. The brave stepped past him and laid his gladius and pugio on the ground by his side at the standard's base.

Marcellinus's legs had stiffened. The brave grabbed his arm and pulled him up onto his feet. Sisika and the chieftain were already walking toward the huge longhouse that capped the mound. Marcellinus took a few steps after them.

Braves in falcon masks converged on him, turning him around firmly. Marcellinus did not resist as they ushered him down the steps of the mound and tethered him to a tall cedar pole.

Marcellinus awoke at dawn lying on the ground, his body stiff and aching. His eyes were stuck shut, and with his wrists lashed together it was hard to raise his fingers to rub the sleep out of them. He felt a tacky dampness at his shoulder and leg where his wounds had reopened and a fierce throbbing pain along his arm from the Cahokian liquid flame.

They had bound his wrists and hobbled his ankles with a fine sinew that cut into him when he moved. A short rope held him fast to the pole of red cedar that stood just inside the open gates of the palisade, the same gates he had run through the previous day, near the battle's end.

With some difficulty Marcellinus rolled onto his back and peered up the steep slope of the Master Mound. He saw no one.

He grasped the pole and levered himself to a sitting position. Through the gates, the early sun lit the straw-thatched huts, turning them golden. Native men and women walked back and forth between them, rubbing their eyes. Marcellinus rubbed his own eyes again. The Cahokiani were a people who in the heat of summer did not wear very much. Many of them were clad only in breechcloths—and some in even less.

A woman limped past, her long gray hair in braids. She was dressed more modestly than the younger women in a fringed tunic that might have been deerskin. Her hip clearly troubled her, for she had a rolling gait and rubbed her hip bone and grumbled as she walked.

Seeing Marcellinus, she stopped dead in her tracks. Her expression hardened. Pursing her lips, she turned and hobbled back the way she had come.

Moments later a grim-faced brave walked through the gate. His head was shorn at the sides, leaving a sharp spiky crest of hair that jutted up from his scalp and hung down his back in a long braid. His shoulders were decorated with dark feather tattoos, and a jagged pattern of blue and red war paint adorned his chest, smudged where he'd slept on it. The stink of battle was still on him.

Halting in front of Marcellinus and not meeting his eye, the warrior raised a chert knife.

Marcellinus tilted his head back, baring his throat. He would welcome whatever death was his due, and a quiet dispatch in the dawn was as good as any, but he would prefer the slash to be quick and sure-aimed.

The brave grabbed his hands and sawed through the sinew that bound him. When Marcellinus still didn't move, the man pushed his wrists apart a little impatiently.

"Maybe I should stay here," Marcellinus said.

The brave grunted and hacked away the sinew binding Marcellinus's ankles. The older woman reappeared and quacked at him peevishly, dragging Marcellinus to his feet with only belated help from the brave. She only came up to his shoulder but was considerably stronger than she looked.

The woman's hut was only a couple of hundred yards outside the gate, but every step sent shooting pains through Marcellinus's legs and spine. He tottered like an infant, muttering in profane Latin and bleeding gently into the dust. Just as they arrived, the cramps in his muscles started to ease.

Outside the hut a much younger woman nursed her baby, bare-breasted and long-legged. She gaped at the Roman, then stood and strode away. The brave called after her, but the harsh set of her shoulders was answer enough: yesterday's enemy was hardly welcome at their house. "I don't blame you," Marcellinus said.

The old woman returned bearing a bowl of water. Marcellinus bowed his head to drink, but the woman's shriek brought him upright again in short order. She gestured, hands flapping and braids bouncing, and he finally understood. Dipping his palms into the bowl, he splashed water onto his face and rubbed his hands together, did it again, and a third time.

The water quickly turned dark and bloody. Marcellinus touched his face more gingerly, trying to locate the gashes in his skin so he wouldn't irritate them further.

The old woman slapped his hands away from his forehead. Startled once again, Marcellinus sat quietly as she dabbed at his brow with the corner of a small blanket that itself looked none too clean. Satisfied, she babbled another stream of words at him and emitted an explosive *psssht!* of disgust at his continued lack of comprehension.

Meanwhile, the brave pushed a smaller clay bowl of water into his hand. Marcellinus hesitated, wary of breaching etiquette again. The brave understood and gestured, lifting his hand to his lips.

Marcellinus drained the bowl in two large, painful swallows and held it out for more.

As the sun rose higher, Urbs Cahokiani came to life at its own speed. People moved slowly and dallied to chat with one another. Their motions seemed aimless to Marcellinus's eyes. It was nothing like the purposeful bustle of the castra.

Braves and women blinked at him as they walked by. Children stared openly, and many would have stayed to stare longer if not urged past by their parents. Some people had started the work of their day while the air was still relatively cool. A man carved strips of meat from a deer hung up on a wooden frame, a dog at his feet hoping for scraps. Two women outside the hut opposite began to grind corn on a dish-shaped rock, glancing at Marcellinus covertly out of the corners of their eyes. Outside another hut a little farther away, a plump older woman turned clay in her hands, fashioning it into a bowl; the fired and half-painted pots by her blanket showed her to be something of a craftswoman. She had a colored blanket draped over her shoulders, but most of the other

Cahokians wore tattoos, body paint, breechcloths, and not a great deal more.

Marcellinus frequently glanced back toward the gates where he had spent the night, but no sudden consternation erupted at his absence from the pole, and no warriors came dashing down the steps of the mound to collect him. The Master Mound and the rest of the area inside the palisade seemed empty.

Of course, the warriors and ordinary folk of Cahokia were also awakening the morning after a ferocious and exhausting battle. A battle that Marcellinus himself had brought upon them. The paradox that he could be sitting eating some kind of corn mash in the morning light, unmolested and practically ignored in the middle of an enemy city he had just the previous day waged brutal war on, became even more acute.

And with that thought came another wave of delayed terror and nausea at the loss of his Legion. Marcellinus stopped chewing and swallowed hard.

He could casually eat breakfast on a morning like this? While the tormented souls of thousands of Romans still shimmered in the air around him?

The old woman reached out her hand in concern. Obviously his despair had shadowed his face, and how could it be otherwise?

Marcellinus stood abruptly.

He had presided over one of the greatest Roman defeats in history. This was his Teutoburg, his Carrhae, his Cannae. Today marked his entrance into the pantheon of the cursed: Roman generals whose incompetence had wiped out their entire commands, legates who had failed so disgracefully that their names were held in contempt for centuries.

What would his father and family think of him now? His daughter?

At least those other blighted generals had had the decency to perish in their final wars. Publius Quinctilius Varus. Marcus Licinius Crassus. Lucius Aemilius Paullus. All had fallen in battle with their men. Why should Gaius Publius Marcellinus go on living with this dark hole at the center of his soul?

Without even a nod to his hosts he stepped away from their hut and strode blindly forward into the heart of the Urbs Cahokiani.

People moved out of his way. As he limped past house after house, Cahokians fell silent and watched him go, and still nobody raised a hand against him. It all blurred around him: white walls, golden thatch, staring faces, soil and sand underfoot. The sun, already beginning to burn his face.

Then there were no more people and few houses, merely the twin stenches of burning and death.

His foot bumped into a corpse, and he stopped.

Marcellinus stood at the edge of yesterday's battlefield. A sea of broken bodies stretched out before him, Romans and Cahokians piled in a mass of slaughter. The stink of viscera wafted over him.

Marcellinus grunted and shoved up the sleeves of his tunic. He had work to do.

The Cahokiani had made a noble start on the grisly work the previous evening. They had at least dragged the bodies away from their Great Plaza and the huts that surrounded it. But the battle line had extended for hundreds of yards beyond that, and the melee had ranged far and wide as the Romans had scattered under the assaults of the Thunderbirds and the warrior horde on the ground.

A few dozen grim-faced Cahokiani were already walking among the dead, lifting the broken bodies of their warriors and carrying them reverently away from the battlefield. As each body was moved, a small swarm of flies took to the air. By the nearest stand of trees Marcellinus saw a neat line of Hesperian corpses, their smashed bodies straightened as well as they could be, their weapons placed on their chests. With much less care, another team of Cahokians stripped Roman bodies of arms and armor. Children carried blood-streaked swords and breastplates off the killing fields and added them to the growing piles of steel at the edge of the plaza.

The spoils of war. Marcellinus could imagine how useful the Roman weaponry might be when pressed into service against local foes. Perhaps he had already changed the balance of power in the region.

What of that? He put the thought aside. He cared nothing for tribal politics. If the Cahokiani wanted to go off and slaughter Iroqua with Roman steel, more power to them. He walked forward and bent over to pick up the body of the first Roman soldier he came to, a fine blond-haired boy with green eyes open in surprise, his face unmarred but his intestines a mass of dark blood and flies.

Someone seized him from behind. Marcellinus tried to react, but he was hampered by the corpse of his countryman and the dizzy ache of his own limbs. He sprawled backward onto hard Roman armor, the dead lad's weight across his knees.

Above him stood a Cahokian warrior, his face still daubed with war paint. Spiral tattoos covered his arms and shoulders. He held a Roman gladius awkwardly in both hands, the point of the blade bobbing in the air scant inches above Marcellinus's unprotected chest. From his belt hung strips of bloody hair, the scalps of dead Romans. His features were distorted, and a few drops of his spittle alighted on Marcellinus's cheek.

Belatedly, Marcellinus realized that the warrior was screaming at him and had been screaming for some time. His fugue state of despair apparently had rendered him insensible to the sounds around him. Nor had he been truly conscious of the terrible, fetid smell of the battlefield that burst upon him now, flooding his nostrils. He rolled aside, spilling the dead Roman boy off his legs, and vomited onto the bloody ground.

He stood and took up the body once more. Again the Cahokian struck him down. Marcellinus tasted blood: fresh blood here where there was already so much. He thought of bearing his breast to the man. Thought of goading him, fighting back just enough to force his own death.

The brave pointed to the tattoos on his chest and arms, spit on the ground, pointed at the dead men around them, the jabs of his fingers rough and accusatory.

The sun blinked. Another brave had leaped over Marcellinus and seized the screaming warrior by the shoulders. More men arrived, shouting and gesturing, shoving at one another, some pointing at Marcellinus and snarling, others pointing toward the Great Mound. Marcellinus sat up and wiped his mouth, put his head in his hands, and waited for the argument over his fate to be resolved.

. . . And still they didn't kill him.

Morning gave way to afternoon. Marcellinus took no break, stopped for no rest, accepting only a bowl of water a woman halfheartedly held out to him around noon.

The charnel pit was a long walk off to the east, a shallow rectangular grave that already contained several hundred Cahokian bodies. At first Marcellinus wanted to protest, although he had no words to speak that they would comprehend: the grave was not deep enough, the dead would be defiled, the Cahokians' dogs and other wild animals would dig up the corpses, human bones would proliferate through the area, disease would spread.

Then he looked around, and the answer became obvious. A mound would be built here over the valiant Cahokian dead, a permanent memorial to their sacrifice.

He nodded, spit the flies out of his mouth, and trudged back to the battlefield to hoist another corpse onto his shoulders.

But now, logical thought having restarted in his brain, he had another idea. He walked out beyond the plaza, back the way the Roman army had come, until he came to the carts they had hauled across the continent. The baggage train was still loaded just as he had last seen it; the Cahokiani had no use for Roman tents, and they needed none of the Romans' dwindling supply of corn, hard cheese, and wine. There was no sign of the slaves who had hauled the carts across Nova Hesperia. Even the horses had disappeared. Whether the beasts had been freed by the Cahokians, escaped by themselves, or been slaughtered for their meat was beyond his power to guess.

Marcellinus had thought that the carts could be unloaded and pressed into service to ferry the dead to their final resting place, but once again he could not make himself understood. Unsurprisingly, the few braves nearby ignored all his gestures, and unloading a wagon and hauling it to the battlefield was quite beyond the efforts of one man.

He took a long drink of wine, unwatered. Its brackish, sour taste helped cut the gummy residue in his mouth and throat but sent a cloud of dizziness over him again. He clutched the tall wheel of the cart until it passed, took a second swig, and went back to work.

As a professional soldier, Marcellinus found it a little galling that so few of the dead bodies on the battlefield were Cahokian. As a human being, he felt oddly comforted.

For his dead Roman legionaries, there would be no memorial mound. The charnel pit dug for the Romans was a converted borrow pit out in the marshland, and their bodies were burned in batches once they had been stripped of weaponry and armor. Marcellinus was dourly content. They were just empty husks now, broken forms that his valiant men had no further need of. Better that they be burned and have their essence rise into the Hesperian air than rot in the damp earth. Their memorial would be in his mind, where it would loom greater than any grass-covered mound.

More upsetting than the burning of the corpses was the scalping. As Sisika had promised months before, the Cahokians often cut off the Romans' hair, carving it whole off the skull beneath. Many of the legionaries Marcellinus doggedly ferried to the Roman charnel pit had the characteristic red band hacked out of their heads, in some cases blackened and stale, in others still weeping blood. It was also clear that many of the Romans had been strangled.

Aside from Marcellinus, the Cahokians had not spared the wounded.

By midafternoon all the Roman corpses on the battlefield had been stripped of their helmets and breastplates. At least Marcellinus did not need to perform that task. He did, however, find a pugio the Cahokians had missed, ground into the blood-soaked dirt beneath the body of a Hispanic auxiliary from Fabius's Seventh Cohort. The soldier had been so comprehensively butchered that Marcellinus had almost left him where he lay for someone else to deal with, but perhaps the dead Roman's blade was his reward for gritting his teeth and honoring the man's sacrifice. Marcellinus slid the grimy dagger inside his tunic before dragging the auxiliary to his final resting place.

At day's end they were still not done. Marcellinus trooped off to the broad and winding creek that ran just north of the city with the rest of the Cahokian workers and dipped his aching body into the water to sluice off the worst of the dried blood and muck. By now he received little more than dull, resentful stares from the Cahokians.

It seemed that outside the heat of battle none of them would even stoop to murder him. So be it.

Marcellinus stumbled and fell on his knees from exhaustion several times on his way back into the city. Today's heavy exercise had reopened his wounds, and scabs of new blood now caked them. His stomach hurt, a hard knot of pain and emptiness at its center, but he could not have faced food even if any had been offered. He walked through the palisade gates of the Great Mound and curled up on the bare ground where he had awoken that morning, at the base of the pole they had bound him to. He was sound asleep well before sunset.

He awoke to the same old woman shaking him by the shoulder. Her gray braids tickled his chest. The sun was already well above the trees and river bluffs to the east as she guided him, hobbling badly, to her hut.

This time the young mother and her baby had already made themselves scarce. Marcellinus splashed his face with water; swallowed sour tea and some corn gruel, this time supplemented with beans and a pulpy yellow vegetable he could not identify; then pushed himself unsteadily to his feet.

He meant to bow to his benefactor to express his thanks the only way he knew how, but once he bent forward at the waist, he lost his balance and kept going, toppling to the ground. He was dimly aware that she rushed to his side, shaking him, but he had no strength left to tell her to stop, that he was not worth the trouble, that it would not make any difference, anyway.

He lost consciousness with her worried babble filling his ears and did not awaken all that day or all the night that followed.

Marcellinus opened his eyes. He was lying on a straw pallet in a Cahokian hut. Three children stood in the doorway.

Disoriented, he sat up. Pain lanced through his forehead, and the walls shimmered. He squinted through it. The inside of the hut was bare, and so was he, almost; he was wearing a breechcloth that only just preserved his modesty.

His tunic lay at the foot of his bed, neatly folded. It had been rinsed out after a fashion but was still brown in patches, streaked with his blood and the blood of countless others. Also on the bed were a clean Cahokian-style deerskin tunic and the small golden lares that had been tied into the pocket of his tunic for luck and safekeeping. He was most surprised to see the pugio he had stolen from the battlefield, its blade and hilt scrubbed clean of the gore that had caked them.

The oldest boy said something in a clear piping voice. The girl added a few words in a strained tone but then smiled nervously. Marcellinus realized that it was the sound of her voice that had awoken him several seconds earlier.

Their words did not sound like the Algon-Quian that Fuscus and the other Powhatani had spoken. Another belated realization, something else Marcellinus had been aware of without consciously articulating: the Cahokian language was different from that of the Powhatani. That meant, he supposed, that Sisika must speak both tongues.

The boy took a step down into the hut and raised his hand, said something else. The smallest child, who had not yet spoken, gasped in fear and tugged at the taller boy's arm until he reluctantly stepped safely back outside the doorway.

"Give me a moment," Marcellinus said. He swung his legs off the bed. They felt rubbery, and once again the walls danced around him. "Uh, wait outside. Go away." He made shooing motions, but not un-kindly, and the children retreated into the bright world outside his door and let the animal skin that covered it fall back into place.

The hut was smaller in area than his Praetorium tent but, oddly, taller. It had no windows. Rafters supported a peaked roof of rushes and prairie grass, and light came in through a broad hole in the roof's center, directly over what looked like a fire pit with a hearth of rough stones. The walls were of wooden struts covered with reed mats. The sleeping pallet and its mattress were the only furniture.

There was no chamber pot. What was he supposed to do? He stood and took a few experimental steps. When he touched his face, his hands did not come away bloody. In fact, it looked as if somebody had smeared a paste or salve of some kind over his wounds.

Marcellinus stood under the chimney hole and inspected his legs and arm. Sure enough, a white substance had been plastered over the gashes. Flexing his leg, he realized that his wound had been stitched up while he slept, before the salve had been applied. The paste smelled fresh and natural. Beneath it, of course, Marcellinus stank, but at least he stank of good honest sweat and not of pus or gangrenous infection. He would be keeping all his limbs.

He pulled on his stained Roman tunic, leaving the alternative Ca-hokian garment where it lay, After a moment of thought he slipped the clean pugio inside his tunic; if he was allowed to own it, presumably he was allowed to carry it. His Roman sandals were nowhere to be seen, leaving him little choice but to slip on the moccasins at the foot of his bed. He went to the door. Its doorway was to the south, with the sun cutting through it obliquely. It must be morning, then. The floor level in the hut was a good nine inches lower than the ground level outside, perhaps to help keep the hut cool in summer and preserve its heat in winter. Clumsily, he stepped up and out.

He was well away from where he'd lost consciousness, on the opposite side of the plaza from the old woman's hut. Beyond the plaza rose the Great Mound, solid and imposing in the early sunshine. By its palisade, immense stacks of Roman armor and weapons glinted a burnished silver. The skies were filled with puffy clouds, and some of the humidity had dissipated. At any other time Marcellinus might have called it a lovely day.

The three children sat on the ground to the left of the door. On seeing him, they rose bashfully. The youngest child was a boy, he saw now; it had been difficult to tell earlier, as his hair was just as long as the girl's.

"Uh, bathroom?" Marcellinus said. "Latrina? A pot to piss in? Um?"

The eldest boy raised his right hand, palm out, as if he were telling Marcellinus to stop, but the next moment the other two children did it, too. A greeting, then. The boy pointed to his own chest. "Tahtay," he said, self-importantly.

"Yeah," said Marcellinus, looking around. The nearest stand of trees was some distance away.

The girl pointed at herself. "Kimimela."

"Gaius," Marcellinus said. "Look, wait here a moment." They padded after him regardless. "No! No. Stop. Sit down. Stay right there. Stay!"

"Tahtay!" said the boy, aggrieved.

"Yes, yes, Tahtay. Gaius." Oh, hell. He mimed inexpertly what he needed to do, and the girl spun away with a blush and a screech. The boys cackled, and the smaller one pointed at a hut set apart from the others, a couple of hundred feet away.

"Uh, sorry," Marcellinus said. "Look . . . I'll be right back."

Marcellinus had no particular affinity for children; he had stopped talking to them at roughly the time he had stopped being one himself. He had treated his own daughter, Vestilia, like an adult from the time she was six.

The tallest boy was eleven winters old, and his name was indeed Tahtay, which when mimed meant "the storm" or perhaps just "the wind." Kimimela's name meant "butterfly" based on the shape she drew in the dirt and the way she fluttered her arms, and she was eight winters old. The smallest of the three was called Enopay, which meant "bold" or "brave" or "defiant" or some other idea synonymous with standing up straight and strutting around with his fists up, and none of the three knew how old Enopay might be.

They were disappointed that his name, Gaius Marcellinus, didn't mean anything and couldn't be mimed, and they seemed dubious about the number of winters he claimed. They addressed him as "Gaiss" to his face but referred to him as "Hotah" or "Wanageeska" or "Eyanosa" when they discussed him among themselves. When Marcellinus, with some trepidation, tried to inquire what those words meant, they—predictably—just pointed at him and grinned.

They had obviously been sent to learn his language, and Tahtay, above all, took his task very seriously. As soon as Marcellinus had walked back to them from the latrine, Tahtay had pointed to his legs and said a word, then pointed for Marcellinus to sit, then said another word. Jumping to his feet and walking, Tahtay repeated the first word, where-upon Marcellinus said "Tahtay ambulas," and Kimimela clapped her hands in delight and made a sign with both hands that had to mean the same thing: walking.

After that the work began in earnest, with Tahtay miming an action or an idea, saying a word, and then inviting Marcellinus to say the word in his own tongue. Their young brains soaked up his Latin like sponges.

Their efforts to teach him spoken Cahokian in return were an abject failure. Marcellinus could hold a Cahokian word in his mind only until Tahtay said something else, and then the first word slid out of his head as if it had never been there. He did much better with the gestural language, the hand-talk as Kimimela called it, because the gestures had their own logic; the sign for *water* involved pretending to drink from your cupped hand, *sleep* had him resting his cheek against his hands, and the sign for *question*—the most useful gesture of all and one he used constantly—required him to hold up his hand with his fingers open and waggle it at the wrist.

Even so, by noon Marcellinus was wearying of the effort, and the weight of his guilt was growing inside him once again. He swallowed the last of the chewy hazelnut cakes they had brought him, raised his hands in surrender, and stood.

"Hand-talk," said Tahtay sternly in barely comprehensible Latin. "Sit, hand-talk hand-talk."

Marcellinus swung his hand back and forth in the gesture for *No* and gestured *Walk, graves.*

"Walk to river," Enopay counteroffered in Latin.

Walk graves, then walk river, signed Marcellinus.

Kimimela grimaced and gestured *No.* "Kimi hit food," she said aloud.

"What?" Marcellinus said, and knocked twice on his right forearm with his left fist, which was the sign they had developed for when someone needed a definition.

Enopay mimed it. Kimimela, seeing what he was doing, mimed the same thing faster, as if competing or trying to catch up. "Huh," said Tahtay, a grunt he had picked up from Marcellinus.

Marcellinus thought he understood. He pointed to Enopay's arms. "Grind?" He pointed to the space beneath. "Corn?" He mimed eating to try to confirm it.

"Kimimela grind corn. No walk graves, grind corn," said the girl.

"That's quite a lot of Latin for one day," Marcellinus said.

"Hand-talk!"

Marcellinus stood. The inactivity had rendered his leg muscles almost immobile. He tried not to let the children see how stiff and weary he was, wondering what the word for pride was. "Enopay," probably.

He bowed solemnly to her. "Farewell, Kimimela."

Kimimela laughed and ran, her pigtails bobbing.

Having gotten rid of the girl, Tahtay and Enopay were keen to enlarge their vocabularies still further, with the result that in short order Marcellinus had learned the Cahokian words for urine and feces. Oddly, they stuck in his mind much better than the other words. However, Tahtay's next mimed question was even more vulgar, a bridge too far for one so young, and Marcellinus shook his head in embarrassment and took a step away. "Gaius walk graves."

Obligingly, they jumped up to escort him.

Marcellinus wasn't sure about taking the boys to the battlefield, but he couldn't imagine how to parse a sentence complex enough to ask whether their parents would object. He hadn't yet taught them father or mother and, put to the test, couldn't think of a suitable mime for those words at that moment.

He gestured *No*. "Enopay, Tahtay. Sit. Gaius walk." He took a few experimental steps, shooed them away.

It didn't work. "Tahtay walk graves."

He walked across the plaza with a boy on each side. Cahokians carrying pots or straw glanced curiously at them; the boys strode along, proud of their important task, and Marcellinus nodded as politely and solemnly as if they were promenading on the Capitoline Hill on a fine Roman afternoon.

The heat was building, and the air was growing fetid. Marcellinus would have given anything for a trip to a good honest bathhouse. It might take hours of sweating, oiling, and scraping to get all the muck and dirt out of his skin.

As they walked past a small mound with a house perched on its flat top, Marcellinus had a sudden thought.

"Tahtay?" Marcellinus knocked twice with his fist on his forearm and pointed upward to indicate the path of something flying up off the Great Mound. He gestured a small wing with his hand, then demonstrated the might of a full Thunderbird using his outstretched arms and pointed back at the Great Mound.

"Catanwakuwa," said Tahtay for the smaller falcon craft and "Wakinyan" for the Thunderbird, and those words too burned themselves immediately into Marcellinus's brain, never to be forgotten.

The battlefield was empty. Ominous dark patches littered the soil and sand, but the acres of dead had vanished. Marcellinus was surprised and impressed at how much the Cahokians had managed to achieve while he had been unconscious. Had he perhaps been out of action for two days instead of one?

As it turned out, there was equally little to see at the graves. The Cahokians had made excellent use of the time Marcellinus had spent in his exhausted slumber, and a two-foot layer of soil already covered the trench grave of the Cahokian warriors. A desultory stream of men walked in from the other direction carrying baskets of soil that they dumped out onto the rising mound, glowering at Marcellinus. It might be weeks before they built a full mound at that rate, though perhaps it was work that need not be hurried. Overseeing them was a stocky older man wearing a feather cloak and copper earrings. Delicate, complex tattoos adorned his wrinkled skin; tassels, amulets, and a wooden mask with a long nose hung from his belt. When he caught sight of Marcellinus, the man backed up and raised what appeared to be a flyswatter in defense against him.

A shaman if Marcellinus had ever seen one. He knocked on his arm again and pointed at the man. The shaman flinched, and Tahtay said "Youtin" in a tone that did not seem unduly reverent.

"Youtin," Marcellinus repeated. Perhaps a man worth watching.

The earth carriers and Youtin resented his presence, as well they might, and Marcellinus did not linger. He walked on, turning down the path that would lead him to where his legion lay. Too, it seemed that the last Roman corpses had been dragged to their own charnel pit; unable to shake his young honor guard, Marcellinus did not walk right up to it, but the smell of smoke and burning had drowned its previous aroma of death and decay. A plume of greasy smoke still arose into the heavy sky, but a bank of soil had already been piled up ready to bury the site forever once the embers of his legionaries had cooled.

Very well. His dead were in their final resting place. No work remained for Marcellinus. It was done.

He nodded and tried to turn away from the grave but failed. The draw of his perished cohorts was too strong. Even as he stood in the bright early afternoon, the familiar darkness welled up in Marcellinus's soul; his breathing became ragged, and he swayed. How far was it to the damned wagons from here? Would the wine still be there?

"So many gone," he said. "Aelfric. Pollius Scapax."

Marcellinus had no rites to perform. No prayers to offer up to chilly Cybele, no penitence to offer the austere and forbidding Christ-Risen, and if Jupiter Imperator had been a real god and not merely the symbol of Roman Imperium, he surely would have stopped the breath in Marcellinus's throat already. Marcellinus stood by the ashes of his men with no gods to comfort him, with guilt and isolation his earthly punishment.

Now would be a fitting time for it to end. Perhaps he should take his own life, right now. Fall here once and for all and write the last line on the history of the Fighting 33rd.

For a moment he was very aware of the pugio inside his tunic, its blade warm against his stomach.

He looked back. Tahtay frowned into the trees, his hands over Enopay's eyes and nose. Enopay stood, suffering it calmly, his head bowed.

"I'm sorry," Marcellinus said. "Gods, what am I thinking? Why would they let me bring you here? Is everyone in this tribe of barbarians insane?" His voice faltered.

"Hand-talk," Tahtay said gruffly.

This was intolerable. Marcellinus had to find a way out. Of Cahokia or, if necessary, of his life.

Gaius walk to river, he signed. He strode away with the blood pounding in his ears, and a few moments later the boys ran past him like the wind, boldly, back to the plaza, and waited there for him to catch up.

As the boys guided Marcellinus westward through a seemingly endless suburb of the fine white houses, all crested with yellow reed thatch, his pulse raced. He had almost expected not to be allowed in this direction, would not have been surprised if a passing brave had halted him and forced him back the other way. For the river meant potential escape. And also . . .

Once past the Great Mound, Marcellinus looked back and inspected its broad slope. From here he could see the north face of the earthen pyramid that had been at the reverse as his army had marched into the city from the south. From the north side, the Cahokiani had launched their nimble Catanwakuwa and mighty Wakinyan to rain death and destruction on the 33rd Hesperian Legion. Before he died, Marcellinus wanted to know how that was done.

Alas, he could see almost nothing. A pair of long wooden rails braced by struts extended up the side of the mound to its flat top and extended another twenty feet farther up into the air from there. However, his view of the foot of the rails was obscured by the tall stockade that encircled the mound and the area near its base. There must be a mechanism of considerable power that he could not see, but it was either hidden behind the wooden wall or dismantled and packed away to keep it safe from the elements until the next time they needed to deploy it. Any substantial wooden apparatus would, after all, eventually warp in the damp heat of the Hesperian bottomlands.

Some kind of giant ballista or onager, Marcellinus was betting. Either tension power or torsion. But in truth, the launching mechanism was not so much a marvel as the controlled flight of the wings once hurled into the sky and their pilots' uncanny ability to ride the air currents and maintain their height.

From within Cahokia it was hard for Marcellinus to deduce the layout of the city. He knew that it was bounded just north of the Master Mound by the winding Cahokia Creek, with only a crescent-shaped lake and a few homesteads and fields beyond that. From his moments on top of the Master Mound he also knew that the city sprawled off farther in a westerly direction, toward the mighty river, than it did to the south and east. But it was only now that he noticed that the Master Mound, the Great Plaza, and the subsidiary plazas and platform mounds that flanked them were all oriented along a north-south or east-west axis. The longhouse on low stilts that they passed as they headed toward the river—a storehouse for grain, with the wooden blocks keeping the floor raised against damp and rodents—was similarly aligned north-south. The common houses that surrounded the mounds and communal spaces, however, were not, apparently scattered with more care given to social convenience than to the cardinal points.

As he went by those houses, Marcellinus kept his eyes averted, for clearly he was not beloved by their occupants. Some spit as he passed, though fortunately behind him into his footprints. Others called out comments in Cahokian that Tahtay and Enopay chose not to translate. Children gaped, frozen in place by his proximity until their parents or elder siblings ran to pull them out of Marcellinus's path, generally hurling harsh-sounding words at him even though he had made no hostile move. Even their dogs barked at him.

Tahtay and Enopay remained calm. Their faces showed no shame or embarrassment, though their pride at their assignment seemed muted in the face of such Cahokian enmity.

Half a mile past a midsize plaza to the west of the Great Mound, the boys guided him around a large clearing. Here five or six dozen tall poles defined a circle measuring perhaps four hundred feet across. The poles, of the ubiquitous red cedar, were of a uniform height and had carvings on them and other items tied to them that Marcellinus could not identify. A central pole well over a hundred feet tall towered over them all, and from here the motif of its carving was easy to recognize: the human-size carved figure atop the pole was a birdman, a falcon warrior with wings extended.

"Nice," Marcellinus said, and pointed. Enopay opened his eyes wider and gestured *No*, urging him past the wooden monument into the next area of houses. Indeed, a few nearby warriors had perked up their attention visibly at Marcellinus's interest in the cedar circle. Clearly this was a sacred space for the Cahokians, and nobody would be happy to see him trespass on it.

He remembered how the aquiliferi honor guard had reacted when Sisika had shown interest in the Roman Aquila of the 33rd. Some mysteries were best not meddled with.

From here the journey to the river was a long flat slog through even more houses arranged around a succession of small plazas each centered with its own cedar pole and studded with conical mounds and the occasional ridge mound. At one point they detoured around a broad lake with a suspiciously even shoreline that Marcellinus took for a flooded borrow pit. All the soil that formed the giant mounds of Cahokia had to have come from somewhere.

As they walked, the sinuous curve of the Cahokia Creek swung down to meet them, and the boys steered him leftward, to the southwest. Here there were only a few houses, and much of the land was given over to agriculture, mostly the broad Cahokian corn and what looked like herbs and even flowers. Ahead of them, the western complex of Cahokia seemed almost a separate town to Marcellinus, subordinate to the main city in the size of its mounds, granaries, and houses.

Marcellinus held up his hand. He badly needed to rest. Over the last three days he had endured a battle, the grueling cleanup that had followed, and a day of complete inactivity, and his muscles were complaining. Discreetly, he examined his wounds to check for blood or other leakage, but the stitches and salve were holding up well.

So, ten thousand people or more in the main urbs of Cahokia plus another three or four thousand in the smaller suburbs that lay ahead. Hundreds or even thousands more spread around in the more sparsely populated areas of the floodplains out to the river bluffs, and then who knew how many more in the rural populations in the hilly uplands and spread out in homesteads to north, east, and south, tending to the huge Cahokian fields.

It added up quickly. All told, he must indeed be sitting in a metropolis of twenty thousand people. Larger than many of the principal cities of the Roman Imperium, though meaner in architecture aside from those mighty earthen pyramids. Many months ago on the shores of the Chesapica, hearing tell of a "great city," Marcellinus had not imagined anything like this.

The boys were fidgeting. "Onward," Marcellinus said.

As they entered western Cahokia, a warrior stepped forward brandishing a spear. His body was a mass of tattoos from his waist to his eyes, and a shell gorget hung around his neck, bouncing on his chest. With a derisive laugh the warrior pointed at the top of Marcellinus's head and then his own, and then at his waist.

Hanging from the warrior's loose belt were three fresh scalps, presumably Roman.

Tahtay spoke sharply, wagging a finger at the much taller Cahokian who confronted them and then reaching back to point at the Great Mound, now perhaps five miles behind. The warrior laughed again and surged forward.

Enopay, of all people, stepped into the warrior's path in Marcellinus's defense.

"Come back!" Marcellinus cried. "Enopay, no!" But the warrior had already backed up and now turned to stalk off between the houses, still calling out in a mocking tone. A few seconds later he was gone, but the men and women he had left behind him still stared at Marcellinus, not blinking.

Marcellinus said to Tahtay: "My life wouldn't be worth a bent straw if not for the speech your chief made on the mound, would it?"

"What?" Tahtay said. "Hotah walk to river," and they set off again.

No other Cahokians challenged them, and Marcellinus redoubled his efforts not to make eye contact with people or look at what they were doing. Eventually they passed through the last lanes of the western city and approached the river's muddy shore.

Getting to the river had required a much longer walk than Marcellinus had expected given the view from the top of the Great Mound, and the reason was easy to deduce: the river was the biggest he had yet seen in Nova Hesperia, much broader than the rivers they had forded or floated across on makeshift rafts on their epic journey through the Appalachia and then through the never-ending forests and plains.

"Mizipi," Tahtay said proudly.

"Frumen," Enopay added, equally proud of knowing the Latin equivalent.

"Flumen," Marcellinus corrected him absently.

It was over half a mile across, broader than the Tiber and muddier as well. On the river's far shore were a few dozen small mounds and a smattering of houses; certainly several hundred people lived over there, but for all intents and purposes Cahokia stopped on this side of the river and at a safe enough distance from the shoreline that nobody's home would be inundated when the river burst its banks. Marcellinus gazed dolefully at the water. A tough swim and not much to look forward to on the other side.

Its current also disappointed him. The Mizipi was broad and well established, and its waters did not move swiftly. Its shoreline wound sinuously off into the southern distance, with few trees in sight. His thoughts of stealing a canoe and rushing downstream to make landfall and disappear into the wild were clearly unrealistic. The Mizipi was too slow, and its banks too well populated. Any flight downstream would be so ponderous as to be comical, and it would be a simple matter for a couple of braves downstream to paddle a few hundred feet out from the bank and intercept him.

Compounding the difficulty, the unattended canoes he could see on the riverbank did not have paddles in them. Canoes and dugouts of various sizes were abroad on the river, some drifting on the current while their owners cast a line for fish, others riding up- or downstream laden with corn and beans. As they stood and watched, he saw two other cargoes. A team of four men staggering under the weight of bundles of Roman armor and swords finished loading a broad canoe and headed northward in it, making impressive time against the current for a craft so laden. Coming in the opposite direction, a lone man floated downstream in a large canoe half full of furs, a trader perhaps. Seeing Marcellinus, the man paddled a little closer to shore and eyed him with his mouth open wide. The Roman's tunic and skin tone marked him as a foreigner, and the merchant clearly did not know what to make of him. Nor did he wait around to find out, applying more effort to the tempo of his paddling until he was safely past.

"Mizipi," Tahtay repeated.

Marcellinus was tired, depressed, and hungry. A large but backward city. A greasy river. Only children to talk to. Even in the best case, in which they did not flay him alive at their next feast day and he did not die of malnutrition or infection or some terrible disease, his future was bleak.

He signed *Gaius walk house*, and they started the long journey back.

As the Master Mound came back into sight over the thatched Cahokian roofs, a thought came to him. He waved *Question*. "Sisika?"

Tahtay and Enopay looked at him, waiting for a mime or a gesture. Tahtay knocked on his arm, inviting a definition. Marcellinus pointed at the mound and tried again. "Sisika?" He tried the sign of the hawk wing. "Catanwakuwa, woman?"

Tahtay shrugged, baffled. "Yes? No?"

As yet, they had not established the word for "chief," and doing so proved to be more difficult than Marcellinus had anticipated. For the next mile of the walk he was sure the boys did not understand him, but they finally established to everyone's satisfaction that yes, "Great Sun Man" really did mean "chief."

All right, then. He gestured *Question*, said "Sisika," and followed it with the gestures for "Great," "Sun," and "Woman."

"No," they both said, still baffled, perhaps even offended, and then they reached the plaza.

Marcellinus had not seen Sisika since the evening of the battle and did not really know why he was inquiring after her; she had shown him only hostility, and he could have expected nothing else. But it felt important.

The boys had lost interest. Enopay yawned, and Tahtay bopped the smaller boy on the head. Campfires were being lit outside houses all around the plaza, and his interpreters abruptly ran off in different directions with a wave, leaving him alone.

Marcellinus set off again, then stopped and scratched his head, confused. In the end he had to go back to the Great Mound and then outward again to locate the hut in which he had woken up.

On finding it, he did not enter. He could not. He just stood there, time spilling around him, lost in thought, until someone walked up and tugged at his arm.

It was the young warrior he had first seen at the palisade gate and at the old woman's hut. Marcellinus followed him blindly, and then the old woman was offering him a bowl of beans and some of the odd yellow and green vegetables these people ate that were all skin on the outside and only seeds and air within. Just as before, the younger woman sat outside the hut feeding her baby until Marcellinus appeared and then stormed inside.

He ate in silence, hating himself for having to subsist on handouts like any indigent living off the grain dole in Roma. Afterward he stood, offered thanks in mime, and hiked back to the Roman wagons. No one stopped him, and the wagons looked untouched when he arrived, their supplies still intact. He climbed up one of the wheels—how astonishing that these people, this whole civilization, did not use the wheel!—and sat on top of a wagon as the sun drifted slowly down toward the western river bluffs.

Somewhere on one of these two hundred wagons was a kit bag with his name on it, containing his spare clothes and the other limited possessions he had brought with him to Nova Hesperia. He had no idea which wagon it would be on. That was what his adjutants had been for, and they were all dead. It might take weeks to uncover it, and really none of its contents were relevant anymore. His old life was over.

Eventually he opened a wineskin and swallowed about a pint of the wine as night fell and turned the trees and the other wagons into silent silhouettes.

He trudged back into town past the house they had provided for his use and through the gates of the palisade. The pole they had tied him to had been removed, but he obstinately curled up there on the grass anyway.

The ground was too hard, and Marcellinus was not tired enough. The wine he had drunk hindered sleep rather than helping. He shivered.

He rolled onto his back and gazed upward. The skies had thickened with cloud, but it was not truly dark; the moon must be illuminating them from behind. By him rose the tall wooden stakes of the stockade.

Tilting his head away from them, he could look up the long slope of the Great Mound.

The mound was truly gigantic. Its base must cover a dozen acres. It was no mere lump of soil but an engineered structure of packed earth and silty clay, practically a pyramid. On a wet floodplain like this, the Cahokians who built it must have known something about drainage or it would have subsided. How long would it take even a legion to construct such a thing?

A figure loomed over him. Startled, Marcellinus sat upright, pulling a muscle in his side and sending shards of pain through the stitches in his leg. He expected a brave with a knife; he always expected a brave with a knife . . . but it was a woman, and not the one with the gray hair and the sore hip who fed him but someone young and lithe.

Women could be killers, too. Marcellinus scooted backward on his rump away from her. But the girl's eyes in the night showed only disgust for him, her body language only contempt. She made a throwing motion, and a blanket landed on Marcellinus's ankles.

And then she spit on him.

The wordless moment stretched between them, strangers, enemies, and then she turned and stalked off without a backward glance. At last he recognized her from this familiar act of walking away: it was the young mother who avoided him when he came to eat, that nameless woman full of loathing who surely must have been persuaded to bring him the blanket under sufferance, commanded by the older woman who must be her mother or mother-in-law.

She did not fear him. To her, and perhaps to all of them, Marcellinus was vermin, a war captive not even worthy of the sacrifice, fit only for the company of children who had been ordered to learn his language to communicate with future Romans. Marcellinus, a Roman Praetor and commander of legions, was reliant on the charity of a haughty, scornful, dirty people. He had no place here.

And even now Marcellinus could be slain at any time. Enough Cahokians had made their hatred of him very evident, and the young woman had worn a knife at her belt. If she had found him sleeping unprotected, might she have used it?

Despite his weariness, he could not stay here a moment longer. They were not even going to guard him? Fine. Then let them lose him.

Leaving the blanket where it lay, Marcellinus stood and walked out through the gates of the palisade, across the plaza, through the neighborhood of dark and silent houses on the other side, and on into the night.

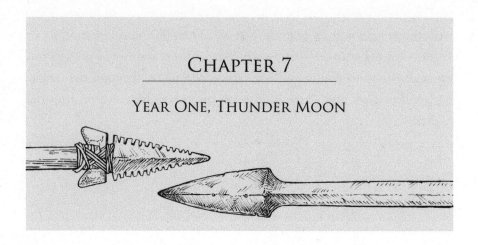

CHAPTER 7

YEAR ONE, THUNDER MOON

Marcellinus walked straight as a Roman road through the city, past the wagons, and onward. This was the way his army had swept into town, and it was the way Marcellinus left it, heading southeast. Due east technically would have been even more direct, but that route would take him through an area unknown to him: more neighborhoods, perhaps damp ground or marsh, and eventually the escarpments of the river bluffs, a challenge to navigate by night. This was the way his Legion originally had been guided into town by the Cahokians. There was a road that led through a break in the bluffs; this was the way he knew.

At any moment he expected braves to appear and bar his way, perhaps at the city's edge. Surely someone must be watching him. What manner of people would let an enemy roam their city unguarded, with free access to their women and children? But no one came.

Let them try to stop him. He would walk around them. If they knocked him down, he would stand up and walk again. If they trussed him with sinew and carried him back, he would wait an hour or a day and then leave again. He would wear them down until they let him pass. Or killed him outright.

Marcellinus had decided that he would not idle away his days in captivity at the pleasure of barbarians. He would not be their tame language tutor. He would not keep the company of children, however engaging. They could kill him or he would march through the night, sleep through the day, and eat berries until he was killed, starved to death, or made it back to the sea. And given the huge distance ahead of him and the savagery of the tribes in his path, the odds of his ever seeing the Mare Chesapica again were laughable.

This time there would be no horse to carry him. He did not need one. He had no duties and did not need to think. He was responsible for no one but himself.

He would not rest until dawn.

Marcellinus walked.

The wan light from the shielded moon was barely sufficient to light his way. For a while he walked by the extensive fields of Cahokian corn that fed thousands, the plants rustling quietly in the gentle breeze. Though well worn, the road he followed was Hesperian, not Roman; as often as not he found his foot dropping several inches into a hole or catching on a root. Every time it happened, he cursed silently and walked on.

Worse was the wooded area he came to next: copses of chestnut and hickory, oak, and birch. The crowns of the trees masked what little moonlight there was. Cahokians did not maintain their forest floors as free from brush and undergrowth as the Iroqua, and his legs were constantly being scratched and scored by unseen thorns.

He came out of the copse and crossed another cornfield, this one flanked by a cluster of four Cahokian houses arranged around a small head-high conical mound. The clouds were shifting, and the moon, long past full, was dropping toward the horizon. However, Marcellinus's night sensitivity had improved, and now the growing darkness troubled him less. He tripped rarely now, taking the natural rise and fall of the land beneath him in stride. He picked up the pace when he saw the next stand of trees in his way.

Through to the other side of it, he saw no further Cahokian houses. A small field separated him from another stretch of trees. His mood lifted just a little.

He heard a faint clicking.

Marcellinus knew the sounds of animals and already had heard the rustlings of owls and field mice. He was familiar with the whisper of the breeze as it shifted the ears of corn. This noise was none of those.

He was currently walking into a small, shallow bowl of land; this close to the Mizipi floodplain the topography was all minor, yet he was clearly on a gradual downhill incline, the horizon lifting around him by a few degrees. There was nothing nearby any taller than a knee-high bush. He had seen no human beings since he had walked away from the plaza. Yet his senses told him someone was near.

The inhabitants of Cahokia were not night walkers. The Great City had slumped into inactivity just moments after the end of twilight. And out here there were no dwellings; no one would wander this far afield through insomnia or bodily needs.

Maybe Marcellinus had not left Cahokia behind, after all. Was he being trailed?

Then, *ahead* of him at the edge of the next copse, he glimpsed the faintest of motions.

It was not the wind in the brush, and Marcellinus did not think it was a deer. But he did not understand how any braves who were supposed to be following him had managed to get so far ahead or why they would need to unless it was to lie in wait and apprehend him.

Or kill him.

Reaching the lower limit of the bowl-like depression, he found the tiniest of streams flowing through it. He slid to the ground in a single movement, collapsing as smoothly as a dropped tunic.

Marcellinus had been walking southeast, so if he followed the path of the stream, his options were now to crawl north or south. He chose south solely because the four houses and the small mound had been to his right when he had walked past them twenty minutes before and because beyond them had been a more extensive stand of trees. To the north there was no significant cover within crawling distance, and eventually the Cahokian creek might block his path. Therefore, he crawled southward, but long before he came to trees, road, field, or houses he came across a pair of opportunistic bushes growing out of the side of the gully cut by the stream and alongside them a deeper cutaway ditch. There he stopped and lay still.

Perhaps it had been suicide for him to try to leave Cahokia. Well, so be it.

Time passed. The moon set. And then they walked right past him, no more than twenty paces away, six braves in a line. One of them muttered something, and the Hesperian in the lead made a curt gesture, the hand-talk for "no." Clearly, grumbling was not permitted on this expedition.

They looked to right and left as they passed him, all alert, but Marcellinus was doing such a superlative impression of a lichen-covered rock that none of them even paused for a second glance.

Marcellinus waited. Now what?

After two hundred breaths, he raised his head. Three more groups of braves were moving through the open area, six men per group. Behind them, nothing and nobody so far as he could tell.

Well.

Wearily, he placed his face down in the dirt. Opened his mouth to let the sultry water of the stream dribble into his mouth and cool his throat.

For long moments Marcellinus had no idea what to do. His mind was blank, his muscles quivering in reaction, his heart pounding. This was the last thing he had expected.

Pursuit from behind would have been no surprise. But these braves, two dozen in total that Marcellinus had seen so far, had not been on his trail. They probably had not even seen him. Because they were heading in the opposite direction, heading toward Cahokia from the east.

And over the last few days, even Marcellinus's tin ear had grown accustomed to Cahokian consonants and the natural rhythm of their speech. The words muttered by the passing warrior had had a different cadence altogether.

Stealthily, Marcellinus pushed himself up onto his hands and knees and made ready to hunt the Iroqua war party.

Back toward Cahokia he went, toward the city where he was neither a guest nor a captive, ignored rather than honored, and absorbed with condescending ease. Back toward a life he had forsworn just hours earlier.

On reaching the edge of the cornfield, the group of Iroqua stopped and huddled. Marcellinus used the extra time to skulk across behind them, closer to the trees. He still would not get to the houses before the Iroqua did but would perhaps at least be near enough to raise some kind of alarm.

Dividing again into their squads of a half dozen men, the Iroqua glided along the tree line so effortlessly that Marcellinus many times lost sight of one or other of the parties. He did not have time to stop and seek them out when this happened; the warriors were moving so quickly that they would outpace him if he delayed. By taking the sensible line instead of the most direct, the Iroqua would make it to the outskirts of the Great City in less than half the time it had taken Marcellinus to walk away from it.

And as that fact sank in, he registered another: one of the bands of Iroqua was now only four braves strong.

Marcellinus took a step back toward the trees, but it was too late. They were running at him from his right quarter, two dark ghosts flowing through the cornfield at astonishing speed. They had been galloping bent forward, almost in a squatting position, but once it was obvious he'd seen them, they stood up straight and ran at him even faster, still utterly silent and almost too tall to be human.

Marcellinus swung away and ran into the forest. Once they left the cornfield and hit the leaves and twigs of the forest floor, he could hear their footfalls right behind him. He reached into his tunic for his pugio, swerved as if to avoid a tall oak that loomed up out of the night, and then swerved back toward it at the last instant.

He jumped, turning in the air, and his back slammed into the tree trunk with spine-cracking force. He blew out air as he hit it, controlling the shock to his breathing. His knife arm was already up, extended back the way he had come.

The first Iroqua ran onto the pugio blade while Marcellinus's gasp of pain was still spilling from his mouth. The blade penetrated the man's gut with such force that the Roman's hand followed it beneath the flesh into the Iroqua's stomach. The man crashed into him, flattening him into the oak, and Marcellinus felt an intense flare of agony as one of his ribs snapped.

The Iroqua howled. Marcellinus wrenched at the pugio's hilt, but it was slick now and jammed solidly in the brave. He let go and grabbed at the man's head, trying to smack it into the tree, but his hand came free: the Iroqua's feather headdress that had made him appear so preternaturally tall in the night had come off in Marcellinus's hand.

The Iroqua was winded, too, and slid down Marcellinus's body. Marcellinus grabbed at the spear in the brave's right hand, but the Iroqua maintained a tight hold on it and it slipped from the Praetor's grasp. All Marcellinus could do was jab at the man's eyes with his stiffened fingers as he toppled.

The second Iroqua's full-speed momentum had taken him past the tree. Marcellinus shoved the first warrior away to his right, hoping to impede the second one's approach, but that was not the way the second brave came on his return; he looped around the tree and appeared to Marcellinus's left. Hot flame scored Marcellinus's stomach, but it was the broad slash of a blade, not a killing stroke. The Iroqua whirled the ax around his head as Marcellinus threw himself to the right; the warrior's ax blade cut deeply into the tree. Wood chips flew.

The first Iroqua seized his right ankle. Unbalanced, Marcellinus fell forward onto the forest floor, and as he did so, the Iroqua sank his teeth into his calf. Marcellinus lashed out with his left foot and caught the man under the chin. Momentarily the pain in his leg multiplied fivefold, but the Iroqua's head slammed back into the tree trunk as Marcellinus heard the man's skull crack with gruesome finality.

Marcellinus rolled and came up holding the first raider's spear. The remaining Iroqua left his ax embedded in the tree and reached behind him for the chert-studded club that hung from his shoulder on a leather strap. But at last the fight had become equal. Marcellinus leaned back to open up space and jabbed at the man's left flank with the spear's tip. The Iroqua tried to knock the spearhead aside with his club and step past it, but in committing to the move he opened up his right side; Marcellinus whipped the spear around and plunged it deep into the brave's chest. The second Iroqua stumbled back over the unconscious body of the first. Marcellinus shoved hard and, releasing the spear, jumped forward.

Still impaled on the spear, the Iroqua hit the tree. With a head butt Marcellinus broke the man's nose, then punched him in the throat. As the man gagged and struggled, the Roman yanked his ax out of the tree and swung it, splitting the Iroqua's skull from forehead to cheek.

Marcellinus folded into a crouch. Adrenaline and battle fever had pushed the pain away but now it flooded him: broken rib, bleeding stomach, bitten leg, bruised spine. His ears still rang.

Four ragged breaths and he was up again, pulling one of the sweaty Iroqua headdresses over his head so the feathers stuck up toward the sky. He grabbed the spear and the ax, but the ax was heavy and clumsy, and even lifting it put an unbearable stress on his chest and gut.

Swearing, he dropped the ax and dived his hand into the first corpse, up to his wrist. It took two tries, but he managed to pull out the pugio. He wiped it on the ground and got to his feet once more.

Still in shock, Marcellinus started running in the wrong direction but by the tenth step realized his mistake. He turned and ran back out of the tree cover and into the open.

Throwing all pretense at stealth to the winds, he ran as quickly as he was able. The jabbing pain from his broken rib mingled with the chronic fire from his stomach, but the rib was not near his lung and the stomach cut was painful rather than dangerous. He tried to lope like a Hesperian, spear held horizontally, in the hopes of fooling any Iroqua who might glance back at him, but the hissing of his breath through his teeth was so loud that he doubted anyone would really take him for a native.

Moreover, he could not see them. In the time it had taken him to slay his Iroqua welcoming committee, the rest of the war party had disappeared. He kept running through the next stand of trees and into the next clearing.

They were just emerging from the little four-hut farmstead. One troop of six already was jogging on in the direction of Cahokia; the second and third were exiting the huts and forming up into lines. Marcellinus ducked quickly to his left, putting one of the huts between himself and them.

He had to slow down. If they sent a second pair of warriors to deal with him, it would be all over; he was too exhausted to fight them. Marcellinus panted, his mouth open wide to reduce the sound, and slowed to a walk as he came into the settlement from the rear.

At first, he thought only the dead were there to greet him. Six Cahokian men lay torn and strewn on the ground, their throats cut or their necks broken, the hair hacked from their heads in a bloody swath. A seventh dead man knelt against the small ceremonial mound that centered their farmstead, naked and scalped, with his intestines sprawled on the ground in front of him. The Iroqua had been brutally efficient.

Then he heard the sounds of muffled sobbing and found the women. Four of them were trussed at wrist and ankle with the same type of heavy sinew that had bound Marcellinus on his first night in the city. Marcellinus's pugio made short work of it, though he left smears of Iroqua guts on their skin. With shrieks and wails, the women ran to the bodies of their men.

Marcellinus left them to their sorrow and trotted on. Again he had lost sight of the Iroqua. His wounds flared once more as he pounded through field and forest, and the night eroded into a battle with himself as his senses reeled and unconsciousness threatened to claim him.

He tripped on a root and a moment later heard himself scream aloud at the jolt of pain it sent through his body. Appalled, he clamped his mouth closed and raised an arm to clout himself on the side of the head. Was he sliding into some kind of waking nightmare? The noise continued.

Two of the women from the farmstead were running up behind him, sprinting on fleet legs and fast overhauling him. Each had one arm longer than the other; clubs, they carried clubs. They did not scream from anguish. They were raising the alarm. He could recognize only one of the words they shouted, but that word was "Iroqua."

Marcellinus wondered if they would kill him when they caught up to

him, if they could really tell him from an Iroqua in the darkness of the
night, especially wearing his stolen Iroqua headdress. But one thing he
knew: he would not defend himself against them, not if it meant any
harm to them.

He ran slightly to one side and slowed to a jog. The women sprinted
past him.

Ahead, Marcellinus saw the silhouettes of six men in tall headdresses,
turning. Beyond them the Great Mound of Cahokia loomed.

Howling their battle cries, the women crashed into one of the Iroqua
war bands. From the left another group of Iroqua appeared, the group
of four, dashing back from the environs of the city. Marcellinus knew
they had seen him and stopped running. He gulped air deep into his
tortured lungs and lifted the spear, bracing himself and trying to summon back the blood fever he had felt earlier. He had almost nothing
left. But he had gotten lucky before. Perhaps he could be lucky again
and drag one of the Iroqua down into death before the rest of them
chopped him into pieces and took his scalp.

As they ran toward him and his breathing calmed, Marcellinus heard
shouting from the city. Dogs barked, and the next moment brought the
clangor of stone being beaten against metal. Cahokia was rousing to
face the Iroqua; the enemy war party's nighttime killing spree was over.
But any Cahokian aid would arrive much too late for Marcellinus.
Wounded, without armor, armed only with a spear and a dagger, he
now faced four Iroqua warriors.

An arrow sped past his shoulder and embedded itself in the ground
just a few feet away. Marcellinus actually heard its whooshing sound as
it cut the air. More arrows came, and the Iroqua scattered, ducking and
weaving but still running toward him.

Marcellinus hurled his spear. Pain affected his cast, and the spear
wobbled in the air. It was neither as heavy nor as sharp as a Roman
pilum; it struck the chest of the nearest Iroqua and knocked him to his
knees, but the man wrenched it away and pushed himself upright again.

The next warrior barged Marcellinus's shoulder and sent him sprawling. An ax blade swished by dangerously close to his head. Marcellinus

tried to grab the arm that held it but missed. His pugio had been knocked from his hand, and he was disarmed, too winded to fight.

His only hope was that the Iroqua brave would cut his losses and flee from the Cahokians. That hope was dashed when he felt the Iroqua's knee pressing into his chest, holding him down. The native headdress he still wore was ripped away, and a rough hand yanked at his hair. Marcellinus was about to be scalped, still alive.

Marcellinus punched at the man, a glancing blow that was largely ineffectual. Dizziness claimed him. Perhaps twenty feet away he heard another man's bellow of pain, a woman's scream of rage and triumph.

All at once the night was full of sparks.

A burning arrow exploded into the ground to his right, setting the grass afire. Marcellinus felt the thud through their joined bodies as a second arrow buried itself deep in the Iroqua's back. His face contorting with surprise and pain, the Iroqua tumbled onto him, sending another flare of agony through his rib cage.

The hawklike shape of a Catanwakuwa flew over them, its baleful eye glowing. No, not an eye but a lantern, and as Marcellinus tilted his head to watch, its pilot dipped an arrowhead into the light and sent another flaming arrow earthward.

Two more Cahokian wings swooped by. Their lanterns enabled them to see each other, removing the threat of a midair collision as well as providing flame for the arrows. Fire-lit arrows helped them establish range and correct their aim.

Marcellinus lay still, panting, as those fireflies danced. The body of the Iroqua rested on top of him, quivering as his life drained away into the dirt. Marcellinus savored the man's death. His part in this battle was done, and if he shoved the body away and tried to stand, he risked getting a flaming arrow in his own back for his pains.

At least one of the Cahokian women had survived the fight. Marcellinus could still hear her voice, calling up to the falcon warriors who circled overhead.

Hawks landed, their pilots running in midair before their feet hit the ground. Bows up, the tattooed Cahokian warriors surveyed the scene.

One of them nocked an arrow and took careful aim. His shot clearly flew true, for he did not need to shoot again. Turning, he saw Marcellinus.

The falcon warrior approached him. The wide wing structure still rested on his back, blocking out the sky.

Rather feebly, Marcellinus waved.

"Gaius fight," Marcellinus said. "Iroqua-Iroqua, trees, dead Iroqua. Gaius run. Man, seven . . ." Damn. He did not know his numbers in Cahokian, so he held up fingers, then gestured a throat cutting. *Woman-and-woman . . .* He mimed being bound at the wrist and pointed at the woman from the homestead who was thirty feet away, weeping, babbling her own story through her tears.

He sat on the southern edge of the Great Plaza. The Cahokians had dragged him there with scant ceremony, along with the corpses of the Iroqua. Marcellinus wanted to see how many Iroqua dead there were to make sure they were all accounted for, but his Cahokian captors shoved him back onto the ground when he tried to stand. The hubbub in the plaza was considerable, confusion still reigned, and the four grim-faced Cahokian warriors who stood over him had their weapons at the ready.

Marcellinus tried again, doing the hand-talk as he spoke. Most of his speech lapsed into Latin, for he remembered few of the Cahokian words the children had taught him. His gestures should have conveyed his meaning, but he knew he was only partially understood.

Around him Cahokia was alive with lanterns. Dozens of wings still soared overhead, scouring the outskirts of the city for other enemies. In the relative cool of the night the Catanwakuwa had little opportunity to gain height, and many falcon warriors walked their wings back to the mound to be launched again.

A tall, well-muscled brave appeared and said something to Marcellinus's guards. At his arrival the men stopped hurling questions at the Roman and handed him a pot of water instead. Marcellinus drank deeply and on lifting his eyes again saw Tahtay running toward them as fast as his legs could bring him.

"Thank Juno," Marcellinus said.

"Hand-talk, hand-talk, hand-talk," Tahtay panted, and Marcellinus began it all again. Every few sentences Tahtay would stop him and babble away to the tall Cahokian, then beckon impatiently for Marcellinus to continue. To his frustration, it was at this late stage that Marcellinus discovered that Cahokians and Romans used different methods for counting on their fingers and that his numbers were being misunderstood, so he drew lines in the dirt to indicate the number of Iroqua instead.

"Question, two Iroqua, dead," Tahtay said once they'd struggled through to the end of the story together. "Where?"

Marcellinus pointed into the night. Tahtay gestured *No* and pointed at the ground.

"Really?" said Marcellinus. Would the Cahokians understand a map?

Apparently so. He sketched it out in the sand of the plaza; a pebble became the Great Mound, a small square he scratched out with his finger became the plaza where they sat. He thought a little, then drew in the features he had run past. "Trees here. Trees. Corn. Trees. More corn. Four houses, men of Cahokia, all dead. Women, that." He pointed at the woman who, as it happened, was pointing at him at the same moment in her own much more coherent retelling of the tale. "Trees. The Iroqua-Iroqua I killed, dead, here. Here."

"Question, dead?" Tahtay pointed vaguely at his body.

Marcellinus touched his gut and the back of his head. "Iroqua One." Then he touched his chest and mimed a spear point going into it. "Iroqua Two."

The tall man grunted and went to talk to the woman.

"Hotah?" Tahtay said. Marcellinus was holding his stomach, probing at his damaged rib. It hurt like hell, and he was having trouble taking a full breath. He knocked twice and taught Tahtay the Latin for "pain," "cut," and "wound," learning the hand-talk in return. These were the words they needed right now.

Having heard the woman's story, the tall warrior returned and spoke again. Tahtay said, "Question. Gaius fight Iroqua?" He gestured, shrugged, hand-talked the gesture for *Question* again, and shook his head.

Well, why *had* he done it? It was a fair question. Marcellinus stared out into the night, at the milling braves, feeling the pain of every one of his wounds.

"Hotah? Gaius?" Tahtay poked his shoulder.

"For gods' sakes, Tahtay . . ."

"Why Gaius fight Iroqua?"

"Because . . . Because I did not want any more Cahokians to die. All right?"

Marcellinus paused. He hadn't done the hand-talk, and Tahtay generally relied on the combination of both, but the boy had understood and was already explaining it to the tall brave.

The brave stared at the Roman for a long moment, then spoke an order. The man carrying the pugio placed it at Marcellinus's feet, and two of his guards jogged away into the night while the remaining men stood at ease, looking around them at the mob of their fellow Cahokians.

"Good," Tahtay said. "Finish. All done. Gaius sleep."

Gratefully, Marcellinus lay down on the hard-packed dirt and sand. His mind still buzzed and his body was a single living mass of pain, so he knew he would not really be able to sleep, but the rest was welcome.

Yet when he opened his eyes, the dawn light was already coloring the plaza pink and gold, the men and Tahtay had gone, and a young woman he had never seen before had cut away his bloody tunic and was dressing his wounds.

Marcellinus stirred, but the woman pushed him back down. Would nobody in this town let him be? Irritated, Marcellinus hand-talked *I, See, Cut,* and reluctantly she let him twist his head up to look.

His stomach wound was several inches long. The Iroqua's chert blade had not scored him deeply, but the edges of the cut were ragged. "The dangers of a blunt instrument," said Marcellinus, relieved.

The woman gestured *No* in incomprehension, and Marcellinus lay back down and let her wash and bind it and apply the thick white salve from a pot. *Wound*, he signed, pointing at the rib so she would know about that, too, though no salve she could apply would help it heal. Then, in the growing light of morning, she saw the bite mark in his calf and grimaced, raising her hand up to her mouth.

Being alone with her made Marcellinus uneasy. She was slim, strong-featured, and attractive, and he was unable to meet her eye. A few other Cahokians were coming out of their houses to fetch water and firewood, but none were anywhere near them.

She said something, pointed at his leg, made a slashing motion. "Really?"

She pointed again and grimaced.

Marcellinus nodded and handed her the pugio. She washed the blade thoroughly, gave him an apologetic look, and began to cut into his calf.

Even though he knew her intention, he had not expected it to hurt so much. He cried out and grabbed at her, almost knocking her over.

She put her hands on her hips and lectured him in Cahokian, braids bobbing on her shoulders.

Marcellinus sucked in a deep breath, trying to fill his lungs despite the pressure from his damaged rib. He wasn't a child; he understood that bite wounds could easily get infected. He wasn't going to get any better medical attention than this. He should be grateful someone was even trying.

He ducked his head and hand-talked, *Sorry. Thank you. Yes. Sit, Leg. Cut*, and she understood. Resting all her weight on his thigh to stop him from flinching away from the blade, she bent to her task again.

The pain was awful, but Marcellinus withstood it without embarrassing himself any further. Once she had removed an Iroqua tooth and cleaned up the wound to her satisfaction, she painted it with a dark liquid from one of her pots that stung like Hades and then sewed it with five stitches of a bone needle and thin sinew and bound it with the white salve.

In the meantime the bright sun of Nova Hesperia had risen to bathe the Cahokian plaza. People were watching. Marcellinus felt embarrassed.

The woman stood and reached down to him. He tried to get up without her help, but the pain was excruciating. She had to put all her weight into it to haul him onto his feet, and then he had to lean on her for the long walk back to his hut. She was dusty and sweaty and smelled very female, and Marcellinus was humiliated to realize that this was the closest he had been to a woman in many years.

In his hut she lowered him gently onto the mattress, lifting his legs as if he were a geriatric. Marcellinus tried to shake off his shame.

"Gaius," he said.

She looked at him thoughtfully. He said it again, pointing at himself, and gestured *Thank you.*

Unexpectedly she grabbed his chin with her thumb and forefinger and looked deep into his eyes. Marcellinus cringed at her unblinking gaze. She turned his face to right and left, studying him in a wordless interrogation. Again Marcellinus felt uncomfortable at being alone with her and deeply saddened. "Stop," he said, and hand-talked, *No, Please, Stop. Please.*

Sniffing, she looked instead at the dressing over his stomach and probed the wound on his calf. Poked briefly at his older leg and shoulder wounds, shaking her head again at the mess he was in. She gestured, *No Walk. Sleep.*

As she stood, Marcellinus found there were tears in his eyes.

She half turned in the doorway and gave him another long stare. Again he avoided her eyes, staring at the ground.

She waved to attract his attention. Pointing to herself, she said: "Chumanee."

He hand-talked, *Thank you,* but she was already gone.

Chumanee woke him again when the sun was high. Wiping the salve off his leg, she washed the bite wound even more thoroughly, daubed more of the dark liquid on it, and bound it again with the salve and a length of woven cloth. Marcellinus kept his eyes closed throughout.

When she was done, she did not leave but stood and waited.

"She say, 'Why you fight us?' "

Marcellinus opened his eyes. Chumanee stood before him, mute. Behind her stood Tahtay.

"Uh," said Marcellinus.

"You, big army. Why fight us, Cahokia?"

Marcellinus did not reply. He had no answer for her.

"We do nothing. No blood between you and us peoples."

Marcellinus struggled to sit up. Chumanee did not help. The hut quivered around him.

"The Iroqua killed many of my men," he said, and even now felt a brief surge of anger at the cowardly sneak attacks his legion had suffered.

Chumanee spoke. Tahtay said, "We are not Iroqua."

"I know."

"Why fight—"

"I had orders to take your land. Uh, my chief, say, fight . . ." Hesitantly Tahtay began to translate, but Marcellinus held up his hand. "Wait. No. That's not a reason. Or an excuse."

"Huh?" Tahtay said. "What say?" He knocked on his arm.

Marcellinus did not want to speak. The truth of it was that he had needed Cahokian corn to feed his army over the winter. He had needed to take what these people had so he could give it to his own troops. The military equation had been brutally simple.

And it shamed him that he had allowed it to come to that. Here in the wilderness of Nova Hesperia he had found a city. Considered barbarians by his superiors in Rome, clearly, but nonetheless a people proud and well organized enough to face his Legion in battle on equal terms. Perhaps "barbarian" was an uncharitable term, after all.

And they had defeated him, using flying machines that a year ago would have been beyond his wildest imagining. For that, if for nothing else, they deserved Marcellinus's respect.

That, he realized at last, was why he had turned back. The Cahokians had slaughtered his Legion, but they had done it fairly, with military might, skill, and honor. The Iroqua had butchered his men in the trees and tortured and burned his scout.

It was because of Marcellinus that the Iroqua were testing the Cahokians' inner defenses. *He* had potentially weakened the Cahokians and made them more vulnerable to Iroqua predation.

The Cahokians had his grudging respect. Enough of them had died already because of him.

He hand-talked: *I, Speak, Bad. Wrong words.*

"What are right words?"

He thought about it. Eventually he said in Latin, "Sometimes, when two armies meet, big warriors, they must fight. We had come so far. Long way. Yes? Many moons."

Tahtay did not translate. He just stared.

"What?" Marcellinus said.

"Those are right words? I say to Chumanee?"

"No. Those are the wrong words, too." He turned to Chumanee. "Look. It just got away from me. The march, the heat, and the impossible distances, the constant hoping for gold. The need for supplies. The Iroqua attacks. Corbulo's mutiny. By the time we got here to Cahokia . . . there were no choices left."

Chumanee stared. Tahtay shook his head. "Hand-talk?"

"Tell her Gaius is sorry. But Gaius has no answer for her."

Chumanee was standing very close. Her face was dark; he thought she might slap him. He did not move.

Once, not so very long ago, any native woman who struck him in anger would have died instantly. But Marcellinus was no longer a Praetor.

Instead she touched the back of his hand as if checking to make sure he was real, and at the delicacy of her touch Marcellinus did flinch away from her. She spoke now, very quietly. A chill of horror went up Marcellinus's spine. *Gods*, he thought. *Please let her be vowing to slit my throat in the night. Don't let her pity me. Please.*

The boy coughed. "She say you are good man among bad men, Romans. She say that why you . . ." Tahtay waved his hand around his head.

"Confused? Crazy?" Marcellinus closed his eyes. "No. That's not right. I'm not a good man, Tahtay. Tell her that."

The Cahokians spoke again. Marcellinus felt the movement of the air as Chumanee stood, caught the aroma of her on the air, heard the rustle of the deerskin as she pulled back the door curtain and stepped up out of his hut.

He opened his eyes. Tahtay was looking at the floor, acutely embarrassed.

"You don't have to tell me," Marcellinus said.

"Chumanee say, 'Maybe tomorrow you will be.'"

The room hazed up around him again.

"Go now, Tahtay," he said quietly.

"More outside," the boy told him.

Marcellinus shook his head. He neither understood nor cared. "I'm sure there are. Go now. I need to rest. Gaius sleep."

Looking uncertain, Tahtay left.

Marcellinus tried to breathe deeply. His damaged rib curtailed the effort, and he gasped.

This was not the first cracked rib Marcellinus had ever suffered or even the third, and he knew it would take a month or more to heal. That was the worst of it, though. He might have white salve splattered all over him, but he would survive. Provided he could avoid getting himself into any more fights, that is.

The gloom of his hut oppressed him. Before he slept again, he needed to see the sunlight. Limping slowly to the door, Marcellinus pulled the deerskin aside and looked out into the early afternoon.

There he found a squad of Cahokian warriors waiting for him.

They sat patiently on the ground in the open space outside his hut, nine of them, all young and fit with the feathery shoulder tattoos. The seven men had their hair shorn at the sides and were naked to the waist to show their war tattoos. The two women wore tanned leather tunics and tightly braided hair and looked just as muscular and hard-bitten as the men. Off to one side was a small pile of burnished steel: Roman armor, Roman shields, Roman gladii and pila.

"Oh," said Marcellinus.

The warriors appraised him. Two of them nodded, impressed at the severity of his wounds. The larger of the women smiled broadly. Marcellinus preferred not to guess why. He looked around, but his translator children were nowhere to be seen.

One of the warriors stood. *Teach*, he gestured in hand-talk: *Fight*. Picking a gladius from the pile, he shook it clumsily. He pointed at Marcellinus and then at the warrior group and bowed. The rest of the warriors bent at the waist from their sitting position.

Bowing was not a normal action for Cahokians. They were using his own gestures to honor him. Marcellinus felt embarrassed at the mimicry; he hardly deserved such respect from them. "Um. Wait. Stay there."

At least he knew the hand-talk for "pee'" now. As he hobbled away to take care of business, they stayed exactly where they were and patiently awaited his return.

Even as Marcellinus limped back to them, he knew it was hopeless. He could barely stand, and walking was a trial. His bitter aches at calf, thigh, stomach, ribs, back, shoulder, and head vied with one another in intensity even as he walked. He could not lift anything larger than a pugio without opening his stitches; a sword or a shield would be hopeless. Even if he could communicate effectively, drilling them would be all but impossible.

And he was glad of it. Flattered as Marcellinus was that a few Cahokian warriors would seek his training in methods of fighting with Roman weapons, he was queasily uncertain about providing it. It might be fair enough to arm them against their local enemies and keep Cahokia strong—clearly the mound builders and the Iroqua shared no love for each other. Should the rest of the world stay absent, his personal distaste for the Iroqua might just be enough for Marcellinus to throw in his lot with the Cahokians. But when another Roman force arrived in Nova Hesperia next year or the year after to face not only bombardment from the air but Hesperians with Roman weaponry, trained in Roman tactics?

Where Nova Hesperia was concerned, Roma's earliest and worst mistake had been in killing the Norse and losing the vital information they had held in their heads. On the trek inland, aside from trusting Corbulo too much and Aelfric too little, Marcellinus's biggest blunder had been murdering Fuscus. Had he kept the scrawny Powhatani alive, he might have been able to talk to the local Cahokians during the days of the final approach to their city, perhaps even make some kind of treaty before his hand was forced. Fuscus was a coward and an opportunist, but just maybe, keeping him around might have made all the difference. If Marcellinus had kept his temper, perhaps he would even now be awakening each day to a different world, a world in which his 33rd Legion still lived.

But that was a big what-if, and Marcellinus would never know the answer to it.

Meanwhile, the Cahokiani had not made the same basic error. Marcellinus was alive, and it looked like he might stay that way. Why? Well, that was becoming increasingly obvious.

Despite the Romans' tragic showing in the attack on Cahokia, the 33rd Legion had owned sophisticated weaponry and displayed a military discipline the Hesperians had not seen before. Marcellinus had things he might teach them about warfare. He probably was being kept alive for just that purpose, just as Marcellinus himself had vowed before the battle to preserve some of the Cahokiani pilots to teach him about the wings and the liquid flame. In which case it might be Marcellinus's duty not to play into their hands.

It was a conundrum, and Marcellinus was loath to try to solve it on three or four hours' sleep after the most traumatic week of his life.

Here he stood, in front of a group of Cahokian warriors. Their faces showed him that they had not grasped the full magnitude of his wounds until now. The leading brave stood and held out a sword to him anyway, hilt first, more in hope than in expectation.

Marcellinus did not reach for it. He took his hand from his ribs with some difficulty and signed, *Today, No. Cut. Wound.*

He shrugged and looked sad. The brave signed something back, but it was too fast with too many gestures, and Marcellinus didn't catch it. He shook his head and limped on to lean against the doorway of his hut.

Enopay ran across the plaza, sobbing his heart out, and sat down at Marcellinus's feet with a bump. The warriors looked at one another, embarrassed.

"Um." With some effort Marcellinus crouched. "Enopay? I'm all right. See?" He raised his arms, which made him wince in pain; unfortunately, it was a poor demonstration of his robustness.

Enopay's large eyes swam in tears. He jabbed at the Roman's good shoulder, perhaps intending it as a petulant blow for putting himself at risk.

Marcellinus signed, *Gaius good*, and wiped the boy's eyes and nose with the corner of his tunic. Other than that, he was at a loss. He really should have spent more time with Vestilia when she was young.

Another small figure was marching toward him with her chin up, displaying much more dignitas than should have been possible for a child of eight winters. On arrival Kimimela made a shooing motion at Marcellinus, ordering him into his hut, and started to lecture the braves rather imperiously; their eyebrows went up, and several of them tried hard to stifle their grins. The leading brave, however, listened to her gravely, signing *Yes, yes* as she spoke and holding her gaze as if she were a great chief.

Nodding ruefully at Marcellinus, the squad piled their Roman weapons against the outside wall of Marcellinus's hut and made to depart.

From his other side came another female voice, lower in timbre but just as insistent. Marcellinus turned his head with injudicious speed, winced, and swayed.

Grabbing his arm, Chumanee hustled him into his hut, and Kimimela followed them in.

Marcellinus sighed. A fig for his dignity and warrior reputation: today it was his destiny to be bossed around by women and children.

And it wasn't over yet. Chumanee had barely gotten him settled on his mattress before the old woman, whose name he now learned was Nahimana, arrived with a bowl of corn, beans, and vegetables for the invalid. Her price for supplying this bounty was the opportunity to tut-tut and fuss over him, poking at each of his wounds in admonishment and disbelief that he had managed to damage himself even further. Her demeanor suggested that she thought Marcellinus must be very, very clumsy.

Marcellinus rested the bowl on his lap. Rather desperately he signed: *Thank you. Gaius eat. Gaius sleep.*

Then, knowing that the women would not understand, he said quietly to Kimimela in Latin: "Gaius eat, then three children come back, hand-talk hand-talk hand-talk."

His stomach was growling as if he hadn't eaten for a month. He needed the food and maybe several times as much of it as Nahimana had brought. But after he had taken care of that, what Marcellinus needed most was not rest but information.

Not for the first time, he had a lot of work to do.

For the next two weeks Marcellinus rarely stirred farther than twenty paces from his hut. But over that time he made huge progress.

Improving his ability to communicate was his first priority. Without bridging the language divide, Marcellinus could not effectively teach anyone to fight or even to bring him food he liked. Without being able to teach, he could help neither the Cahokian people nor himself. Without being able to navigate the social etiquette of Cahokian society or understand the political situation in the region, he was powerless.

Fortunately, "his" children had an inexhaustible enthusiasm for Latin. The first week was an avalanche of words, ideas, and gestures interrupted only by his exhaustion and by Chumanee's frequent visits to check up on his wounds and scold him. In the second week Marcellinus started to rein in the children and concentrate on sentences and the flow of ideas; nuance and accuracy of expression became more significant than the sheer volume of vocabulary. The children still used the infinitive verb form for everything—Marcellinus was not about to force young Hesperians to conjugate Latin verbs—but it mattered little when their store of words was so great.

Unlike the children, however, it did not take long for Marcellinus to saturate on language. A couple of hours and his brain was full; he could no longer retain any but the most basic hand-talk signs, and he could pick up only two dozen words of spoken Cahokian in a day.

But Tahtay, Kimimela, and Enopay were unstoppable. Even when Marcellinus could stand it no more and drove them away so he could rest, he heard them outside drilling one another and reviewing vocabulary. After the first week they talked exclusively in Latin among themselves. Even when the boys played chunkey, a game that seemed to involve rolling a stone disk along the ground and then throwing spears at it, they shouted their scores and argued the points in Latin. Marcellinus even taught them some boyish Latin insults to make it more interesting.

"And all in Cahokia use hand-talk?"

"All use hand-talk. All, everywhere."

"Everywhere?"

"Yes. Cahokia, Algon-Quian, Iroqua, People of the Grass, People of the Hand. All peoples hand-talk."

He asked them who their parents were and where, but they just shook their heads. Marcellinus persisted, but after a while it felt pointless; they weren't going to tell him, and that was that. Orphans, perhaps? Had Marcellinus been mobile enough, he might have tried to follow them home. But he wasn't, and in a way he was content not to know.

For the first few days of his convalescence he was as weak as a kitten and despaired of ever regaining his strength. When Nahimana brought him what was obviously intended to be a chamber pot, he swallowed his pride, thanked her, and then used it regularly. But with the old woman's cooking and Chumanee's visits, his health gradually improved.

Toward the end of the first week he managed to get outside again. His first complete circuit of the local neighborhood felt like a milestone, and even that became a learning experience; on the lee side of every Cahokian house was a tiny garden that grew corn, with beans and the strange vegetables they called askutasquash all jumbled up, with the beanstalks climbing the corn and the vegetables growing close to the ground in their shade. Most of the Cahokians' produce came from the huge fields, and corn was doled out freely, but each family's garden helped and seemed to be a source of pride. In addition, they grew flowers on the sunny sides of their houses; particularly commonplace was a tall plant with a broad yellow flower that burst into bloom during Marcellinus's recovery that Kimimela, appropriately enough, called "sunflower."

Still he saw no visible signs of leadership, no elite, no government or ruling class. He never saw anyone giving orders, and the old shaman, Youtin, seemed almost invisible in the community. As far as Marcellinus could tell, the organization of Cahokia proceeded by group consensus. The children talked of Cahokian elders, but they surely must operate with a light touch. Events somehow gained their own momentum from within. Marcellinus had never seen anything like it.

And still nobody recognized Sisika's name. Marcellinus began to wonder if he had imagined her.

If the power structure of Cahokia was obscure to him, at least the clan system was transparent enough. The families of Cahokia were broken down into hereditary clans in a way roughly analogous to the gens of Roman society.

Over dinner one night—his first with real meat—he learned that Nahimana and her warrior son Takoda were of the Bear clan. Takoda's young wife, who once had spit on Marcellinus and still wouldn't speak to him, was Kangee of the Turtle clan. Other clans among the menagerie included Wolf, Deer, Raven, Duck, Beaver, Hare, Chipmunk, and Fox. To his surprise, all the clan chiefs were women. Clan membership was a point of pride and cheerful rivalries, and young men and women were expected to marry outside their own clans.

The most prestigious clans in Cahokia were those that flew, the Hawk and Thunderbird clans, but these were neither rigid nor hereditary, as they regularly accepted new members. Marcellinus privately reasoned that their mortality rate was probably so high that they had little alternative but to recruit; they were really more like guilds than clans.

Now that he had established that, Marcellinus's interests turned further afield to their enemies, and here he once again had to bring Nahimana into the conversation. As they sat eating outside Nahimana's hut one night, with Tahtay oiling the wheels of conversation, they revealed to Marcellinus that the hated Iroqua were not the monolithic enemy force he had supposed but a confederation of five tribes: Seneca, Caiuga, Onondaga, Onida, and Mohawk.

It amused Marcellinus no end that one of these tribes apparently owned the same name as one of Roma's most famous philosophers and orators. It amused him rather less to discover that the Iroqua raids were continuing. During his convalescence, sneak raids by Iroqua war parties had plagued the outer reaches of Cahokia. The first war party obviously had been sent to reconnoiter deep into the heart of Cahokia, perhaps to report back on the extent of the death and destruction wrought by the Roman army. Subsequent parties were less ambitious and did not attempt to penetrate so close to the Great Plaza, but hardly a day went by without a vicious Iroqua raid on an upland village or a Cahokian outpost farther upstream or downstream on the Mizipi. Farming families from outlying areas began to migrate into the city for their own protection or move across the Mizipi to the emptier and relatively safer farmlands there.

It was growing clear to the Cahokians that having already driven a wedge deep into the lands formerly under the control of the various scattered Algon-Quian tribes, the Iroqua next sought to expand into the territory of the mound builders. They did not have this all their own way; sometimes the skirmishes went against them and squads of Cahokian braves descended upon them and hacked off as many Seneca and Caiuga scalps as they could. But that only brought an even more savage response from the Iroqua. Marcellinus learned that this series of running battles between the two nations even had its own name: the Mourning War.

Meanwhile, the torturous heat of summer had finally broken. The days were growing cooler. Autumn was just around the corner.

Marcellinus's rib was still his most serious problem, but it had transitioned gradually from the sharp stabbing pain into a dull ache he could mostly ignore. He could raise his arms over his head now and even swing his arms around. He could walk to the gates of the palisade that led to the Great Mound and back again across the entire thousand-foot length of the plaza without feeling that he needed to crawl into a hole and sleep for a week afterward. It was time to take the next step.

"I am well," he declared. "Gaius not sick. Ready to work."

Tahtay cheered. Kimimela looked dubious. Enopay looked resentful. Marcellinus sighed. "Tell the warriors to return tomorrow."

"Who warriors?" Tahtay prompted in Latin, unsure whether he understood.

"The nine warriors from before." Marcellinus pointed at the Roman swords and armor that he had made the children bring inside his hut and pile in the corner to preserve them against theft and the elements. Despite that, the steel badly needed cleaning. "I teach? Fight with Roman spear, sword?"

Kimimela poked him in the stomach. The slash he had sustained there was mostly healed, but still he winced, and she raised her eyebrows at his response. Marcellinus poked her right back. "Stop worrying. Are you my mother now?"

"Eyanosa kill Iroqua?" said Enopay, and Kimimela cringed. Only Enopay called the Roman Eyanosa. Eventually Marcellinus would find out what it meant.

"Well," said Marcellinus. "Gaius sit down in winter, kill Iroqua in spring."

"Huh," Tahtay said.

Marcellinus turned to him. "What? Nine warriors not want to learn now?"

"Not know," said Tahtay. "Maybe warriors not here. Maybe they away, fight Iroqua."

Despite Tahtay's dismissiveness, Marcellinus told the children to spread the word. The following dawn when he awoke and went to his doorway, he found sixty-five Cahokian warriors sitting cross-legged outside his hut and Tahtay and Kimimela sitting among them, grinning from ear to ear.

The more Marcellinus had learned about the Cahokiani, the easier his decision had become.

After the battle Marcellinus had not sacrificed his life by falling on his sword. Since then he had continued to show weakness in abundance, if only to himself; he had drunk wine to try to float the shame from his mind, and then he had made a rash—and, to the Cahokians, baffling—choice in walking out into the hostile night of a continent he barely understood.

If Marcellinus had believed in the Fates, he might have said that he was meant to intercept the Iroqua war party, that the battle and its consequences were foreordained or a sign from the gods indicating what he should do. As a good Stoic, he acknowledged it as merely a chance encounter. But either way, Marcellinus had been lucky to survive, and he was not eager to repeat the experiment now that he knew how many Iroqua enemies lurked out in the hills and bottomlands, so close to Cahokian city boundaries.

Today he saw nothing sane or valiant in striding alone to an Iroqua death. And since he could not get back to Roma, he would have to work with what he had right here and now.

Let Roma come to him.

Let another legion or two make the long, exhausting trek. Romans surely would be back eventually—Marcellinus could not imagine Hadrianus III giving up his claim to Nova Hesperia simply because a single ragtag legion had failed. It was just a matter of time. And once the new Romans arrived, let them witness what Marcellinus had done with these people in the meantime.

The next Roman army must not make the same mistakes Marcellinus had made. If Marcellinus did not want another legion to suffer the fate of the 33rd or the Cahokians to be slaughtered at their hands, he had a lot of work to do. Cahokia had to be prepared, and then Roma would have to be persuaded of the strategic and economic benefits of waging peace rather than war.

The Cahokians had wings but no idea how to run an army. They had no tactics, no strategy, little metal, and no steel. Their "roads" were laughable, and because of that they had no use for the wheel. They had no writing. No baths.

Marcellinus would help with all that.

Cahokia would hardly be the first province to be hauled out of an older time by the civilizing power of Roma. There was more than one way to conquer a people.

Besides, he could not sit idly by. Marcellinus was not a man given to passivity. He was used to a structured life of military discipline, order, and regulation. He had to work, and he had to show leadership. And really, that was all there was to it.

He would make them a province worth having, for Roma. Even if the first thing the next Romans did when they arrived was execute him for his pains.

That evening, after his first training session with his Cahokian braves, Marcellinus walked out to the Roman wagons. He felt weak but nowhere near as achy as he had feared.

He took every single wineskin he could find and poured all the wine out into the dirt. It took quite some time.

The wine was growing vinegary, anyway. And he did not like the way he had leaned on it like a crutch. From now on Marcellinus would drink water.

Returning home, he built a little shelf at the back of his hut by bending up the bottom of one of the reed mats and set up his lares, the little golden household gods that traveled with him.

Marcellinus folded his destroyed Roman tunic and put it on the floor under the shelf. On it he placed his pugio and the Iroqua tooth that Chumanee had dug out of his leg. Aside from his weapons and the Cahokian clothes that he was wearing at that moment, he was looking at the sum total of his possessions.

Marcellinus had no incense or candle to light, but he wafted the air as if he had and performed a small daily ritual over the lares. It was not that he believed that little golden figurines could aid him or guide his future, more that the ritual helped him maintain his Romanness here in the wilds of barbarian Nova Hesperia.

Or rather, here in the center of Hesperian civilization.

For Marcellinus no longer thought of them as faceless natives. Training with them that day, teaching them the positions of the sword and how to stand in ranks in open and close order and, gods help him and them both, how to march in step, he had come to know them as individuals. Paradoxically, in the middle of drill, which was designed to remove individuality from a group of soldiers and create a corps of comrades instead, Marcellinus had felt the uniqueness and humanity of each person under his "command."

His legionaries were gone. There was no one else who spoke tolerable Latin in whole sentences within a thousand miles, maybe five thousand. Marcellinus's enemies had become his keepers. And his keepers were not a mass of barbarians but a motley collection of human beings. Whatever rituals they spoke before their own gods before they went to bed were surely no wiser or more foolish than the words Marcellinus had just spoken to his "toy persons," as Sisika had termed them all those moons ago.

And so Marcellinus lay himself down to sleep after his first day as a Cahokian drill sergeant, almost intolerably weary but—at long last— a little more at ease about his survival and purpose deep in this alien land.

CHAPTER 8

YEAR ONE, FALLING LEAF MOON

On the night of the first frost, two of the Cahokian granaries burned.

Once again the streets and plazas of the Great City came alive in the middle of the night. Marcellinus pulled his tunic over his head and ran from his hut as the first alarm was sounded with the pounding of drums and the clash of rocks against large copper sheets on the Master Mound. Outside, Cahokians stumbled blearily out of their houses into the chilly air; Marcellinus had to push his way through them to get to the plaza.

The burning granaries were to the west and east of the Great Mound, bracketing it with twin fiery calamities. Smoke streamed into the night sky, and the reek of burned corn filled the air.

Shielding his eyes from the blaze, Marcellinus peered between the houses, across the city. It looked hopeless. Obviously the two granaries had not set themselves aflame, but the culprits were long gone. The Iroqua arsonists had presumably fled the scene long before the fires had become established.

The western granary was nearer. Marcellinus began to run. His Praetor's instinct was to try to take control, to bring order to the chaos, but he did not know the right Cahokian words for this crisis and he was an outsider here; no one would listen to him. In any case, once Marcellinus navigated his way through the crowd to the granary, order had somehow already appeared from nowhere. Bucket chains had formed of their own volition; men and women were passing large pots of water all the way from Cahokia Creek past the Master Mound to the granaries. In partial states of undress, their sweating faces reflecting the baleful light from the conflagration, they were a stirring sight to Marcellinus.

Stirring yet potentially desperate. Cahokia had a dozen granaries spread across the city, but the fall harvest had been disappointing, and that corn had to feed a city of twenty thousand people through what Enopay had told Marcellinus was expected to be a long, bitter winter.

The granaries were the same kind of structure as many other huts and lodges of the city but much larger, with floors raised on stout wooden beams to deter vermin and keep the corn dry. Several of the western granary's support beams had already sheared, and the rectangular building slumped like a drunkard. A woman thrust a sodden blanket at Marcellinus and ran by him to step up into the blaze; he could already see other men clambering through the burning wooden struts, beating at the flames with wet blankets and rugs in a futile attempt to bring the fire under control as other Cahokians continued to hurl water into the building.

Memories uncurled, galvanizing Marcellinus into action. He dropped the blanket and ran forward, screaming and waving his arms. "No! Get off granary! Away, all away! Very bad, very bad!"

His warning came much too late. The water on the burning grain in the confined space had already done its work, creating a flammable gas. Now that gas ignited. The granary exploded, sending a plume of flame into the sky and bowling Marcellinus off his feet, backward into the dirt.

It took until dawn for calm and order to return to Cahokia, but this time Marcellinus was one of the many men and women circulating through the plaza explaining what had happened and helping with the dead and wounded. Close to dawn he came upon Chumanee tending to the burns of one of the braves caught in the blast from the western granary; she peered up at him, dirty and weary, and he nodded to her as he went by.

A new crowd had clustered around the still smoldering eastern granary, and Marcellinus walked over. A tall brave was speaking, the same man Marcellinus had been forced to explain himself to with Tahtay's help the night the Iroqua war party had raided the outskirts of Cahokia. Fortunately, Tahtay was already there and could translate, for the tall brave was not using the hand-talk. Currently he was stating the obvious, which was that the Iroqua had sneaked into their city like cowards to attack their winter grain and weaken them and saying the things a leader should say: this outrage would not go unpunished, Cahokian vengeance would be swift and sure, and so on. The crowd cheered, but Marcellinus wondered exactly how they would get vengeance on sneak thieves, murderers, and arsonists who performed acts of sabotage and then melted away into the night.

The tall brave finished his oration and strode on toward the wreckage of the western granary.

"So," Marcellinus said to Tahtay. "Chief, that?"

"That was Great Sun Man," Tahtay said proudly.

"Really?" The brave wore the same kind of tunic as any other man, and his hair and tattoos gave no clues to his rank. Without the clothes and regalia of office that Marcellinus had seen on top of the Master Mound, there had been no way for Marcellinus to tell him apart from any other Cahokian warrior.

Marcellinus had assumed that Great Sun Man lived high up on the Master Mound, just as an Imperator might hide himself away on the Palatine. But it was the reverse: Great Sun Man lived with his people, just a man among men, emerging from the throng only in times of crisis when someone needed to take control. It was an unusual style of leadership that Marcellinus would need some time to think about.

Tahtay was beaming while watching Great Sun Man's progress through the crowd. Suddenly it all made sense. "So, Tahtay? Great Sun Man?"

"War chief. In peace, elders and clan chiefs make law. In war, war chief. And today-now, always war."

"Yes, yes." Marcellinus knew that already from his evening conversations. It was rather like the difference between the Senate and a general. But now the rest of it had fallen into place.

"Tahtay? Gaius think Great Sun Man is your father."

And Tahtay puffed up his chest and grinned at him.

"The Seneca, that tribe is the western door. Mohawk, that tribe is the eastern door. The Onondaga, that tribe holds central flame of the Haudenosaunee League. Flame? Is like fire. The light."

Marcellinus chewed and swallowed. Wachiwi, the woman now describing the many tribes that made up the Iroqua, was young, gorgeous, and distractingly unclothed; her breasts bobbed as she pointed at positions on an imaginary map in the air and bobbed again as she reached into her bowl for a piece of duck meat or a slice of askutasquash. But she was also the most knowledgeable about Iroqua geography and politics, being of Iroqua descent herself; Wachiwi had been born into the Onida tribe, captured during a raid and adopted by the Cahokians as a child of only six or seven winters.

Kimimela was eating with them tonight, as was Tahtay. Nominally they were there to help with translation, but Marcellinus suspected them of baser motives. Tahtay was clearly mesmerized by Wachiwi, studying her lessons in geography and politics a little more avidly than their content deserved. Kimimela was just as clearly the reverse, resentful and distrusting of this charismatic new creature in their midst and glowering at Marcellinus whenever she thought he showed the woman too much attention, which was most of the time. Enopay was there, too, but was fast asleep on the floor of Nahimana's hut.

All the people in Marcellinus's small clan by adoption—Nahimana, her warrior son Takoda, the children, and now even Wachiwi—knew more Latin than Marcellinus knew Cahokian, to his continuing shame. Only Takoda's young wife, Kangee, retained any haughtiness toward him. She never spoke in his presence but would make functional hand-talk when it was impossible to avoid communicating.

"So, five tribes," said Marcellinus. "Tribes with big territories all in a line. And these tribes, all friends, never make war with one another, tribe with tribe?"

"Friends," said Wachiwi, looking into his eyes. "Make talk, make . . ."

"Laws," said Tahtay.

"Treaties," Marcellinus said, and turned to the children. "Treaty: agreement between nations. Law: agreement or duty inside nation."

"Treaty," Wachiwi said. "Tribes Haudenosaunee, treaty." She pushed the hair back behind her ears and smiled.

Kimimela sighed.

"Rules: duty within family," Marcellinus concluded, and said more quietly, "And Kimi, here we have rule of no pouting."

"Tell Wachiwi that. And Kangee," she muttered. Marcellinus was impressed that she had deduced the two different kinds of pouting—sultry and sulking—without any explanation from him.

"Be nice," he muttered back. "I need to know these things." He looked up. "So anyway, ask her: Iroqua tribes never fight, Iroqua with Iroqua?"

Tahtay translated, almost blushing under Wachiwi's gaze, and then relayed her response: " 'They fight all time. But small fights. Not like with us. Haudenosaunee are against all People of the Mound, whether Cahokia people or other cities along big-river Mizipi.' "

Oddly, this idea had never occurred to Marcellinus. "There are other mound cities as big as Cahokia?"

"No," said Wachiwi, and gestured in hand-talk, *Cahokia, big, best.*

"Really?" Marcellinus turned to Tahtay. Wachiwi had a tendency to exaggerate.

"Cahokia, uh, ten-and-ten . . . ?" Tahtay said.

"Twenty," said Nahimana.

"Twenty thousand mans and womans. Other mound-builder cities two thousand, four thousand biggest. And many are just two hundred, four hundred. And farmsteads, villages. Cahokia best city anywhere."

All right. "And how many Iroqua?"

They did not know that, of course. How could they?

"Very many," said Wachiwi, and signed *large, many.*

"*Too* many," Tahtay said, proud of knowing how to say that.

"Fewer next year," Nahimana said, offering more food around the small gathering, "when Wanageeska help us kill them."

They all looked at him. He kept his expression calm. Really, by now the die was cast. "Yes. I will help Cahokians kill Iroqua."

"Good," said Nahimana. "Because that why Great Sun Man say to keep you alive, from the Great Mound. Otherwise, no."

Tahtay frowned at her reprovingly, and everyone else looked away, embarrassed.

So there it was, a bald confirmation that Marcellinus had been spared from death solely to help Cahokia wage war. He had expected nothing different, but to hear it stated so matter-of-factly was still something of a shock.

Wachiwi held his gaze and leaned forward. "Wanageeska eat more duck. Wanageeska need be strong, kill Iroqua."

"Uh, thank you." He felt himself redden. Nahimana cackled to herself, and on the blanket beside him Kimimela sighed again.

Catanwakuwa dipped and swirled above Marcellinus's head. The Hawk pilots were subjecting his five dozen warriors to aerial bombardment while they trained. It was good practice for his ground troops to maintain discipline with missiles falling out of the air onto them, and good target practice for the falcon warriors. Naturally, though, Marcellinus was a more tempting target for them than the Cahokian braves, and he carried no shield to deflect the missiles. By now he was completely soaked and begrimed with mud.

Had they been strafing Iroqua, the falcon warriors would have hurled pots of liquid flame. As it was, they threw pouches of muddy Mizipi water of around the same size and weight. And had Marcellinus's men been in real battle, they would have been trying to shoot the birdmen out of the sky; instead, a series of straw targets formed an irregular line a couple of hundred yards in front of them, with additional targets to their left and right, and they fired at those.

"First Cahokian, trade!" Marcellinus bellowed, and another mud bomb slammed into his right shoulder, knocking him forward onto his knees.

Even over the sound of battle, the high-pitched giggling from the sidelines was easily audible. Marcellinus stifled his urge to turn and throw mud at Kimimela and Enopay. Maybe later.

His first rank of archers had just fired a swath of arrows. Some of them had even struck the human-shaped straw men. His second rank stood, took three steps forward, and became the first rank; arrows already nocked, they prepared to release.

"Centurion, order them to fire!" Marcellinus said.

Half of them released their arrows, as they always did, unable to tell the difference between an actual order to shoot and Marcellinus's order to his centurion. Irritated, Akecheta berated those who had fired early in abrasive Cahokian.

"Um, Centurion?" Marcellinus called. "Now *nobody* is firing."

"Fire!" Akecheta shouted, and those in the first rank who had not already loosed an arrow did so, along with those men in the second rank who had just gotten impatient.

Marcellinus sighed. "First Cahokian, trade!"

The second rank marched through and dropped onto one knee, all firing as one despite never having received the order.

"Gods," said Marcellinus. "The Iroqua are going to eat you all for dinner."

"Fire!" Akecheta shouted just to drive home the point that no one could, then wagged his finger at them accusingly.

Marcellinus strode forward. "First Cahokian: spears!"

The first rank reached behind them. The men in the third rank leaned forward to hand each of them a Roman pilum. That, at least, worked well enough.

"Set spears!"

The first rank grounded their pila in the dirt at their feet, points up and out, as if a war party of screaming Iroqua were barreling toward them at full speed with axes and chert-studded clubs.

"Second rank: spears!"

The third rank passed pila forward to the second rank, which held them up in the gaps between those of the first rank. The Roman pila were heavy javelins, similar in size to the Cahokian spears but thicker and sturdier, and the Cahokian battle line was now an impenetrable wall of steel. If only Marcellinus could train them to use shields at the same time, they would be invincible. Unfortunately, bows, pila, gladii, and shields were at least two items too many for his Cahokian troops to wield effectively at this early stage. Besides, to most Cahokians holding a shield was just a waste of an arm and negated their natural fleetness of foot.

Mud rained down on them. There had been a long pause in the bombardment, but the falcon warriors had now flown overhead in formation and let loose a sudden barrage all at once.

Marcellinus wiped gunk from his eyes and spit. He had not taught the falcon warriors that trick. They had apparently learned it from watching the group drills below: a single coordinated surge of missiles was much more effective—and more deadly—than when everyone shot when he felt like it.

The birdmen, at least, learned quickly.

All right. They had been at this for several hours now, and Marcellinus should stop them soon for a break and a drink of water. The weather was much cooler these days, but he still didn't want anyone passing out from overexertion.

"First Cahokian, prepare to charge!"

The braves liked charging. All soldiers did, at least when there wasn't a real enemy in front of them. They leaned forward as one. Akecheta bellowed at them, reminding them to keep their heavy pila straight out and pointing at their imaginary foes, not sagging toward the ground.

"Hold!" called Marcellinus. "Hold . . ."

The First Cahokian seethed, impatient. But if there was one thing Marcellinus had vowed to ensure that his next army was capable of doing, it was waiting.

"Hold," Marcellinus repeated.

The Hawk wings came around in formation for another strafing run. Marcellinus said nothing. He watched and waited.

Then: "First Cahokian! Charge!"

They were off and running, howling at the tops of their voices, pila

still held out in front of them. Even at a full run they preserved a re-
markably straight line. For some reason this had been much easier for
them to learn than maintaining discipline while firing arrows. Marcellinus still hoped to get them into a steady progression, move-fire-move-
fire-move-fire, with flights of arrows going off more quickly and
efficiently than the men could manage firing at random, but at this rate
it wouldn't happen till next summer.

Cahokian warriors charged *fast*. At his age and with the vestigial
aches of his many wounds, there was no way Marcellinus could keep up
with them.

They hit the straw men head on, still running full tilt. The steel spear
points went straight through the straw men and into the ground on the
other side. Around half the troops drew gladii and raised them above
their heads, some of them hacking at the remains of the straw figures.
The other half dropped to one knee and covered them, as they were
supposed to. In a real battle they'd be down there taking scalps, anyway.
Marcellinus would never be able to train them out of that.

Some of his troops were more coordinated with the steel blades than
others. Eventually Marcellinus would arm all the men and women in
his century with a gladius, but many of them needed more individual
sparring practice before he could risk it. Right now, the chances of them
disemboweling one another by accident in their excitement were too
great.

Even with the swords only in experienced hands, the hacking was
getting overenthusiastic.

"First Cahokian! Retreat!" Nothing happened. "First Cahokian, to
me!"

Marcellinus ran forward. "Centurion! Akecheta! Order the retreat!"

Akecheta spun around, looking confused, and one of his own men
nearly stabbed him in the thigh with Roman steel.

"Gods preserve us," said Marcellinus.

A falcon warrior swooped over the front rank and shouted down at
the warriors. They stood as one, turned, and began to jog back toward
Marcellinus.

Akecheta arrived first, panting, and Marcellinus gave him a companionable punch on the shoulder. "Lunkhead! Not supposed to retreat when *enemy* tells you to!"

Akecheta grinned, unabashed. The "enemy" Catanwakuwa banked low over them and dumped a torrent of water and mud down Marcellinus's neck.

By the time he released them for the afternoon, Marcellinus looked as if he had been thrown into a bog. Small children scattered at his approach, screaming in delighted mock terror.

He could tell already that discipline would be a persistent issue with his new army. He was smiling nonetheless.

By Marcellinus's best guess, he had two years. But he might have only one.

If all had gone as planned and Marcellinus had taken Cahokia, he would have sent dispatch riders back to the Roman beachhead garrison at Chesapica well before the end of the campaign season, and a small longship would have been sent back to Roma to tell Hadrianus the news. It was now October, and Marcellinus had no way of sending news of his defeat to the Chesapica. But the Imperator and the Senate well understood the immensity of the Atlanticus and the difficulties his legion would face in a new continent. If a longship did not come to Roma or arrived with no real news of the 33rd, they would wait till the next spring. It might take until after the Ides of Maius—the Planting Moon, by the Cahokian calendar—before serious doubts began to register, and that would already be very late to summon, prepare, and dispatch another legion to Nova Hesperia the same year. In those circumstances it probably would be the following spring—nearly two years hence—before the Romans returned.

But if Roman survivors made it to the Chesapica, if his errant but skillful scout Isleifur Bjarnason learned of the destruction and made haste to the east, or if the garrison somehow learned of the loss of the 33rd Legion from the Powhatani or the Iroqua, Hadrianus might still receive the news this coming winter.

What happened then would depend entirely on how the war with the Mongol Khan was going and whether the Imperator himself was campaigning with the Roman army on the front line—adding to the length of time it would take to get dispatches to and from him—or had returned to Roma. It also depended on whether a legion could be spared and where that legion currently was.

In all likelihood, then, two years. Perhaps even more. But if all the pieces fell into place, if Hadrianus learned the news of the massive defeat quickly and acted swiftly to avenge it, if a new legion was sent and came thundering west along the very trails and bridges that the 33rd had blazed through the land . . . Marcellinus might have as little as six or eight months.

He would need every day.

The two lines of braves crashed into each other. Half of the first line fell over. "Halt!" cried Akecheta with the absence of timeliness for which he was now renowned.

Marcellinus groaned. This afternoon, no one in the First Cahokian was concentrating at all. He had no idea why.

His troops helped one another to their feet, having the decency to look a little embarrassed.

"All right," Marcellinus said. "Now let's—"

"Present arms!"

Akecheta's suddenly barked command in Latin cut off his thought in midstream. There could be only one reason for the interruption: Marcellinus was outranked. He turned.

"Leave tomorrow," said Great Sun Man, striding up to him. He wore what Marcellinus thought of as his kilt of office, with the blocks of geometric patterns carefully dyed into it. Serious business was afoot, then.

"Where you go?" Marcellinus asked, wiping his face with a blanket. It was the nearest these people got to a good honest towel. Then he saw the expression on Great Sun Man's face. "What, me? I must leave Cahokia? Why?"

"You. Me. Many warriors. Kill Iroqua."

Marcellinus looked around for Tahtay or Kimimela. By now he knew a few hundred basic conversational and combat words in Cahokian and could sign and understand much more complicated gestural sentences, but Great Sun Man knew no Latin and rarely deigned to use hand-talk with him. This conversation might quickly exceed Marcellinus's language skills.

"Joke? Ha-ha?"

"Not joke." The war chief eyed him suspiciously and then looked around at the First Cahokian. "Fight."

"So we fight? Where?"

"Sunrise." Great Sun Man pointed east in the Cahokian style by turning to face the sun so that his left side was aligned eastward. "Mizipi, then Oyo, and then," he gestured, "Iroqua long camp."

"What?"

"Iroqua build winter? No-no. We fight. Kill Iroqua."

Marcellinus couldn't follow this. "Uh, wait, sorry, where's your son?"

Tahtay's excitement at the news was infectious. "Cahokia scouts have found Iroqua war camp, past Snake Mound along Oyo River, long-way. They, Iroqua warriors, build up camp there for winter. A place called Woshakee. We cannot let them stay so close. We go now, destroy Iroqua long camp before winter, kill much Iroqua."

"We all?" He turned to Great Sun Man. "Tahtay come, too, Iroqua battle-fight?"

Great Sun Man said something Marcellinus didn't understand, then, seeing the Roman's baffled expression, simplified his words. "Yes. Tomorrow before dawn, we go. Many warriors. You and your—" He gestured at the men around them a little quizzically. "—fighters. We see what you do. And Tahtay, for words, my son Tahtay, for man, for battle. I have spoken."

The war chief walked off abruptly; the conversation was always at an end after "I have spoken." Marcellinus shook his head and turned to Tahtay. "What did Great Sun Man say?"

He hardly needed to ask. Tahtay was grinning from ear to ear. "Great Sun Man say time for Tahtay to come to war, time for Tahtay to become a man!"

"Really?" Marcellinus was appalled. A boy of only eleven winters? Even his signiferi in the 33rd Legion had been several winters—several years—older than *that*.

"Eat well today," the boy advised him with the air of a seasoned professional. "Food on warpath very bad, hard meat and berries."

He meant dried deer meat pressed into small cakes, tough and unappetizing. Marcellinus had seen it before. "Yes. I will eat well."

Tahtay ran off, skipping in a most unwarriorlike way, and it was only then that the true import of Great Sun Man's words sank in.

Marcellinus was going to war against the Iroqua. With the Cahokians. *Leading* Cahokians by the sound of it, or at least his own small unit of them.

After a long and sometimes frustrating convalescence, Marcellinus was certainly ready to see some action. But the First Cahokian? His efforts with them to be tested so soon?

The consequences of failure might be huge. Fatal, even if he survived the Iroqua. Marcellinus was under no illusions: he was still very much on probation with the Cahokian war chief.

"Great Juno . . ."

He looked up at the sun. It was midafternoon. There was still time.

"Akecheta!" He ran back toward his men. "Akecheta! Centurion! Warriors, fall in!"

CHAPTER 9

Rather than build a winter camp, the Iroqua had stolen one.

"These, Mohawk Iroqua," said Great Sun Man as they paddled down the Mizipi. The war chief took his turn at the oar just as often as any of his men. Marcellinus had been quickly exempted from rowing duties; he could not match the power and precision of the Cahokians, and the repetitive nature of the paddling put strain on his shoulder, his ribs, and even the wound in his stomach. So, much to his humiliation, he got to loll around in the war canoe for hours on end while the other warriors propelled them vigorously down the Mizipi. Even Tahtay got to paddle from time to time.

At least it kept them warm. The chill had long ago crept into Marcellinus's bones. Along with being hotter than Roma in the summer, apparently this Hesperian latitude was all set to be colder in the autumn and winter as well.

"Mohawks." Marcellinus nodded. "And long camp?"

Great Sun Man spoke to Tahtay for what felt like several minutes. Marcellinus looked at the flotilla of war canoes that followed in their wake. Great Sun Man's canoe had been the last to push off from the riverbank at Cahokia but by now had passed through the formation to take the lead.

With so few leaves on the trees, the conspicuousness of their passage was making Marcellinus nervous. They were sitting ducks out there, and the breastplate he was wearing against arrows would drag him deep into the water if their canoe capsized in an attack. Even though the Cahokians assured him they had many days' travel ahead before they encountered the Mohawks, Marcellinus felt ridiculously unprepared. He wanted all the details of what they were up against.

"The Mohawk take a city," Tahtay said. "Small city, fives-of-hundred mans and womans. City of our people."

"Cahokians?"

"From Cahokia, no, but our people. People of the Mounds, most along the Mizipi but also the near rivers. Mohawk take that city, Woshakee, by creep, by sneak. They kill the warriors, take the womans and children. In the Mourning War they need children to replace braves they lose, need womans to make more children."

"Very nice," said Marcellinus. "So, this city?"

"City has palis . . . ?"

"Tall tree logs around it, like a wall? 'Palisade.' Or 'stockade.'"

"Yes, palisade, to stop attack. But Mohawks big clever and walk in with traders, then kill by night. So now they have a town close to Cahokia, with corn and many womans, and they can grow fat over winter and then rise and raid us, kill us quick when the first thaw come."

"But we will kill them quick instead. Now."

"Yes."

Marcellinus was going with a couple of hundred Cahokian warriors to besiege a walled city. He wondered what their chances were. "This happen before, Iroqua steal a city?"

"No. This new."

"Do your enemies build stockades around their cities, too? Cahokians have attacked cities with stockades before?"

"No. This new, too."

Marcellinus grimaced. "It would have been good to know this before we left Cahokia, Tahtay. We could have prepared, made special weapons and practiced drills for this. If we have to beat our way through a palisade, we need battering rams or borers. Did we bring liquid flame?"

"Yes," Tahtay said. "We have liquid flame in clay pots. Some. On canoes, not safe bring much."

"And do Iroqua have liquid flame?"

Tahtay had been translating over his shoulder so his father would hear the conversation, too. Great Sun Man responded. "Yes. Iroqua use it before. Iroqua liquid flame not good as Cahokian liquid flame."

Well, of course not. "And I suppose a couple of score of good siege ladders would be too much to hope for? Even some picks and crowbars?"

At least they had brought shields. Against Great Sun Man's protests that they would weigh down the canoes and slow them down, Marcellinus had managed to bring four dozen of the tall rectangular shields for those of his men whom he'd trained in their use late in the afternoon before they left. That last-minute training looked even more fortuitous now.

"Yes, they have the flame, too," Tahtay added superfluously. "But why we need break stockade? Mohawk will come out and fight us. Why not?"

With a perfectly good fort around them? Marcellinus doubted it. Iroqua honor and Cahokian honor were two very different animals. "We'll see. Tell me more about city, about land around it. How far from river? There are trees, hills, what?"

Tahtay asked Great Sun Man, who seemed impatient at the question. "No. He never go. I never go."

Marcellinus stared. "Has *anyone* in this canoe been to the city we're going to relieve?"

Tahtay inquired, but Marcellinus could interpret the brief head gestures and grunts of the other fifteen warriors in the canoe for himself.

"Juno, protect us all," he said.

"Change paddle men," Great Sun Man said. "Change!"

And they did, with great nimbleness, walking up and down the canoe in midstream as if they were on land, nobody falling in the water or even needing to grab on to anything for support. That, at least, was impressive.

"You people could teach the Norsemen a thing or two."

" 'Norsemen' is what?" Tahtay asked.

"Never mind."

It took them twelve days to travel to the vicinity of the captured city, Woshakee. For the first three days they paddled down the Mizipi, going with the current. During that time they passed several Cahokian-style villages and towns positioned up against the river, their reed-thatched roofs surrounding mounds of various sizes. The larger towns were protected by full palisades, but without firing platforms, and the villages had only low fences that looked like they would fall to a strong sneeze. Tahtay told Marcellinus that those fences were made by weaving branches together and then painting them with mud; as in some areas in northern Europa, they were fit only for keeping cattle in . . . if these people had had any cattle.

On the second day the Mizipi narrowed to flow through a rocky bottleneck. Here the Cahokians stopped for a few minutes to pay tribute to an immense rock that sat in the water near the riverbank. The rock was covered with petroglyphs: spirals, painted eyes, and falcon glyphs and figures of men, and weaving through them all the sinuous form of a snake that extended all the way from the crown of the rock down into the water and, presumably, beyond. The rock must have weighed a dozen tons, and the glyphs looked older than anything Marcellinus had seen in Cahokia, which meant older than anything he'd yet seen in Nova Hesperia.

Kiche, the shaman acolyte, climbed onto the rock and lit six fire bowls, dedicating them to north and south, east and west, above and below, while the canoes maintained their station in the current with some difficulty. The other warriors, at least the ones not paddling, bowed their heads in reverence and chanted briefly.

"Sky," Tahtay said, pointing upward, and "Land under," pointing down, far down by the way he was emphasizing it.

"Yes," said Marcellinus. He had moved to the stern of their canoe half out of respect for the Cahokians' traditions and half out of embarrassment at their superstition; even now it was hard for him to square the pragmatic and down-to-earth everyday aspect of the Cahokians with the more superstitious and pagan side that came alive during their nighttime ceremonies and the occasional daytime rituals like this.

"Is Rock of Thunderbird and River Snake," Takoda said with a reproving air as the men moved back to their positions in the canoes and prepared to go on.

"So I see," said Marcellinus.

"Water and air join here with the earth, and we thank them."

"I'm glad." Marcellinus was aware he was failing a test, but he didn't believe it was a critical one, and he really had no choice. He could not pretend to an animist faith his own people had mostly left behind centuries ago. What he wanted most of all was not the blessing of the air and the underworld but to make faster progress across the water.

On the fourth day, after looping through a series of long oxbows flanked by lush woodlands, they came to the confluence of the Mizipi and Oyo rivers. The river junction was guarded heavily on both sides by stockades manned by scores of dour-looking warriors dressed like Cahokians but with less elaborate tattoos and little distinctive finery—no copper ear spools and only a few shell necklaces—and the weapons they carried were mostly chert-studded clubs and plain spears.

"Ocatan, this," said Tahtay. "Fort, yes? On the water."

At Ocatan they picked up another ten canoes' worth of warriors, their boats riding out to join the Cahokian force and slotting neatly into the formation as it paddled by. All somehow prearranged.

Once they made the turn, the going got harder. The Oyo was a much broader river than the Mizipi and with bluer waters, and they were now paddling against the current rather than with it.

"How much farther?" Marcellinus asked, pointing behind them, much to Tahtay's confusion. "What I mean is Oyo and Mizipi join here to make one river. How far is the mare, the big water, south down the Mizipi, that way?"

Tahtay didn't know. He asked Great Sun Man, who replied, "One moon."

To Marcellinus the riverbank had appeared to be rushing by as their shallow-draft canoes were paddled vigorously by a dozen men at a time. "No. A month? Thirty days paddling from here?"

"Maybe longer, maybe farther."

Even now, Marcellinus was daunted by the scale of Nova Hesperia. "And how far upriver?"

Great Sun Man shrugged and spoke to Tahtay, who reported, "Another moon. Until cold. And then, forever."

The evening before they reached Woshakee, the canoes pulled in to the shore at dusk. By this time Marcellinus was weary just from watching other men work.

It would be futile for Marcellinus to warn them against setting a fire. They wouldn't listen to him anyway, and at this time of year they could hardly survive the night without one. With careful selection of fallen wood the Cahokians kept the amount of smoke that rose above the trees to a minimum, and they did not cook over it to avoid flavoring the wind with the scents of their food. Nonetheless, Marcellinus was sure that the Mohawks would know they were coming.

Marcellinus picked at his dried meat and berries with the rest of them. Normally he was not a man to fret the night before a battle, but normally he had the weight of several thousand well-trained men at his back. By contrast, this small Cahokian skirmishing force worried the hunger right out of him. His orders might prove to be a dangerous distraction to the men he supposedly commanded. What if he failed again? What would he do if Tahtay was killed the next day or, worse, if something Marcellinus did *got* him killed?

When the fire died down, the men all huddled together for warmth, rather too close for Marcellinus's taste, though he had to admit it helped keep the night chill at bay.

The next day dawned frosty. Marcellinus was already awake when the rest of the braves stirred; he had volunteered to take third watch with half a dozen other warriors and had blinked his way sleepily through to the coming of the sun. He went and splashed his face with chilly river water to wake himself up.

"Here," said Great Sun Man.

Marcellinus had been expecting food. Instead he was presented with a tall young warrior who blinked owlishly and scratched himself. "Yes?"

"This man, Mahkah. He know the city the Mohawk have taken."

"Ah, good. When was he last there?"

"When last?" Great Sun Man frowned, and Tahtay, returning from his morning ablutions in the bushes, had to ask that question for Marcellinus.

"Twelve winters," was the reply.

Marcellinus eyed his informant. "And how old is Mahkah?"

"Seventeen winters."

"Tahtay . . ."

"No worry," the boy said blithely. "Later we get you another."

As it turned out, Tahtay was right. Marcellinus had pumped Mahkah for all he knew about the lay of the land at their destination. It wasn't a lot, and Marcellinus suspected that Mahkah was following the established Cahokian custom of making up answers when he didn't know for sure. But after two hours paddling along the Oyo the meaning of "we get you another" became apparent.

"Canoe," Marcellinus said tersely. "Get bows, arrows?"

On the southern bank the branches of a willow hung down low over the water, half its brown leaves already shed but still providing a little cover. From beneath it a small canoe was gliding out.

"Arrows?" said Great Sun Man with mild contempt. "Shoot? No. Our men, that."

And so they were. The canoe held three young Cahokian warriors, obviously scouts sent ahead to check the terrain and now waiting there for the war party to arrive. Marcellinus grinned. Even now it was surprising how often he failed to ask the right question and how often nobody around him understood him well enough to provide the right answer regardless. But at least their little army would not totally lack for information.

"Make plan while paddle," Tahtay said.

The other canoes moved in and bunched up, the formation closing.

The men in his canoe shipped their paddles as canoes slid into position on either side. The braves on the outer edges of the formation continued to paddle. Behind them, similar bunches of canoes moved up against them, gentle as a kiss. Paddling and momentum carried them up the Oyo.

Great Sun Man turned to his scouts, who began to talk about the city ahead, the layout of the land around it, and the number and disposition of the Mohawk warriors.

"Paint, my son," Great Sun Man said. Tahtay looked serious and excited at the same time as his father applied blue and red war paint to his cheeks.

Marcellinus looked around him. Many of the men had been painted for war since they had left Cahokia but were now making final preparations. As the male warriors stripped to the waist, he saw again the jagged patterns of the war tattoos and paint on their chests and arms. Some men attached feathers to the ends of their braids. Hanska, the only woman among them, wore shells braided into her hair and a buckskin jerkin, her arms as tattooed as the rest. The archers were strapping on leather wrist bracers. Many men donned wooden or reed mats against their chests, the simple armor Marcellinus remembered from his battle against them. Others, mostly the members of his First Cahokian, pulled on Roman breastplates.

Memories resurfaced of the wild melee in which he had cleaved many such mats with Roman steel and sent warriors crashing dead into the dust. With those memories came a surge of energy and an equal surge of guilt.

Marcellinus did not push those emotions away but collected them and refined them in his heart. He was about to go into battle. The oddness of his situation must not distract him. He was as likely to die in today's fight as in any he had ever fought, and he needed his wits about him. A seasoned campaigner made use of whatever energies he could muster.

Marcellinus was a peculiar hybrid these days: Cahokian tunic,

Roman breastplate, Cahokian belt with a Roman sheath and a Roman gladius hanging from it, Roman army sandals on his feet. He had a Roman helmet, too, not the shiny gilded steel helmet with the fancy crest of a Praetor that he had once worn but one from a simple legionary. A dead man's helmet.

"Paint, Wanageeska?" Great Sun Man asked.

The war chief was talking to Marcellinus. His fingertips were daubed red and blue.

"No," Marcellinus said by reflex. Go into battle painted like a wild man?

Then again, it was their battle he was fighting. And Great Sun Man was frowning.

"Yes, sir," said Marcellinus. "You honor me."

If he was to fight shoulder to shoulder with Cahokians, he needed them to treat him as one of their own, at least for a few hours. Why stand out even more than he did as a creature alien to them? And if there really was any special energy to fighting in paint, why reject it?

Great Sun Man's fingers worked deftly on his cheeks and across his forehead. As far as Marcellinus could tell, the chief was applying the same simple pattern of paint across his face that Tahtay had. He wondered briefly whether he was being adorned with the pattern of a boy's paint rather than a man's. But when he looked around at the other Cahokians, every man's paint was different. Tahtay's was not inferior to anyone else's. And nobody was laughing at Marcellinus; to the contrary, he saw nods and distracted half smiles, the self-absorbed camaraderie of soldiers around the world preparing for combat while accepting the companionship of the men around them.

"Thank you," he said.

"One thing more," said Great Sun Man, and reached into the long bag at his feet where he kept his ax and club.

He drew out a gladius and a pugio, shiny Roman steel. They were Marcellinus's original weapons: the gladius with the ornate hilt he'd had specially made for him before he had set off as a newly minted tribune to make war against the Khwarezmian Sultanate and carried ever since and his more straightforward standard-issue pugio with the nicks in its pommel where he had used it as a hammer to fix his sandal one afternoon during the long march through Appalachia. He had not seen those weapons since he had laid them down in surrender on the Master Mound months before.

"Is good?" Great Sun Man asked, eyes narrowed.

Marcellinus understood his caution. Like Romans, Cahokians took omens seriously. Perhaps Marcellinus might not want back the weapons he had wielded in defeat.

But Marcellinus did, and the trees bounding the river shimmered a little in his vision as he took his old gladius and raised it up in front of his eyes.

A lump formed in his throat. He took and absorbed the energy of that, too, once again focusing it outward. Suddenly Marcellinus felt strong and ready to fight and kill.

"It is very good," he said. "I thank you, Great Sun Man."

The breeze picked up on their final approach to Woshakee. It blew northerly, scattering ripples across the waters of the Oyo and tending to push the canoes leftward toward the riverbank. For the Cahokian war party this was the least favored direction the wind could have taken; was even the air in the pay of the Iroqua despite their rites at the great rock? Great Sun Man grimaced.

Mostly flat for the past few days, the land had begun to crumple up around them over the last twenty miles. The southern bank was sparsely lined with trees. They were within arrow range but just barely, and so the Cahokians kept careful watch on those trees for Iroqua archers. The northern bank swelled into a gentle slope that steepened to end in a low ridge several hundred yards away. The land cover was grassy rather than cultivated; according to the scouts, the Woshakean cornfields lay east and north of the city, in fields that were more level and easier to till, and also east and south on the other side of the Oyo. It was pretty, well-behaved countryside, and if the Legion had marched through more land like this on its long trek west, Marcus Tullius might not have been quite so scathing about Romans wanting to farm Nova Hesperia one day.

Though in order to give away land parcels to Roman veterans or civilian migrants, they'd have to evict the local farmers who were already there. Marcellinus shied away from that thought.

Once again Great Sun Man's canoe led the Cahokian flotilla, with the rough-and-ready boat of the three scouts paddling alongside. One of those scouts raised his hand in a signal that Marcellinus didn't understand, a Cahokian warrior sign, not a gesture in the hand-talk that all Hesperians understood.

"Next bend," came the whispered word through the lead canoe, and the signal was passed by warrior sign back through the canoes that followed. The rearmost five canoes broke away and headed in toward the shore. The remainder maintained position in the center of the river.

The bend was a long, slow turn to the right. As they rounded it, the landscape that the scouts had described came into view. The occupied mound-builder city of Woshakee sat on the left, northward bank about a half mile distant. The stockade that surrounded it came within a dozen feet of the Oyo. Obviously, here the river did not make a habit of bursting its banks. Trails of smoke rose above the stockade, dispersing in the breeze, but it was the orderly thin smoke of fire pits, not the vicious black smoke of destruction. Although the wind was wrong, Marcellinus caught the distant aroma of meat simmering in a pot. His mouth watered even though his stomach was tight with anticipation.

Perhaps two hundred feet inside the stockade he saw a mound thirty feet high, topped with a longhouse. Unlike Cahokia, in this city the chieftain had actually lived on the city's main mound until he was scalped and burned alive by the Mohawk. Marcellinus was sure that the longhouse now served a more pragmatic purpose for the invaders.

The Mohawk would be watching. It was unrealistic to hope that the approach of the Cahokians had gone unnoticed. Woshakee had been taken by specialists in war, essentially professional warriors, the expansionist arm of the Haudenosaunee League. Such men would not be caught napping in their stolen houses with their stolen women. Yet there was no sign of Iroqua readiness to fight. Certainly they were not all lining up outside their palisade ready for battle in the way the Cahokians had awaited the Romans.

And it was impossible, of course, to tell how many Iroqua there were behind that palisade, within that city that normally might have housed five hundred or a thousand people. The Cahokian scouts' description of the land had been excellent, but they had not been inside and did not know the size of the Iroqua force.

Roman history was full of sieges in which a few hundred defenders inside a fortified city had successfully held off armies of many thousands for weeks or even months. Those cities had often been built of stone and usually had a river or some underground water source flowing through them. Nonetheless, even if there were as few of the Iroqua as there were of the Cahokians, the defenders held a strong advantage over Great Sun Man and his warriors.

But the Iroqua were not armed with Roman steel.

Marcellinus looked again at the north ridge. No movement from up there yet. Far behind him, the five Cahokian canoes already bobbed empty against the riverbank. To his left, five more canoes pulled ashore carrying the heaviest of the Cahokian war items—Marcellinus's precious shields. Those canoes contained members of his First Cahokian Cohort, including Akecheta and Takoda. The remainder of the men he had trained were distributed in canoes all around him. Marcellinus itched to get onto shore himself and get his cohort into formation before something happened.

And then something did.

Within the city, beyond arrow range, a man clambered up on top of the longhouse and gazed out at them. He appeared calm and unsurprised, with the solid demeanor of a war chief. Great Sun Man grunted, obviously coming to the same conclusion.

A second figure appeared, climbing the wooden steps to the top of the mound and passing something up to the chief. A spear? The war chief knelt to take it and held it high for all to see.

Yes, a spear. And impaled on its point a bloody head.

The man gestured widely in the universal hand-talk of Nova Hesperia, a simple message that even Marcellinus could understand.

Tahtay translated it anyway. " 'You die.' " He cleared his throat. " 'You all die. Come, fight, die.' "

From the crest of the hillside to the north, a Hawk wing rose into the air. It hung in the wind, then dipped into a big loop to the right, angling for altitude. Whatever mechanism had thrown it up there, it was not as powerful as the launching rail of the Cahokians, but it would certainly be enough to give the Iroqua the air advantage.

"Keep your eyes up," Marcellinus said to Tahtay. "See everything. Assume nothing."

The boy swallowed. His face was pale, his eyes wide.

"Stay calm. Keep thinking. Never panic. Be brave, be ready, be fast. If you are attacked, dodge a blow rather than blocking it. If a Mohawk is down, show him no mercy. Stay with your father. Make him proud."

"All that?" Tahtay asked.

Marcellinus grinned tautly. "And more."

The Cahokians had passed a copse of oak and hickory on the northern bank a hundred yards back. From those trees came a sudden fusillade of Iroqua arrows.

Great Sun Man shouted, but the Cahokian warriors already on the bank were prepared, raising Roman shields. The Iroqua had their range right away, but the arrows bounced harmlessly off glinting steel.

Now the canoes themselves came under arrow fire. Many fell short or long—range was harder to establish for boats on water—but two braves in the rearmost Cahokian canoe took hits in the arm and leg, respectively, and the first wounded howls drifted in the air.

But they were not down and thrashing as his legionaries had been, back in the Appalachian pass. "No poison," Marcellinus said in relief.

Three more Hawks had taken flight from the top of the ridge and now swooped down across the water, sleek and fast. Small gouts of liquid flame erupted on the riverbank near the advanced landing party. The Hawk pilots carried pots of the incendiary rather than bows and arrows.

Mohawk archers popped up to line the top of the Woshakee palisade, probably standing on a newly built scaffold of some kind. Those archers began to nock and shoot arrows of their own.

The Cahokian landing party was now pinned between assaults from their front and rear plus occasional firebombs from above.

The canoe bearing Marcellinus and Great Sun Man swung in at speed, ramming the bank. As soon as it hit, Marcellinus jumped to shore and ran into the midst of his men. An Iroqua arrow banged into his chest plate, startling him but bouncing away harmlessly. Behind him the other Cahokian canoes were crashing ashore, warriors splashing through the shallow water and up onto the land.

Tahtay slipped and stumbled, then pulled himself onto the bank in a defensive crouch before running to join his father. Marcellinus put the boy out of his mind. He could no longer afford to be distracted.

"First Cahokian, to me! Two lines, back to back!"

Under Akecheta's urging they were already doing it; a double line of warriors already faced the copse behind a solid rank of shields while another double line fell in behind them, raising shields in the opposite direction, toward the city. Akecheta, resplendent in Roman breastplate and leg greaves, stood at the uphill end of the First Cahokian, and Marcellinus took his place at the downhill, riverside end. The rest of the Cahokian force was fanning out under Great Sun Man's command, already firing arrows into the city while racing to gain the higher ground. This brought them within easier reach of the birdmen, and one Cahokian fell to an Iroqua arrow. Another, splashed with liquid flame, shrieked and fled at full speed into the river.

Marcellinus nocked his bow, aimed well ahead of the Iroqua Hawk warrior, and fired. He missed, but the Hawk swerved and headed cross-river to land on the other bank, unable to regain altitude, now effectively out of the battle.

"First Cahokian, advance!"

They had settled beforehand that "advance" meant toward the city, and his warriors now did exactly that, walking along the bank behind their shields toward the palisade while the men facing the other way backed up to guard their rear, the men with no shields shuffling along between the lines. In a very small number of paces they would be out of range of the arrows from the trees behind them.

But now those arrows were ceasing as battle was joined. The warriors from the five Cahokian canoes that had gone ashore early were storming the copse, slaying Iroqua in hand-to-hand combat. Even from the scouts' description of the land, the copse had been an obvious hiding ground for a Mohawk ambush, and preparing a secondary assault force to take care of business there had been one of the first orders Great Sun Man had given during their on-river planning.

Beyond that, their powers to predict what would happen had been limited. Hawks from the ridge had been another obvious danger, but the Cahokians had had no chance of forestalling that possibility. Sending a team of warriors to sneak around and take the ridge from the rear would have added another day to the attack and spread their forces too thin.

The sounds of cheerful slaughter from the copse continued, and now Cahokians began to run from the copse to join their fellows out on the open riverbank. Fresh scalps bobbed from their waists, splashing blood onto their legs and the grass as they ran. The danger from the Iroqua archers having passed, the rearward-facing unit of Marcellinus's First Cahokian began to shuffle around and slot themselves into the forward line even before Marcellinus or Akecheta gave the order; Marcellinus shook his head at their acting on their own initiative, but it was the correct thing to do.

Fortunately, the wings from the ridge were few and far between. Marcellinus suspected the Mohawk had not brought many pilots with them; the central part of Nova Hesperia lacked the crags and hills of Appalachia, giving little reason for the Iroqua to have brought a substantial force of aerial warriors. Nonetheless, the birdmen they did have were wreaking a fair degree of havoc. The Cahokians with shields to spare raised them when the Hawks came over, and some of his other soldiers even lifted shields that were supposed to protect them against arrows from the city to guard against liquid flame from above. It was clear which danger the Cahokians feared the most.

Marcellinus's cohort continued to advance, firing arrows in rotation for every ten feet of ground covered. Having a live enemy firing back had done wonders for their concentration, and they sent off coordinated flights of arrows almost without a hitch under Akecheta's bellowed orders. Two hundred feet from the palisade, no one in the First Cahokian had fallen, none had dropped out of line, none had even spoken except to relay orders. Their faces were set in focused glares. Akecheta had not yet given them a confusing or ambiguous order, and none of the individual warriors had botched anything. Marcellinus was grimly proud of how the battle was going so far, and how well the men were using the shields given how little practice they'd had with them.

The larger force of Cahokian Wolf Warriors with Great Sun Man had made it far enough up the hillside that they could fire more easily down into the city. Men with slingshots hurled the Cahokians' liquid flame over the palisade. Many firebombs smacked into the wood of the stockade; the fire spread quickly over the surface of the tall, well-packed poles but burned only where the bombs hit. Beyond the splash zone the wood did not catch fire the way Marcellinus had hoped it would. The stockade was not visibly covered with pitch, but the Iroqua had treated it somehow to make it fire-resistant. That was disappointing.

With a few gestures of warrior sign, Great Sun Man split out four groups of six warriors from his force and sent them up the hill toward the crest where the Hawk wings were being launched. The warriors ducked and weaved as they ran up the hill, using the occasional stands of pine and hemlock for cover, howling for blood with convincing ferocity. Marcellinus felt sorry for any Iroqua they encountered on the ridge.

But the city itself was their main problem. Though the Cahokians had plenty of arrows, they were hitting few targets. The Iroqua could feel quite comfortable tucked away behind their sturdy ramparts of wood. Few Cahokians were falling under Iroqua arrows either. This battle would not be over quickly. Each army could gather and reuse the arrows of its enemy, and neither army was inflicting or suffering significant losses.

Presumably the Iroqua had many more warriors than the few dozen

Marcellinus could see; they probably would man the palisade in shifts, with the bulk of them able to rest between bouts of action. At some point the Cahokians would need to retreat out of range and rest as well.

The siege of Woshakee might not be resolved today or even this week unless something drastic was done.

Marcellinus moved in behind the line of the First Cahokian to benefit from the shield wall. In the din of men shouting and arrows plinking off metal, he tried to think.

Once his men found out what he was thinking, he was pretty sure they wouldn't like it. He didn't like it himself. It was really too soon to try something this complicated with such an untrained squad of soldiers.

But he was also convinced that it was the only plan that made sense.

Marcellinus looked up the hill. No birdmen had flown for maybe a quarter hour—it was hard to keep time in the blur of battle—and the last few to strafe the Cahokian force had been ineffectual. These Iroqua Hawks flew low, with wooden armor covering the body and legs of their pilots, and after releasing their liquid flame or arrows over the Cahokians, they generally landed back inside the city. Without the armor, their birdmen's hopes of survival would be poor; at the heights they were flying the battle would become a duck hunt. However, the armor spoiled their aim with the bow, and their pots of incendiary were injuring several but killing no one. Maybe it wasn't as good as Cahokian liquid flame, after all.

Marcellinus could not assume that the Hawk threat was over. It was too soon for the four Cahokian war bands to have made it to the crown of the ridge, especially against opposition. Waiting a little longer might make his Cahokians safer from air attack. But they had been in battle for close to an hour now, and there was a limit to how long he could wait before his men grew tired or their nerve cracked.

Or his own did.

"First Cahokian, group for orders!"

This wasn't Marcellinus's battlefield. Great Sun Man was Marcellinus's superior officer. But Great Sun Man was three hundred yards away, working his own force of Cahokians up the slope around the north side of Woshakee, where they could launch their arrows from slightly above the line of the palisade and perhaps even throw fire onto those Iroqua shooting at the First Cahokian. Marcellinus needed to take advantage of that before the Iroqua could adjust their tactics and provide covering fire of their own.

The First Cahokian formed a tight huddle inside a ring of steel. Tersely, Marcellinus told his men what he wanted. Then he told them again. Then he drew it in the mud beneath their feet. He was pretty sure they got it the third time. The older warriors looked grim, the younger ones a little startled. Only half a dozen looked cheerful about it, but those men hooted and punched the sky, and some of their enthusiasm spread. Privately, Marcellinus thought they must be men of little imagination; this would be a bold move but one that could easily and quite literally collapse into disaster. His men would learn quickly or it would be all over.

"I'll be right there with you," said Marcellinus. "Wanageeska will lead. Wanageeska will be first. I ask none of you to do a thing I would not do myself."

They looked uncertain. He had used too many negatives in that sentence to be safely understood. Rather than try again, Marcellinus grinned fiercely. "Maybe you will not keep up with me! Maybe I will win big glory! And maybe I will fall! In that case, futete! Fuck it!"

That, he got a cheer for.

He coached them in the three orders he planned to give. With various gestures they assured him that they understood.

He looked at Akecheta, who wore a slight frown. Marcellinus swallowed. This was the moment when Akecheta could refuse his command, and it would all be over. "Are you with me, centurion?"

" . . . Yes," said Akecheta. "Got it."

"Got it, *sir*. You're sure now? Yes? Go?"

Akecheta pulled himself up to his full height. Three arrows plunked off the shield that covered him. "Yes, sir! Got it! I have spoken!"

"Axes? Liquid flame?"

Seven men and Hanska waved them to prove they had them at the ready.

"Then First Cahokian, fall in!"

"First Cahokian!" Akecheta shouted, showing teeth and punching the sky. "Fall in! Futete!"

Akecheta wasn't Pollius Scapax. He would never be. But he would do.

Chapter 10

Year One, Beaver Moon

The First Cahokian Cohort advanced toward the wooden walls of Woshakee in a diamond testudo formation. The men walked forward as a close group, the outermost warriors holding shields to guard the left and right flanks, those within holding them over their heads, overlapping and tightly locked. Tucked into the front apex of the group, Marcellinus could smell their fear, but no one flinched even when the din of missiles landing on metal rose sharply. They were just fifty feet from the palisade, and the Iroqua were flinging rocks instead of firing arrows.

Marcellinus had six dozen men under four dozen shields. Against the onslaught of liquid flame that could spill from a Wakinyan it would not have worked. Against sticks and stones, if every warrior kept his head and was not distracted by his bowels, it just might.

Marcellinus just hoped the Iroqua didn't know as much about siege offensives—and how to protect against them—as he did.

Behind him two men crumpled onto their knees, and the formation faltered. Somebody cursed in Cahokian. Marcellinus turned and helped shove the men back onto their feet. They were unwounded—one of them had merely tripped on a rock, taking the man next to him down as well—but their faces betrayed their terror.

He clapped each man on the shoulder and grinned that fierce smile again. He knew it must make him look slightly insane. "Forward!"

"Forward!" Akecheta cried.

On they went. As promised, Marcellinus was again at the head of the diamond, right at the prow of this land ship they were sailing together along the grassy riverbank. His biggest fear was that the Iroqua would swarm out of Woshakee and turn this into a melee. He hoped that they would not think quickly enough or move quickly enough to do so. There was no gate in the stretch of wall the Cahokians were approaching. The main city gate was on the northern side, the inland side, and the archers of Great Sun Man were bombarding it. The scouts had told of another, much wider gate on the river side that gave easy access to boats in happier times. That gate was currently unobserved by anyone in the Cahokian war party. If warriors came running around that corner, Marcellinus would get half an eye blink's warning and then be in hand-to-hand combat, his men clustered tightly together.

It didn't happen. The prow of Marcellinus's testudo ground into the palisade and flattened. The men at the back dropped onto their knees, deliberately this time; those at the front held their shields up higher, and the testudo became a triangle with its long edge up high against the palisade and a slanted roof. Rocks, pots, and grinding stones hailed down on them thick and fast, their clanging raising a racket over which he could not shout orders, but the First Cahokian had retained enough presence of mind to remember what they were supposed to do next.

Seven men and a woman with axes of steel and chert wormed their way forward under cover of the shields and subjected the wall in front of them to a barrage of blows. Wood chips and splinters flew, and for a heartening moment Marcellinus thought perhaps they were under more threat of injury from shards of wood than from the external danger.

Then the external danger changed with a loud splash. The Iroqua had hurled a cauldron of boiling water down over the testudo. Men screamed.

Marcellinus screamed, too. "Hold firm! Hold firm!"

A second giant splash sent scalding water across Marcellinus's forearm. Above him, shields wavered. Akecheta drew his pugio and waved it, shouting and snarling. Marcellinus had no doubt that his centurion was threatening to slay any man who let his shield drop. And in truth the boiling water was no threat to the formation; its value was more psychological. Battle in such cramped quarters was not to Cahokian taste. Under this wall of steel, his warriors had no idea what might be coming next.

And come it did. Heavier objects crashed down on the shields, bowing and buckling some of them even as the men held them high. But the First Cahokian stood firm.

Now came the hot flare of fire from the Cahokians themselves.

"Step left!" Marcellinus shouted. All he could do was point and bellow. "Left-left-left-left!"

They did it in some semblance of coordination just as the foremost Cahokians hurled liquid flame into the broken wood of the palisade and it exploded right in front of them. That made everyone else move to the left a lot more quickly, especially those men perilously close to the splash zone, but they still managed to keep the formation.

The wood burned. Hacking away the top surface of the palisade had removed whatever protection the Iroqua had applied. A whole band of wood twenty feet wide and a foot high caught fire in an instant.

Marcellinus had no real hope of breaking through the palisade. Wood took a long time to burn, and it was clear the testudo formation would survive only a few more moments. But now the psychology of the situation was reversed: the Mohawks' protective wall was aflame, black smoke billowed upward, and they heard the bang and splash as the Iroqua diverted their panicked attention to deal with the new threat.

"First Cahokian, attack!"

"Attack!"

Either they would remember, understand, and follow him or they would not. He had no time left for doubts.

Marcellinus roared like an arena lion and raced out from under the protection of the massed Roman shields. He had to duck as the rear end of the formation was already dropping; still he caught his helmet a glancing clang as he exited.

After the cramped space in the testudo, to be out in the open air was almost a blessing. It was less of a blessing that he appeared to be alone. He caught the merest glimpse of the larger Cahokian force up on the hillside staring down at him in stupefaction.

Then Marcellinus spun, still bellowing his war cry, and ran up the shields.

The Roman shields formed an inclined slope, an embankment that stopped four feet shy of the top of the palisade. A dozen Iroqua faces painted in purple and red ocher gaped over it at him, showing pink mouths and white teeth. The shields bobbed under Marcellinus's sandals, but he kept his balance, did not need to drop a hand to stay upright. Gladius in hand, he surged up toward the foe.

He was no longer alone. Akecheta ran up the shields next to him, and behind Akecheta came four other warriors of the First Cahokian, the tallest and fiercest, the best fighters in the best armor, the ones most likely to survive a frontal assault on the enemy position. Mahkah was one of them, howling like a berserker.

Marcellinus shoved his gladius into a Mohawk mouth and through the neck beyond, snatched it out again as the man fell, and whirled the edge of its blade into the shoulder of the enemy warrior next to him. By his side Akecheta's studded club crunched down, making a broken egg of an Iroqua skull.

Marcellinus teetered at the very top of the inclined testudo. Over the palisade he saw that the ground of the city within was swarming with Iroqua. They ran between houses, bunched up into units. Every man was armed, and every woman as well, and there were far too many of them.

No time to fear. No time even to think. A Mohawk club was swinging toward his head. He decapitated the Mohawk who wielded it with a roundhouse swing of his gladius and vaulted over the palisade. On its inner side and four feet down, a narrow walkway lined the wall. Marcellinus landed well, took an arrow on the chest plate, and raised a steel-greaved arm in case a second arrow was winging toward his face.

Akecheta landed with him, and another Cahokian beyond the centurion. Nobody came over on Marcellinus's left side; a Cahokian warrior tried to make the leap but tumbled off into space with a squawk. Another man replaced him, almost falling the other way six feet onto the ground inside the Iroqua-held city. It was Mahkah, eyes wide and teeth bared; Marcellinus grabbed and steadied the youth, then spun him around and pushed him unceremoniously toward the Iroqua who was running at them along the walkway. Mahkah met him ax to ax with a howl of sheer hatred, and his second blow drew an arc of scarlet blood from the Iroqua's neck.

The women inside the city were armed, but they were not Iroqua. Taking their chance to rebel against their captors, they assaulted the Mohawks right and left with adzes, pots, even grinding stones. They were able to snatch up only the occasional ax or club, but the confusion they created in the Iroqua ranks was immense.

Marcellinus swayed. Directly beneath him were three Iroqua braves. It was a toss-up whether he would get his knees cracked with a club before or after he was hamstrung with a bronze ax. *Bronze*, he thought. *Where on earth did they mine the tin?* Then he ran the eight short feet that separated him from Mahkah and flung himself past the young brave into space, rolling to his feet on the ground inside the city and slashing, parrying, kicking, killing.

The Iroqua outnumbered the Cahokians perhaps two to one, though the several dozen scrappy Woshakean women helped even the score. More important was the suddenness of it all: within two hours the Cahokians had arrived, neutralized the squad of archers in the copse, gained the high ground, set the palisade ablaze, and come over the top of it whirling weapons of steel, using a stratagem never before seen in Nova Hesperia.

Up the shields and over the wall after Marcellinus had come twenty more Cahokian warriors. After that it had become more difficult, and the embankment of shields collapsed a minute or two later. The men left outside then formed a human pyramid, one man standing on two other men's shoulders and helping to pull warriors up and over him, over the palisade. At the same time, Great Sun Man's warriors raced down the slopes and hurled themselves into the fray. Then someone opened the gates—probably one of the Woshakean women or children, since none of the Cahokian warriors bragged about it afterward. That was the beginning of the end for the Iroqua.

Just seven Cahokians had died, and none of them were members of Marcellinus's First Cahokian Cohort. Marcellinus had led a charge over an enemy parapet and lost nobody, although four of his men had received deep flesh wounds, another man had a dislocated shoulder, and most of the rest had earned the usual gashes, bangs and burns, broken fingers, and broken noses. Many had twisted ankles from falling off the palisade on one side or the other. But Akecheta, Mahkah, Takoda, and Hanska were almost unscathed. For this low injury rate, Marcellinus was deeply and profoundly grateful to whichever set of gods had taken an interest in this frantic scramble for control of a minor city—by any civilized standard, really a rather small town—on the banks of a nondescript river in the middle of nowhere.

Ninety-five Iroqua were dead in battle. The vast majority of the rest, including the Iroqua war chief, had claimed discretion as the better part of valor and escaped out of the eastern gate. Several dozen Cahokians and more than a few of the women had run after them, roaring and screaming, but terror had given the Iroqua wings, though not of any useful variety. They were quickly gone. Another score or so Mohawk warriors had been beaten unconscious or maimed in the fray; those men were summarily scalped and strangled where they lay by the women of Woshakee, eschewing the even more vicious and drawn-out retribution that was their right, and their bodies were thrown out of the town gate to be burned on the morrow.

"Are you now glad that we brought the shields?" Marcellinus asked half an hour later.

Great Sun Man grinned and shook his head. "Too heavy!" he said. "Much too heavy!"

"Then maybe next time we'll carry you home on one," Marcellinus said. He knew the joke wouldn't translate, but some days just making himself laugh was enough.

More than enough.

The bulk of the Woshakee houses were intact. It turned out that most of the Woshakee women and children were alive and unharmed. The Iroqua hadn't butchered them, hadn't even violated them.

Perhaps that kind of venomous, systematic violence against women was a thing only civilized armies did.

The men of Woshakee were all dead or had fled. The capture of the city had taken place in such turmoil that nobody knew whether some of them might still be hiding in the forests somewhere. Everyone hoped so.

"And how did Tahtay like it, being a warrior?"

The boy gave him a complicated look and didn't reply.

They walked through the narrow streets. Marcellinus was interested to see that here in Woshakee, where space was tight, the houses had been built in rows as neat and orderly as any castra or Roman town. It was a way of getting as many houses as possible inside the small compound defined by the palisade perimeter. Yet even here the central platform mound had its plaza in front of it, sufficient for the whole town to congregate. Smaller mounds flanked the plaza, only ten feet tall but still conferring status on the houses that topped them. Every house had its little plot for corn and beans, squash and sunflowers, now fallow.

Compared with Cahokia, Woshakee felt cramped and provincial. Marcellinus was glad he lived in the bigger city.

"Tahtay?"

The boy averted his eyes as they passed a scalpless corpse not yet disposed of, his hand drifting up to cover his nose. "I did not fight. Mostly watched. Or not."

"I know. But you were here, risking as much as anyone."

"Yes." Tahtay sighed. "Being a warrior is good. Seeing here, what Iroqua did. That is not good."

"Worse than what Romans did?" Marcellinus asked quietly.

"Much worse."

A woman walked by them carrying a grinding stone and hmmphed when she saw the corpse. Forthrightly enough, the Woshakee women were trying to put their city back in order, and the Cahokians were helping. Shortly, Marcellinus would return to helping, too.

"You should have killed more of them," Tahtay said vehemently. "Next time I will help you. Tahtay will learn how to kill."

Marcellinus wondered how Great Sun Man would have responded to this. But Great Sun Man was busy managing the refortification of Woshakee, talking to the clan chiefs, making sure the injured were cared for, and organizing squads of his men to evict the Iroqua dead, bring the canoes into the city, help prepare an evening meal, and set watches. Straightforward enough work, but Marcellinus knew from experience how any administrative task could take many times longer than it should, especially when half the men were wounded and everyone was dazed and inattentive after a fight.

Tahtay looked up at him sharply. Marcellinus had not yet answered. But Tahtay's future was not in doubt. "You will be a mighty warrior," the Roman reassured him. "You are tall and strong, and your father before you is mighty—wait, what is this?"

Two stout Woshakee women hauled a boy out of a house, one of them on each arm. The boy was squirming and crying for help in what sounded like a combination of Iroqua and Cahokian. He jammed his heels into the ground, and when that failed, he kicked the older woman in the thigh. The woman slammed her elbow into his head, and the boy went down.

The younger woman put her knee on the boy's back and looped a length of deer sinew around his neck.

Beside Marcellinus, Tahtay watched with a sick fascination. With his last breath, the boy begged for mercy in fluent Cahokian. The woman tightened the sinew, and the boy's cry became a gurgle.

Marcellinus strode forward. "Wait. Wait!"

The young woman's eyes widened at the sight of Marcellinus. The boy gasped as she loosened the cord, then howled again as she put all her weight on him to hold him down.

The older woman shouted at Marcellinus, hands on hips, her words tumbling out more quickly than he could follow. He took a prudent step back. "Tahtay?"

"This boy, he was hiding under the floor in their grain store. He had a knife. He is Iroqua."

"Is he? He sounds Cahokian. Did he try to hurt them?"

Tahtay and the woman babbled at each other, and Marcellinus knelt. The boy studied him through narrowed eyes and then said some words in an oddly inflected speech that was neither Iroqua nor Cahokian.

"Now what did he say?"

The boy switched back to Cahokian. "I ask where you come from. You are different."

"I am from the east, across the big water," said Marcellinus, and the boy looked startled.

He was tall and skinny but barely a single winter older than Tahtay. "Do we kill boys now?" Marcellinus said to the younger woman. "Do we?"

"He came with the Iroqua as a speaker of words," said Tahtay. "He stood by and laughed with the Iroqua as Woshakee men died. He did not fight, and he had no weapon. But he hid like a snake in the floor, and who knows what he would have done if he had not been found?"

"I am not Iroqua," the boy said. "My name is Pezi, and I am from Etowah."

"Etowah?" said Tahtay.

"Ha!" The younger woman clouted Pezi over the head. Losing patience, Marcellinus pushed her off and helped Pezi to his feet.

"Thank you," said the boy. "I am yours."

"Etowah is a big mound-builder town," Tahtay said. "It is far from here, far, to the south and east. It is not Iroqua."

"I am from Etowah. I was born farther south, nearer the Market of the Mud. I was captured by Iroqua from Tuscarora. I have been theirs for two years." Pezi spit. "I am glad they are dead."

The Tuscarora, Marcellinus knew, were a tribe affiliated with the Haudenosaunee in the more southerly lands. Probably, many of the Iroqua who had harassed his legion early on the trek had been Tuscarora. "You speak Cahokian, and Iroqua, and . . . ?"

"The words of the People of the Hand. Not well. But men of that tribe would come to my village when I was young."

He was young now. Marcellinus shook his head.

In Latin, Tahtay said, "I do not trust him, Hotah. Look at him. He would say anything to live."

"I am looking. I see a boy like you."

"Like me? No." Tahtay paused. "He belongs to the women, and they want to kill him."

Marcellinus thought briefly of Fuscus dying at his feet. "Perhaps he belongs to Etowah. And good translators are useful. Great Sun Man should decide."

"We do not kill boys." With no great enthusiasm, Great Sun Man agreed that Pezi should live and return to Cahokia with them.

It was growing late in the afternoon. The Cahokians would sleep inside the palisade tonight and maybe the following night, too. Then most would return to the Great City, but others would stay here a few weeks longer, or perhaps even all winter if they chose, to lend further assistance. For any brave without strong family ties to Cahokia, Wosha-kee might represent an opportunity.

Great Sun Man had offered the people of Woshakee safe passage to Cahokia under the war party's protection so that they could overwinter there. But the clan leaders, who were all women and had all survived, spoke otherwise: it was their city, it was their home, and they would stay. They asked only not to be forgotten and for more good Cahokian men to come and visit them in the springtime. Otherwise, the inhabitants of Woshakee would take it from there.

Marcellinus admired their resolve. Secretly, too, he admired Tahtay's strength. Marcellinus himself had been a pretty tough kid at the age of eleven winters, but he had never been forced to experience a full battle against a numerically superior foe, had never witnessed a town bearing up in the aftermath of that bloody warfare, with menfolk slaughtered, homes wrecked, and enemy corpses littering the streets.

Woshakee was still vulnerable, and Marcellinus did not feel safe even inside its wooden walls. The sooner they got home to Cahokia, the happier he would be.

One of Great Sun Man's warriors ran up and handed him a long band of rolled-up fabric. Marcellinus took it, uncertain. "This is what?"

From there, the warrior hand-talked, pointing up at the ridge. *For fly the Hawks. Look. Pull.*

Marcellinus tested it. When he tugged at it, it stretched, and when he let it go, it snapped back to its original length.

"Interesting. Some kind of animal gut?" He didn't think so, but no matter; he could study it further on the long paddle home.

Perhaps they should take home one of the Iroqua Hawk wings, too. Marcellinus wondered if he should try to persuade them that it was worth the effort to find one in good condition and pack it up to carry it with them just in case the Iroqua had come up with some other innovation the Cahokians hadn't thought of yet. Although he was pretty sure he could predict Great Sun Man's response to this idea: "Cahokian wings, fastest and best!"

The war party beached its canoes and entered Cahokia in triumph. Tahtay marched at the very front with his father, accepting the accolades of the Cahokians as if he had raised the siege of Woshakee all by himself. Behind them the other warriors hooted, howled, and danced their way into the city.

Marcellinus left the preening to the others and walked in almost anonymously in the rear of the group with Pezi. He did nod to one person in the crowd: Chumanee, the healer, who was wearing a fine buckskin he had not seen before. Her hair was in one braid instead of two, and until she waved at him, he did not recognize her.

She walked alongside him as the war party made its way to the Great Plaza and made a great play of scrutinizing his arms and legs. "You not wounded," she said. "This very strange. You not at the battle?"

Marcellinus grinned. "Oh, I was there. But this time, clever. See, few of the men I fought with have bad wounds either."

Marcellinus was inordinately pleased. There could be no better validation of the Roman methods and armor than this. And Great Sun Man had been much less curt with him on the journey home.

"Perhaps you all run away," said Chumanee.

For a moment he was irritated. But Chumanee was just joking. She was not a warrior and did not know how insulting that suggestion was.

And then they were at the Great Plaza, and the clamor of the cheering crowds drowned out whatever else Chumanee might have tried to say, and Nahimana was there, and Enopay, and then Kimimela came running at him screaming like a little girl, which she wasn't quite, not anymore. Wachiwi appeared from nowhere and startled him with a hug, and Marcellinus gave himself up to the joy of the moment.

He had never thought to have friends again, and now he had them. Those gods he didn't believe in had smiled on him beyond any consideration of his merit or worth. He had gone from being the unluckiest Roman in the Imperium to being the luckiest Roman out of it.

Did he deserve it? No, absolutely not. But as Chumanee had once said, maybe one day he would.

"It was a good fight. It was not enough."

The elders stilled and looked at him. Marcellinus began to speak again, but his mouth was dry from the smoke. They waited for him to stop coughing and drink water and begin again.

For the first time, the chiefs and elders of Cahokia had invited Marcellinus into their sweat lodge on the Mound of the Smoke. Both names were well earned; the fire pit in the center of the lodge warmed the air almost to the scalding point, and only a small fraction of the smoke made it out of the hole in the eastern side of the lodge's ceiling. As if that were not enough, from time to time one of the younger braves would pour a wooden cupful of water onto the hot hearthstones that surrounded the fire, adding a gout of steam to the air with a hiss and crackle.

Even worse was the smoke from the red flint-clay pipe the elders were passing from hand to hand. Marcellinus did not know what it was, but he knew how to mimic the man who had held it before him. After he sucked deeply, his lungs filled up with fumes that had made his mind buzz almost audibly while at the same time making him want to throw up the venison and askutasquash he had feasted on not an hour before.

He looked around them all again. The sweat lodge was circular, built on a frame of arched willow poles that formed a dome over them. Around him a dozen or so elders sat in a circle, stripped to the waist or simply dressed in tunics. Most were tattooed and scarified, although Marcellinus no longer found the sight of such damaged skin remarkable. Aside from the marks on the men's bodies they displayed no signs of rank or insignia of office. Great Sun Man stood out from the others only by his relative youth.

Tahtay was not there, of course, and Marcellinus keenly felt the lack. Here he had to rely on his limited Cahokian vocabulary and his slightly more extensive hand-talk.

"Good to fight for Cahokia," Marcellinus said. "For your farms, your people. But your farms, people are *here*. Woshakee was your city, now freed. Now we must go *there*. Strike Iroqua in their lands, in their center. Strike at Iroqua hearts."

He turned to Howahkan, one of the principal elders and the one who was paying the most attention to his ravings. "Look now. If my anger is with you—*if*, I say; I make story, I . . . compare. Yes? If my anger is with Howahkan, do I fight his corn? Do I pull thatch from his roof? No. My anger with you, my fight then with you."

Half of them got it. He had lost the other half. Marcellinus struggled on. "Cahokia's fight with Iroqua warriors, Iroqua nation, not with . . . family, women." Suddenly the heat squeezed his chest, and he could not go on. Tears were flowing down his cheeks freely now and dripping to the floor. He ignored them; perhaps the men farther away might mistake it for sweat. "If my anger is with you, is it enough to keep you out of *my* house? Stop you kicking *my* dog, breaking *my* pot? No. My anger is with you, I come to *your* house.

"Our battle is with warriors. With Iroqua chief, Iroqua city. We take fight there. To Iroqua city."

They laughed at him.

Damn. Immediately crestfallen, Marcellinus bowed his head. "I speak too much, wrong words. I am sorry."

"No, is good," said Great Sun Man. "Wanageeska's heart is strong. Elders make laugh because Iroqua have no city."

"Shit," Marcellinus said. "Really? No city?"

"Small town, village, farm. No mounds. No big city."

"Huh." Marcellinus yielded the floor, feeling stupid. How had that never come up before? Why had it never occurred to him to ask before shooting his mouth off in a council of the Cahokian elders?

More to the point, how could you fight an enemy with no center, an enemy that was everywhere?

Well, he knew that one.

"Give me pipe." He sucked the fumes greedily, and his mind sharpened again. "This is . . . good pipe . . ." They all laughed at him again with companionable good nature as he coughed and tried not to retch, and once more he had to swallow water to keep his gorge down. His ears rang like a bell. The nausea faded.

So the mound-builder civilization of Cahokia was centralized . . . just like Roma. And the Iroqua were decentralized like many of Roma's historical enemies. Of course, the traditional Roman way was to pillage and lay waste to the land, forcing the enemy to consolidate and form an army against them. But even if Marcellinus had the stomach to ravage Nova Hesperia to the north and east, he was pretty sure the Cahokians would balk.

"All right. Then we make Iroqua come to us, bring big army. Pretend to be wounded deer, bring hunter. Then we turn on them like lion. Um, I mean like wolf, like bear. Just like you Cahokians, uh, defeated my army."

A broad-shouldered elder whose name Marcellinus could not recall stirred and raised his hand to be heard. "Iroqua know we have Wakinyan. Iroqua not bring army here."

"I . . ."

Perhaps Marcellinus should shut up now. He bowed his head, exhausted. There would be other nights; with luck this would not be the last time he was invited to smoke by the elders. So long as he did not completely embarrass himself tonight.

Great Sun Man prodded him. "Wanageeska say more."

The mental sharpness instilled by the pipe remained. He obviously needed to know more about the Mourning War, but fighting was not Marcellinus's only skill. His ambitions here were greater than just the bloody slaying of Iroqua. They were the immediate problem, but a future wave of Romans would be the ultimate threat. Marcellinus still had his duty to the Imperator.

If he were legate here and not merely a tolerated prisoner, what would he do next?

"All right," Marcellinus said. "I will say more, ask some questions, tell you things I know. Things I think we might do . . ."

The sweat lodge broke up some two hours later. By then even the Cahokians were hoarse and beginning to nod off. It was a cold, crisp night, and Marcellinus walked into the middle of the plaza. A dog lying across the threshold of a Cahokian home awoke and studied him suspiciously before resting his head back down on his paws. Aside from the elders ambling home, no one was afoot, although Marcellinus knew sentries were now keeping watch, looking out from the top of the Master Mound and patrolling the perimeter of the Great City. Never again would Cahokia be caught by surprise by raiders and saboteurs in the night.

It was good to feel the sweat drying on his skin, to feel the energy of the smoke drain from his body, to be replaced by a healthy solid weariness. Good to look up at the stars in their familiar shapes and constellations even this far from home.

Marcellinus drank his fill of the heavens, then turned and gazed on the Great Mound of Cahokia, tall and stark against the night, surrounded by its palisade of wooden logs.

Another palisade should encircle the whole city, at least the central square mile or so. With bastions and lookout posts every few hundred feet. Even with the new sentries Great Sun Man had assigned after the granary burning, Cahokia was ridiculously vulnerable to a night attack. It was something else to think about over the winter.

His skin was grimy. He reeked of smoke. After the palisade, the next thing Cahokia needed was a bathhouse.

Walking toward the mound, he followed the line of its palisade around to the right. Beyond it snaked the Cahokian creek, and despite the chill of the night air and the even sharper bite of the water, Marcellinus waded in and splashed his legs, arms, and chest until the layer of stale smoke was almost gone. Then he realized it must be in his hair as well and, before he could talk himself out of it, ducked his head into the icy creek.

Baths and a basilica. The plebs of Urbs Cahokiani should have the right to hear the decisions of their leaders, not just the patrician classes, or at least their local equivalents in the sweat lodge.

A proper forum. The central plaza was a good start, though it was more like the Campus Martius or an arena without seating than a real forum. Theaters next, amphitheaters and circuses, and then aqueducts, sewers. The march of Imperium was surely irresistible.

He ran through the list of items he had shared with the elders in the sweat lodge, attempting to commit it to memory before he slept, since this city had no parchment or wax tablets on which he could take notes. And he realized that of all the things the Cahokians needed, a forum and law courts were among the least of them.

Marcellinus walked back to his house, savoring his solitude, looking forward to his blanket and his mattress. Only then, approaching his front door, did he consciously realize that despite everything, despite his own extensive personal failures, he was no longer unhappy.

It was something of a revelation, and he did not know what to make of it.

Pulling aside the deer hide that covered the door of his hut, he stepped down into the darkness.

A warning bell rang in his head. His nose, ears, and soldierly instincts all reacted at once. Marcellinus was not alone in the hut.

He reached for his belt, but of course his gladius no longer hung there. It was in the corner of his hut, where he had left it hours before.

She sat up on the mattress, rubbing her eyes. Marcellinus's first thought was that she had been crying, that something had happened.

Then she stood, and the blanket fell away, leaving her naked.

"Wachiwi?" he said.

Wachiwi reached for him. Now it was she who smelled and tasted smoky; she had warmed herself by the fire pit earlier that evening.

"Is this really a good idea?" he murmured, but the hand-talk had deserted him and his hands were already busy of their own accord. His fingertips had itched to explore Wachiwi since the first night she had shown up for dinner. She was pretty and not so young that it felt indecent. And, very obviously, she was here because she wanted to be.

She kissed his neck, murmuring in Cahokian as her fingers stroked his chest and then ran up his arms to his shoulders, lingering on his scars. Marcellinus shivered even as his hands traced the curve of her hips and moved up her back.

He didn't know what she was saying aside from his names. Early on as she looked up at him with sparkling eyes and tugged him back toward his bed, she called him Wanageeska, and the music of her low voice and the unknown Cahokian syllables flowed over him like water. Then, later on, as she moved fiercely against him, trying not to cry out, then she called him Gaius.

Wachiwi eventually went back to sleep with her body sprawled across his, and Marcellinus gazed up into the roof of the hut at the small part of the night sky he could see through the smoke hole. He had had many women before; as a Subura youth and a young centurion stationed in Galicia-Volhynia there had been almost too many to count, and then had come his wife Julia, Vestilia's mother, for four wonderful years followed by six more of increasing unease, with resentments building up on both sides, compounded by her dalliances during his constant absences. After they parted, there had just been long intervals of giving himself over fully to the Imperator's work, punctuated by occasional commercial transactions in the brothel districts of distant cities where nobody knew him. Now that Marcellinus had the leisure to do the arithmetic, he realized it must be ten years or more since a woman had actively sought his company in bed.

He supposed he should have thought Wachiwi a triumph, quite literally: a heroic battle won, prestige earned with the elders, and to the victors went the spoils. He ought to be feeling contented, even rejuvenated, but he did not. Instead he felt a nagging guilt he would not name, not the usual one of blood and soldiers and death but something more subtle.

Half awake in the early dawn, he felt Wachiwi's hands moving over him again. This time he yielded all restraint and became animalistic with her, hard and rough, and this time her happy squeals must have carried halfway across the Great Plaza, but Marcellinus gave no thought to that in the desperation of the moment, and it was only after their third and final coupling that he felt truly spent.

In the afterglow, Wachiwi rolled him over and kissed him long and hard, scoring his thigh with her nails, drawing blood from his lip with her teeth. For a while, he let her have her way.

He got out of bed. Wachiwi lay there watching him. She said something in a low voice, eyes slitted, hands moving over her own body. It sounded dirty, and back came Marcellinus's internal censor, back came the guilt. This was not what he had expected, not, despite the physical satiation, what he had wanted at all.

And that was the day Sisika returned.

CHAPTER 11

YEAR ONE, BEAVER MOON

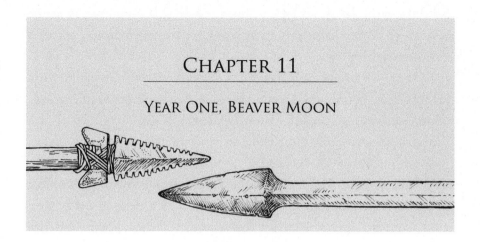

They dressed in silence. Marcellinus was starving. "We should go separately," he said. "To breakfast. Uh . . ." He resorted to hand-talk. *Breakfast, first me, then you. Gaius, go, Wachiwi stay. Then, after: Wachiwi go. Yes?*

She laughed at him, and they went together.

Breakfast that day was quiet, just Nahimana and Takoda, Wachiwi and Marcellinus. The Roman would not have given much credence to Takoda's perceptiveness, but to his chagrin the young warrior picked up on the new development within a few moments and could barely eat for the grin on his face.

"I go," Wachiwi said. "Wash, grind corn." She gave Marcellinus a smoldering stare and, as she went, bopped Takoda lightly on the arm.

"Did Wanageeska sleep well?" Takoda asked as soon as she was out of earshot, and grinned even more widely.

Nahimana grunted. "Why Gaius choose Wachiwi?"

"I did not choose," he admitted.

Her eyebrows went up. "No? Then Gaius is a fool."

"Wachiwi is your woman now?" Takoda broke in.

Marcellinus did not know how to answer. It was hardly his intention to take a wife, but he could neither deny nor reject what had just happened. He felt an almost inconceivable awkwardness. Once again he had acted rashly, with no facts at his disposal, this time literally in the dark. How old would he have to be before he learned common sense? "I don't know."

"You are without eyes," Nahimana said. "Without ears and foolish. But this," she continued, lewdly swinging her hand between her legs, miming something dangling there. "This, Gaius has."

Marcellinus cringed, mortified.

When he arrived at the plaza, Akecheta was running sword drills with a couple of dozen warriors. Marcellinus was happy to see some new faces in the Cohort, less cheered to see that Takoda was there before him, still smirking. Three other people had made kissing noises behind his back as he had walked there from his hut. Marcellinus had not deigned to give the culprits the satisfaction of reacting.

Akecheta might be a journeyman where discipline was concerned, but he certainly had the positions of the sword down cold. Marcellinus let him carry on and himself walked up and down the lines of Cahokians, adjusting a grip on the hilt here and the position of the feet there and greeting the new arrivals. It was still early in the morning, and no one's enthusiasm was yet getting the better of him. That was good.

Tahtay showed up, chewing on a corncob and looking worried. "Be happy," Marcellinus said, waving at the sweating ranks of gladius-wielding warriors. "No one dead here yet."

"Wachiwi?" the boy demanded.

"What?"

"The women are saying. You and her."

"No one has anything better to think about?" Marcellinus said in some desperation. "We beat Iroqua! We made Cahokia safer! But more work to do. And people say to me, Wachiwi?"

Tahtay grimaced, shrugged.

"You should learn sword, get strong," Marcellinus said. "You are a warrior now. Get a sword. I give you numbers."

Tahtay moved closer. "What was it like? Wachiwi is . . . good to look at."

"Juno's sake, Tahtay! What are you, eleven winters? We'll talk when you're older. Go and fetch a sword."

"Near twelve winters!"

After another hour Akecheta called a halt. Even in the chilly air the men were sweating. As they took swigs from their water skins, the centurion walked over to Marcellinus. "So, *sir*. Good sleep?"

He grinned widely.

Marcellinus raised his eyes to the heavens.

At exactly that moment, a Wakinyan soared into the air off the top of the Great Mound. An urgent babble of conversation instantly broke out. Many of his warriors stood, their water skins falling to the hard ground unnoticed.

"Merda," Marcellinus said. "Akecheta, what? Is it an Iroqua attack?"

Even now, surrounded by Cahokians, the sight of the giant Thunderbird sent a stab of fear down Marcellinus's spine and through his heart. For a moment he almost felt sorry for any Haudenosaunee army that might be foolish enough to assault the city. But as he watched, colored streamers unfurled behind the Wakinyan. At the same moment the cheering and jubilation of its twelve pilots reached him. This was not a battle but a celebration.

Launching at a run, a half dozen Catanwakuwa drifted from the top of the mound and followed in the Thunderbird's wake, flying in a credible straight-line formation. With only the small cooking fires of a Cahokia morning to provide hot updrafts their range could be only a few hundred feet. But that was apparently sufficient for today.

Following his warriors, Marcellinus jogged to the south edge of the Great Plaza. From there they could see a dozen Cahokian braves walking into the city. From their posture it was obvious they had walked a long way, perhaps all night, but they did not have the look of men who had been in a fight. They were proud, weary, happy to be home.

As they neared, Marcellinus saw that they formed an honor guard around a small figure with a falcon mask draped casually around her neck.

The Hawk wings spilled air and landed gracefully around the woman and her party of braves, stepping into the group to walk with her. The Thunderbird roared by overhead again only a couple of hundred feet up. Marcellinus ducked, still daunted by it, but it passed quickly beyond Cahokian city limits and came down to earth.

People cheered. Everyone was smiling, including Tahtay.

"Tahtay!" Marcellinus pointed accusingly at the woman at the center of the warrior escort. "*That* is Sisika! Why you pretend to not know Sisika?"

"Huh?" said Tahtay. "What is Sisika? She? That is not what she called."

Sisika had given Marcellinus a false name. The very first thing she had told the Romans had been a lie. Marcellinus felt oddly indignant.

Sisika's honor guard of braves and birdmen took her to the gates of the palisade, which swung open for her on cue. She walked on, alone, up the cedar steps of the Great Mound.

At the top stood a tall brave in a headdress and a colored tunic. Great Sun Man was there to greet his, what, "daughter of chieftain"? Or had that been a lie or a misunderstanding as well?

It seemed like the whole city was cheering. In terms of the Cahokian response, Sisika's arrival outstripped the return of Great Sun Man's triumphant war party the day before. She was clearly an important and popular person.

Marcellinus couldn't even pick out the braves of his First Cahokian Cohort anymore in the crowd. He guessed today had just become a holiday.

Well, all right, then. After his conversations with the elders the previous night, Marcellinus had a lot of questions for Tahtay.

His heart lurched. Kimimela was running toward him, but she looked terrified, as close to panic as he had ever seen her.

From behind Marcellinus two men appeared, tattooed in the warrior fashion. Their heads were shaved except for a broad crest of hair, and they carried Roman pila. Even on this cold and breezy morning they were naked to the waist.

"Wanageeska," one of them said, and took his arm roughly. "Come."

The second warrior stepped in on his other side. Their intentions were very clear.

Kimimela's mouth twisted. "Oh, shit . . . !"

"Kimi!" Marcellinus said. "Bad words!"

The warriors hustled him away.

Marcellinus was not taken in through the front gate of the palisade; his was not to be a public welcome. The warriors pushed him through a narrow side gate under a firing platform and made him clamber the eastern face of the Great Mound in ignominy. The autumn sun was a pale echo of its summer intensity, but nonetheless Marcellinus dripped with the acrid sweat of exertion and fear by the time he made it to the top. Despite having fought two battles for the Cahokians against the Iroqua, he could tell that this meeting would not be a happy occasion.

The longhouse was two stories tall and wider than a granary. As he got there, the six birdmen from Sisika's entourage arrived, too, and carried their wings into the building. Behind them walked Kimimela, her eyes downcast, visibly shaking with fear.

Not a promising sign.

Marcellinus took a deep breath. Just a few months ago he had been quite ready for these people to slit his throat in sacrifice or inflict whatever other dire and final tortures they could devise. Unwilling to die at his own hand, he had been prepared to perish at theirs. But since then, that Stoic frame of mind had evaporated, and now he felt only an aching sense of disappointment.

Would they really take him to war and then into their sweat lodge only to slay him the next morning? Well, they might. Perhaps they had done him honor after the battles only to drain his blood now. Perhaps they felt they had learned all they needed from him. Marcellinus still knew almost nothing of their traditions. Anything could happen.

Maybe Wachiwi had been their final gift to him before his slaughter. Or maybe he was to die for polluting a Cahokian woman.

More likely, of course, something had definitively changed with the return of Sisika to Cahokia.

They made Marcellinus wait for quite a while, far enough from the plateau's edge that he could not see down into the Great Plaza. He wondered where Tahtay was and whether the boy knew what was going on. If Tahtay were here in Kimimela's place, Marcellinus would have asked for his insight. But Kimi stood forlorn and trembling twenty feet away, lost within herself, and Marcellinus did not disturb her.

He heard raised voices from inside the longhouse. A man and a woman were arguing in fast-paced Cahokian. Now Kimimela raised her head to look at Marcellinus, wide-eyed.

Before he could ask her what she had heard, Sisika and Great Sun Man came out to confront him.

Sisika's presence brought a further chill to the heavy autumn air. By her side even Great Sun Man appeared muted.

Marcellinus stood patiently among his bodyguard of braves. Whatever happened, he would not show fear. The last few weeks rolled back for Marcellinus. He was no longer merely himself; once again, he was the Imperium's sole representative. If these people were to know only one Roman, let him be a man of dignitas.

Sisika looked leaner and tougher than when he had last seen her. Where had she been all this time?

She spoke. Kimimela's head snapped up in sudden attention. Marcellinus waited.

Kimimela cleared her throat. "She say: 'You have healed from your wounds.'"

"Yes," said Marcellinus. "Thanks to Cahokian kindness."

Poignantly, Kimi did not recognize the Latin word for "kindness." Marcellinus mimed a painting action to his shoulder and thigh, a hand on his forehead, indicating the medical help he had received. Kimimela nodded, and he caught the name "Chumanee" in the words she said next to Sisika and Great Sun Man.

Sisika spoke again.

Kimi said, "She say: 'I should kill you. But I will not.'"

Sisika's face was ominous. This was not a joke, then. Marcellinus did not smile. He had been aware of the ironic similarity between his current situation and that of their first meeting even without that.

"And she say: 'You carry death Powhatan. Then you carry death Cahokia.'"

"Yes," he said very quietly.

"'Many thousand of Powhatan graves. Families. Many men die. Women.'"

"Yes."

"'Romans kill many of Cahokia.'"

"Yes."

"'Why you live?'"

Marcellinus looked at Kimimela, uncertain of her meaning. She was staring at the grass at her feet, translating scrupulously without interjecting any of her own thoughts. He doubted Tahtay would be so single-minded in his duty. Perhaps that was why the boy wasn't here.

Marcellinus knocked twice with his left fist on his right forearm for clarification.

Kimi bowed and offered hands as if giving a gift. Touched her heart and her head, uttered a Cahokian word, made a symbol in the hand-talk.

The best he could fathom from this was, *By what right do you live?*

He almost laughed. They were asking him? It was a question he could not answer. Perhaps it was meant to be rhetorical. He waited.

The litany continued. "'Many Roman die.'"

"Yes."

"'Many Cahokian die.'"

"Yes."

"'Haudenosaunee die.'"

He was mute.

Kimi looked up. "Wanageeska kill Haudenosaunee. It is Iroqua name for themselves. She mean: 'Wanageeska kill Iroqua.'"

These days Kimimela always called him Gaius. Marcellinus felt unaccountably sad. "Yes, I know. Yes."

"'You fight Cahokia Roman warrior Iroqua.'"

He shook his head, unsure.

Kimimela met his eye and said it more slowly. "You fight." He nodded. "With Cahokia, you teach, Cahokia, to fight like Roman. Kill Iroqua." She mimed sword moves, the fifth and sixth positions of the gladius.

Marcellinus turned to Sisika. "Yes. I help Cahokians to fight Iroqua. Yes, I do that."

Kimi repeated it in Cahokian.

Sisika spoke, looking sour.

Kimimela cleared her throat. "'So, if Gaius is taken by Iroqua, Gaius then fight Cahokia.'"

Aha. Now he understood.

"No," Marcellinus said, stepping forward to address Sisika directly. His warrior guard looked horrified and glanced at Great Sun Man for orders; Great Sun Man held up his hand for calm, allowing it. Marcellinus continued. "I should not have fought Cahokia. I take the blame; I did it, but I did not wish it. I did not welcome the killing here. But the Iroqua . . . they strike from hiding. Sometimes they use . . ." He did not know the Cahokian word for poison. "They are wild and have no honor. Wanageeska will always kill Iroqua."

Kimi translated as best she could. Sisika eyed him impassively.

He tried again. "Now I fight for Cahokia. If Iroqua take me, if Caiuga take me, or Mohawk, or any Haudenosaunee, I will die fighting against them. You understand? Gaius will never fight *with* Iroqua *against* Cahokia. I never fight Cahokia again. This I swear."

"Uh, Wanageeska," Kimimela said. Terrified, she knocked twice on her arm, at the same time saying, "Hand-talk?"

Marcellinus smiled at her ruefully. She was right. He could say this with his hands much more easily. He signed, *Gaius kill Iroqua, kill Iroqua, kill Iroqua. Gaius not kill Cahokian. No. Many-winters-and-many-winters. Never kill Cahokian.*

Sisika laughed scornfully. The sound cut him to the core. She gave a command, and her two warriors grabbed him and pulled him back away from her. Marcellinus bowed his head and didn't resist.

One of them punched him in the gut, knocking all the wind out of him; he gagged, dropped onto his knees, and stayed down.

Kimimela screamed and ran to him. He felt her hand on the back of his neck; through the tears that streamed from his eyes, he saw her turning to confront the braves.

"Oh, gods, Kimi," he gasped. "Just let them do whatever they're going to do."

One of the braves leaned down and grabbed Kimimela by the arm. She screamed again.

"No!" Marcellinus shouted. "Leave her alone!"

Great Sun Man barked out a single word in Cahokian. Everyone stopped moving.

Across the plateau three of the Hawk pilots stared, mouths wide.

The brave let Kimimela go and stood back.

The silence lasted for a long time. Still on his knees, Marcellinus sucked air painfully into his lungs. If the brave had punched him in the ribs, he would have been out of action for another month or more. Small mercies. He patted Kimimela on the arm.

Sisika said something, and another brave came forward carrying—of all things—blankets. The brave spread them on the ground.

Kimimela turned to Marcellinus. Sweat dripped off her nose. She raised her eyebrows and then, unseen by everyone except the Roman, winked.

"She say: 'Wanageeska sit.'"

Apparently Marcellinus had just passed some kind of a test. He did not completely understand what had happened. But if he was to live after all, there was something he had to clear up. And perhaps a fresh start might be in order. Pointing to himself, he bowed at the waist as best he could. "Gaius." Then he made hand-talk signs: *What call, you?*

Sisika's mouth twitched. It was as close as she had yet come to a smile in his presence. "Sintikala."

"Is name of bird," Kimimela said, sitting down beside him cross-legged. "Bird who fly very fast."

"Sintikala," he repeated. "So, Sisika . . . ?" He hand-talked the sign for *Question*.

"Algon-Quian, Sisika. Cahokia, Sintikala." She waved around at her surroundings. "Cahokia." Pointed at herself. "Sintikala."

"Ah." Marcellinus smacked his palm against his forehead in the universal gesture of stupidity. Of course. She had translated her Cahokian name into Algon-Quian for Fuscus. And perhaps, as a chief of Cahokia far from home, it would have been imprudent to use her real name. Marcellinus felt foolish.

"Sintikala is chief of Catanwakuwa clan," Kimimela added.

Well, that explained her high status here. Marcellinus bowed to her again. "Sintikala." Another bow. "Great Sun Man."

Formal introductions over, Marcellinus thought they might ask him about the plans he had spoken of the previous night in the sweat lodge. Wasn't that, after all, why they were keeping him alive? Surely they were interested only in what he could provide for Cahokia. Surely that was why they had sent a team of children to learn his language.

Instead, Sisika's—Sintikala's—next words, as translated through Kimimela, were, "I travel east, into the sunrise."

Marcellinus's interest quickened. "How did she travel?" he asked Kimimela.

"No interrupt," she whispered.

"Sorry."

Sintikala spoke again, and Kimi said, "'I cross Appalachia. Many Iroqua. I travel to Chesapica. I see what Romans have done there. Many Powhatan dead. Many-and-many.'"

Marcellinus nodded. There was no denying the havoc the Romans had wrought at their eastern landing. But if she had been to Chesapica . . .

"Roman have big . . . canoe?" Kimimela looked at him.

"Ship," he said to her. "Big canoe is 'ship,' carry many, thousand-and-a-thousand Romans."

Kimi's eyes widened. "Sintikala say: 'Big ship is broken, down under the water; other ships, not so big, have gone away. Maybe gone back where they came.'"

"So no Romans still there?" Marcellinus asked.

"Only dead Romans. Iroqua kill."

Marcellinus nodded grimly. It was not hard to imagine. After the 33rd Legion had passed through Appalachia, the Iroqua must have followed their road back east to the Chesapica and cut off their retreat, sinking at least one of the Roman troop transports. The small Roman garrison he had left behind would have sustained heavy casualties; either they had been slaughtered to a man or some of them had managed to escape in the Norse longships. Marcellinus might never learn the whole truth of it.

He had often thought of that garrison on the east coast. Their destruction was one of the possibilities that had kept him awake early in his stay in Cahokia. But he had possessed no way to communicate with them, so their fate had been in their own hands.

He shrugged, upset but also impatient. Nothing had changed. Either some men would have found their way back across the Atlanticus to Roma or they would not. Either way the end result was likely to be the same: the Imperator would know for a fact that his legion had perished or make that assumption.

Marcellinus tried to explain all this to Sintikala and Great Sun Man as completely and as honestly as he could. It was quite a challenge, and he had to teach Kimimela many new words and ideas to get through it all. During his long exposition, four Cahokian women brought a dish of food for Sintikala, corn and beans and fish, which she gobbled down quickly. She obviously had used up a lot of energy out on the trail.

Nobody brought food for Marcellinus, and the Cahokians were silent. So he kept talking, telling them what he planned to do next.

In the cold light of day, some of his ideas seemed a little wild. Marcellinus was only one man, and there were limits to how quickly he could do what needed to be done and teach the Cahokians all the things he wanted them to know.

As Marcellinus gestured, supplementing his words with hand-talk, he felt the pugio shifting inside his tunic, where he always carried it. He'd had it with him all along. Fortunately, it had not occurred to him to draw it earlier in that brief confrontation when it had looked as if his life was in danger. He drew it now, slowly and carefully, warning them first that he was about to do so and using only his finger and thumb. Even so, the warrior guards looked nervous.

He laid it on the blanket before the chiefs. "This is 'pugio.' Made of? We call 'steel.' Hard." He rapped on it with his fingernails. "Almost unbreakable. Many things Cahokia can make with steel. Weapons for war. Tools for peace. Right now, you have much Roman steel in the weapons you took from us. I may be able to make even more for you. But to try it, I will need iron and fire. Iron is . . . like this, metal, but heavy. Fire like . . . kiln? A kiln is where you bake pots. But much more: hotter-and-hotter than kiln. And also, we will need charcoal."

He went through it all again, everything he'd said to the elders in the sweat lodge the previous night: how to make steel and what steel could do for them.

Great Sun Man looked at Sintikala hopefully. She appeared skeptical.

Now that he had apparently won over Great Sun Man, at least for the time being, it was Sintikala's good opinion that Marcellinus wanted to earn. It seemed unlikely he ever would. For it was also only Sintikala who had seen him in his full glory as Praetor, surrounded by the trappings of Roman power, only Sintikala whom he had bullied and threatened and taunted and then almost contemptuously released. Only Sintikala who had seen firsthand the devastation the Legion had brought to the Chesapica.

Marcellinus vowed silently that one day he would impress her. He would toil night and day, and he would see her eyes widen in approval or die in the attempt.

He went on to describe his next idea, but there Sintikala raised a stern hand to stop him and steered the conversation right back onto the territory that was most uncomfortable for him.

Kimimela looked worried. "Sintikala say: 'I ask you again.' "

Marcellinus took a deep breath. "All right."

" 'Why Wanageeska not hate Cahokia? We killed a thousand-and-thousand of your warriors.' "

"That was war," Marcellinus said tightly.

" 'You kill much Powhatan. Not in war.' "

He bit back his first bitter response and said instead, "That was expediency."

Trying to mime "expediency" defeated him. He just shook his head.

He sensed that they didn't really care about the Powhatani. They were just trying to understand him. But how to explain Roman culture to Hesperians? Their world was completely different.

Sintikala waved away the impasse and asked a different question. "The battle we fight, Romans-Cahokia. What if Cahokia lose and Roman win? What happen next, to Cahokia?"

Marcellinus sat back on his heels. This was a question he had not seen coming. He was a pragmatic man. He rarely wasted time mulling over the road not taken, the choices not made. Or maybe in this case he had shied away from the thought.

But Sintikala had no mercy. Her will was remorseless. Unlike Great Sun Man, she had seen what the 33rd had wrought, and she had not seen Marcellinus fight at Woshakee. Her perception of him was completely different from the war chief's.

Marcellinus tried to answer honestly, but not so honestly that they would slit his throat where he sat.

"If we had won . . . I would have taken over the city. Made myself chief."

Sintikala gestured, *Go on. More.*

"Cahokia would be province of Roma. Province?" He worked on translating that concept for a while with Kimimela, stalling for time, until Sintikala waved impatiently. *More.*

Well, what else? Marcellinus would have quartered the 33rd Legion in Cahokian houses. He would have fed his men with Cahokian corn. It would have been Roman soldiers he drilled in the Great Plaza. And he would have scoured the entire city for gold and found none.

Then? Then, with some time left in the season before winter came in, Marcellinus probably would have taken the bulk of the 33rd Hesperian onward into the west, perhaps leaving a cohort and a tribune— Aelfric, perhaps, or Corbulo or Tully, if in this scenario they had never mutinied—as a garrison to hold the city. As Praetor, his duty would have been to march onward, blazing the trail across Nova Hesperia, until the cooling weather brought him back to overwinter at Cahokia.

After *that*, imagination failed him. It depended on too many things that he did not know, events that had never come to pass.

Halfway through his halting explanation, Sintikala held up her hand and spoke to him directly in pidgin Latin. "Cahokia be . . . slave."

Marcellinus bowed his head, sick at the thought. Who had she learned that word from? Fuscus?

"Cahokia, woman. Romans . . . use."

Here Sintikala used the Latin word she had learned in his presence months ago. And Kimimela made the hand-talk for it, a coarse and obvious gesture Marcellinus had learned from Akecheta in ribald banter and was a little horrified that a girl so young would know.

"No," said Marcellinus. "No. No. No."

"Yes."

He looked rather desperately at Sintikala and at Kimimela.

"And, next: death."

Creeping, reptilian, it began to uncoil inside Marcellinus, the horror of how it might have been.

"No!" he said. "Roma rules provinces . . . wisely. Brings law. Peace and trade. Baths, even. All peoples . . ."

He stopped. That was true enough. Roma's provinces did reap extensive benefits from their alliance with the Imperium. But not right away. And certainly not if they had resisted annexation.

"Slaves," Sintikala said again, in Latin. "Slaves. Slaves."

There was no escape. Marcellinus lifted his head. "Yes."

They stared back at him.

If he had defeated them in battle . . . as enemy chiefs, Marcellinus probably would have had Great Sun Man and Sintikala chained. Eventually even taken them back to Roma as prisoners. For successfully conquering Nova Hesperia, Hadrianus would have awarded Marcellinus a triumph. These two, and other elders of Cahokia, would have been dragged through the streets of Roma behind Marcellinus's chariot and then publicly strangled in the Forum.

But it had not happened, and it would not happen, and he said so. "We did not win. Instead, you kill all of my Romans. All except me. And now—"

"'You would make slave of my daughter?'"

"What?"

This time Kimimela had said the words in direct translation of what Sintikala had said.

Marcellinus stared at the girl. Kimimela stared back at him, terrified, the tension in her body betrayed by the veins in her neck and the set of her shoulders.

Rage flooded him.

He leaped up, and they all recoiled except the warriors, who stepped forward ready to slay him in an instant if he threatened their chiefs. But that was far from Marcellinus's intent. He turned and walked away blindly, his mind filled with a murderous fury directed only at himself.

Kimimela hurt. Kimimela enslaved, at the mercy of his Legion. The idea was unbearable. The images seared him.

The earth gave way beneath him. Marcellinus fell and rolled several yards before he stretched out his arms and brought himself skidding to a halt. He had walked off the level plateau of the mound and tumbled down its side.

He lay still and did not try to get up.

Marcellinus never cried, but his face contorted and he bent forward. Breathing was difficult. He brought his knees up to his chest.

"Stop. Please stop."

Kimimela stood on the edge of the plateau with the two warrior guards standing warily a few feet behind. Marcellinus squinted up at her, silhouetted against the clouds, then turned his face away.

"All right. Wait up there. Wait for just a moment."

Great Sun Man and Sintikala were packing up the blankets, talking quietly. The braves watched Marcellinus through narrowed eyes as he approached.

"Sintikala. Great Sun Man. I have more to say."

They stopped and looked at him.

"I have killed Algon-Quian. I have taken slaves. I attacked Cahokia. I brought fear to Cahokia. I did that, and I accept full . . . responsibility? For that. You beat us. That was . . . fate. That was meant to be."

Kimimela steadily translated as best she could. Sintikala listened calmly and spoke through her daughter. "'Cahokia never feared you. We pitied you. We knew you could not win.'"

Marcellinus swallowed. "I am sorry for waging war on your people. It was not well done. But now I am here for a purpose. I can help you."

Sintikala was a statue. "Today, you say so."

"I say so today and tomorrow, and winter and summer."

"And if Romans come?"

"Romans?"

"She means another army," Kimimela explained. "If more Romans come here, to Chesapica and then to Cahokia? If Romans come, then you will fight for Romans, against us?"

"No," Marcellinus said.

The atmosphere was brittle. Sintikala cocked her head. The braves had their spears pointed at him, waiting for the word, but Marcellinus would not lie.

"I will not go back to Romans and fight against Cahokia. And I will not fight for Cahokia against Romans. I will try to help Romans and Cahokians make peace. I want no more fighting between Roman and Cahokian. Believe me." He took a deep breath.

What he really wanted was to re-create Cahokia in the image of a Roman provincial city and for Nova Hesperia to be ultimately a civilized ally of Roma. But that would be an almost impossible idea to convey to Sintikala and Great Sun Man. He would have to work up to that gradually.

An uncomfortable gray area remained unspoken. The fact was that Marcellinus was arming and training Cahokians who might one day fight against Romans if this went badly.

He elided it in his mind. No solution was perfect.

There could be no doubt that the Iroqua were a more imminent threat than the Romans. Marcellinus had to make the best choices he could on each day that was given to him. No one could demand more of him than that.

He closed his eyes for a moment. "And as I have lost my Legion, all my Roman warriors, the new Romans may take me prisoner and kill me anyway."

Great Sun Man and Sintikala were still silent, so Marcellinus spoke again. "If you want to make me slave, I will be slave. I agree that it is what you might be if . . ." He gestured back and forth. *If our positions were reversed* was much easier for him to mime than for Kimimela to translate.

"I will be slave. Either way, I help you now. And every day, I learn."

Sintikala's eyes drilled into his skull like a pilum. He stood and accepted it.

Eventually she nodded once.

Turning, the two chiefs walked away into the longhouse.

Unhappily, Kimimela watched them go. Marcellinus was surprised that she did not follow her mother. Then he realized that at no point during this long morning had Sintikala shown any affection toward her daughter. She had not leaped to Kimi's defense during the tense moments with the warriors, had not spared her a compassionate glance during the most painful parts of the conversation. Marcellinus had shown Kimimela more care and attention than Sintikala had.

Someday he would learn more about that. But not today.

The braves still stood close by. Not knowing what to do, Marcellinus signed, *Question?* They bowed and pointed toward the main steps that led down the Master Mound.

More evidence that the Roman bow was catching on in Cahokia.

"Come," he said. "Come, Sintikala's daughter."

Kimimela shrugged helplessly. If Tahtay took pride in his father, Kimimela's feelings were more complicated.

They walked together to the edge of the mound and onto the steps, side by side.

"And so you are Sintikala's daughter. And Sintikala is Great Sun Man's daughter?"

Kimimela recoiled in surprise, perhaps even horror. "No!"

"Oh," he said. "Sorry."

Not "daughter of chieftain," then, after all. Or was Sintikala the daughter of some other chieftain? Marcellinus gave it up. He had no more energy for the complexities of Cahokian society. He blew out a long breath and tried to relax the taut feeling in his shoulders.

Then, halfway down the mound, Kimimela tapped him on the arm and screwed up her face as if she'd chewed a lemon.

"Question," she said. "Wachiwi?"

Nahimana and Tahtay waited for them at the gates, looking relieved.

"Hotah not dead, then," said Tahtay, straight-faced.

"Not today." Marcellinus was about to explain, but the boy had already turned to Kimimela and asked her something. She shook her head wryly. Tahtay sighed and looked sympathetic.

To Nahimana, Marcellinus signed, *Gaius is well. Thank you for coming.*

Nahimana glanced at the unhappy children and said firmly, "Food."

It was a good call. Marcellinus was starving.

And exhausted. It was not yet noon, but it felt like he'd been awake for a week. Facing Sintikala was tougher work than fighting Haudenosaunee.

CHAPTER 12

YEAR ONE, LONG NIGHT MOON

Marcellinus hit his first major snag the very next day: he needed bricks to make a kiln and a kiln to make bricks.

It was frustrating. He had assumed that the Cahokians used kilns to fire their pottery. But they did not. Instead, they put their unfired pots and bowls into a hole in the ground; filled the hole with logs, sticks, and twigs; and lit the whole mess on fire. It worked surprisingly well—the Cahokians' pots were beautiful, and their pottery making was a fine art—but Marcellinus could not easily make bricks in a pit, let alone steel. To make steel he would need a proper furnace and bellows, and a hole in the ground would not get hot enough or give him enough control over the process.

With Tahtay's help he talked to a number of women who specialized in making pots but could not interest any of them in his project. They spent their days fashioning beautifully shaped and painted bowls and had no interest in putting that aside to make and fire hundreds of flat, boring slabs of mud. However, Cahokians rarely decided anything quickly, and it took a while for Marcellinus to realize just how lost his cause was.

As they walked home, dejected, from the western suburbs, Kimimela ran over to find out why they wore such long faces. Tahtay explained it to her. Kimimela turned to Marcellinus and said simply: "Boys like fire."

"Well, yes," said Tahtay.

Exit the craftswomen, enter the street urchins; by noon the next day Tahtay and Kimimela had rounded up a good thirty boys—and girls— who liked playing with fire and were eager to be in at the beginning of something important. Two days later brick production began in Cahokia, first in rough-and-ready ones and twos that often broke from not being heated evenly and then in the dozens, and it did not stop even though Marcellinus had enough bricks for five kilns within the week.

Iron would be the next problem, and it would take far longer to solve. After hearing Marcellinus talk of iron at some length, the elders had confidently assured him that there were caves just three days' run southwest of Cahokia where you could get all the iron you could ever need if only you were strong enough to carry it back. However, since no Cahokian had previously had a real use for it and three days' run in summer translated to a very long and cold walk in the winter, it proved difficult for Marcellinus to be sure that anyone truly knew where those caves were and impossible for him to persuade anyone to go there before the ground unfroze the next spring. In the meantime he pulled the iron fittings off the Roman wagons and also assembled sets of Roman tools— hammers, saws, punches, picks, files, and tongs, even an anvil.

He had plenty of broken Roman swords that could be beaten into plowshares. Marcellinus was confident that once he had won the Cahokians over with the virtues of plentiful steel, getting them to bring iron for him to make more would be straightforward enough.

Turning his dreams into reality proved to be a lot harder. He started playing with his new forge, assisted by Tahtay's warrior friend Dustu and by Hurit, the big-eyed tomboy Tahtay's age whom the Cahokians had adopted from the Algon-Quian. However, he made such poor initial progress that he had to swear them to silence. Marcellinus had spent a lot of time with blacksmiths and metalworkers; he could forge, punch, cut, and weld iron with a reasonable degree of skill. But he had never before tried smelting, and it turned out that this art was much more complex than it appeared. Even with a fine brick furnace and a reasonable supply of charcoal, all he succeeded in doing was making the existing iron more brittle. New steel would be a long time coming.

In the meantime he created the world's largest, clumsiest, and least efficient wheelbarrows.

The Cahokian elders had dismissed Marcellinus's wild claims for the wheel, and by and large they were right to do so. Without Roman engineers and the Imperium's massive work crews of soldiers and slaves, the trading paths that crisscrossed Nova Hesperia would never be wide enough or level enough for a wheeled wagon. Nor did the continent possess the horse, donkey, ox, camel, elephant, or any other beast of burden capable of hauling human beings around on a regular basis. But that did not mean that the wheel was worthless to them.

The iron wheels on the Roman carts were half as tall as a man, and it took Marcellinus and his willing team of child labor several hours to unload the carts and then figure out how to unhitch the wheels from their axles. After that nightmare, it was relatively straightforward to strip planks off the carts and hammer them together to make the barrow part, in the process realizing that after bricks, axes, and hoes, the next items he needed to learn how to mass-produce were nails.

His first wheelbarrow was long and tall, and it took two men to lift it, steer it, and keep it stable against toppling. Two men or six boys, for Marcellinus had learned his lesson well and realized that the children of Cahokia had a much greater appetite for novelty than did the adults. In short order he had to make a second wheelbarrow the same size as the first, so that at the end of the day, when all the bricks had been hauled out of his furnaces and wheeled to central Cahokia, his teams of urchins could race the unlikely vehicles back and forth across the plaza.

The wheelbarrow races caused a sensation, but it was short-lived. Cahokians might let their eleven-year-olds tag along on battles against the Haudenosaunee, but they drew the line at letting them risk their necks in Marcellinus's chariot races.

Nonetheless, the wheelbarrow lesson had been learned. Cahokians built mounds religiously but slowly; there were always several being built at any one time, and the rectangular mound over the mass grave of the warriors who had fallen to the Romans was still only waist high. Until now the primary method of earthmoving had been the bask and building a tall mound could take years. A few words in the right ears and three more wheelbarrows were quickly made and pressed into service to haul earth.

Marcellinus could only imagine how quickly they might build mounds once he could make even better wheelbarrows. But a better wheelbarrow required a smaller wheel, which required a proper iron-working furnace to cast the wheel rims, not to mention thinner planks of wood and many more nails.

And that was just wheelbarrows, the smallest and most trivial invention that Marcellinus had in mind for his new community.

Arriving at the brickworks one morning, Marcellinus discovered that he had just missed Pezi.

"He wanted to come in, look around," Dustu said darkly. "To learn. To be useful."

Marcellinus had seen almost nothing of Pezi since they had returned to Cahokia after liberating Woshakee. "So?"

"I told him to go and drown himself in a borrow pit. He is interested in too much."

Marcellinus shook his head, bemused. "He speaks languages. We might need him."

"Huh," said Dustu. "My fist speaks languages, too."

Dustu was a year younger than Pezi but strong and capable. He already had his first warrior tattoo, from a skirmish with the Iroqua to the north. His hair was long and full and gleamed with deer fat, with feathers braided into it with a care that his casual nature belied. Marcellinus had seen him sparring with a gladius with Mikasi and Hanska as well as with Tahtay. If he was matched against Pezi, with or without a weapon, Marcellinus had little doubt who would be victorious.

"If you want to keep him out, keep him out," he said. "But try not to damage him. One day he might be useful."

"Others can talk to Iroqua," Tahtay said.

"He also speaks the language of the People of the Hand."

"And when do we need to talk to them? We cannot trust him. It is dangerous to trust people who speak out of both sides of their mouths."

"Does he?"

Hurit propped herself up on one elbow and pointed at Marcellinus. "The Wanageeska was dangerous, and we kept him alive."

"So far," said Dustu. "And not everyone agrees about that, either."

Marcellinus winced. "Let's get back to Pezi. You can talk about killing me when I'm not standing here with you."

Hurit stood and stretched. The two boys eyed her, but she held Marcellinus's gaze steadily. When Hurit was older, she was going to be dangerous herself, and not just with a sword. "Ojinjintka says that Pezi wants to fly Wakinyan. What do you think?"

Ojinjintka was the chief of the Wakinyan clan, an old woman who looked as if she might blow away in the breeze of a Thunderbird's passing. Tahtay and Dustu both snorted. "No," Dustu said. "Pezi stays on the ground where we can see him."

"Maybe he just wants to help," said Hurit. "To belong. He has already gotten himself adopted by the Deer clan."

"Probably because he's so good at running away," Marcellinus said without thinking.

Dustu and Hurit gasped in disbelief. Tahtay looked around them quickly and then shook his head. "Wanageeska. We three here, we know that you speak lightly, but better not let a warrior of the Deer clan hear your words or you will find yourself eating them."

"Of course. Sorry." Marcellinus cleared his throat. Mahkah was of the Deer clan, and many other good men he knew. "That was stupid of me. Anyway. I brought Pezi here, and that may not have been wise, either. But I made a mistake once before in . . . disposing of someone who could speak many languages. Pezi can be useful as long as we keep him under control."

Later, Marcellinus ran Pezi down in the neighborhood where they made adzes, bows and arrows, and other tools for peace and war.

"What are you doing here, Pezi?"

The boy shuffled his feet. He had the talent of looking guilty even when—perhaps—he was not. "If I want to eat, I must work for Cahokia. Here there are no words to be spoken. Perhaps working wood is not so hard to learn as other things. But no one will teach me."

Marcellinus studied him and came straight to the point. "Pezi, you say you are from south of Etowah, and you lived in your village and in Etowah until the Iroqua captured you."

"It is true."

"Yet Ojinjintka says you do not speak Cahokian like a man of Etowah."

"I try to speak it the way they all speak it. I have known many men of Cahokia. I know many languages. I grew up learning them."

"And you know the language of the People of the Hand, who never came so far north as Etowah."

"We fought them, my people of Etowah. You think I lie?"

Marcellinus looked at him appraisingly. "That's the thing, Pezi. I don't know. Anyway, why are you here? What do you want?"

"I want to live," the boy said. "I want to be free. And I do not ever again want to be any man's . . ." He made a coarse gesture.

Marcellinus flushed and looked away. He could not have been a Roman commander without knowing of such things, but still they made him uncomfortable. "The Iroqua asked that of you?"

"Asked? No."

"I am sorry, Pezi. That will not happen to you here."

"I know. I just want to work so I can live here and not always be taken from place to place and war to war, and then . . ." Pezi shook his head. "What I can do is speak words. Perhaps I can learn to speak yours."

"Latin?" Marcellinus had already considered it. The boy would undoubtedly be quick to learn, but Marcellinus didn't have the time and inclination to teach him. He might have tried to persuade the children to teach him, but Tahtay had taken an instant dislike to the translator that had quickly rubbed off on Kimimela and Enopay.

Marcellinus had brought Pezi here, and he had to keep the boy out of mischief somehow. He sighed. "You want to learn to turn wood? All right. Let me talk to some people."

What Marcellinus needed first and foremost was good axes. And because iron was so hard to work into steel, he turned to the idea of making bronze. Certainly there was no shortage of copper; the women wore disks of it in their ears, and the men around their necks. In the ceremonies Marcellinus mostly avoided, he had seen dancers wearing large beaten sheets of the metal. It came from the Great Lakes, far to the northeast of Cahokia, mined there in its natural form and shaped using cold hammering rather than smelting.

He already had tin. Tin was light and flexible and abundant in Europa; most of the Legion's pans and cooking utensils had been made of it. Eventually he would need a local supply, but for the time being he mined his own carts and came up with thousands of tin pans, dishes, and spoons. It became another game for the endlessly useful children of Cahokia to ransack the Roman wagon train and separate out the tin.

Bronze could be made at a much lower furnace temperature than steel. For steel getting exactly the right measure of charcoal and air into the mix was crucial, but for bronze the proportions were more forgiving—one part tin to nine parts copper, a bit of care with the melting and mixing, and that was all there was to it. Before midwinter Marcellinus was turning out bronze ax heads and hoe blades by the score.

If he had stopped there, he would already have redeemed himself in the eyes of most Cahokians. But Marcellinus had the bit between his teeth. Fully recovered from his wounds, working all the daylight hours and some of the night too, he was a man possessed.

By the time the spring festivals rolled around, Marcellinus planned to be living in a whole new Cahokia.

Marcellinus did not live a life solely of innovation. It was winter, and the landscape around them was icy and unfriendly. Everyone had to pull his or her weight. So in addition to his teaching and his experiments with brick making and smelting, Marcellinus carried water and chopped wood and hauled grain in his wheelbarrow to the families that were too elderly to fetch it themselves. Marcellinus had never been too proud to get his hands dirty, and as the sole representative of the Roman people, he wanted the Cahokians to think well of him.

And they did, if only for his kilns; many was the day Marcellinus would show up to supervise the results of his latest experiments in smelting and discover dozens of people sitting around the structures, warming themselves by the radiating bricks.

Naturally that opened up another possibility, and Marcellinus had soon persuaded several of the able-bodied to help him build a large brick house with half a dozen rooms near the Cahokia Creek on the downstream side of the Master Mound. He built it with a raised floor in the style of the granaries, but underlaid the structure with brick rather than wood and did his best to seal the outside. The real trick was getting the hot air from the furnace room to circulate under the floor. He managed it eventually, though it required bribing children to pump the bellows of makeshift fabric for him from time to time.

Unfortunately, the Cahokians would forever be limited to bricks and crude mud-and-clay mortar for their heavy construction. Roma had the best concrete in the world, but much to his embarrassment and frustration, Marcellinus had no idea how it was made.

The first deep snows came halfway through the Long Night Moon. Marcellinus was alarmed; officially, the following month was the Snow Moon and the month after that was the Hunger Moon, so they obviously had quite a bit of winter left ahead. The ground froze hard every night, and it was often midmorning before people ventured out to melt snow over their cooking fires and make their tea or bean broth. In the afternoons Marcellinus pressed on with his military school. His warriors were eager to keep practicing with the unusual weaponry and to keep up their strength and fitness. And so, of course, Marcellinus indulged them. He suspected that by the time the Hunger Moon waned their enthusiasm might wane with it, and he wanted to make all the progress he could.

Finally, once the land truly descended into the grip of Old Father Winter, there were the reading lessons. Marcellinus's reading class attracted two dozen at the outset, dwindling to fourteen once people realized how many letters there were to memorize. Enopay, Kimimela, and Tahtay were there, of course. But Akecheta, Takoda, Napayshni, and Hanska also showed up—four of the smartest warriors in his First Cahokian Cohort—plus Pezi, who was quick with languages and keenly interested, and six of the men and women responsible for keeping track of the winter grain and making sure the food did not run out before the Crow Moon. These were precisely the people Marcellinus had hoped to entice into his mystery cult of message sending and record keeping, and he was encouraged by his success.

On several more nights, and especially as the weather grew harsh, Wachiwi would be waiting in his hut when he returned. Sometimes Marcellinus was too exhausted from his wood chopping and building and smelting and teaching to do any more than collapse into her arms. Usually, though, she could entice him into further diligent efforts that were rewarding for both of them and helped keep the chill of winter at bay.

Nonetheless, with each night Marcellinus realized the error he had made in tumbling into bed with the first woman to present herself. Wachiwi made few further attempts to speak his language and grew bored with his attempts to speak or hand-talk hers. Their bond had only one purpose, and although Marcellinus was fond of her in a rather functional way, he knew it would not last and should not. The sniggering among the Cahokians had faded away, and he no longer feared that some warrior relative or clan chief would appear from the woodwork and force the two of them to wed at spear point. But his heart was not in it, and it did not feel right.

And so he had tried to explain and ask her not to come to his house again. Wachiwi had pouted briefly but had not made a scene. She had pulled her clothes on and left within minutes, and he had not seen her again since.

This time Marcellinus climbed up the central southern stairway of the mound with Great Sun Man at his side and Tahtay scampering up the stairs ahead of them, waiting for them to pass him, then running by them again. As the cedar steps were thick with packed snow, this was not without its risks, but neither Tahtay's father nor Marcellinus felt inclined to restrain the boy's enthusiasm.

Marcellinus was dismayed at how hard he found the climb. The long winter was leaching away his physical conditioning. If as a Praetor he'd seen a legionary having this much difficulty toiling up a simple hill, he'd have ordered his centurion to have the man run six miles in full gear every afternoon until he shaped up or dropped dead.

At the first plateau he turned and looked out across the city. In the Great Plaza, several games of chunkey had broken out; stone disks were rolling, spears flew, and men and boys shouted in good-natured competition. Over to the west the Cahokian crowds still milled around in the sacred circle of the wooden poles, where they had just celebrated midwinter, the shortest day of the year.

As far as Marcellinus could tell, the Cahokians deduced the date of midwinter with the help of the spacing and orientation of the tall cedar poles. Standing at the center pole and looking outward, specific poles in the outer ring had some significance in terms of where on the horizon the sun rose and set on key days of the year. It was a giant calendar in wood, a sundial of the seasons, and although it was all worse than Greek to Marcellinus, the Cahokians relied on what they learned about the sky from Youtin to decide when to plant their corn and when to harvest it. Since it now looked as if the winter corn would last till springtime despite the losses from fire, Marcellinus supposed all that astronomical wizardry must be good for something.

Marcellinus was partly worried to find out they were only half done with winter and partly relieved that he still had as much time ahead for his brick-making and metalworking activities as he'd had already. He was also cheered that there would be a feast that night, a welcome relief from an early dinner standing in front of Nahimana's hut, shoveling stew and flat bread into his mouth and stamping his feet against the cold, followed by a tactical retreat to his hut with a few fire-heated stones for his hearth.

He also was cheered by this: an invitation to climb the mound with the war chief in much friendlier circumstances than his last visit, with an opportunity to see inside the Longhouse of the Wings.

The view from the top of the mound was dreary, with snow-covered fields stretching away in all directions and visibility so poor that they could scarcely see the icy snake of the Mizipi curling in the distance. Still, at least the wind wasn't blowing.

"Bleak," he said, pointing around him, and Tahtay said a Cahokian word and made a sign that may or may not have been the appropriate translation for bleakness.

Marcellinus turned away from the winter-gripped countryside. On his last trips to the top of the mound, he had been too distracted to realize how large the longhouse really was. It was a monstrous thing, a basilica of a building that sat on its own slightly raised soil platform a foot or so above the level of the rest of the plateau.

"Made of?" he said to Tahtay as they approached.

"House? Wood," said the boy. "Stout poles of wood. Then smaller wood, like weaving? And then clay."

Still wattle and daub, then, even though it looked so solid and permanent. Constructed with much more care than the pole and thatch style of Cahokian houses, though similar in appearance to the granaries, which had the same need for good insulation. Probably susceptible to damp, but that could be managed with care. No falcon warrior would want to hurl himself into the sky on a wing that might be suffering from rot.

"In spring, take it down," Great Sun Man said.

"Down?"

Tahtay nodded. "All of it. The mound, here? Every year we put more clay and soil on, make it bigger. Make," he said, gesturing, "straight, tidy. And new reeds for roofs here and in houses in the city. Big time of building and making new."

Marcellinus was still catching up. "The whole longhouse, you take it down? Add earth to the mound? And then put up the building again?"

"Of course," Tahtay said.

Then they took Marcellinus inside the longhouse, which swiftly curtailed his architectural musings.

He was surrounded by wings. The entire building housed a single room, and dozens of Hawk wings hung from the rafter in browns and greens and yellows, swaying in the breeze caused by their entrance. It

was like being surrounded by a flock of stately bats hovering and curt-
seying around him.

"Holy Jove," he said reverently.

Each wing dangled from a rope. Great Sun Man lowered one for him
to examine. It was surprisingly light and felt fragile.

"How it folds for launch?"

Great Sun Man shook his head and made a face. "I should not.
Maybe I break it."

"Hmm." Marcellinus reached out a finger and pushed gently at the
fabric.

The war chief looked at him shrewdly. "So. How you make this better?"

"Stop."

Sintikala stalked into the longhouse dressed all in leather, the tanned
deer hide outfit she wore to fly. A falcon mask hung from her hand. She
moved like a panther.

Marcellinus had not seen her for weeks. Great Sun Man came often
to watch him drill his Cahokian cohort. He had even spent a while
learning how to cut and thrust with a Roman gladius before declaring
himself happier with his war ax, whereupon Marcellinus had, rather
rashly, promised him a better ax one day. But Sintikala he did not see.
Perhaps she lived up here, alone in the Longhouse of the Wings.

To Great Sun Man she said in Cahokian, "What is the Roman doing
here?"

Marcellinus could not fully follow Great Sun Man's response, though
its gist was clear: he was showing the Wanageeska the wings, teaching
him more about how the Cahokians flew, so that he could help them fly
better. Marcellinus also picked out the unmistakable Cahokian words
that guided so much of what they did these days: "Kill Iroqua."

Sintikala walked over to them. Marcellinus and Great Sun Man towered over her, but her taut power made the size difference irrelevant.
Her physical presence was daunting. Marcellinus could not imagine
how he could have been so oblivious to it when she had been brought
into his Praetorium tent as Sisika a lifetime ago. Now she was liquid

flame, a razor-sharp ax, a Coliseum lioness. He looked down at the floor, disturbed by his strong reaction to her.

"Look at eyes," she commanded, and reluctantly he lifted his head.

This was the second time he had been forced to stare deep into Sintikala's eyes. They were a deep brown and very clear. She gazed into his in return. Neither of them blinked. Time stood still.

"All right," she said. "Teach him."

"Yes?" Great Sun Man ventured cautiously.

"*You* teach me," said Marcellinus.

Sintikala raised her eyebrows in disbelief.

"When you . . . launch," he said, and stopped. He had said "launch" in Latin, and she wouldn't know that word. He tried again, using hand-talk. *When you fly, in sky, Hawk. Question: How . . . ?* He folded his arms around himself and ducked to mime what he meant.

"How do you fold wing around yourself?" Tahtay said in Cahokian.

Sintikala nodded. Pulling the Hawk wing up from the floor, she hoisted it up over her head. Ungainly by itself, it slid over her shoulders like a glove and became part of her body. She deftly fastened the straps that held it to her torso and reached into the wing. Then she scrunched and dropped, rolling onto her back, and wrapped the wide wings around herself like a ball.

"Now, *that's* impressive," Marcellinus said.

She said something, her words muffled by the layers of fabric that enclosed her like a seed. Opening the wings, she lay there on her back.

"She need help now," said Great Sun Man with more than a trace of amusement, and Tahtay added, "That is position when she launch. But without launch, now she cannot get up without hurting the wing."

"Funny," Marcellinus said, though he didn't smile in case Sintikala took offense. Great Sun Man lifted the wing carefully from the top, with her on it, and Tahtay guided her feet back under her so she could stand again.

Freeing herself from the straps, Sintikala shrugged the wing off. She hooked it back onto its rope and hoisted it up into the rafters. "Just for 'launch.' In sky, like bird. On ground, is like—" She mimed it.

"Beetle, that," Marcellinus said to Tahtay, who translated unnecessarily, since it was obvious what Sintikala was imitating.

"Put it back on. Please? Show me how the wing locks rigid in flight. How it stays . . ." He gestured. "And when you twist to turn in the air, what do you do?"

Sintikala looked at Great Sun Man. Great Sun Man nodded. She sighed. "All right. Pull over the bench, there. I need to lie down. In air, I am flat."

She donned the wing again and lay on the bench on her front and for the next several minutes showed Marcellinus how she controlled the wing, how she gained and lost height, how she circled and swooped, how she landed.

Marcellinus struggled to hold it all in his mind. He had to force himself to concentrate; what he was learning was mechanical, not magical. But also not simple.

"Incredible," he said. "Incredible."

"What?"

"Very good," he amended. "And how long can you fly for? How long you stay in air?"

She sat up and looked at him icily.

"Next, Gaius see Wakinyan," Great Sun Man said hurriedly. He looked to Sintikala for confirmation. "Yes?"

Sintikala pulled off the wing and attached it to the rope once more. "You big war chief. Show him what you like."

They made their way through to the back of the Longhouse of the Wings. Now that he was less blinded by the broad spread and multicolored beauty of the Hawk wings, Marcellinus noted the piles of falcon masks that lay on the floor on either side of him, the empty pots ready to hold liquid flame, the bows and thigh quivers of arrows, everything the well-equipped Cahokian birdman or birdwoman would need. And he also finally made sense of something else he had seen. Before the battle between Cahokia and the Legion, he had seen the falcon warriors take off from the top of the mound and spiral down to the ground. The warriors surely had been warming up for battle, but once equipped they also had been dropping down to ground level so they could head around to their launch area at the base of the Master Mound.

Walking out into the cold air, Marcellinus found himself at the top of the long parallel wooden rails that rested on the northern side of the mound. The rails glistened; the single finger he brushed against the smooth rail came away coated with some kind of oil.

"Steel will make a better rail," he said. "Stronger and straighter and less friction, uh, smoother. And narrower. The oil is what?"

"Flower like sun," Tahtay said. The sunflowers, then, that grew by many of the Cahokian huts and out in the fields. Their oil was useful for more than cooking.

Below him now, within the mound's palisade, he could see this launch area and also a huge low building that he had not been able to see from the outside that must be the hangar for the great Thunderbirds of Cahokia.

They would be kept at ground level because they needed to be launched from there. A Wakinyan was launched rigid, already in its flying position, rather than being tossed into the air like a rock as the Catanwakuwa were. As he had just realized, the falcon warriors needed to warm up before their dangerous launching by jumping off the mound top; that would hardly be possible for the Wakinyan pilots, even if they could have hauled or carried their cumbersome craft up the steep Master Mound.

They walked down the mound, trying not to slip and slide. Here on the north side the steps rarely saw the sun and were more slippery, with only the greasy rails to grab on to. Had Marcellinus been unobserved, he might have scooted down the slope on his rear end as Tahtay was doing, but that would have lacked dignitas in front of his adult hosts. He was, however, gratified to see that Sintikala and Great Sun Man skated and stumbled on the icy ground just as often as he did.

Despite the wintry cover, the long trenches at the foot of the mound where the launching machinery was usually installed were very obvious. The footprint of the mechanism was broader than it was long, but there was no sign of where it attached to the runners. Tension or torsion? With the Nova Hesperian emphasis on bows and arrows, Marcellinus was betting it would be a tension-based apparatus.

There was also a large open space at the base of the mound. Obviously a Thunderbird itself would take up a lot of room, but the length of the open area seemed excessive. Either they lined up the Wakinyan there in a row waiting for takeoff or . . . surely they didn't use human power to assist with the launching.

"Men run here, to pull the birds up?"

Yes. "Men run, and also . . ." Great Sun Man gestured at the indentations where the machinery had lain. So, human power allied with some kind of mechanical power.

Safely down off the mound, they entered the Longhouse of the Thunderbirds, and here Marcellinus found he had been wrong in one regard. Directly inside a wide door that looked like it could be taken out in a single piece, he found a long, narrow winchlike arrangement. It was a torsion device after all, a complex-looking skein of hemp and hair and what might be catgut, currently not under tension but capable of being twisted with a system of levers to a high degree of strain. It was the same principle that made an onager kick a stone into the air but substantially larger.

"How many braves, to move this?"

Great Sun Man waved his arms, hand-counting: *Fifty.*

"And you say you have no use for the wheel," Marcellinus said.

"Wheel push back when launch," Tahtay said, effectively miming recoil.

"Not if . . . well, let me think about it," said Marcellinus. "Anyway, we can do better than this, twisted rope, we can do better."

"Twisted rope *and* braves," Great Sun Man said.

"Better would be a giant frame and counterweight," said Marcellinus. "Uh, big heavy thing that falls, using gravity to pull . . . Maybe even springs . . . but we'll need to be able to cast iron first, and steel would be better. I will work more with iron, and then later, when the Grass Moon comes, maybe I show you."

"You big clever," Sintikala said. "More clever than Cahokian." Her voice carried an edge.

"No, no. Roman people have just been around longer. Roma, very old. Romans use many ideas from other peoples: Greeks, Moors, Parthians. Other very large nations. And we have more metal." He pursed his lips. It still sounded patronizing.

"All those nations. All like Roma?" Tahtay asked.

No, he wanted to say; Roma is bigger and better than any of them. But he had already stepped over the line into hubris, as the Cahokians themselves sometimes did. "Not like Roma."

"But Romans do not have wings," said Sintikala.

"No, Romans do not have wings."

"And Romans do not win battle here."

"Sintikala," Great Sun Man said reproachfully, as if she had called Marcellinus's mother a bad name.

"Roma has many wonders," Marcellinus said. "Big buildings of stone, roads, bridges that carry water." He stopped. The Cahokians had no frame of reference for things like aqueducts, bridges, amphitheaters, forums. "Many things. But no, Roma does not have wings."

Marcellinus hardly wanted to end up sounding like Great Sun Man: "Roma biggest and best!" Embarrassed, he turned and found himself standing nose to beak with a Thunderbird.

He had seen them flying in battle, in training, in salute. He had never before approached one on the ground, up close like this.

It was colossal. Well over a hundred feet from wingtip to wingtip, it sat resting on two splayed wooden trestles that looked uncannily like claws. Its wings were swept back to help it cut through the air, and their natural upcurve made the bird appear predatory even in repose. Its frame was wooden, with thicker struts than those of the Catanwakuwa. Skins garbed the wings, probably deerskin, but scraped and treated so carefully that they were all but unrecognizable and so seamless that they appeared as a single fine sheet spanning the entire machine.

From beneath the Thunderbird hung the twelve bars that the warriors who flew it would hold on to, shoving left and right to steer it.

Above each bar was the harness that held the pilot's body in the prone position, facedown to the ground he soared over. Nearby were the empty sacklike shapes where they carried the incendiary bombs that could destroy hundreds of men in an instant.

A third of the way out from the spine and a quarter of the way back from the nose, Marcellinus saw two large clips that attached the Thunderbird to the rail for launch. For the first time, he realized that during this launch the pilots' bodies—and their faces, and the deadly liquid flame!—must be suspended mere feet above the surface of the mound. Until the mound fell away, leaving only empty space beneath them and warriors dangling hundreds of feet above the trees.

Marcellinus had known that the Thunderbirds were large, but seeing them from afar, launched from the Master Mound and wheeling in the sky, had disguised their true immensity. And although huge and substantial, they also seemed perilously frail for the task of carrying human beings into the sky.

He must have turned pale, for Great Sun Man said, joking, "So, Gaius fly on this?"

Marcellinus shuddered. Very gently, he caressed the wood frame of the Wakinyan. "No."

"You afraid?" Tahtay asked.

"*You* dangle up in the air under the damned thing, then," Marcellinus said rather more forcefully than he intended.

"All together," said Sintikala. "All go: boy, man, and war chief." She laughed, the first Marcellinus had heard from her, a surprisingly free and joyful sound for one so daunting otherwise, and added something Tahtay did not translate.

"What?" Marcellinus asked.

"She say you do not have, um." He gestured rather lewdly and said a Cahokian word that Marcellinus had heard previously only from Wachiwi.

Balls. Sintikala was saying Marcellinus lacked manliness, did not have the courage.

Marcellinus flushed red and turned on her. "Yes? You say so?"

"Wanageeska not have to go," Great Sun Man said quickly.

"But I will. If you offer, certainly I will. To help you, I must understand it all."

Sintikala held his gaze, still grinning. "Tonight is Midwinter Feast. You fly, Spring Planting Festival. I have spoken."

"Of course."

Marcellinus swallowed. To cover his unease he walked away from her, between the Thunderbirds. The immense low building contained four of the giant frames, all fully constructed and apparently airworthy, and several additional wings and struts and sets of frames and harnesses that either were spare parts or could be assembled to make even more of the things.

In all likelihood these were the very same Thunderbirds that had destroyed the Fighting 33rd Legion, yet Marcellinus felt no antipathy toward the machines now. Only awe, and the creeping terror of being thrown high into the air aboard one.

As if he weren't awake enough at nights with regrets and guilt and plans cascading around his mind; fear of flying was all he needed.

"Thanks a lot, Sintikala," he muttered.

CHAPTER 13

YEAR ONE, LONG NIGHT MOON

No alcohol had passed Marcellinus's lips since the day he had walked out into the wilderness for his fateful encounter with the Iroqua war party. Nor had he missed it; he had never much favored even the finer Falernian wines, let alone the cheap, sour stuff they had hauled across Nova Hesperia. But legionaries liked their wine and many of them shunned simple water as a debilitating beverage, and Marcellinus had to admit that wine dulled the senses most usefully when one was out on the march.

That evening, standing by a roaring fire outside Nahimana's hut, he was introduced to the second drug of choice he had encountered in Cahokia, after the rather obnoxious tabaco weed that they smoked in their flint-clay pipes in the sweat lodges. Tonight's was a kind of corn mash beer.

At his first taste, he nearly spit it over Nahimana. Swallowing it was one of his most heroic acts of the winter. He immediately felt the alcohol hit his system.

"What?" he demanded of the people around him. "This is corn, yes, and also what?"

Nahimana and Takoda were laughing openly. Even Kangee, the woman who hated him, smiled a little vindictively as she rocked her baby boy, Ciqala, in his basket cradle by the fire pit.

"Tree," Kimimela said importantly. "Juice of tree."

His eyes narrowed. "*Which* tree?"

"Any tree. All tree." Nahimana mimed something he didn't follow, and he shook his head.

"Here, here," said Kimimela to make him look at her as she mimed. "Here is tree trunk. Here is ax. Here is pot. Water from tree, juice of tree."

"Sap, that," Marcellinus said, and took another cautious swallow of the evil beverage.

"We put sap in big pot," Nahimana began.

"Jar," Kimimela interjected.

"And wait."

"Oh, *Juno*," he said. "Fermented tree sap? If I only knew how to brew real beer, I'd teach you."

"Want more?" Kimi asked mischievously.

"Gods, no," he said. "And don't you drink it either."

Dusk had soaked the Cahokian Great Plaza in a gray half-light; the sky was too cloudy for shadows. Yet despite the lateness of the hour and the chill in the air, no one was thinking of sleep. The streets around them thronged with passersby, and the plaza was a hubbub of activity. Rows and rows of blankets defined lanes around the edge, leaving the central area empty. Lanterns were being lit, along with the occasional flaming, oil-soaked brand. In the distance, outside the palisade of the Master Mound, food was being cooked in big pots—jars—over giant fires. Even this far away, the aromas of forest herbs and burned corn wafted on the breeze. Tonight was midwinter; it would be Marcellinus's first Cahokian feast.

"Tea," said Nahimana, handing him a cup, which he accepted gratefully. It smelled much more fragrant than the mash beer and almost took the taste out of his mouth.

"We should go," he said.

Marcellinus had been summoned to dine with Great Sun Man and the clan chiefs and elders once night fell. He supposed it was a compliment. At least by now he was confident they weren't going to slice him open and roast his internal organs as a delicacy before his eyes. Despite her taunts and frostiness toward him earlier that day, he was excited to see Sintikala again. It would be the first time he had eaten a meal with her.

"I just hope the drinks are better at the top table," Marcellinus said for his own amusement rather than with any hope that the joke would translate. "Up, Kimimela. Let's go."

"No," she said, her face suddenly somber. "I not called for."

Marcellinus shook his head. "Your mother is your mother. She doesn't need to call for you. Come. Tahtay is already there."

"Gaius." Nahimana stepped forward. "Don't be, um." She said something to Kimi.

"Embarrass," said Kimimela. "She say not embarrass me."

"Gaius, don't be embarrass," Nahimana said.

Marcellinus shook his head. Obviously two gulps of that awful so-called beer was two too many. "Look, I don't understand. Why can't Kimi come?"

"I not called for," Kimimela said stubbornly. "I eat with Enopay's people, like always."

"Like always?" Marcellinus had assumed that when Kimimela wasn't with him, she was with her mother or other family members. Every Cahokian he had asked seemed to have an extended family too complicated to describe. "Kimimela?"

Nahimana grabbed his arm and marched him away from the girl. "Stop it," she muttered to him. "You say wrong words."

"I'll damned well decide what's wrong about this," Marcellinus said, but allowed himself to be guided away and across the Great Plaza.

Their progress was slow, as Nahimana rolled as she walked. Nowadays Marcellinus could even decode most of the curses she addressed to her sore hip under her breath. As they neared the mound, Marcellinus could just pick out Great Sun Man's voice from the general hubbub. The war chief was speaking on the mound top, which was lit by an extravagantly flaring torch; Marcellinus could see the same ceremonial feather headdress and the kiltlike garment around his legs that Great

Sun Man had worn when the Roman had first seen him after the battle. Amazingly, the war chief was bare-chested despite the many degrees of frost. Beside him stood the slighter figure of Sintikala, bundled up more sensibly against the midwinter weather. On Great Sun Man's other side huddled the gaggle of elders and clan chiefs. It was to them that Great Sun Man was speaking, not the people of Cahokia, who were largely going about their business and ignoring whatever ritual was taking place above them. Clearly it was not a night to make the city stand and listen to a speech.

"We must be early," said Marcellinus.

"Nearly over," Nahimana said. "Too cold to flap mouths for long."

On the mound, Youtin, the shaman, spoke next. His voice did not carry down into the plaza, but it was clear that he was the focus from the way he lifted his hands and from the direction in which the chiefs and elders were looking. By his side stood Kiche, who one day would take his place as head shaman.

The other elders raised their arms, perhaps in response to something Youtin had said, and a chant began. Around them in the plaza the babble of voices stilled, and the people paused to face the mound.

Great Sun Man picked up the flaming brand, and for an instant the firelight glinted off the Aquila of the 33rd Hesperian. Then the war chief and Sintikala walked forward, and a roar arose from every Cahokian throat, wordless, almost deafening. Glancing at the women by his side, Marcellinus could see that their mouths, too, were open in acclamation, but the din battered so hard at his ears that he could not hear their voices.

The two chiefs began the long walk down the stairs, the elders following behind more gingerly, and the roar faded.

Tahtay stood at the palisade gate waiting for his father. Seeing Marcellinus's approach, he bounced on his heels, looking first up the mound and then across the plaza, trying to keep warm but obviously relishing the thought of the evening ahead. But Marcellinus still had a bitter taste in his mouth, and it wasn't just the crappy beer.

A small figure walked up behind him. "Gaius?"

He turned. "Kimi?"

Nahimana looked back and frowned.

"He wants me here," Kimimela said, pointing at Marcellinus. "He has spoken. And so I am here."

Marcellinus reached for her hand and squeezed it.

"Kimimela has balls," he said to Nahimana in Cahokian, very quietly.

"Well," Nahimana said. "This will be fun."

Great Sun Man's speech on the mound to his elders and clan chiefs was the sum total of the ceremony. By the time he and Sintikala and the others reached the base of the mound, they were once again talking and laughing among themselves. Families were taking their places on the blankets, friends were calling to one another, and mock fights were breaking out, with braves rolling on the ground and laughing while their families scolded them. The odor of the awful mash beer was already quite marked. A man walked by holding five pots of the stuff between his arm and his body; seeing Marcellinus without one, he thrust a pot into his hand and laughed cheerfully. Marcellinus took the pot with a gracious smile and touched it to his lips with his breath held.

Great Sun Man and Sintikala approached, the former bantering with the elders while the latter called out to friends as she passed. Tahtay arrived ten paces ahead of them, as was his custom. He looked quizzically at Kimimela and then came to stand beside her in very obvious moral support.

"See?" Marcellinus murmured. "One big happy family."

"Huh," said Nahimana.

Great Sun Man sat down as soon as he arrived, sprawling on the blanket. He was far from drunk—his eyes were as alert as ever, and his speaking was quick and incisive—but he was certainly more relaxed and happy than Marcellinus had ever seen him. An elegant woman, robed and befeathered, separated herself from the gaggle of elders and sat down next to Great Sun Man, and Great Sun Man started talking to her as if they had been separated for mere moments. Sintikala stood on

Great Sun Man's other side, ignoring Marcellinus and Kimimela, and launched into a fast-paced conversation with a man who had crossed two blankets to speak with her. The man wore a cloak of fur that he casually left open to show the falcon feathers etched on his shoulders and the painted spirals and jagged scarifications across his chest.

"That is who?" Marcellinus said quietly to Kimimela, indicating the woman. "Mother to Great Sun Man?"

She tutted at him, scandalized. "That is Huyana, oldest wife to Great Sun Man."

Marcellinus studied her with more interest. "Then she is mother to Tahtay?"

"No, no." Kimi tutted again. "Mother to Tahtay is Nipekala, third wife to Great Sun Man. Nipekala eats with her clan tonight."

As did Great Sun Man's second wife, no doubt. Marcellinus wondered why he even bothered to ask about Cahokian family life, since the answers merely confused him. "I have not seen her before. Huyana, I mean."

"Huyana is very often with spirit men."

"Ah. Very useful." Cahokia's shamans, or priests. Youtin presided over the ceremonies at the cedar circle and apparently had played a role tonight but seemed happy to delegate most of his other spiritual duties to his young acolyte Kiche, especially if those duties would require him to go anywhere near a battle. In addition, Youtin was never present at the sweat lodge. Marcellinus had never known a culture in which the priests were so content to lurk in the background. If Huyana was equally spiritual, perhaps it was no surprise he had never seen her before. Or if Cahokian shamans were anything like the priests of Roma's great religions, perhaps Great Sun Man had tasked her with keeping them out of his hair.

Rather casually, he asked, "And that warrior who Sintikala talks with?"

"He is Demothi. Hawk clan. Strong warrior, mighty flier."

"Mighty flier," Marcellinus muttered, and took a sip of the mash beer after all.

"My mother has many falcon warriors."

"No doubt." As Marcellinus eyed the man's physique again, another warrior took his place, then another after that. Marcellinus told himself that these men were merely coming to pay their respects to their clan chief.

Sintikala still had not acknowledged Kimimela, who was now chatting with Tahtay. As always, they were relaying the words they had learned that day, trying to outdo each other with obscure Latin phrases, and trading insults in odd and pointless ways that reminded Marcellinus how young they were.

Marcellinus tried to relax. He was not about to make headway on the whole mysterious business of Sintikala and Kimimela tonight. Instead, he gave his attention to his conversational Cahokian, which certainly required all the focus he could bring to bear.

Despite being cooked in huge pots by a chaotic squadron of not entirely sober women, by Cahokian standards the food wasn't terrible. Marcellinus had eaten so much corn and beans and squash over the last months that most meals were a chore. But tonight the inebriated cooking squad had added an array of herbs to the stew and also small pieces of meat.

After the food some of his First Cahokian came by. Akecheta was the first to pay his respects, and then it became a steady stream; Takoda, Napayshni, Yahto. Mahkah jumped at Marcellinus from behind to surprise him, laughing a little drunkenly. Hanska arrived with Mikasi, and Marcellinus greeted them with interest, as he had not previously known the two warriors were lovers, had not, in fact, suspected that Hanska favored men at all. As the others had done, they said some words to him and then bowed and tactically retreated.

"You know many names now," Nahimana said.

"I do," he said.

"Your warriors are not just warriors to you."

He looked askance at her, not sure how to respond, but was saved by the arrival of the younger crowd, a few children from the brickworks and his reading classes. Enopay arrived fortuitously at the same time as

Hurit, meaning that when Tahtay immediately abandoned Kimimela to talk earnestly with the other girl, Kimimela could turn to Enopay for conversation.

"Why only one feast in winter?" Marcellinus waved around him.

"Only one midwinter," Nahimana pointed out.

"Yes, yes. But. Why not do this once for each moon? Make everyone happy more often."

Nahimana shrugged. Marcellinus changed the subject. With a captive audience, maybe he could learn something more interesting here. "I have many names," he said.

"What?"

Marcellinus clapped to draw attention to himself, and the folk around him looked up from their conversation. "Tahtay say 'Hotah.'" He pointed to himself and said it more loudly. "Hotah." Nahimana smiled, and the others nearby looked mildly impressed and gave the sign for yes.

"Well?" he said. "Hotah means?"

Nahimana pointed to his arm and his leg and then around her. Sintikala's belt was white, and Nahimana pointed at that as well. White.

"Aha," Marcellinus said. "All right, then. And Kimimela and Great Sun Man say 'Wanageeska.'" Again, he pointed at himself, and again they clapped; there was more pointing at the white salved areas of Marcellinus's body, and some additional hand-talk revealed that Wanageeska meant "white spirit."

Enopay was fidgeting, beginning to look nervous. Marcellinus skewered him with a look. "And Enopay? Enopay say 'Eyanosa.'" He pointed at himself. "Eyanosa?"

At this, all of them within earshot broke down and laughed until they cried. Great Sun Man guffawed, and even his wife cracked a smile. And when Sintikala laughed, it changed the whole shape of her face; for the briefest of moments she was no longer a warrior but a young woman, sparkling and without cares, quite beautiful.

Marcellinus waited for the hubbub to die down, cheered to be the source of such merriment. "And 'Eyanosa' means?"

"Big," said Nahimana.

"Big up, big out," Kimimela offered.

"Means big in *all directions*!" Enopay clarified valiantly.

Marcellinus nodded and laughed. It was certainly true that he was taller and broader in the shoulder than everyone around him except Great Sun Man, though surely many of his warriors were nimbler and stronger.

"Ah, Enopay!" he said. "Enopay the Bold! Eyanosa will fight Enopay!" And much to the amusement of Great Sun Man and the other elders and the open-mouthed amazement of all present, Marcellinus got up and chased the happily shrieking child around and around the blanket.

Soon after this, the drumming began. As the throbbing beat started up in several areas of the crowded Great Plaza, Great Sun Man received a formal deputation of six well-muscled young men with exquisite body painting that must have taken all day to apply. Behind the men came women bearing their face masks of copper and wood, their feather cloaks and turtle-shell rattles, and all the other paraphernalia of Cahokian ritual.

Marcellinus stood. By day, Cahokians were the calmest and most pragmatic people he had ever lived among. By night they were either asleep or pagans; on special nights the deerskin drums and the flutes of cedar and walnut wood would come out and the sacred dancers would cavort in their masks and bright, extravagant clothing and headdresses, their deer antlers and eagle feathers and birdman outfits, their bodies artfully scarred and extravagantly painted. Sometimes the dances would be so sufficiently complex and well choreographed that they were a joy to watch even if their meaning was obscure. On other occasions the dancing would quickly devolve into chaos and bacchanalia with masked men and women cavorting in increasing abandon and disarray, often joined by the ordinary people of Cahokia. Although Marcellinus saw no overt sexual license at such events—for all their summer disdain of clothing, the Cahokians were straitlaced about public displays of affection—his military training and Stoic nature made him feel uncomfortable at their lack of self-control. After watching his warriors caper and pretend to be their totemic animals by night, he found it almost impossible to look them in the eye in training the next morning.

Besides, the meanings of Cahokian ceremonies and festivities were lost on him. Cahokia had a pantheon of gods just as bewildering as the Roman collection, which had been assembled painstakingly over the centuries from a wide variety of other cultures. In Cahokia, Marcellinus had heard tell at various times of the Corn Mother; the Evening Star (who may or may not have been the same deity as the Morning Star); Keshari or sometimes Heyoka, the sacred clown; and especially Red Horn, a mighty mythical warrior who wore human heads as earrings. Oddly, it was a representation of Red Horn's head with his large nose that Great Sun Man wore in his ear spools at various ceremonies. Marcellinus perceived something of an impiety about this, but he knew that in religious matters logic often took a seat at the back of the temple.

"Thank you," he said to Nahimana as the dancers donned their finery.

"What?" she mouthed. Even before the dancing had begun, the drumming had built to fever pitch. Perhaps it was a good way to keep warm.

He hand-talked *Thank you*, and she replied, *Why? For talk me*, he gestured. *For us company, here.*

The dancers started to caper, snorting. They rocked back and forth to the drumbeat, bending so low that their heads almost touched the ground. Around him Cahokians were singing. He understood none of the words, could not tell what animals the dancers were supposed to be, if they were even mimicking animals.

Great Sun Man and Sintikala were on their feet, swaying in time to the drums. Tahtay and Hurit, with breathless youthful daring, were holding hands. Enopay was nowhere to be seen, and Kimimela was gone, too.

Marcellinus looked around, seeking her, but she had vanished into the Cahokian night.

Her mother danced, and Marcellinus could watch no more. He stalked from the plaza and went to bed.

Marcellinus slipped twice on the steps of the mound. The sun was still low on the horizon and had done little to warm the ground or disturb the layer of ice above it. To either side of him the grass was frozen and brittle. Off to his right, within the palisade, he could see the foundations for the new brick armory they were building to store all the Roman weapons.

Nobody stopped him from climbing the mound, and he saw no one on the plateau at the top. He walked to the door of the Longhouse of the Wings. "Sintikala!"

No reply. He was reluctant to enter unbidden. Instead, he walked around the outside of the building and peered down toward the Longhouse of the Thunderbirds. "Sintikala!"

As he did so, she walked out of the back door of the Longhouse of the Wings. "I hear you," she said. "Up here, no shout. What you want?"

"I look for Kimimela."

Sintikala looked surprised. "Kimimela not here."

"I know. I just left her with Nahimana."

She shook her head. "I not understand."

"Sintikala, why is your daughter not with you? Why is your daughter *never* with you?"

Turning on her heel, she walked back into the Longhouse of the Wings. Marcellinus followed. "Sintikala!"

The giant forms of the Hawk wings swayed above them. Sintikala hissed: "Shut up! No shout here! I have spoken this to you already two times."

"You did not speak me why your daughter is not with you."

"That is not for you to know."

None of Marcellinus's business? Well, that might be so, and it might not be.

"Sintikala, if you do not want Kimimela as your daughter, then I will take care of her as my own."

Her mouth dropped open. She gaped as if he had lost his mind.

But these were not words spoken impetuously. Marcellinus had thought about this long and hard. Kimimela had been Marcellinus's guide for many months; she had a lively mind and a strong heart, and the thought of her being shunned by her own mother and orphaned in her own city was unbearable to him. He could not stand idle while Kimi was neglected in the same way he once had neglected a daughter of his own.

But now Sintikala strode toward him, fury rippling across her face, fists raised.

He stood his ground. "Sinti—"

His back slammed into the floor. Almost quicker than a thought, she had hooked her bare foot behind his ankle and shoved, felling him instantly. It was quite a trick for someone barely two-thirds his size, but before Marcellinus could react she was on top of him, punching the air from his lungs. Pain flared in his chest; she had not rebroken his snapped rib, but she had come close.

She knelt with all her weight on him, and her hand slipped into his shirt like an eel. Snatching his pugio out of his tunic, she held it to his throat. The cutting edge pressed against the main artery of his neck rather than the windpipe. Sintikala knew how to kill quickly. Marcellinus froze, very aware of the blade's sharpness.

"Oh, you do not fight now?" she said.

"I do not fight Cahokians. I told you."

"You come just to shout?"

"I came to talk."

"No. You come to take my daughter. You come to insult me."

She jerked the pugio away from his throat and pressed it against his hairline. Once again Marcellinus was in danger of being scalped with his own weapon.

"You say you have a daughter?" he said. "Really? Then why—"

The blade was back at his throat, biting into the flesh. "No speak."

Marcellinus said nothing. She leaned closer and looked into his face, studying his eyes, his nose, his lips. Over her shoulder the brooding

Hawk wings rocked in the air, wide and alien. She was breathing heavily, and her breath warmed his cheek.

Again she jabbed the pugio blade into his skin. "Eyes to me!"

Reluctantly Marcellinus met her acid stare. She looked deep into his soul once more. His heart jumped.

Sintikala rolled off him and stood, leaving his pugio resting on his breastbone. He sucked in a long, painful breath.

"Go now," she said. "Do not talk of this again. I have spoken. Yes?"

He struggled to sit up.

She surged toward him dangerously. "Wanageeska! Yes?"

"Yes. Yes."

She stalked away, out the back door of the longhouse, and Marcellinus did not follow her.

"And now I am *nine* winters," Kimimela concluded.

"And I am *seven* winters!" said Enopay.

Nahimana looked at him skeptically. "Yes? You sure?"

"Winter only half done," Marcellinus objected. It was the day after his confrontation with Sintikala and still only two days after the Midwinter Feast; he wasn't sure this counted as living through a winter.

"And *you* are a hundred winters, Eyanosa!" Enopay said.

"Beat the child for me," Marcellinus said to Nahimana, and Enopay screeched cheerfully.

Lessons had restarted after the midwinter break. Today the four of them were writing together; Tahtay was off bossing around the other boys and girls at the brickworks.

Marcellinus considered. Everyone was in a good mood, and he was not going to wait forever. Now was as good a time as any.

"Kimimela?"

"Yes?"

"Where is your mother?"

She shook her head. "At the Great Mound? I not know."

The resentment welled up inside him again. "And why is your mother not a mother to you?"

"Gaius." Nahimana leaned over Enopay, guiding his hand as he smeared charcoal over bark. His early proficiency with writing had faltered a little; learning the alphabet was one thing, but spoken Cahokian was light on some consonant sounds, R, B, and V for three, and sounds that Enopay didn't recognize well with his ears he forgot to write with his fingers.

Kimimela shook her head.

"Kimi, where is your father?"

Nahimana stood, thunder on her face, charcoal clutched tightly in her hand, and Marcellinus was sure that if the children hadn't been present, she would have thrown it at him.

Good. He must be on the right track.

"My father killed by Iroqua," said Kimimela. She said it quietly and almost formally, as if still reciting a lesson, but her eyes were suddenly hooded and tired.

He thought about it. "Were you there when he died?"

"No."

"Was Sintikala?"

"I not know."

"How old were you?"

"Two winters. Three."

"So, Sintikala could not . . . blame you?"

"Gaius," Nahimana said.

"No."

"But, perhaps you look like him?" Marcellinus said. "Or Sintikala was protecting you when . . . it happened?"

"I not know. How I know that?"

Nahimana stepped up, inserting herself between him and the girl, eyes flaring. "Yes, Gaius. Yes. Kimi look like him. Now *shut up.*"

Kimimela's father, Sisika's husband, killed by the Iroqua. And the daughter reminded Sisika too much of the father. The older Kimimela got, the more she would resemble him. A constant reminder. Could that really be all it was?

"Damn it," Marcellinus said. "The Iroqua. Always the damned Iroqua."

"No, no," said Kimi. "Gaius, not be angry, please . . ."

"I am not angry with you, Kimimela."

"Not be angry with Iroqua," she said unexpectedly.

"Please," Marcellinus said, and Nahimana stepped aside.

Marcellinus sat down next to Kimimela. She dropped her gaze, and he put his hand under her chin, gently raising her head to look in her eyes as Cahokian women had so often done to him. "No?"

"No. Do not join the Mourning War."

He did not understand. Had he not already killed scores of Iroqua? "Too late. I already joined."

"But do not be angry," she said in a voice he could barely hear. "Do not be killed by Iroqua, Gaius."

" . . . Oh." His mind stalled.

Nahimana cleared her throat. She was looking past him. He turned, and there she stood in the doorway to his hut: Sintikala.

In his mind she would always have two names. Marcellinus could certainly address her as Sintikala, the warrior, a daughter of a chieftain and the leader of the Catanwakuwa clan, but part of her would always be Sisika to him.

Even if Sintikala hated Marcellinus forever, he would still owe a debt of feeling to Sisika.

Kimimela did not react to her mother's presence. Looking down, she again calmly started work on her writing.

From the doorway, Sintikala stared long and hard at Marcellinus. The fur-lined cloak she was wrapped in made her look small, but Marcellinus could still feel the abrasion at his throat where she had forced his own pugio against his skin, the commanding strength with which she had trapped him on the floor of the longhouse.

"Yes?" Marcellinus said.

Sintikala looked at her daughter. "I came to speak with Kimimela."

"Really?"

Sintikala's eyes narrowed. "Really."

He could not read her intent. He hardly ever could. Kimimela's face was similarly unreadable. "Kimi? Is it all right?"

"Yes," the girl said almost inaudibly.

For the first time, Marcellinus realized it was entirely within Sinti-kala's power to ensure that he never saw Kimimela again.

He swallowed and stood. "Fine. Enopay! Come. We must check the heating in the Big Warm House. Make sure we do not cook any elders."

The boy did not laugh; the tension in the room was high enough to quench even Enopay's natural exuberance. Soberly, he stood and fol-lowed Marcellinus out into the sharp, icy light of the day.

Nahimana moved to leave, too, but Sintikala held up her hand, and Nahimana stayed. For that, at least, Marcellinus was grateful.

"Here it is like sweat lodge, always," said Ohanzee the warrior to Mar-cellinus via Enopay, a sneer on his face showing his contempt. "Make men weak."

"Wait till you old," retorted Howahkan, one of the elders of Ca-hokia, with white hair and a face like leather. "You strong now, nothing harm you. You make many winters, then we see what you say."

"Huh," said the brave, and pointed at Marcellinus. "You don't fool me, Wanageeska." And with that, he stalked off toward Cahokia Creek.

Howahkan hobbled around the Big Warm House with Marcellinus, watching him raise his hand up to the bricks, searching for cracks in the mud-and-clay mortar where heat might escape. "You don't fool me, Wa-nageeska," he mimicked, and cackled.

"He was certainly in there a long time, making sure the house was so terrible," Marcellinus said, and had to wait for the belated laugh once Enopay translated.

"Yes. He is a careful fighter, Ohanzee is. Studies his enemy long and hard."

"Is that one my enemy?" Marcellinus was constantly surprised at how few enemies he seemed to have. In his first few days in Cahokia the animosity toward him had been so great, he had felt like he was swimming through it, but those days were long behind him. Today, many grumbled about the pace of change, many made sarcastic com-ments, and occasionally people asked him painfully pointed questions about his past. But with the possible exception of Sintikala, none were so genuinely antagonistic that Marcellinus felt he needed to guard his back.

"Ohanzee talks only. He will not become one of your ass-licking warrior boys, but neither will he harm you or plot against you."

Marcellinus looked at Enopay in astonishment. Enopay looked back at him innocently. "Howahkan said that. I only translate."

"Not in front of the boy, Howahkan," said Marcellinus reprovingly, and walked into the Big Warm House.

It certainly was warm, warmer than he had intended, and the air was stale. None of the thirty or so Cahokians who were sitting in there chatting seemed inclined to complain, though. "Question: Here, too hot?" Marcellinus asked.

"Much," said Enopay, pulling his tunic off over his head.

"Not *you* . . . Ask *them*."

The older folk were all happy enough with the humid, foggy atmosphere in the house. Marcellinus supposed Howahkan was right; when he was their age, perhaps a room like this would be exactly what he'd need to thaw out his old bones after a night spent huddling in a hut around a dying fire. For a moment he wondered whether he'd survive long enough to feel the cold quite that badly and whether he'd still be living here in this mounded city when he did.

"This is a good house," Enopay was saying to Marcellinus, pointing at the graying Cahokian woman who originally had said the words. "Last winter, and last-last winter, many more people die than this year. This house saves our old and clever." A man spoke next, and Enopay pointed at him. "Now we live longer to irritate our grandchildren. Eh? Eh?"

Marcellinus laughed, nodded cheerily to the creaky Cahokiani who were still conveying their polite thanks to him either through hand-talk or through Enopay's good graces, and moved on. In the furnace room he gave instructions to the boys who were keeping the fire going that they could afford to work a little less hard. "Go for a swim or something instead," he said, and they all cheerfully shouted "Brrrr!" at him.

"Come, Enopay," he said. "We go foundry. Play with some iron!"

But Enopay pointed and said, "Daughter of chieftain."

She walked across the plaza toward them, head down, arms wrapped around herself against the cold. The wind had picked up out of the east while Marcellinus had been in the Big Warm House, bringing clouds with it. It probably would snow again this afternoon.

"Ah. Off you go, Enopay," Marcellinus said, and the boy grimaced and discreetly walked away.

Sintikala stopped and regarded him with those vivid eyes.

Marcellinus cleared his throat. "I say wrong words before. Your daughter is your daughter. I am sorry."

A long silence fell. Marcellinus suspected that Sintikala could tell he was merely saying the words, was not really sorry at all, not for any of it. And if she brought out a blade again, Gods help him, Marcellinus would do his best to take it away from her, peace pact or no. He would not hurt her, but this could not go on. He eyed the ground to see where the snow was thickest, where footing would be the least treacherous.

"It is a good man who helps children," she said, and his eyes swiveled up from the ground to meet her gaze again.

"Walk," she added, and set off without waiting.

Marcellinus followed.

They cut off the corner of the Great Plaza by wading through the foot-high snow that separated them from the northward path to the creek. Marcellinus's moccasins let in a little snowmelt, but early on this winter he had raided the wagons for some Roman-style leggings and his feet stayed warm. The leggings looked a little odd when worn with a Cahokian tunic. Then again, Marcellinus looked odd to the locals whatever he wore.

The trail led them by three tall platform mounds, obviously not grave sites since each one had a single house atop it. Sintikala pointed at the leftmost of the mounds. "I live there."

"Oh?" said Marcellinus, and pointed back over his shoulder at the Master Mound. "I thought . . ."

Sintikala was shocked. "The longhouse? Nobody lives up there!"

Marcellinus had hardly seen her anywhere else. "Natural mistake."

They came to the creek. It was frozen over for most of its width; only in the central few feet did open water still run, though in several places near the bank people had broken holes in the ice to collect water.

Sintikala turned along the creekside path. They were headed, Marcellinus realized, toward the charnel pit and the growing mound where a thousand years ago he had helped bury the Cahokian dead.

"Kimimela likes you," she said. "So I won't kill you."

She turned, birdlike, and twitched her face briefly. Perhaps it was supposed to be a smile.

"Thank you."

"And so, you want to know of my husband now?"

She was like a coiled spring next to him. Marcellinus cleared his throat. "No. He is not my concern. That is your life."

"Yes. And so?"

Above him, the loaded clouds. Beside him, the Hawk chief. Within him, sour memories of long ago.

His wife, Julia, had found love elsewhere and eventually left him because of his long absences on campaign. Julia had poisoned Vestilia against him, and Marcellinus had never stepped forward to try to mend the breach between them. Now he never would.

For his whole adult life the army had been all-important to him. He had done his duty; he had put Roma's fortunes above his own and in the process risen to be a tribune and finally a Praetor. But now his legion was destroyed and the wreckage of his family was ridiculously remote.

Marcellinus could barely put it into words for himself. He certainly could not explain it adequately to anyone else.

So he chose simple words. "Sintikala, I had a daughter once. I was often away from home, fighting battles. We grew apart, and now we do not know each other. She . . . despises me now. I was foolish."

Sintikala nodded. "And so you say I am foolish."

Marcellinus would have tried to smile, but his face was frozen. "Perhaps you are."

She looked at him searchingly for a long moment. Marcellinus braced himself, knowing how quickly she could move. Any moment she could take his legs out from under him. He would need to lash out and counterattack immediately rather than trying to break his fall.

Eventually she said, "I will tell you something. Something Kimimela does not know. And if you tell her, I will kill you. It is for me to tell her, one day. Yes?"

No, he wanted to say. He was already out of his depth. But . . . Sintikala was ready to trust him with something. "All right."

"My man was Cahokian, but he was half Iroqua."

This was a surprise. Marcellinus felt questions on his lips but swallowed them and waited for her to say more.

"That is how I speak some Iroqua words. And my man wore Cahokian war tattoos and went in a war party to revenge on the Iroqua when they raided our homesteads upriver on the Mizipi, nine winters ago."

Nine winters. "All right."

"I was not there. I could not go." She touched her stomach. "I had Kimimela, ready to be born."

"And you should have been with your man. Fighting beside him."

She looked at him oddly. "Beside?"

" . . . Above." Watching over him, thought Marcellinus, and felt an odd, painful stab of jealousy.

"I was not there because I was here," she said, as if lecturing a child.

"You could not be everywhere."

"I had never thought to be a mother. I tried for two winters to be . . ." She stopped. "I could not. I am not a mother. I am a warrior."

And that, at last, Marcellinus could understand.

Again she skewered him with her eyes. "You do not speak."

"Because you are right," he said sadly. "I did the same. I went where my duty took me. Thank you for telling me this."

Sintikala nodded. "And now, you and me."

"Us?"

"We have made crimes. You make crime on me. I make crime on you." She was using the Latin word for "crime." She must have asked Kimimela for it.

Sintikala went on. "Iroqua make war on Cahokia. Each Iroqua crime, we hurt Iroqua more. Each Cahokia crime, Iroqua hurt us more. And again-again. Yes?"

Escalation. It was the definition of the Mourning War, a long, slow vendetta of blood between two nations, each side forcing the other side to mourn its dead again and again. Marcellinus had spent a long time talking with Tahtay, coming to understand it.

Sintikala stopped and faced him. "Iroqua, Cahokia . . . will not stop now. Mourning War always. I wish it was not so. But Gaius, Sintikala? Yesterday-and-yesterday . . ." She made a sound very much like a raspberry. "End. Finish. Behind. Yesterday. All-done." *Question: Agree?*

She had reverted to a combination of simple Cahokian, Latin, and hand-talk, but Marcellinus thought he understood. The two great Hesperian nations had come too far in hatred ever to make peace. He and Sintikala had not.

"We make treaty," she said.

It was more than he had anticipated. More than he had any right to expect from her. Marcellinus was moved. "I would like that."

She frowned at him, unsure of his words, and made the hand-talk again for *Question.*

"Yes," he said firmly. "Treaty."

They walked again. Snowflakes began to drift from the clouds, alighting on the fur of Sintikala's hood and the tip of Marcellinus's nose.

"Yesterday, I think you are Roman enemy chief. Yesterday-and-yesterday, here"—in her heart—"to me, you are . . . as Iroqua. You understand? But today-here I think you are not that man. Not the same."

"I will always be Roman. But no longer an enemy, today or tomorrow. Never an enemy to Cahokia. Never an enemy to, uh, Sintikala. I have spoken."

She halted again. They had not yet reached the mound of the Cahokian dead. "Good. We turn now, go back. Yes?"

He shivered. "Yes."

They said nothing more until the row of three mounds came back into view. Marcellinus had a hundred questions, but he kept himself in check. This was the first time he had walked with her in peace and friendship, the first time they had been together without antagonism and distrust spilling over. He did not want any new misunderstandings to damage the moment.

"Wachiwi is your woman?"

Marcellinus flinched. "No. For a while, a moon ago or more, yes. Today-now: no."

She frowned. "Wachiwi make good wife for Gaius."

Marcellinus was at the same time startled that Sintikala had accepted him enough to urge a Cahokian wife upon him and alarmed at having his life so quickly mapped out for him. And she had called him Gaius.

"I think Wachiwi may not think so," he said carefully.

The Hawk clan chief twitch-smiled again. "I think Gaius is good chieftain of men. Of children. But no-good chieftain of women."

That was undisputable. He was silent.

"I will speak to Wachiwi," Sintikala said.

He hand-talked *No*. "Wachiwi should choose her own husband."

"Yes. But I will speak to her."

"Sisika—Sintikala—I do not hurry to take a wife. Wachiwi is not right for me. If I take a wife, I will wait . . . make the right choice."

They had reached the foot of the mound where she lived. Now she stopped and reached up for his chin with cool fingers, pulling his face around and down so she could see his eyes. Not for the first time, Marcellinus felt her gazing past his flesh and bone and straight into his soul.

His heart lurched. Too late, he tried to look away.

"Oh," she said.

He cleared his throat. Sintikala had seen what Marcellinus still hardly dared to admit to himself: his growing attraction to her. He felt absurd, and his face flushed in humiliation.

"I am not for you," Sintikala said. "Take Wachiwi."

"No," he said obstinately. "Not Wachiwi."

She sighed. "Gaius, my husband is dead. I want no more husband. I am broken."

"You are not broken. You are a warrior."

"Many warriors are broken."

That was true enough. She looked up at her house. It was snowing quite hard now.

"I will wait," Marcellinus said.

"You go," Sintikala said, pointing at the snow falling around them. "I go. I make food. Kimimela eats here tonight."

"What?" Marcellinus said. "Really?"

"I am still not a mother. But I know how to train warriors."

Their eyes met again, and for once Marcellinus read the message in hers. He smiled and nodded. "Kimimela will make a fine warrior."

"Yes, she will. I have spoken," she said, and began to climb. Although the slope of the mound was gentle, the new snow had made the wooden steps slick, and she had to climb with her hands as well as her feet. It lacked dignity, and Sintikala must have been aware of it, for she turned a third of the way up and waved him away with a shooing hand motion. "You go!" she said, and he grinned and turned away.

"Take Wachiwi!" she called after him, but Marcellinus walked on as if he had not heard.

The snow was falling thickly by the time he got back to his hut. All around him Cahokians were scurrying for home, pulling their door skins closed. Trails of smoke arose from Cahokian smoke holes near and far.

A large piece of fresh bark rested at the foot of his bed. He tutted; the children were supposed to keep their charcoal smearings on the schoolhouse table he had so laboriously constructed. He picked it up. On it, in the looped sprawl he recognized as Kimimela's handwriting, it said, "Kimi thank Gaius."

Marcellinus sat in his doorway for a while, watching the other huts appear and disappear in the swirling snow. Then he got up, put Kimimela's piece of bark onto the shrine with his lares, and set about laying a fire for the long, quiet evening ahead.

CHAPTER 14

YEAR TWO, GRASS MOON

The Mizipi burst its banks in the Grass Moon, flooding the low-lying plain that surrounded Cahokia. Briefly the Mound of the Flowers and the Mound of the River became islands in the muddy flow, forlorn and oddly rectangular. On warm days children Enopay's age swam out to the Mound of the Flowers and scaled it, running or rolling down its shallow slopes to splash into the waters at its base.

Not Enopay himself, of course. Enopay was busy at his studies, writing and figuring.

Meanwhile, many of the adults were busy stripping and rebuilding their homes. The Cahokian huts lasted about ten winters at most before they grew rotten and drafty. Tearing down houses and building them up again was a communal activity that appeared to happen randomly to Marcellinus's eye. Randomly but efficiently.

After the rebuilding came the renewal ceremonies and ritual purifications. For several days, Cahokia was alive with prayers and tabaco smoke as well as the happy shouts of children.

Having dealt with the homes that needed repair, the Cahokians turned next to their mounds and the Great Houses that sat upon some of them. Using a combination of mud and finer clays, they built up the tops of the Master Mound, the Mound of the Sun, the Mound of the

Smoke, and many others. It was, as Great Sun Man had promised, a "big time of building and making new."

The wheelbarrows helped with that, of course.

"If Iroqua have no city, if Iroqua are not mound builders, then Iroqua have no Wakinyan."

The elders nodded as if Marcellinus had said a very wise thing, which meant they were humoring him.

"Only Cahokia has Wakinyan," said Matoshka. In the damp heat of the sweat lodge, sitting right next to him, Marcellinus could smell the rancid bear fat that the old warrior smeared into his hair. He took a long pull of the tabaco pipe, sucking the smoke deep into his lungs. It burned a little as it went down and it still made him cough, but after every puff his mind sang. It seemed that the more of it he smoked, the better he understood Cahokian and the less the other odors of the sweat lodge perturbed him.

"No other mound-builder cities have them?"

"No other. We make them here. We keep them here."

"Good," said Marcellinus. "Good. But *why* do Iroqua have no city? Why?"

He looked around him. Two of the elders were nodding off, but the rest were all with him. "Kanuna?"

In his late fifties, Kanuna was the youngest man there after Great Sun Man and Marcellinus himself. Respect for the more senior elders often muted Kanuna, but his brain was sharp and he had traveled farther up and down the Mizipi than most Cahokians. Kanuna rubbed his ear and said, "Those are the wrong words."

"Why wrong?"

"Iroqua villages are small, and they move them often," Howahkan interrupted. "Clear land often. Twenty winters, long time for Iroqua village. They are north, and their corn does not grow in big fields like here."

"They move when their land grows . . ." Great Sun Man hand-talked a gesture that literally meant "old bread," which Marcellinus took to mean "stale" or "bad."

"But you do not," he said.

"We have the river mud," Kanuna said. "And we move the crops from field to field. Today corn, and next spring sunflowers. Then maybe tabaco. And some years, nothing in the field, for the earth to rest."

"Cahokians are wise with the land," said Great Sun Man.

More important, Cahokia also had a river that burst its banks every spring and spread a rich and fertile silty soil across the whole bottom-lands area. Marcellinus resisted the urge to tell them about the Nile in Aegyptus and the Indus in Sindh and the early flush of the civilizations that grew up around those rivers. It was the Iroqua's loss that their land did not include such a river.

"And that is why your words are wrong," Kanuna explained. "The right words are, 'Why does Cahokia have a city?'" He raised his eyebrows and smiled.

"All right," said Marcellinus, eager to avoid getting into a long discussion of the wisdom of their fathers' fathers or, worse, off into some irrelevant creation myth, either of which could easily happen when the old men got to sweating and smoking. Their forefathers had chosen to build Cahokia here for a reason, and they obviously had executed their plans with precision; the mounds and plazas must all have been laid out at the same time to be so regularly aligned. Cahokia was a planned city. "Good, good. But if Iroqua have no cities, how do they talk? They are one nation; they are Haudenosaunee. A league, a treaty. Five tribes, all agreeing?"

"Yes," Kanuna said. Howahkan shrugged. Matoshka blew a gout of smoke over their heads, passed the pipe, and cleared his throat.

They didn't get it. Marcellinus leaned forward. "What do you do when you want to talk to your neighbors down the Mizipi?"

"We visit them. Or they come here and feast. Cahokia provides to all."

"Yes, yes. So my words are these: to make a league between five tribes—five!—the Iroqua must meet and talk and smoke. And afterward they must feast."

"Yes."

"So where do they feast?"

"Ah," said Great Sun Man, but Kanuna had figured it out ahead of him and was already saying, "Powwow."

Ogleesha was offering him the pipe. Marcellinus took it but did not put it to his lips. "Yes, yes? What is powwow?"

A big meeting, they told him.

"All the tribes, in one place?"

"Of course."

Like the folkmoots of the Germanics and the Celts. Marcellinus sat back.

"But, but . . ." Great Sun Man poured water over the hearthstones, which sent up a sizzling gout of steam. Boiling water splashed Marcellinus's forearm, but he managed to keep still. He didn't want to flinch in front of these grand old men of Cahokia. "But Haudenosaunee powwow is deep inside Iroqua land. No Cahokian army could go so far."

"An army can march a very long way. If it's the right army." Marcellinus grinned at them narrowly. Some things he would be proud of to his dying day, and even the Cahokians could not take that away from him.

But Great Sun Man was right. It would be impossible for a Cahokian army to march deep into enemy territory, living off the land and building a castra every night. They could not make roads as they went and would not enslave men to haul the giant wagons such a trip would take. To do all that, not only would Marcellinus have to teach them Roman methods, they would have to *become* Roman. That wasn't going to happen in anyone's lifetime.

Well, then, time to put that aside and focus on something more likely.

They needed to protect and support the other cities down the Mizipi. They needed much quicker communications. And they needed all those things while remaining Cahokians and not magically turning into Romans.

As with all things, he would have to start at home.

"Iroqua will come soon," said Marcellinus. "Maybe tomorrow. Maybe next week. But soon."

Great Sun Man looked around him as if he expected to find a Senecan brave reaching for his scalp that very moment. "Yes?"

They stood on the shore of the Mizipi. Cahokian birch-bark canoes and dugouts navigated carefully around the mudflats. It was the first quarter of the Grass Moon, and the river was already swollen with meltwater and much higher than usual. In days it would flood the low-lying areas of Cahokia; the first market would be held the following week, and the Spring Planting Festival two weeks after that. Ducks and other waterfowl had recently returned and now quacked cheerfully in the shallows. The air was tart with smoke from a controlled burn of the scrub in the copses to the south of the city.

"Iroqua? You know this how?"

"Because it's what I would do." Marcellinus sketched it out to Tahtay and then walked to a canoe while Tahtay explained it to his father.

At Woshakee, the Cahokians had hit the Iroqua squarely in almost the last week the rivers had been navigable. They had struck the last blow of the season, and the Haudenosaunee League would have spent the whole winter angry about it. They would want to make redress and cause some mourning of their own as soon as they possibly could.

Also, if they had been able to scout the Cahokians at all over the winter, the Iroqua would know about the much larger stockade that even now was growing up around the city. But it would take several more months and thousands more logs to complete, and the Iroqua would be eager to burn the wall that already existed before it was long enough to form a substantial defense.

Great Sun Man and Tahtay joined him at the canoe. "And we must keep their traders away," Marcellinus added.

"Traders?"

Despite the war, the Cahokians still traded with the Iroqua. They traded with everyone. They traded with the Hurons of the Great Lakes to the north for the copper they used for their ceremonial face masks and their ear spools and necklaces and now for Marcellinus's bronze. They traded with tribes all the way down the Mizipi as far as the giant river delta where the river flowed into the sea; here they got the conchs and other seashells they prized for necklaces, gorgets, headpieces, and masks. They imported dried fish from the north and east to supplement the trout, catfish, and carp they pulled out of the Mizipi, furs of beaver and fox from the north, and from the western grasslands they obtained more furs and meat and horn culled by the tribes there from the large buffalo-like creatures that apparently abounded, creatures Marcellinus had yet to see with his own eyes.

Even as Marcellinus spoke the words, he knew it would be impractical to keep the Iroqua traders out. Yes, sure as eggs, some of them would be taking intelligence back to the Iroqua war chiefs. But Cahokia thrived on commerce, and no one would be willing to inhibit trade.

He relented, but only a little. "We must keep outlanders from the kilns and the foundry, at least. And the armory as well. Just as you already keep them from the Longhouses of the Wings and Thunderbirds. I have spoken."

"All right," said Great Sun Man, which from him could mean either "yes, absolutely" or "yes, yes, I heard you." Marcellinus made a mental note to mention this to Kanuna and Matoshka and Howahkan and the other elders who might support him on this, as well as the warriors and boys who jealously preserved their own status in running the forge and the brick kilns. It would not hurt to tell Sintikala and Ojinjintka, the chiefs of the Hawk and Thunderbird clans, either.

"And the steel weapons," he continued. "In the autumn I caught Cahokians trading away Roman breastplates and Roman daggers. We spoke of this." In fact, Great Sun Man had not taken the matter as seriously as Marcellinus would have liked, and Marcellinus had ended up raising his voice to the war chief in an attempt to make him fully understand the danger. The canny old warrior Matoshka, at least, had stood at his shoulder on this issue. "Now, as the rivers open again, just yesterday I found Cahokian women gathering Roman helmets and speaking of trading them at the market next week."

"But we must make trade for Cahokia," Great Sun Man said.

"Not with steel," Marcellinus insisted. "Never with steel, whether it be pilum or pugio or shield or breastplate or helmet. We must trade none of these things."

Tahtay cleared his throat. "Father. Think of an Iroqua war party raiding one of our upland homesteads with Roman helmets to protect them against the clubs of our Cahokian farmers. A Caiuga wearing a helmet cannot be scalped. Wanageeska is wise about this."

"Steel is our major advantage," Marcellinus said remorselessly. "The Iroqua do not have iron and steel. We must guard our advantages jealously."

"Some of the weapons already go to other cities," said Great Sun Man. "Our mound-builder cities upriver and downriver. To protect against Iroqua."

"Yes," Marcellinus said. "But we agreed to send those weapons after much talk in the sweat lodge. And those cities must account for those weapons and produce them when we ask."

"All right," said Great Sun Man readily, knowing as well as Marcellinus did that such an accounting would never occur.

"Kimimela," Tahtay said, and pointed.

Marcellinus knew something was up as soon as he saw how Kimimela was walking. These days, determined to seem grown up and preserve her dignitas, she was having difficulty not skipping with excitement.

"So, what?" he said as the girl arrived.

"Sintikala, she tell me to tell you. Today you fly."

Marcellinus glanced upward involuntarily. Puffy clouds hung lazily in the sky. The last snows had melted away several weeks since. But Marcellinus had been by the sacred Plaza of the Cedars as often as anyone else, and he knew what the date was, at least in Cahokian terms. "What? No. Spring Planting Festival weeks away, tomorrow-and-tomorrow."

Kimimela shrugged and grinned. "Sintikala," she said, as if that were the only justification needed.

"But today we will cast an arm. I mean, at the foundry we make a long metal pole, like a bow. I must be there to watch over the metalworkers . . ."

"Sintikala say you come now. She say we must be ready, maybe tomorrow Iroqua come. Gaius must know how we fly."

As the hurry-up logic matched Marcellinus's own, it was inescapable. "Damn."

"Unless you frightened, of course," the girl said innocently.

Marcellinus wiped the sweat off his forehead. "You're your mother's daughter, you know that?"

"Yes," Kimimela agreed. "Come now?"

"We shoot you," said Sintikala. "In air." She pointed upward at forty-five degrees and made a whooshing sound. "Shoot you up, you fly down. Big brave Roman falcon warrior birdman. Yes?"

She was teasing him. It was still an unusual feeling. Marcellinus tried to take it in stride. "Hawk? No. Maybe tomorrow. But Wakinyan, yes, today. Why not?"

"Why not?" she mimicked in Latin, and walked with him around the base of the Great Mound.

The doors were already off the longhouse, and a Thunderbird had been dragged out of it almost as far as the rail. Ten warriors still wrestled the heavy launch machinery into place, and the launch cable had not yet been put under tension. Akecheta and Mahkah, of all people, were helping to lug the mechanism out, grinning. A couple of falcon warriors ran to help them install it in place at the end of the launcher. Nearby, four Thunderbird warriors pulled on flying tunics and sang their preflight rituals. Ropes and cables were strewn all across the ground.

Birds were singing as well, and much too cheerfully. "They do not look ready. Maybe I come back later," Marcellinus said.

Sintikala took his arm. Marcellinus jumped as her fingertips touched his skin, but the chief of the Catanwakuwa clan was all business. She ushered him through the door of the Longhouse of the Thunderbirds to the back wall, where more flying suits hung. "Choose," she said.

"You have a mask that covers my eyes?"

"Ha ha," she said. "No mask for you. Battle mask, the armor for face: that has to be . . ."

"Earned," Kimimela said from the doorway behind them. "Earned in fight. Fight in air. Not yet for Wanageeska."

"Oh," Marcellinus said. "Are you coming up into the air with us, Kimi?"

"Me?" Kimimela shivered in mock fear and made big eyes. "You joke? Not me!"

"But you're a butterfly!"

"Butterfly fly near ground," she said.

Sintikala looked at her daughter appraisingly and said something in Cahokian that Marcellinus didn't catch.

"What?" Kimi asked.

"You my daughter," Sintikala said to Kimimela in Latin with a sideways glance at Marcellinus. "You want to fly, you fly. Go with Roman. Fly high in air."

Kimimela's mouth dropped open, and her eyes lit up. "Yes? Merda!" She clapped her hands.

"Kimi!"

Sintikala looked at him quizzically. "Merda means what?"

"It means she's happy about it," Marcellinus said diplomatically. "Happier than I am, anyway . . ."

They fastened the Thunderbird to the rails. Then they fastened the pilots to the Thunderbird.

Marcellinus watched as they lifted Kimimela into place and strapped her to the underside of the wing. They had no leather tunic small enough for her, so she wore her everyday tunic with extra ties at the wrists, waist, and ankles to keep them from billowing in the air. Sintikala tied her daughter under the broad strut of the Wakinyan herself. Marcellinus tried to console himself that if this flight were truly dangerous Sintikala would hardly put Kimimela at risk, but the knowledge did not reassure him.

Then it was his turn. Smiling broadly, three braves hoisted him bodily off his feet and latched him up under the wing on the right-hand side. Cinching broad leather straps across his chest and waist, they pushed his feet up under a retaining bar that held him firmly at the ankle. Now Marcellinus dangled prone, a few inches below the wing, three feet off the ground; a thin wooden bar hung down in front of his chest not for his safety but so that he could help steer the bird. His flight tunic was uncomfortably hot and tight and already chafed him at the neck. What would it be like to wear such a thing in the heat of summer?

Fully loaded, a Wakinyan held twelve people. Today only ten would fly, so there was an empty harness beside Marcellinus, closest to the wingtip, and a similar gap on the opposite side of the bird beyond the warriors. They had lightly loaded four of the bomb sacks before fastening the pilots in place for balance, and the nearest sack partly blocked his view of the opposite men hanging below the left wing.

The Thunderbird rocked as the other warriors were installed into position. The crewing of the bird was happening a little too fast for Marcellinus's comfort; a steadier pace would have helped him come to terms with being strapped under a wing that was about to be thrown into the air.

Into the air . . . Even now it seemed impossible.

Kimimela squeaked with excitement. She was on the same wing as Marcellinus, slightly forward of his position. She rocked in her harness, shaking the whole Thunderbird and earning her a terse "Be still!" from the lead pilot, who was right then checking his own straps in the front left harness position. Kimimela aside, Marcellinus knew none of the Thunderbird's crew: braves all, broad and muscular, tattooed and painted.

Sintikala ducked under the bird one final time, checking each harness and footrest and slapping each of the crew on the shoulder as she passed. She treated her daughter and Marcellinus in the same casual way.

The Thunderbird jolted. Marcellinus almost cried out, but the support crew was merely tugging the nose of the craft upward and attaching the twin ropes to hooks near the prow. What would happen to the bird if those ropes failed to disconnect after launch, as the bird passed over the top of the ramp? Yet again, Marcellinus realized he should have invested a little more time in advance study and preparation.

The bird slid forward and up to match the angle of the mound. Marcellinus now dangled directly over the torsion device that would launch the craft. Its tightly twisted cable creaked. Behind him he saw a row of legs; a line of men were pulling a rope taut. Steadying the craft? Auxiliary power?

If a signal passed between the ground crew and the pilots, Marcellinus missed it. He had no warning. One moment he was facing the ground with the first new light green grasses of spring waving in the breeze beneath him, his nerves stretched almost as taut as the ropes and cables. The next instant the world was in furious motion.

Marcellinus cried out as the grass blurred and the wooden blocks of the launch mechanism vanished. The ground skidded by, jarringly close to his face. A roar filled his ears: friction against the wooden ramp, the howl of the ropes, the air beating against his ears, the whoops of the warriors around him.

Impossibly close, the Longhouse of the Wings flashed in front of his eyes and was gone before he could even react.

The ground disappeared. The din vanished. He looked down at a quilt of green and gold, bumps and ants. Somehow he had been plucked out of reality altogether.

His breath caught. He was aloft, dizzyingly high, dangling beneath a Thunderbird.

Marcellinus was flying.

The triumphant war cry that erupted from him startled his copilots and rocked the whole Wakinyan.

He had feared throwing up. He had feared panicking, or losing consciousness, or falling out of his harness, or losing his mind, or doing something foolish that would send the Thunderbird plummeting to the ground. Nothing of the kind had happened. A huge serenity filled him.

Cahokia was laid out beneath him like a map. The shape of the city, formerly guessed from walking the streets and surveying it, was now clear: a sprawling mass with irregular curving edges and three clusters of huts marking the population centers. The Master Mound was behind him and to the left, with the giant square of the Great Plaza laid out before it. To his right was western Cahokia and another concentration of houses around a longhouse he had never come across on his earthly ramblings. The organization of the smaller mounds in the city was also apparent from this height: hundreds of them, arranged sometimes in lines or groups but more often scattered at random. The Mizipi curved away to the south, the Cahokia Creek almost invisible behind him, and as the pilots shoved their bars to the right and leaned left, the Thunderbird veered leftward and brought the Oyo River into his view on the far horizon.

Kimimela's voice floated across to him. "Gaius? Good?"

"Spectacular. Incredible. Very, very good." His tone would have to convey the less familiar words. There could be no hand-talk up here.

The Wakinyan banked, continuing its graceful turn. Marcellinus was chagrined to see how small the Big Warm House looked from this height. For a moment he had trouble picking out the kilns and his foundry, but when the Thunderbird passed over them, there was no mistaking its upward lurch as the bird rode the rising thermals from his early attempts at industry.

If Marcellinus could only build enough foundries, a Thunderbird might stay aloft over Cahokia forever. But today, in the cool of springtime, they had already suffered a considerable loss of height in just a single arc over the city.

With this, Marcellinus began to pay more attention to the other pilots and to imitate their actions and body positioning more closely. After all, he was up here to learn.

The lower the Wakinyan descended, the more precarious his position seemed. At altitude Marcellinus had felt invulnerable, as if he were gazing out of the window of an impossibly high tower. Swooping lower over the houses of Cahokia, back toward the plaza, brought home to him how fast the bird was traveling and how exposed they were, dangling beneath it like grapes on a vine. The slightest miscalculation would smear them across the ground.

Just how *did* one of these colossal Thunderbirds land, anyway?

It happened fast and totally beyond his control. The Thunderbird roared over the last houses of the city, their thatched roofs blurring, and the ground leaped up to meet them. A fast heartbeat before Marcellinus was convinced they were all dead, the nose of the craft bobbed upward. He saw a flash of blue sky right in front of his face, and the giant wing flopped down onto the ground with an abrupt hip-cracking bang.

As they skidded to a halt over the grass and gravel, Marcellinus tried desperately to keep his face off the ground. He heard a very bad word in Latin that he had never taught Kimimela, followed by an almost hysterical giggle that broadened out into a belly laugh.

The laughter came from the other pilots, and he was the source of their hilarity. Marcellinus opened his eyes to discover that the braves were all standing comfortably on the ground.

Ah. Apparently, on landing, Marcellinus should have kicked his feet free of the wooden rod that had held his legs up and his body prone. He could then have swung upright and helped absorb the impact of the landing with his legs. But with Kimimela's legs being too short and Marcellinus's being still up in the wing, the whole right side of the Wakinyan had rammed into the dirt, with them in it.

Kimimela was fine, hanging beside him comfortably and giggling fit to burst. Being on the outside, Marcellinus had of course acquired several new cuts and bruises.

"Well," he said. "You might have told me . . ."

"No broken, no hurt," said Sintikala, walking alongside the Wakinyan as Marcellinus and the others carried it back toward the Longhouse of the Thunderbirds, Kimimela trotting with her.

"If you say so." Marcellinus had to admit that the bleeding had stopped quickly. These days he was always bruised somewhere or another.

"You like fly?"

"I be falcon warrior like Sintikala!" Kimimela said, skipping. "Good fast high clever Hawk!"

"Huh." Sintikala ruffled her daughter's hair. "We talk. You, Gaius, you like fly?"

"Like" was too insubstantial a word for what Marcellinus had experienced today. His life had been changed forever. Again.

"Yes. I like fly. Yes, a thousand. A thousand-thousand."

She grinned. "Cahokia big clever?"

"Yes," he said. "Cahokia big clever. Sisika? Thank you."

She shrugged, choosing to ignore the incorrect name. "All right. Now go make better launch arm, better rail, better all-things, fly better. Yes?"

Marcellinus had served the Aquila of the Imperium for his entire life, and in his own way he served it still. But everything else had changed.

For two decades he had led armies. Here in Cahokia, he had friends. He had seen his new world from the skies, and now he was back on terra firma on his own two feet and bleeding only a little.

And when he looked down at Sintikala and Kimimela, he felt something move in his soul that he had thought was long dead.

Perhaps he wasn't so old, after all.

"Definitely," Marcellinus said. "And I already know where to begin."

CHAPTER 15

YEAR TWO, FLOWER MOON

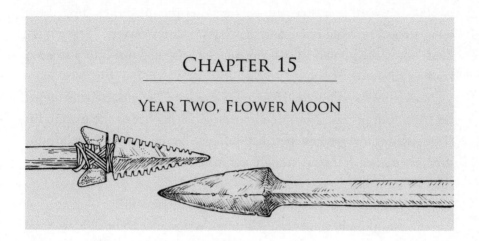

The braided rope of hemp and sinew creaked under the strain of considerable torsion. Gingerly, Cahokian warriors settled a rock into the cup at the end of the onager's arm.

"Loaded, sir," Akecheta said.

"Back," said Marcellinus. "Really, all of you. Back farther."

Braves shuffled away from the machine.

"Fire!" Marcellinus ordered.

Akecheta struck the lever with a hammer and stepped away smartly. The long arm of the onager flew upward, slamming against its wooden top support more quickly than an eye blink. The onager bucked, and the rear of the siege engine's rough-hewn oak frame leaped a good three feet off the ground. Each of the ten-man firing crew jumped backward. Two of them fell over.

High in the air, a rock the size of a man's torso shrank into the distance with almost comical swiftness. Akecheta squinted, shielding his eyes. "Eight hundreds," he said, though Marcellinus and the other men had lost sight of the large stone some time earlier and could not confirm where it had crashed back down to earth.

"So far?" Marcellinus asked skeptically.

Akecheta shrugged. "Cornfield."

A Catanwakuwa whizzed over them, trailing ribbons. Sintikala swooped upward in a tight arc, peering after the rock, then flipped the wing around to avoid a stall and flew back over the onager. "Seven hundred," she called down in passing, and straightened out into a smooth landing run.

Marcellinus swallowed. Her casual stunts in the air almost stopped his heart, but he was determined not to let either her or the men in his siege engine crew see how petrified he was. "Seven hundred, eight hundred, no matter. It throws straight and true every time and much farther than I'd hoped."

"We put Sintikala in it now?" Akecheta said hopefully.

This was the ultimate goal. Although it was nice to be able to pitch a rock into the distance, Marcellinus's dream was to be able to throw a Catanwakuwa to a useful fighting altitude without needing a mound to launch it from. That way they could harry any encroaching Iroqua war parties more effectively and perhaps even serve as an early deterrent to a future Roman legion.

He clapped the man on the shoulder. "Maybe next week."

In truth Marcellinus had no idea whether a Hawk wing could survive the stress of an onager launch without ripping or even whether a human could take a body punch of that severity and still be able to unfurl the wing and fly. But he had confided to the elders his ambition to develop a mobile Catanwakuwa launcher, and now everyone in the city knew it.

He'd build up to it gradually. Start off with the rope at low torsion, maybe lob people gently into the Mizipi on a hot summer's day. The Cahokians would enjoy that. They'd probably line up to try it and beg him to crank it up tighter.

Originally he had thought to throw liquid flame from the onager, but that was impossible. The bags flew unevenly or burst as they were being launched, and with the best will in the world Marcellinus could not make a covered fuse work reliably. Using an onager to launch the incendiary was simply too difficult and dangerous.

Marcellinus had done his level best to learn the secret of the Cahokian Greek fire, but only the shamans knew it, and they weren't telling. It was not made in the city, and for obvious reasons; they mixed it in a carefully guarded location somewhere to the south and east and brought it into Cahokia in jars. One day he had broken open a small pot and poked at it with his fingers—very carefully— and it seemed to be made from a thick oil, like pitch only more gelatinous. From the way it smelled and the brightness of the flame when it was lit, Marcellinus suspected the deadly recipe might also include sulfur and quicklime. But that was as far as he had gotten.

"Once more," Marcellinus said. "Let's land the next rock right on top of the last one." The siege engine crew began to spin the windlass to pull the long bar of steel and wood back down into place and add strain to the rope.

Sintikala strolled up to them. With her wings still strapped to her shoulders she looked like a very broad-winged bat. Bending, she inspected the cup where the rock would lay. "All look good. I should try."

"Maybe next moon," Marcellinus told her.

She glanced up at him. "Walk."

The engine would not be ready to fire again for several more minutes. The rope was hardly creaking at all yet. Marcellinus stepped away.

"Wachiwi is still not your woman," Sintikala said.

He sighed. "Sisika, it's none of your business."

"Business?"

"It is Gaius's worry, not Sisika's worry."

"Throwing engine is your worry," she said.

"Yes, that, too."

She stared into his eyes, putting his heart under considerable torsion. He could almost hear it creaking. Perhaps because he was so much older than she was yet still behaving like a moonstruck calf.

Sintikala *was* strength. She was, quite simply, the most magnificent woman he had ever known.

Women could wield power in Roma. They could lead dynasties, rule great households, sometimes even manipulate the entire Imperium from behind the scenes. Yet none were warriors the way Cahokian women were, and of the warrior women, none was as competent and impressive as Sintikala. She was fast and aggressive, tough, and a little haughty. She captivated and intrigued him.

His wife, Julia, had been her own woman, with that element of deviousness that women in Roman society often cultivated in order to succeed. But Sintikala was not devious. Where Julia had been manipulative, Sintikala was straightforward and brutally honest.

She was also the mistress of a strange new domain—the air. A creature of the world above, she soared over his head, unattainable, strangely magical.

He loved the smell of her sweat. Even her wings seemed normal to him now.

She shook her head. "Gaius . . ."

He knew what came next. "Don't say it again," he said roughly.

"I do not need to. And my name is Sintikala."

She turned to walk away.

"Maybe you should try riding in the throwing engine sooner," he said with just a touch of spite. "Perhaps tomorrow?"

She almost grinned. "Next week."

"But we must have Midsummer Feast," Great Sun Man was saying in the open space outside Marcellinus's hut. "We must!"

"Not unless you will feed them grass," Enopay said rudely. He waved a large piece of bark at the war chief. "Here! Here! Look!"

Great Sun Man could neither read nor cipher Roman numerals and did not take well to being lectured by a child. He stepped forward with his hand raised.

Marcellinus had only recently solved the mystery of Enopay. His mother had died in childbirth, and his father had been killed in the Mourning War two years before the Romans had come to Nova Hesperia. And so Enopay lived with his grandfather, Kanuna, a Cahokian elder and second cousin to Great Sun Man.

Marcellinus inserted himself between them. Family squabbles were none of his concern, but nobody should strike a quartermaster for speaking the truth, not even the leader of a city, not even—or perhaps

especially—when the quartermaster was young enough to be out playing chunkey with the other urchins. "Wait, sir. Enopay is right."

The chief's face set. "People have corn in houses. Always there is more
corn than you know. And young beans on the stalk, berries in the woods."

"Yes, of course." Every Cahokian house had its small storage pit
under the floor, and everyone hoarded a little; it was human nature. But
the burning of the granaries the previous winter had put a dent in the
supplies of even careful folk like Nahimana. "The numbers on Enopay's
bark take account of that. He makes a fair estimate of what we have in
the granaries and what we can expect people to supply from their homes.
We might get through the feast but then would have little to keep us till
the harvest and would be short going into the winter."

"Fish! Berries! Duck! Deer!"

Enopay sighed and pointed to a charcoal scratching low down on the
bark.

Great Sun Man eyed the bark venomously and glanced at Marcellinus's smoldering fire pit. Enopay hastily backed away, clutching his
primitive ledger with both hands.

"Then?" demanded the chief of Marcellinus.

In more abundant years, Cahokia traded its excess corn for copper,
seashells, and other exotic items. To Great Sun Man, his low corn reserve was a serious blow to his prestige. But facts were facts. "Sir, I understand that you wish to provide for your people and show bounty to
all. But Cahokia understands that the Iroqua have destroyed much of
their corn."

Great Sun Man moved closer to Marcellinus. "Do you remember
when I told you of Ituha, the mighty chief and my grandfather-uncle?
He who brought all three parts of Cahokia to be one? But ten winters
after that, when hunger came, when he ask for help with food from the
towns up and down the Mizipi, the people tell him he is no longer chief.
Ituha! The father of Cahokia!"

"Great Sun Man, you face no challenge over this. No other man in
this city wants to be war chief. And none of the clan chiefs would support such a challenge against you."

"We must have feast," Great Sun Man said doggedly. "I have spoken."

Enopay stepped in again. "We *will* have feast. Invite all, freely, as always. But tell them to bring food with them."

Great Sun Man's eyebrows shot up.

"Everyone from outside must bring something," Enopay said. "A rabbit, a fish, a basket of berries, acorn flour, ash cakes. Anything. But something. You and the elders ask them this, people will bring."

"*Tribute?*" Great Sun Man laughed bitterly. "No, no. *Tribute* is for stupid leaders, men of pride. That is the old way. People come here because Cahokia provides! It is the biggest city, the center of the world!"

"Do not call it tribute. Call it sharing with big Cahokian family. The peoples from the upland villages and the plains are all farmers first. They know about family. Here you protect them, and all will be proud to be seen as good farmers and good family. Only this way, you can have feast."

Great Sun Man did not look at Enopay. "Cahokia provides. Cahokia always provides."

"Not this year," the boy said. "I have spoken."

A brittle moment stretched out across several heartbeats. Then, without a further word, Great Sun Man stalked away across the plaza.

"Great Juno," Marcellinus said. "You have balls. You are well named, Enopay the Bold."

"Gaius take this," Enopay said, thrusting the bark ledger at him. "I go away and play now like a silly little boy."

Tears had sprung into his eyes, but his sarcasm was painful. Marcellinus had not seen him play since he had learned to read. "Enopay? Men are measured by their wisdom, and look at you, already winning arguments with chiefs."

"I won nothing. He will probably cut my throat in the night."

Marcellinus laughed. "I do not think so. And why did you win, Enopay? Because your numbers were right."

"Great Sun Man cannot read numbers."

"I will make you a wager, Enopay. I will bet you that Great Sun Man will do exactly as you suggest. And I will also bet you that by the time the sun comes up the day after the Midsummer Feast, Great Sun Man will be able to read numbers."

Enopay scoffed and slouched off to lick his wounds in private, still bruised and shamed.

Marcellinus won both bets.

By midsummer, Cahokia looked very different from above. The Big Warm House had expanded to become a full set of Roman-style baths, with hot and warm pools heated by the brickworks, its floors lined with hypocausts, and a cold splash pool. Once not so particular about hygiene, the Cahokians were now so avid for hot water that the clan chiefs had imposed time limits and no warrior thought it effete to spend time there after battle training.

Now that the mining of iron ore in the hills to the south had been established, the steel foundry had been moved out of the city into a marshy field to the east, there to sprawl untidily over the floodplain, belching heavy smoke. Catanwakuwa pilots who liked to ride the thermals from the steelworks came down coughing, their wings and skin smudged with soot, until Sintikala forbade them to cruise above it.

Through exhaustive trial and error Marcellinus had finally gotten the knack of steel. Ironically, he had found it easier to make using the raw iron ore rather than the fittings from the Roman wagons even though it had now become a three-stage process of roasting the ore in charcoal, hammering it like crazy to force the liquid slag out of the wrought iron, and then heating it again with charcoal to add strength.

All his effort had paid off, though. Respectable human-scale wheelbarrows had largely replaced Cahokian woven baskets for heavy work, and that sped up the spring recovering and reshaping of the Master Mound and the other platform mounds. Steel or bronze human-drawn plows turned the soil in the cornfields. All the little lean-to gardens were bigger this year. The granaries were supported well up off the ground on columns of brick rather than wood, and most now had brick walls as well.

As predicted, Iroqua attacks had begun anew. The mound builders fought three more battles against marauding Iroqua bands in the springtime and won each one tidily. Two were melee actions in which Roman pila, gladii, and armor proved decisive. The third was another Iroqua assault upon a sister mound-builder city along the Oyo River where the residents had marched out in ranks carrying Roman shields to protect themselves against Mohawk arrows and slaughtered the Iroqua with wave after wave of steel-tipped arrows of their own. Marcellinus had been nowhere near this latter action and until he heard the news had no inkling that other nearby cities were adopting the Roman military tactics that he was teaching his First Cahokian Cohort.

Between the innovations and the military victories, all resistance to Marcellinus's ideas had collapsed. The Cahokians' enthusiasm for the creature comforts afforded by brick, iron, and steel had powered them into an immense appetite for novelty. At this dizzying pace, by the time the next wave of Romans crossed the Atlanticus, they might find a civilized province ready and waiting for them.

Marcellinus had not achieved all this alone. The Cahokians had taken his ideas and run with them so quickly that he had difficulty keeping up. Truth be told, he might have liked to spend more time over some of the changes; the siting of the foundry was a prime example, given the evil stench that washed over the plazas whenever the wind blew from the east. But the Cahokians seemed immune to the downsides of their newfound civilization.

The victories against the Iroqua had not made Marcellinus complacent. Around the two hundred acres that marked the central precinct of Cahokia, the new stockade was growing. With their new bronze and steel axes the Cahokians could fell trees at an astonishing rate and had already demolished one of the larger copses Marcellinus had hiked through on the night he had tried to abandon Cahokia and met an Iroqua war band coming the other way.

With some difficulty Marcellinus had persuaded the elders to send the squads of Cahokian lumberjacks north for their trees, to chop them down far from home and float the trunks down the river to Cahokia and so preserve the forests closer to home that sheltered their deer and could be farmed for nuts and forest fruits.

At least, he thought he'd persuaded them. Time would tell.

His Cahokian language skills were now quite functional. At his age he would never be fluent, but with his spoken Cahokian augmented with hand-talk he could make himself understood. For their part, Tahtay, Kimimela, and Enopay spoke excellent Latin, and Enopay could write and figure in Latin better than most quartermasters Marcellinus had known during his twenty-five years in the Roman army. Nahimana's Latin was pidgin but passable, and Latin words were even weaseling their way into Cahokian, with the native tongue having no equivalents for the military, metallurgical, and diplomatic terms that were becoming current. In fact, the First Cahokian Cohort responded to orders given in Latin more readily than they did to those given in Cahokian.

It was, of course, not mere vanity that made Marcellinus drill Latin words into as many Cahokian heads as possible. When Romans came again to the shores of Nova Hesperia, the more Cahokians that could speak to them, the better.

The worst-case scenario—all-out war between a new Roman army and a Cahokia formidably equipped with Roman steel as well as native air power—had to be avoided at all costs, even at the cost of Marcellinus's life and liberty.

And to achieve that, he needed to start his preparations in earnest.

"Sintikala, something is not right."

Twenty feet above him in the Longhouse of the Wings, Sintikala sat cross-legged on a narrow rafter with what looked like a bone needle and sinew, mending a tear in the fabric of one of the Hawk wings. "And," he added, "if it would help, I could make you a steel needle much thinner than that."

She squinted down past the wing. "What is not right?"

"You. And the way we first met, when I was still a Roman Praetor."

Sintikala grinned tautly. "All of that was not right. Perhaps if I had killed you then?"

Marcellinus did not rise to the bait. In fact, he did the reverse, which was to pull up one of the trestles and sit. "My guards would have killed you first. And even if you had managed it, Lucius Domitius Corbulo would just have taken charge. The war between Cahokians and Romans would still have happened."

"Oh, well."

"But tell me this: Back then, when we first met, how did you get to my army so quickly? Where did you really go afterward?"

"Only today you think of this?"

"You asked me to help you make the wings better. I have done a little, but I can't do any more till I know how good the wings are now."

Sintikala tied off her sewing and pulled a Roman pugio from her belt to trim the end of the sinew. Without using her hands, she swiveled on the narrow rafter. She was uncannily comfortable with heights.

"The Catanwakuwa are very good. Light. Smooth. It is the Wakinyan that," she said with a gesture, "pull on the air, come down fast. You help us now with Wakinyan."

She was changing the subject, and both of them knew it.

Bluntly, Marcellinus said, "One day, more Romans will come. Another legion. We must plan what we will do when that happens."

"We?" Their eyes met.

"Sintikala, how far can you fly?"

"Today? Yesterday? Winter? Summer?"

"My legion landed on the shores of the Mare Chesapica. Made castra. Figured out what we were about. We got ready, and we left. And in that time, less than a moon, word of our coming got all the way here to Cahokia, and then you got almost all the way across to the Chesapica.

"And later, here on the mound, you told me that the Romans are gone, all dead. Which means that once again you went to Chesapica and came back here in what, a few weeks? I am not a fool, Sintikala."

She smiled. "But slow in the head."

"Perhaps."

"I will show you. We go outside? I draw it for you. Then sometime, I show you much better."

And making Marcellinus leap half out of his skin, Sintikala dropped out of the rafters to the floor in front of him, a fall that might have at least twisted the ankle of a normal person.

"Yes," he said, a little breathless. "All right."

It had rained that morning, which helped. Sintikala's fingers moved adeptly in the mud, drawing a long, thin snake. She placed a stone by the side of the serpent. "This, Mizipi. The stone is this mound, here in Cahokia."

She leaned toward him and scribbled in the mud, another long line roughly parallel to the Mizipi, with a small flat loop in it. "This is the big water, and here is Chesapica. Where you sit, this is east, the direction of the sun in the morning. You and your army walk here." She sculpted a mountain chain in the mud that ran from northeast to southwest. "Over Appalachia—but see up here? It is easier to cross the mountains here than where you walked. Anyway. Your army came to us this way, across flat, to river flood lands." She scrawled another serpent. "Here is Oyo River, which you cross here, in thinner place."

She drew more, filling out the map. "Much far down here, there is also big water. Market, where Mizipi goes out into big wide water." And farther up. "Here are Great Lakes. All this is Iroqua, to here and to here. If you march souther, you hit Oyo where it is wider, or walk along it. If you march norther, you find more Iroqua."

"And so?"

"Iroqua told us your army come."

Marcellinus had not expected that. *Iroqua?*

"Of course. Why not?"

"Oh, perhaps because you're slaughtering each other in the Mourning War?"

"But also we trade. Furs, hoes, copper, shells. Gaius, it is their land, it is our land. It is not your land. Of course they tell us. Iroqua runners come under pipe of peace, tell us of you."

"All right."

"And then I go to see your army."

"By Mizipi and Oyo," Marcellinus said, taunting her.

She snorted. "Water is for ducks."

"And so you flew."

"Yes," she said. "I flew there."

In spring and summer, the sun heated the ground and made the air rise. The wings could ride higher up into the sky on the heated air. This, of course, was old news; even on the battlefield Marcellinus had seen the Hawk wings soar up from the burning huts, and now he watched them daily, spiraling for height by using the hot invisible column from the brick kilns and, when Sintikala wasn't looking, the steelworks. However, he had never imagined that a Hawk could rise so high and stay up so long using just the heat from the ground.

"Only on some days," Sintikala said. "Days of good, with little white sky fluff?"

"Clouds."

"Yes. And good winds that go where I want to go."

Sintikala had waited more than a week for conditions to be right, and then she had launched in early morning and flown east. By late afternoon she had made it almost all the way to her goal, the Black Mountain in Appalachia, but had lost too much height and came to ground. Two days later, after carrying her wing halfway up the Black Mountain, she launched again; with the wind blowing onto the face of the mountain, she had risen up through the air, looping around and around, spiraling higher. She had followed the Appalachia north, using only the lift from the ridge, and had then found another set of thermal upwellings that had carried her a few dozen miles farther eastward. There her luck had run out a second time, but she had landed just a few days' march west of Marcellinus's army. After she dismantled and hid the Hawk wing, all she had to do was move into the Legion's path and wait.

"So far?" he said, still shocked. "To Appalachia in just one day?"

"Of course," she said. "One other day last year, I never come down until sunset. Only up. Some day is good, others not."

"But still . . ."

"Gaius, I fly. It is all I do. I am clan chief. And so was my mother. All my life I do this. In this one thing, Sintikala is big clever. Other Hawks not as much. I fly higher. No one flies more far than me."

"I bow to you," Marcellinus said, and did so.

"And then," she said with a sigh, "sometimes I have to walk back."

"I'm working on that. We will talk of it. But . . . then, after we met, you walked back through Iroqua, alone?"

"The Iroqua know me. And I am not warrior."

"What?"

"If I carry no weapon, I am not warrior. If I am not warrior, I am safe."

Marcellinus shook his head, not comprehending.

"Yes. Trails are safe for traders, people who travel. To all people who are not warrior. People can walk everywhere in the land. A man or a woman with a child, all are safe if not carry weapons."

Traveling unarmed through barbarian territory was an odd definition of "safe." But Sintikala was the living proof, and so were the merchants who traveled considerable distances to the Cahokian markets or passed through on their way north or south. "All right. So you spoke Algon-Quian and hand-talked with Fuscus. And after I freed you, you warned the Algon-Quian and Iroqua villages in our path. And they avoided us, every single one of them, until the Iroqua warriors were ready to attack us. And you passed safely through all those Iroqua villages without harm."

"Yes."

"And so my plan worked."

"Big clever plan. Brave Roman."

"Yes, yes . . . But even so. And, of course, the Iroqua were happy to let us march on and fight you instead of them."

"We wanted you to go past us, too. You said you would. Pass through to west, you said. But once you saw corn, once you saw Cahokia, we knew you and your hungry men would not pass through. Not leave us in peace. Not ever."

Far above their heads, heavy clouds were gathering. Marcellinus might not have long before their conversation—and their map—was washed away.

"Sintikala, it is now the Flower Moon. For all I know, a Roman legion could already be ashore at Mare Chesapica, in Powhatani lands, or anywhere along the coast to the north or south."

Her eyes narrowed. "You think so?"

"I don't know. But today-now, this is about the very soonest it could be done, if news of my defeat reached Roma quickly."

"And what does Great Sun Man say?"

"Great Sun Man cares only about the Iroqua. He fights only the enemy he can see. He cannot see the Romans yet. They may not come this year or even next, so he does not worry about them. But we must. We need to make a plan."

She nodded soberly. Once again, her perspective was different from Great Sun Man's; she had seen a Roman legion at the peak of its power and efficiency. Great Sun Man had only seen one burned, wrecked, destroyed.

Marcellinus looked at the crude map in the mud again. It had taken his legion weeks to march from Appalachia to Cahokia, and Sintikala had done it in a day? It still boggled his mind. "Well, then. When they land, I must know as quickly as possible. And then I need to get a message to their Praetor, their commander. I will go to them myself as soon as I can, but—"

"You, through Iroqua lands?"

"Yes, but . . . *you* can fly over those lands. When the Romans come, we must get word to them, perhaps a written message, with the finger-talk, words in Latin on bark?"

"You would send me again to a Roman Praetor?" she said, her face dark. "Into the middle of their army of men?"

"With a letter from me . . ." Marcellinus stopped, faintly appalled that he could have suggested such a thing. Send Sintikala into the maw of Roma again, alone?

"A message for the new Romans," she said slowly. "And what would you say to them?"

"That the 33rd Legion was defeated but that I am alive and have allied with you in peace and am . . . helping you. That war is not necessary. Perhaps that Cahokia will feed the Roman troops and help them on past Cahokia and beyond? We can talk with the elders, agree on what to say. But perhaps we would send someone else. Another Hawk. Not you."

Sintikala put her head on one side. "Now you think I am afraid?"

"I think *I* am afraid," he said.

"Other Hawk clan fliers could not fly half the way to Appalachia."

From Great Sun Man, it might have been boasting. From Sintikala, Marcellinus accepted it as simple fact. "Perhaps you fly over them and drop the letter." An aerial messenger would certainly get the attention of any Roman commander.

"Or perhaps if you ask me instead of telling me."

Sintikala was sitting very still. Marcellinus knew her well enough by now to recognize the danger he was in if he said one more foolish thing. "I am sorry. What should we do?"

The Hawk chief brooded, stabbing her index finger in the mud to make an irregular line of holes linking the coast and Cahokia. He thought she was merely doodling until she spoke.

"The Romans will bring their big ships to where you landed. They will want to use the bay, and the road you made. They will not land far north or far south and do extra work. One place." She stabbed the Mare Chesapica with her finger. "And so we send words now to the Powhatan or the Nanticoke, and when Romans come, the tribe chief can give it to the Romans."

"Ah," Marcellinus said. The coastal chiefs would have no love for Marcellinus, but it was certainly in their interest to help if it would prevent further bloodshed.

"Then smoke and runners." She indicated the line of holes. "These are really hills. We put firewood on the hills, and when the Romans come, we make signals. Words in smoke. In these other places we will need runners instead. And so we will know within two hands of days when the Romans arrive and how many, and they will get your finger-talk letter as soon as the local people can take it. You, we can take along the Oyo River in canoes much quicker than you can walk, with some of your First Cahokian warriors so the Romans will see you are still a leader of men."

"I see I'm not the only one who has been thinking about this," he said, and bowed to her again.

Sintikala met his eye. "And then?"

"Then what?"

"You and your Roman Praetor brother?"

"We talk. Sintikala, I will not betray you. I will not betray Cahokia. I swear this."

She grunted. "But perhaps he will not want to hear what you want to tell him."

Marcellinus nodded. That was indisputable.

With extreme good luck, this new incoming Praetor would be a calm and rational man—perhaps even someone Marcellinus already knew—who would accept him as the incumbent legate over the mound-builder cities. He would take the freely offered Cahokian provisions to resupply his legions, maintain discipline in his ranks, and march past the Mizipi and into the west to continue the task of opening up Nova Hesperia.

And ideally the Cahokians themselves would embrace the benevolent hegemony of Roma and even tolerate Roman taxation in return for the advantages in goods, trade, education, and wealth the alliance would bring. They certainly had shown no lack of enthusiasm for the changes in their fortunes so far.

Reality could not possibly be so tidy; it never was. More likely, the incoming Praetor would summarily arrest and execute Marcellinus for losing his Legion and fraternizing with barbarians, and that would be that. Only slightly less harshly, Marcellinus might be taken into custody, formally stripped of his military rank, and kept in chains, eventually to be shipped home in disgrace. Roma was not kind to its failures.

Finally, Cahokia could reject Roma. Marcellinus had never raised the topic of Roman hegemony with them. Could Great Sun Man and Sintikala accept Imperium? Sometimes Marcellinus thought it might work. At other times he thought he was insane for even contemplating it.

But already so much had changed in Cahokia. Marcellinus had to hope.

He pointed to the map in the mud, to the land beyond Cahokia, on the side of the Mizipi closest to her, the western side. "So, what is here? The plains, more peoples, then what? How much farther to the edge of this land?"

"Here are mountains." She used both hands to raise a tall ridge of mud. "Not like Appalachia. *Big.* Big-big, white. Cold with snow."

"And then?"

Sintikala knew that eventually there was another sea. But that was from the casual conversation of traders; she did not know how far, or what the land on the other side of the snowy mountain range might look like. She had never been so far herself.

"A long way, then. A very long march for the Romans. They might be willing to take help rather than fight all the way."

Sintikala looked dubious.

"They must," he said.

Marcellinus looked again at the crude muddy sketch of the giant land he was in and shook his head. So large, yet Sintikala could travel so far through it, flying high in the skies.

Marcellinus was an army man, and his adult life had mostly been nomadic. Aside from the war party to Woshakee, he'd lived in Cahokia almost a year now.

"I show you more." Sintikala stood. "A better map. One day. Not today."

As the raindrops began to fall, Marcellinus traced the line of the Mizipi with his finger. So much here to see, and he had seen so little of it.

"All right," he said. "One day. Thank you."

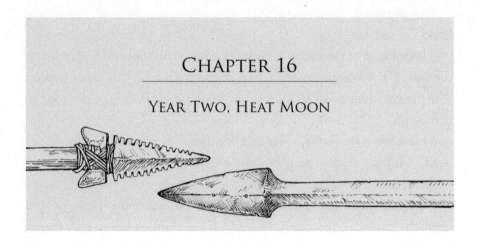

"This pipe? Older than city. Before Cahokia."

Marcellinus took a long pull from the carved flint-clay pipe, and the acrid smoke expanded to fill his lungs. His ears buzzed, but he no longer coughed. It was midnight in the sweat lodge, and his skin already had a sheen of wood and pipe smoke. Perhaps he ought to take a speedy visit to the baths by lamplight after this.

The pipe was carved with the figure of a man. Could it really be older than the city? Marcellinus passed it with exaggerated care just in case. "Great Sun Man, I have been thinking that I need to see more of this land. The river, other towns, villages. I should train centurions in other Mizipi cities and build forges for them so all mound-builder peoples of the Mizipi can be stronger against the Iroqua. They have their Haudenosaunee League. The Mizipi people must have a league, too." And against Roma, he thought unwillingly, but knew better than to speak it aloud.

"Um," said Great Sun Man, caught unaware by the magnitude of the suggestion. "Yes? No?"

Howahkan came to his war chief's aid. "Instead, the warriors from other cities should come here, from north and east, south and west. All could train here together and then return to their cities."

Smoke trickled from Marcellinus's nose and mouth. "Great Sun Man. Speak me the truth. Am I a prisoner here?"

"A what?"

"If Wanageeska wanted to leave Cahokia, you would stop him?"

Great Sun Man waggled his hand at the wrist, the gesture for uncertainty. "Where do you go? Why?"

"I think that you say yes."

"Wanageeska . . . If my son Tahtay wants to leave Cahokia, I would stop him. If my brother Kohana or my mother, Patachee, wants to leave, I would stop them. This is Cahokia. My people belong here."

"Great Sun Man, I will always return to Cahokia. You have my word. I have nowhere else to go. But I will not be chained here. Yes? I mean tied up, bound, as with sinew. Cahokia is just one city, and the Mizipi is long. To help you, I need to know many things."

"Cahokia is best city."

"Cahokia is biggest city. When I have seen others, I will tell you which is best." He punched the chief lightly on the shoulder to rob the words of any sting and indicate that he was teasing.

Great Sun Man frowned.

Quickly, Marcellinus said, "Do not say, 'No, I have spoken.' There are many good reasons why I should see other towns and better understand the great peoples of the Mizipi. So let us talk more of this. Here, and tomorrow, and the day after tomorrow. Yes?"

Kanuna looked from Marcellinus to Great Sun Man and back to Marcellinus. "Yes, let us all talk some more. Pipe?"

Two more hours passed with a conversation that ranged near and far, as was the habit in the sweat lodge. Marcellinus did not raise the subject of his leaving Cahokia again, but others did. Kanuna, the best-traveled of the elders, mentioned towns Marcellinus might visit where he could see things they did not have in Cahokia: canals for irrigation, different designs of gates and bastions for their palisades, rafts, wings of a different style. Ogleesha mentioned the dangers that such travels might bring: bears, rapids, getting lost, roving Iroqua bands. Howahkan praised the initiatives and public works that he would be loath to have Marcellinus ignore for the time it would take to paddle down the Mizipi and back.

To all of this Marcellinus smiled and nodded, satisfied that the topic was at least being discussed and knowing that more direct pressure on his part would be counterproductive. The Cahokian political system had many chiefs and, except in matters of war, largely ran on consensus. By raising the issue in this group Marcellinus had assured that the decision would not be Great Sun Man's alone. Although as far as Marcellinus could see, the only times the elders or the clan chiefs truly owned their power was when Great Sun Man chose to step aside and relinquish his.

Eventually the pipe was empty and their throats were dry, and Marcellinus's head hurt. Ogleesha had wandered home long before, and Matoshka had fallen asleep sitting up. At this point there could be no loss of face in calling it a night. Bowing, Marcellinus got up to leave.

To his surprise, Great Sun Man stood as well. "Come with me."

Together, they walked down off the Mound of the Smoke. At this time of night they were the only men abroad on the Great Plaza. Tonight, with no moon in the sky and his head still buzzing with the tabaco he had smoked, Marcellinus truly appreciated how flat the plaza was. And, he only now realized, water never puddled in it. Clever.

Marcellinus was tired. The bright buzz of the smoked leaf had worn away, leaving him lethargic. He wanted his bed. But if Great Sun Man wanted to take him somewhere, it must be important.

Great Sun Man guided him diagonally across the plaza. On its southern edge were two large mounds, fifty feet high and three hundred feet apart, each with a house at its peak, and before them the war chief stopped.

Marcellinus had been familiar with the sight of these mounds and their houses for as long as he had lived in Cahokia, but it had never occurred to him to ask about them.

"All right," he said. "Who lives here?"

"This is Fire," said the chief. "This is Death."

Great Sun Man pointed to the conical mound on the left. "Here, my father lives."

Marcellinus tried to remember whether he had ever met the war chief's father. Of course, in Cahokia "father" could be a courtesy title for just about anyone, just like "brother" or "sister." Kinship was mutable here, a matter of convenience or respect as often as not.

"You know my father?" Great Sun Man asked sardonically.

Marcellinus grasped it. "He is dead?"

"Yes. And there he is, up there under the house, and my father's father with him, and his father, and three fathers more."

"Only three?" It was Marcellinus's turn to add a glimmer of irony to his tone.

"Before those fathers, there was no Cahokia. Not the city you see now. And other leaders rest here also."

Marcellinus had not realized the city of Cahokia was so recent. Six or seven generations was not so long. Roma had existed for a hundred generations. Perhaps the carved flint-clay pipe they had smoked that night really did predate the city.

He struggled to concentrate. "The fathers are in the mound? Not in the house?"

"Yes, yes, buried in the mound. The house you see is just, well . . . We do not go into such a house."

A mausoleum, then. A sacred place. A ceremonial marker. He nodded.

"Once Cahokia was three cities, all here. The Great Mound and Great Plaza, here, and then another city at western Cahokia, and then west again on the far bank of the Mizipi is another small city with its own great mound and plaza, Cahokia-across-the-water. So, three cities, all very close by, all." Great Sun Man crossed his forearms. "All with chiefs who were like brothers. But soon, less close as brothers and too near to have different chiefs."

Three overlapping cities with three rulers. Echoes, perhaps, of republican Roma, with its three Consuls. Theoretically, those Consuls had shared power over Roma. In practice, they had factionalized and brought the nation to the brink of civil war time and time again.

And further back in history, even Romulus and Remus had been one ruler too many.

Great Sun Man went on. "The chiefs and the three cities, they fight, make war. It is very hard times. In the time of my father's father's . . ." He waved his hand. "You know, much old. We fight each other, and then, when many are dead, we make treaty, and we join cities, have one chief for all. That chief was Ituha, who I have spoken of before. And in here, this mound? The bones of Ituha and the other chiefs, dead."

The bones of Cahokian ancestors lay in the mound before them, sacred relics of Cahokia, with a charnel house and mausoleum set atop them. Dead but still watching over the great city they made.

Marcellinus nodded slowly. Perhaps men were really not so different no matter where they lived. He was preparing a platitude along those lines when Great Sun Man said, "And then they attack us when we are weak. They take our women. We go to get them, but they kill them."

Marcellinus was instantly chilled. "What? Which 'they' do you speak of now? Who attacks?"

"The Iroqua. We were weak, like dogs licking our wounds after fighting. We had become one Cahokia at last, but still we lay in pain. That is when the Iroqua attack, to take our women."

"Merda," Marcellinus said.

"And we chase after, to get them back, but the Iroqua kill the women as they run away and leave their broken bodies for us to find. We carry them home, our dead women, and we bury them in another mound behind these, the low one that you see beyond, with the cedar posts. Fifty women, perhaps. Or sixty."

"I am sorry, Great Sun Man. I am so sorry."

Great Sun Man squinted at him in the gloom of the night. "This is not me. You understand, Wanageeska? I was not there. This is my father's father's . . . a hundred winters since, perhaps."

Marcellinus pulled himself together. "Of course. Yes."

"But there they are."

"And your dead watch over you."

"This is Cahokia," said the chief. His voice and stance betrayed the intensity of his pride. "And here in these mounds is the medicine of all Cahokia. Of the Mizipi. And the other cities, where you would go? They are not Cahokia."

"No," Marcellinus said. "I am sure they are not."

"The bones of my many-fathers. The bones of our women. You will never know more about Cahokia than you do right here, Wanageeska. Right here at the Mound of the Chiefs and the Mound of the Hawks and behind them the Mound of the Women."

Marcellinus allowed the silence to wash over them for a moment. "So this mound to the right is the Mound of the Hawks?"

"The birdmen," said Great Sun Man. "In there are the first Hawks and the first Thunderbirds. The first men and women who make the Catanwakuwa, and make the Wakinyan and fly them up into the sky. Many die in the learning. We bury them here with their wings and with their cloaks of feathers and their beads and their weapons. For they are mighty, too; they are as chiefs, those strong ones who were the first to fly in the air like the birds and protect us against our enemies and help us push back the Iroqua."

Marcellinus nodded, oddly pleased that Cahokia recognized its innovators as much as its kings. How much better might Roma be if it honored men other than Imperators, politicians, and generals?

"We had to understand how to fly well, and fly in war, and fly to protect Cahokia. It was our people who first flew, the People of the Mounds. Although now the Iroqua of the mountains have Hawks too."

"Yes," said Marcellinus.

"The father of Sintikala is here," Great Sun Man told him. "He was a great flier and a great chief. He led Cahokians in war against the Haudenosaunee, along the Oyo, a life and a half ago."

Marcellinus knew he meant a generation and a half, perhaps thirty winters. "He was Great Sun Man before you?"

The chief nodded. "He should be buried in both mounds. The Mound of the Chiefs and the Mound of the Hawks. But he is only one man, and before he die he spoke that he wanted to lie in this Mound, of the Hawks, with those who fly."

"I would have done the same," Marcellinus said, strangely moved.

"One day, perhaps we bury me here," said Great Sun Man, pointing to the left mound. Next, he pointed to the right. "And one day, Wanageeska, perhaps we bury you there."

"Gods, no!" Marcellinus said, appalled. "No, I am not—I make nothing. I was once an enemy and now I am a friend, but I only build things for you that have worked in other places, across the sea. I have invented nothing. And I am not Cahokian."

"Not today. Not yet. But later, when we bury you?"

"I hope that day will be a long time coming," Marcellinus said rather fervently.

"And I, too." Great Sun Man studied each mound in turn as if seeing them for the first time. "Wanageeska?"

"Yes?"

"A moon from now, we must go to Ocatan, I, or perhaps Wahchintonka if I cannot leave, and some of our best warriors. Ocatan is Cahokia's southern door, and any Iroqua who come by river must pass them. We must take Ocatan more weapons and teach them more of the things you have taught us about how to fight. You could come with us."

It was not the trip of exploration Marcellinus had hoped for, but it was a start. "I would like that. Thank you."

"Then, in the winter we will talk more. Cahokia has many friends south of Ocatan, even to the city of Shappa Ta'atan, which is halfway to the Market of the Mud. We should go there to our brothers and make sure that all Mizipian cities stand firm with Cahokia and against the Iroqua. I agree with this. So, not this year, but perhaps next?"

Marcellinus bowed. "Thank you."

"But *this* is why you must always return. Because of what is buried here. Yes?"

He looked into Marcellinus's eyes.

The mounds loomed in the night, silent crypts. Sweat was still drying on Marcellinus's forehead. He took his time and then turned and met Great Sun Man's gaze. "Yes. I will always come back to Cahokia. I promise you this."

"Good." Great Sun Man yawned mightily. "Why are you not tired?"

"I am. I was, anyway."

"Then we should sleep. I have spoken."

And the mighty war chief of the Cahokians turned and strode away as if they had been discussing the weather, leaving Marcellinus gaping after him.

Such an important conversation, right in the middle of the night when he could least take it in, here in Cahokia in the dark, under the stars of a moonless sky.

Then the brooding presence of the giant mounds pressed upon him, and he turned to face them again. Great Sun Man was right; the soul of Cahokia was not on the Master Mound, after all, or even beneath it but here on the opposite side of the Great Plaza. Marcellinus had lived in the city for a whole year and had not known it until tonight.

He shivered.

Yes, Marcellinus was very tired. But he knew that many more hours would pass before he could sleep.

He might as well go to the baths now, after all.

CHAPTER 17

YEAR TWO, THUNDER MOON

They were attacked on the river on the second day out of Cahokia. Without warning, waves of arrows flew from the trees on the eastern bank. Most passed safely over their canoes, and some fell short to splash into the water and float there, swirling in the eddies made by the Cahokian paddles.

Akecheta's response was immediate. He turned the lead canoe toward the shore where the unseen Iroqua war party was hiding and shouted the order to paddle at double speed. Marcellinus, who was taking a turn at an oar, was hard-pressed to keep up with the killing pace set by Mahkah, Napayshni, Hanska, Mikasi, Yahto, Tahtay, and Dustu. From their wake came the war whoops from the other two sleek Cahokian canoes under Wahchintonka's command.

A brief glance reassured Marcellinus that Hurit had crouched down behind him. Only her eyes showed over the gunwale as she scanned the shore for the Iroqua.

Another wave of arrows strafed them. One arrow passed through the thin skin of the canoe just in front of Marcellinus, and another flashed between Tahtay and Mikasi. Pointlessly, Marcellinus ducked.

Now a flight of Cahokian arrows sped in the opposite direction as one of Wahchintonka's canoes returned fire. The other was quickly winning the race toward the shore, powered as it was by fourteen strong warriors whereas Marcellinus's canoe had only eight, including two boys.

The Iroqua did not wait to engage the Cahokians. "Fleeing," said Hurit, the only one with enough breath to speak, but they all saw the two dozen Iroqua braves break cover and scamper up the hill like deer.

"Hold!" Marcellinus shouted, but he was not in charge.

"On!" Wahchintonka cried, and at that moment the foremost Cahokian canoe rode up onto the bank, its warriors already leaping out to sprint after the escaping Iroqua. Wahchintonka's canoe came to shore just a moment later, and the canoe of Akecheta and Marcellinus was alone on the water, left behind.

"Hold!" Akecheta repeated at last, and they coasted and twisted on the gentle current while the warriors panted.

"Bows," Marcellinus said, and Mahkah, Hanska, and Mikasi snatched them up and nocked arrows.

From the woods came a sudden hullabaloo as battle was joined, but Marcellinus could see nothing.

It was a tense and frustrating moment. Marcellinus and his warriors could not land and join the skirmish without leaving the canoes unguarded, and besides, they had Tahtay, Dustu, and Hurit to think of. Given more warriors and more time, Marcellinus could have gone ashore and thrown up quick field fortifications of branches to protect themselves and the canoes. As it was, the nine of them were drifting on the river, sitting ducks.

The din from onshore hushed. For twenty, thirty heartbeats all was quiet. They waited, scanning the bank, checking every tree, every bush.

"A trap?" Tahtay asked. "Luring us ashore?"

"Perhaps." There could easily be more Iroqua than they had seen so far; even now, Wahchintonka's braves could be dead, with Iroqua lurking in wait for the third canoe to land.

Then Wahchintonka stepped out of the trees, followed by the other Cahokians, breathing too heavily to call out but beaming with fierce joy. Four of them clutched fresh scalps, grisly trophies that dripped blood into the mud.

Akecheta's boat erupted in cheers, and Marcellinus breathed again.

"Seneca," Hurit said. "And maybe some Tuscarora from the east, by their tattoos."

"They made me bleed," Yahto said. "But we made them run!"

"Bleed?"

"Women will adore me for my scars and my bravery in battle!" Yahto hooted and waved his arm; it was a mere scratch.

Returning to the canoes, the warriors started plucking Iroqua arrows out of the birch-bark hulls and patching the holes with resin and leaves. Two men he did not know from Wahchintonka's boat were also bleeding, but everyone but Hurit had been wearing breastplates of Roman steel or Cahokian wood over his chest. Nobody was seriously harmed.

"So we are not safe in our own lands," Tahtay said quietly.

Marcellinus gestured around him. "We lost no one. We look safe to me."

"*They* are not safe," Dustu said. "Seneca and Tuscarora come here, skulk like dogs, and then run? Let *them* fear. Let *them* die."

"The Iroqua are cowards," Wahchintonka said from a few yards away. "They can hide in our woods and eat our berries. But once we catch them . . ." He seized a scalp and raised it high.

"Even so," said Hurit for Marcellinus's ears only, "they are still too close, and our people are in danger."

With nothing particularly reassuring to say, Marcellinus nodded and grimaced.

They paddled down the mighty Mizipi, passing the occasional mound-builder village and hamlet on the shores. This time, having no shamans in their party, they made no obeisance to the petroglyph rock but rode the swift currents through the narrows. That evening they camped on the riverbank, with guards posted to warn of any Iroqua incursion. None came.

On the fourth day they arrived at the hill fort of Ocatan that guarded the junction with the Oyo River, where the war party to Woshakee had turned eastward the previous fall.

The war chief of Ocatan was easy to identify. A broad-shouldered man who topped even Wahchintonka by an inch, he wore his full ceremonial kilt and headdress and clutched a spiked chert mace with considerably more heft than the one Great Sun Man had held to accept Marcellinus's surrender almost a year earlier.

Despite the weight of his regalia, the war chief bounded forward to greet Wahchintonka, who wore only a breechcloth, tattoos, and a considerable amount of sweat. "My brother!"

"My brother!" said Wahchintonka. "And all my relatives!" He meant the rest of the Ocatan contingent that had come to welcome them at the riverside.

"And the friend of my brothers." The war chief assessed Marcellinus carefully.

"It is an honor to meet you," Marcellinus said in Cahokian, and for novelty value repeated the sentiment in Latin.

"We hear of the Wanageeska," said the chief. "I am Iniwa. You are hungry?"

Not knowing the protocol, Marcellinus looked around for Wahchintonka, but the leading Wolf Warrior was now talking to the Ocatan elders. Akecheta rescued him. "We thank you, mighty chief, but we are happy to eat when you do, at your time."

"Our walls," Iniwa said. "Are they not great?"

"Your walls are strong," said Marcellinus, and they were. The outer palisade of Ocatan was tall and well tended, with firing platforms every twenty feet. The new defenses Marcellinus was overseeing for Cahokia were not as stout as these. Cahokia, of course, had a much longer and more challenging perimeter. "Strong and new. Last year, when we passed your city on the way to aid Woshakee, your palisade was not so grand."

"We are strong against the Iroqua," Iniwa said. "We will not be Woshakee, stolen by the Haudenosaunee." He held Marcellinus's gaze. "And we are strong against the silver men of your people."

Marcellinus blinked. He was encouraged that the chief of Ocatan was taking the idea of a Roman return seriously. But as sturdy as Ocatan's stockade was, any legion would smash it aside and overwhelm the town within an hour.

"Strong indeed. But I hope that when new Romans come to Ocatan, they will come as friends. As do I."

Clumsy, but the best Marcellinus could manage. Iniwa put his head on one side as if considering it, then stepped away, spreading his arms wide to address the gathering. "And so, you all are welcome! You will enter?"

Wahchintonka replied, "We will enter freely." The sprawling group moved toward the open gates.

The leading warriors of Ocatan now came forward to greet the warriors of Cahokia. But the elders had moved on without greeting Marcellinus, and the Ocatani warriors stepped around him with polite deference on their way to clasp arms with their fellow warriors of Cahokia. None met his eye.

Tahtay had run on ahead with Dustu and Hurit. Stepping to Mahkah's side, Marcellinus murmured, "Stay with me, if you would."

Ocatan was a well-kept town, larger than Woshakee but nowhere near the scale of Cahokia. Marcellinus reckoned the population at no more than four thousand, and that included the smaller and equally fortified outpost on the far bank of the Oyo. Most of Ocatan's houses were the same rectangular wattle-and-daub structures as Cahokian homes, but a significant number were of the simpler pole-and-thatch style.

Its mounds were small but immaculately maintained. And unlike the case in Cahokia, Iniwa lived in a palatial longhouse on the highest mound, the Temple Mound, with ramparts lining its roof. Two wooden rails graced the back of the mound to launch the Catanwakuwa, but the Ocatani Longhouse of the Hawks had been relegated to the mound's base.

Also relegated to the mound's base was Marcellinus.

Above them on the high mound, Iniwa and Wahchintonka were talking, feasting, and exchanging gifts. Akecheta was up there with them. Marcellinus had pointedly been left out and was trying not to feel aggrieved about it.

Worse, most of his other Cahokian warriors had gone to drink beer with old Ocatani friends. Many Cahokians had relatives here; others, like Hanska and Mikasi, had fought alongside the Ocatani in the past. Marcellinus's dinner companions tonight were Tahtay and Hurit, Dustu, and Mahkah. He was, he thought uncharitably, relegated to eating with the children.

Mahkah looked around him. "Ocatan is small, and they do not smile much here."

"Perhaps having Cahokia so close makes them frown," said Marcellinus. For all its strategic importance, Ocatan was merely Cahokia's satellite city, and they must know it.

"I think that perhaps having Iroqua so close is worse," Dustu said.

"The Seneca party on the river?"

"And others like them."

A pair of Ocatani warriors walking past their fire in the dusk eyed Marcellinus and muttered something he didn't catch. Tahtay glared at them and snapped, "You say so?" and Hurit put her hand on his arm. The warriors glanced down at them in derision and walked on.

Marcellinus grunted. "It's all right, Tahtay. No need to go into battle on my account. Perhaps I can win them over tomorrow."

"You will not drill them," Mahkah said unexpectedly. "Iniwa has told Wahchintonka that his warriors will not be taught by you. That will be for Wahchintonka and Akecheta."

"Not drill them? Then why did I come?"

Mahkah raised his eyebrows. "Because you asked? You wanted to see?"

"Many warriors of Ocatan came upriver to help Cahokia in its battle with your people," Dustu said. "And of those, many died. You did not know this?"

"No." Marcellinus was stunned. It had never occurred to him. Why had no one mentioned this before they arrived? Or Great Sun Man before they left?

They were equally startled that he did not know. "Of course. As you marched with your army, we had much time to prepare, and so we called for our brothers to stand with us against you."

"Yes, but—"

A female voice interrupted them. "I would speak with Gaius Wanageeska."

Marcellinus turned. Behind him stood a striking middle-aged woman with a large nose and a scar on her cheek. She wore bird tattoos on her arms and a cloak of black feathers over her shoulders. She seemed familiar, but Marcellinus could not place her.

Without a word, his three young male companions scrambled to their feet and were gone. Hurit had also jumped up, but she nodded formally to the woman and remained standing. Confused, Marcellinus put aside his bowl and stood as well. The woman waved him down. "Sit, Gaius Wanageeska."

"Either of those names will do. Hello."

"I am Anapetu. I am the leader of the Raven clan."

"Yes?"

"In Cahokia, Gaius Wanageeska. Cahokia's Raven clan."

"Ah! Of course!" Now he knew where he had seen her before: standing with the other clan chiefs at the ceremonies. "How are you here? You did not come to Ocatan in our canoes."

"I have been here in Ocatan for half a moon for the birth of my daughter's daughter." Anapetu sat and rearranged her cloak neatly, and at that Hurit sat, too. "I hear that you are a good man and a fine warrior."

He doubted she had heard it from the Ocatani. "Thank you."

"Yet still you are a man without a clan."

"I am," he said.

"And that is why we must talk."

"Ah." Not for the first time, Marcellinus could have used some assistance in social matters. He glanced at Hurit, but she sat in polite deference and said nothing. Tahtay, Dustu, and Mahkah had vanished completely.

Anapetu leaned forward. "Gaius Wanageeska."

At her commanding tone, his gaze swiveled back.

"Great Sun Man has spoken with me, and he and I have agreed. All in Cahokia must belong to a clan. I am to bid you join the Raven clan if you are willing."

"Join?"

Wachiwi, Hurit, even Pezi had been adopted into clans. But Marcellinus was not of the land . . .

The breeze moved Anapetu's feather cloak. "You understand?"

This had to be a direct result of his conversation with Great Sun Man at midnight a month before. The war chief sought to weld him closer to Cahokia.

It was, nonetheless, a great honor.

"Yes, yes. I am sorry, Anapetu. I am still not as familiar with Cahokian customs as I would like. I am . . . I would be happy to be associated with the Raven clan."

"But?" She skewered him with a glare that was, he had to admit, uncomfortably birdlike. "Yes?"

"I am still . . ." Roman? "I have not abandoned my own customs. You understand this? And Great Sun Man?"

Anapetu blinked. Hurit spoke for the first time. "You are still who you were. But now you are also of the Raven clan."

"Then I am honored. What must I do?"

Marcellinus suddenly recalled the rites of passage that Cahokian youths went through to become men. He hoped joining the Raven clan would not involve anything so painful.

His concern must have shown on his face. "Do not fear, Gaius Wanageeska." Smiling graciously, Anapetu placed her hand on Marcellinus's arm. "Come and visit me at my house once we are back in Cahokia. We will drink tea, and we will talk."

"I will look forward to it."

Marcellinus had acquired a new chief. He examined her with increased interest and decided that he had inadvertently done well. Anapetu seemed a force to be reckoned with. The chiefs of the Cahokian Bear and Turtle clans, whom he had met through Nahimana and her son Takoda, were women of much less substance.

Anapetu gestured around them. "Ocatan. You like it little?"

He grinned ruefully. "It is not Cahokia."

"No, it is not."

"And I had hoped to be useful here, but it seems I may not be."

"Useful?"

"With the troops, preparing them to defend against the Iroqua with Roman spears and tactics. And by bringing skills with steel and brick, as I did in Cahokia."

"Hurit, Tahtay, and Dustu are to talk tomorrow with the elders and children of the Fox and Beaver clans here about bricks. That is why they came. Ocatan would have a Big Warm House for its older folk, too."

They had not told him that either. Marcellinus glanced accusingly at the unfortunate Hurit, then looked away.

Anapetu stared at him for so long that he became uncomfortable. "I am known here," she said eventually. "I will speak with Iniwa. Maybe something can be done. I think not, but maybe."

Embarrassed, Marcellinus began, "I would not wish . . . You should not go to trouble on my behalf."

"Trouble?" Anapetu stood, her tunic and feather cloak billowing around her. She looked more like a shaman or a dancer than a clan chief with the feathers and her loose, light clothing. "Nothing is trouble for one of our clan."

The First Cahokian and the First Ocatani were doing mass charge-and-retreat exercises in the plaza. Marcellinus watched from the slopes of the Mound of the Cedars, trying to distract himself from striding into the fray and barking orders. Despite Anapetu's attempts nothing had changed, and a week of inactivity was driving Marcellinus crazy.

Mahkah had been right: Marcellinus had no opportunity to teach the townspeople anything. Akecheta and his Cahokian troops were having the time of their lives drilling the warriors of Ocatan in how to fight with steel and organize attacks in the Roman style. Tahtay, Hurit, and Dustu talked to them of bricks, and within days they had a small kiln up and running on the riverbank. The gifts of Cahokian iron and Roman steel were accepted gladly, but the townsfolk did not jump at the chance to learn how to smelt and forge such items themselves.

"Cahokia always provides," Tahtay said privately. "We give Ocatan hoes and adzes to keep them friends of Cahokia. Now we bring them more shields and spears. Why learn to make something that will come to you anyway if you wait?"

Marcellinus had been frozen out. He had almost forgotten his ostracism by the Cahokians the year before; now in Ocatan he was back to being an unknown quantity, a social pariah.

"Still useless, then?" Hurit plopped herself gracefully down by his side, gulping water from a deep wooden cup. The sun was malevolent today, and it was hotter than Hades.

He scowled at her. "Yes. Anapetu appears incapable of producing miracles."

"Miracles?"

"Never mind." With effort, Marcellinus forced a smile. This wasn't Hurit's fault. "And so we're clan kin, you and I. Fellow Ravens. Birds of a feather."

She looked with some interest at the pugio and wood in his hands. "What are you doing?"

He put down the pugio and picked up the cloth by his side. "Hurit, this is cotton. It is like the wool I wear, but it grows on trees." He considered. "Bushes, perhaps. I found this piece in the market today. I have not been able to ask her yet, but I think it is what Anapetu's tunic is made of."

"Yes, yes," she said. "And?"

"We have this in Cahokia? I have never seen it."

"Because you have no time for our dancers and stories and celebrations," said Hurit. "Our Red Horn dancers, our eagle and falcon dancers? They wear it so that it will flap and fly around them as they dance. The shamans wear it, too. Ordinary people, we do not need it."

"But cotton can't grow around here. The frost and the cold would wipe it out. It grows farther south, then?"

"Down the Mizipi it grows much. In the lands of the People of the Hand it grows even more." She shook her head. "What?"

"Hurit, I have never owned a single piece of cotton clothing. Where I come from, it costs far too much for a soldier."

She raised her eyebrows. "You want some to wear?"

Marcellinus shook his head. If the common people did not wear it, neither would he. Little point in irritating the shamans or, worse, his clan chief by affecting their style of dress.

Out in the plaza the Cahokians bowled over the ranked Ocatani, and hoots of laughter filled the air. Nonetheless, the Ocatani were learning from the Cahokians much more quickly than the Cahokians had learned from him.

"Gaius." Hurit pointed at the frame. "You still have not told me."

"Once we're away from Ocatan, I'll show you." She looked dubious. "Let me finish it first. And we can get more of this cotton somehow if I decide I need it? Lots more? In trade?"

"Of course. If you have enough swords, or shields, or adzes, or furs, you can get anything."

"Gaius Wanageeska?"

"I . . ." Marcellinus stumbled to his feet, his face red. "I am sorry."

Three days later they had set camp on the muddy bank of the Mizipi, heading home, and Anapetu and Hurit had arrived to find him swearing like a longshoreman in several languages.

Anapetu looked coolly at the small wooden frame Marcellinus held. "Explain this thing. Is what?"

"Sorry. When I cannot do something, it makes me angry." He raised the frame. "The cotton, covering this; it has to be very light, lighter almost than the air. And it must not flap. See? It cannot be loose. I need to sew it to the wood and make it absolutely tight."

Hurit squinted at it. Dusk was coming earlier as they progressed into the last days of the Hunting Moon. "It must be tight as a wing? As a drum?"

"Exactly."

"And this is a lantern?"

" . . . Not exactly." Indeed, it did not resemble a Cahokian lantern at all.

The girl raised her eyebrows, a slightly supercilious expression Marcellinus was beginning to find irritating. "What, then?"

"Help me, Hurit? Help me to not pull off my own fingers in frustration, and then I will show you what it does."

Hurit looked alarmed. "Give it to me," said Anapetu.

Marcellinus gave it to her, or rather, Anapetu confiscated it with wry impatience. "We will do this. And you? Go away and do something useful."

"Useful?"

Anapetu had already produced a bone needle and was frowning at the not-exactly-a-lantern. "Not much sun left before dark."

Well, that was true enough. Still embarrassed, Marcellinus left them to it and went to help Mahkah collect firewood.

"We have finished your lantern."

It was much later. The sky was clear, but the iridescent blue of afternoon had faded to gray. Low on the eastern horizon Marcellinus saw two planets, wanderers of the skies. True stars would appear later, once the night was darker.

Tahtay and Dustu sat with Anapetu and Hurit now. Mahkah was arranging firewood into a tent shape, his flint by his side. Soon they would have a fire against the evening cool. Behind and all around them, other warriors were building fires; beyond them, men stood guard, staring into the trees.

Marcellinus examined the lantern. Anapetu and Hurit had done an excellent job. Neat, tight stitches lined the frame, holding the cotton taut.

They had invested a lot of effort in getting it right. It was a shame Marcellinus was about to either throw it away or destroy it.

Perhaps he should have explained.

"It's beautiful," he said.

At the bottom of the lantern was a thin wooden cross-brace so delicate that Marcellinus could easily have snapped it between finger and thumb. He pulled a small candle from his pack and mounted it with care into the center of the brace.

"You want the flint for a spark?" Hurit asked, reaching into her pouch.

"We'll light the fire first and light the candle from that." He looked at Anapetu. "Do you know what this is?"

"No."

"So you don't see where I'm going with it?"

"Going? No. But I hope it was worth our time."

So did Marcellinus.

Mahkah lit the fire. It grew fully dark. Eventually Marcellinus took up a twig and held the end of it in the fire until it smoldered.

"Here we go."

With the utmost care, Marcellinus lit the candle wick from the twig.

The candle flared. The flame leaped into the lantern, throwing their shadows back against the trees. Marcellinus held the lantern steady and talked to it as if it were human. "Please don't burn. Please don't catch on fire." It didn't.

Already the lantern tugged at him. His hands were on either side of the cotton, and warmth flooded his palms. Marcellinus waited till he was sure, until he knew the light was well aflame and the first breeze would not puff it out. He moved his hands apart and let it go.

The lantern drifted upward. It seemed to pause above their heads, to sway and gather itself, then rose again, faster. In moments it was thirty feet up, then fifty, above the trees and still going, a beacon in the night.

The conversations from the campfires around them stilled. Anapetu watched it escape into the sky with the same calm, frowning care she devoted to everything. "Hmmm."

Marcellinus smiled. "Sky Lantern! Flying machine!"

"It goes up fast," Mahkah said.

"Yes!"

"Why?"

"The air trapped inside it is hot. Hot air rises. Catanwakuwa ride that rising air, and birds, too. But when you capture it and hold it close inside a lantern like that . . . Up it goes."

Hurit watched its tiny flame still burning, high in the sky. "Perhaps doing it tonight was not clever. It brings Iroqua?"

"We have guards. And if Iroqua are anywhere near, they already know we're here."

The Sky Lantern soared until it was just a speck, hardly brighter than a star.

"So, Anapetu? What if that lantern was bigger? Much bigger?"

"More bright?"

"Yes. And could lift more than a little lamp. More than a pot. More than, uh, a spear."

He looked into her face, waiting for her to understand.

"More than a canoe. More than—"

Anapetu's eyes widened.

"Yes? See?"

Hurit objected. "But to carry a person . . ."

"Yes, it would have to be very big."

Anapetu peered up into the sky. "Very."

Marcellinus had lost sight of it, too. Dustu had to point it out to them, and even then Marcellinus could glimpse it only by shifting his gaze slightly away from it. The wind at those exalted heights had pulled the lantern westward, and it had moved farther than he thought.

They watched it fly. Soon it was gone, and they sat down by the fire.

Ever practical, Anapetu said, "The very-big one. How do you get it down again?"

Marcellinus hadn't thought about that. "Snuff the flame."

Hurit slapped the ground, making leaves and twigs jump. "Bang?"

She was right. Without its source of heat, it might return to earth alarmingly fast. "Then make the flame smaller? There must be a way. I'll make it work."

"No," Anapetu said.

His heart sank. "What?"

She gazed at him. "Give this to us, Gaius. You have your cohort and your iron and your bricks. Give this to the Raven clan, this thing . . . what, again?"

"Sky Lantern."

"This Sky Lantern. To make the very-big Sky Lantern is the cotton and the wood and the plants and the flowers. You are not good with these things."

Marcellinus had not really thought of a giant man-carrying Sky Lantern as a project of plants and flowers. But Anapetu was probably smart enough to excel at anything she turned her hand to, and Marcellinus was spread too thinly already.

"Also," Hurit added, "you cannot sew without swearing."

Marcellinus laughed. "All right. Wonderful. But Anapetu, everyone, let's all keep quiet about this for now. Because if it works, it might be very important for Cahokia. Perhaps the most important thing since the Catanwakuwa."

The thought was dizzying. After several seasons of merely re-creating things that already existed across the Atlanticus, he finally had invented something new.

Who knew? Perhaps they would bury Marcellinus in the Mound of the Hawks, after all.

CHAPTER 18

YEAR TWO, BEAVER MOON

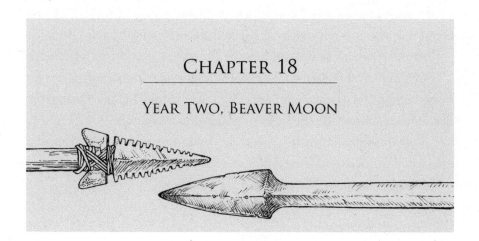

If Marcellinus had harbored any doubts about Anapetu's ability to do the task she had claimed for herself—which he did not—they would have been quickly dispelled, for it took her less than two moons.

Marcellinus was out in the Cahokian farmlands with half a dozen throwing machines—three onagers and three ballistas—hurling giant rock balls and thick bolts of iron-tipped wood what seemed even to him to be impossible distances. In his absence his engineers had lengthened the onagers' throwing arms and increased the weight of their oak frames. In only one case had they been too ambitious and snapped the throwing arm clean off. The new machines were harder to aim, it was true; at these tensions the twisted ropes behaved unpredictably, and the bucking of the onagers at the moment of launch sometimes threw the rocks erratically to one side or the other. There was really no question of throwing a human being until they had worked out the kinks. But in terms of sheer power, the machines exceeded Marcellinus's wildest expectations. It was incredible to see a massive ball being laboriously rolled and lifted onto the cup of a siege engine and then watch it soar away into the middle distance. As for the ballistas, a wheeled crossbow of wood and metal thirty feet wide was a little frightening, with the loud snap of the wires and the huge darts speeding away so rapidly that they almost appeared to vanish.

By the knowing looks his launch crew was giving him, Marcellinus could tell who was approaching without needing to turn and check.

"Huh," Anapetu said. "Impressive. Tomorrow you throw a house."

Marcellinus considered. The balls they were launching were far heavier than a Cahokian house. The trick would be preventing the house from splintering into a thousand pieces at launch.

"Stop thinking about it," she said. "I was not serious. But I need a heavy ball of rock, and I need you to see what we do with it."

"Already? So soon?" he said. "You're kidding."

"What?"

"Teasing. Joking with me."

Anapetu shook her head. "Pick up a ball, follow me."

In fact it took a reinforced wheelbarrow and four men to transport one of the massive two-hundred-pound balls. Marcellinus gave the order, and his men loaded one up and gamely staggered off in Anapetu's wake.

Anapetu had not, of course, done all the development by herself. With Marcellinus's approval she had brought in her sisters Leotie and Dowanhowee, her daughter Nashota, and a squad of other trusted friends to help her with the sewing and Hurit, Dustu, and Tahtay and a half dozen of their young brickworks gang to fetch and carry. All had been sworn to secrecy, and besides, key aspects of how the cotton had been treated and the ensuing construction were known only to Anapetu and her sisters.

Today any last vestiges of secrecy would be scattered to the winds, for Anapetu was leading Marcellinus and his crew toward the Big Warm House and a giant expanse of cloth stretched out on the ground next to it.

The part Marcellinus had expected to be the hardest—getting so much cotton of the quality required—actually had turned out to be the easiest. The traders from south of Ocatan were very familiar with cotton and could acquire it in whatever bulk was necessary in exchange for furs and pelts from the Mizipian cities to the north. Anapetu and other Raven elders had masterminded a complicated three-way deal in which Roman bricks and iron went north and canoes' worth of luxurious furs came south in their place, to then be exchanged for cotton from the southwest, and the haggling and dealing all got done in less than a moon.

When there was something Cahokia really needed, problems melted away. It boded well for Marcellinus's dreams of future Roman commerce. And he liked the exotic look of the furs he had seen. Romans might pay well for those.

Still, Marcellinus had seen few of the Raven clan's preparations firsthand, and this was his first sight of a fully constructed Sky Lantern bag. Even though he had helped with the arithmetic and the details of the design were familiar to him, the sheer size of what they had created was daunting.

The process of inflating the bag had already begun. With the boys' help, Anapetu had redirected some of the hot air from the furnace into a new trench that led out from the side of the house. Above the trench Leotie and Nashota were using sticks to hold up the very top part of the gray bag so that the hot air could blow into it. Nearby, Dowanhowee and two other women stoked a separate fire inside a feast-day cooking jar almost as tall as themselves.

The warm air was certainly building up inside the bag, but seeing how much cotton still lay on the ground, Marcellinus doubted it would rise much farther. He hoped his clan chief was not about to be embarrassed.

He murmured, "You're very confident."

"Confident is bad?"

"You didn't think of making a smaller one first to try it out?"

Anapetu smiled. "You think we did not make a smaller one first?"

He gave up and let her concentrate.

As the bag rose higher, apparently by magic, Anapetu walked among the brickworks boys and gave more quiet instructions, lending a hand to hold up the fabric. The bag now swayed thirty feet above Marcellinus's head, but it was starting to sag. "Huh," said Tahtay.

"Bring fire here," Anapetu said, her voice at last betraying her tenseness. Her sisters manhandled the giant jar closer to the bag.

Marcellinus could now see the opening at the bottom of the bag. Tahtay, Dustu, and the others held the opening up, though the part of the bag between there and the inflated portion still lay on the ground, frustratingly limp.

Marcellinus held his breath. He knew what could happen to cotton that came too close to a naked flame. At any moment the giant bag might catch fire.

"Anapetu . . ." he said, not quite loudly enough.

A large crowd was gathering. Sintikala and five Hawk warriors arrived, keeping out of the way and looking on impassively.

The wind caught the bag and sheared it sideways. Hot air spilled out and washed over them. The bag sagged further.

"More fire," Anapetu said, and winked at Dowanhowee, who produced a small pot and tossed it into the jar.

With a roar, liquid flame erupted from the jar's neck. Leotie and Nashota tossed whole logs in. Through the small holes that had been drilled into the jar's sides, the fire was no longer orange-red but an almost incandescent purple-white.

All at once, the tall bag puffed out. Somehow the cotton still had not caught aflame. Dark smoke billowed into the now-huge body of the bag . . . and gushed out of its peak.

Marcellinus couldn't help himself. "There's a hole, Anapetu. The bag has a hole in the top!"

"Of course!" Anapetu called back. "It needs one!"

Then Marcellinus and the others watching ran forward, because the bag was fully inflated and bucking to be free. The weight of the log-filled jar was not enough to hold it down.

"Wait!" Anapetu said. "Wait! Hold on . . ."

They held it, straining. The boys had already rolled the rock into a strong canvas sling. Now they hooked the sling over the struts that held the jar in place under the mighty swaying Sky Lantern.

"Let go!" Anapetu shouted. "All!"

Everyone jumped back. The hot-air bag lurched upward away from them. It tugged at the sling that held the ball and bobbed ponderously back down. Several people shrieked in alarm.

Hurit ran around the lantern, knocking at people's arms, afraid someone would still be clutching on to the thing, but everyone was safely clear.

Because the bag had risen again, and was rising still. Despite the mass of the jar and the rock ball, despite the bulk of the cotton fabric, which must itself weigh several hundred pounds, the lantern was going up with alarming speed.

The crowd fell silent as it rose to fifty feet, a hundred, with the onager ball still swaying beneath it. The bag was higher than the mound now, and the wind was carrying the whole thing off in that direction, over the mound and north across Cahokia Creek.

It was Sintikala who started the applause then, and soon the shouts and stamping of the crowd became deafening.

Anapetu was oblivious to the din. She stared intently at the Sky Lantern.

The liquid flame was burning out. The lantern had passed over the creek but was losing height, almost imperceptibly at first, but it was certainly coming down.

Anapetu grimaced, and her forehead creased. "All right. Hurit, Dustu, Tahtay, Nashota? Let us go and get it."

The Sky Lantern's first flight had been an unbelievable success. Marcellinus couldn't believe that Anapetu was downcast.

"Too quick." She shook her head. "Only a hundred feet up? Only to the creek? No."

"It was brilliant," he said. "Spectacular. Not forgettable."

"Too heavy." She sighed. "I don't know."

"It didn't catch fire," Marcellinus pointed out. "I mean, the cotton didn't burn."

"That is the clever part. All the rest is just great big hard work. But we had to make many careful fires under the fabric, let special smoke rise through it. The smoke, um, blocks up the tiny holes in the cotton."

Whatever Anapetu had burned, the smoke had sealed the cotton fabric, making it less flammable and much less porous. "Very good."

"Much more work to do."

"Always. Of course. But not a failure. Right?"

Only then did Anapetu smile. "Right! And fun to see it fly!"

The very next week, they threw a Hawk into the air by using an onager. The honor of being the first falcon warrior to be launched went not to Sintikala but to a young warrior of the Hawk clan; this prodigy was skilled enough to unfurl his wings and fly stably from the regular rail launch almost as soon as he cleared the top of the Master Mound, not having to wait for the apex of his trajectory like Sintikala and the rest of the clan. As they were still not in perfect control of the onager during launch, such fast reactions were essential for success. They did indeed fire the warrior out over the Mizipi so that he would splash down into the water if the launch failed, but the precaution was not necessary: the onager fired, the "ball" that was the boy and his wing arced up over the river, and then the youth was flying, banking around over them a couple of hundred feet from the ground and hooting triumphant war cries.

By Marcellinus's side, Sintikala nodded in satisfaction. "Next, me."

"Now?"

She grinned. "Not now. When everyone has gone away. I practice quietly."

As the young Hawk warrior streaked past them again and flared out for his landing, Great Sun Man walked up to them. "So, for Catanwakuwa, very good. How big engine you need to throw Wakinyan?" He laughed.

"Wakinyan are different," Marcellinus said. "For launching Wakinyan, we take the Great Mound with us when we march on the Iroqua."

The war chief smiled again and clapped him on the arm.

"Perhaps not," Marcellinus said. "I will think about it. But Great Sun Man, Sintikala? A Hawk is light and nimble, for one warrior. A Thunderbird is mighty, for twelve warriors. My question for you: How big might an Eagle be?"

Great Sun Man frowned and shook his head, but Sintikala was nodding. "Large enough for two, three? I have thought of such a thing, too. But now . . . small enough for a throwing engine?"

"Perhaps," said Marcellinus. "Eventually. Let us talk more about this."

The weather quickly turned foul. Torrential rains gave way to deep snow and to a pervasive chill that kept that snow on the ground for many weeks, growing dirtier day by day. Cahokia Creek iced over and did not thaw. By the time of the Midwinter Feast the Mizipi had also frozen, though not reliably enough for the children to run and slide on it the way they wanted.

Food was short. Marcellinus's second winter in Cahokia was much more brutal than the first. Nonetheless, it was the happiest time of his life.

The Cahokia steelworks had entered full production, and every afternoon Marcellinus made the long hike over there. However vile the weather, he could rely on finding a large proportion of his budding force of forty or fifty steelworkers, blacksmiths, and engineers in training. In fact, the colder it got, the more people he found there, stoking the crucibles and blast furnaces. They were now turning out wheel rims by the dozen, long segments of rail to be welded onto the existing Wakinyan launcher, the parts for ever bigger and better siege engines, and two or three new swords a week.

Marcellinus was working on a light metal frame that might hang beneath one of the Raven clan's Sky Lanterns; this would provide a safer structure for the fire jar that generated the hot air that kept the lanterns aloft and support a secure wooden platform for a person to sit on once Anapetu could be convinced that they were safe enough to carry people.

The brickworks was going full bore, with Dustu and its other leading lights experimenting with different clays and with adding small amounts of iron, chalk, and lime to the mix for strength and color. Whenever the weather permitted, Cahokian masons were hard at work adding rooms to the Big Warm House. Two more such houses were under construction, one in the plaza of adjacent western Cahokia and another in the burgeoning township of Cahokia-across-the-water—one for each of the three traditional centers of Cahokia.

Marcellinus spent little time at either the brickworks or the building sites. Tahtay, Dustu, and the others ran the brickworks with little adult supervision and had achieved a more uniform brick-baking temperature and an almost perfect success rate. With many months of experience, the Cahokian foremen by now understood the mechanics of building walls, roofs, pools, and hypocausts better than Marcellinus did. This freed him up for more interesting projects elsewhere, although he sorely missed Tahtay's company.

With the test flights of the new three-person Eagle wing under way, Marcellinus had necessarily been spending more time with Sintikala. To be in her company meant also to be in the company of the ten pilots and fifteen or twenty carpenters, tanners, and other artisans involved in developing the Eagles, and most of their conversation was technical and businesslike; nonetheless, he thoroughly enjoyed working with her.

As a direct result, the days leading up to the Midwinter Feast also held the most nerve-racking event of Marcellinus's winter: his first solo Hawk flight.

Marcellinus stood at the top of the Master Mound. The weight of the Hawk wing felt like pig iron across his shoulders. People flew wearing just this? Even now, it was hard for him to believe. He felt that he was two steps away from diving straight into the earth.

And maybe he was.

Behind him stood Sintikala. "It's easy," she said with the note of casual disdain that was as close as she got to encouragement. "You did it before. Just the same now."

He had. As the winter had progressed, Marcellinus had begun at ten feet up the mound and then twenty, each time running downhill till the wing tugged him upward, kicking his heels impotently as he drifted down to skid on the snow at the mound's base.

And then he had run from thirty feet up and had remained airborne for a dozen quick heartbeats, keeping the frame of the wing as rigid as possible before the ground came up to meet him. Although he had been convinced that his heart might stall with fear throughout the flight.

That very same day, Sintikala had pushed him into running into space from the first plateau of the Master Mound, forty feet above the level of the Great Plaza. On this flight Marcellinus had attempted a slow turn to the right, had almost lost control of the Hawk wing, and had twisted his ankle landing at a crazy angle, going much faster than he should have been.

Before his nerve could fail, the relentless Sintikala had insisted he jump off the mound yet again, damaged ankle notwithstanding. He had learned how to bank to the right and even to the left before his next, much tamer landing.

And today she demanded that he take the big leap from the very top of the Master Mound.

"No more play," she said. "Be a man."

"I can't believe I ever *wanted* to do this," Marcellinus muttered.

"Don't think about it," she said helpfully.

A cold breeze flowed from the south. Marcellinus knew that the wind would help him rise and fly even as the frigid conditions would push him toward the ground and keep the flight short. He also knew that the chilly weather was helping to keep the audience minuscule; down at the foot of the mound Demothi and two other men of the Hawk clan eyed him, with Kimimela bundled up beside them in so many furs that she looked spherical and only a scattering of other curiosity seekers on their way to the latrine or the creek or the Big Warm House pausing in hopes of seeing the Wanageeska topple out of the sky.

About as few spectators as he could possibly hope for. Though whatever happened, the story would flow around the city like magic.

He really had no choice. Honor was at stake. And he would rather die than earn any more of Sintikala's scorn.

"All right," he said. "I'm going."

And he did.

Oddly, it was easier from higher up. He took a long run-up, wings bumping on his back. As soon as his feet left the plateau and the earth dropped vertiginously away, Marcellinus swung his legs back and managed to loop his left foot over the bar that held him up horizontally in the prone position.

He was flying the wing, not just hanging beneath it like a child. Presenting a flatter shape to the air around him made his slow banks right and left much smoother and more controlled. It was almost as if he knew what he was doing. And it was only when he pushed up the nose of the Hawk and his feet slid in the icy muck that covered the plaza, skating gracelessly to a halt back on terra firma, that Marcellinus realized he'd been cursing in a mixture of Latin and Cahokian for the entire flight.

His arms and legs quivered as if he had palsy. At the same time he experienced almost more terror than he had felt at the top of the mound, a disbelief at what he had just risked, and a strong sense of peace and rightness.

"Futete!" he said, ending his stream of invective.

Sintikala flitted down to land alongside him. Her Hawk wing rested on her shoulders as if it were part of her. She barely even skidded in the snow. "See?"

He had the exhilarated urge to hug her, but he knew it would not be well received. Besides, their wings might get entangled.

"Easy," said Marcellinus, the blood still thundering in his ears. "You were right."

"Again, then?"

"Not today." He breathed. "I don't think I'll make a habit of it."

"Ha. Tomorrow morning you will awaken and want to run out here and put on your wing."

"We'll see," he said.

CHAPTER 19

YEAR THREE, CROW MOON

Kangee's new baby was born early in the Crow Moon, with Nahimana, Chumanee, and Nashota in attendance. Men were both unhelpful and unlucky at such times, and it fell to Marcellinus to keep Takoda as far away as possible so he would not hear the screams and sobs of his young wife as she gave life to their second child. To do this Marcellinus had to enlist the aid of Mikasi and Hanska, since under no circumstances could the midwives tell Kangee that her husband was with Marcellinus. Kangee still despised the Roman with a passion, and never more so than during the erratic mood swings of her pregnancy.

Marcellinus's first thought was that they should take Takoda to the baths. The man was already sweating so much that it seemed like a good idea to freshen him up before he greeted a new infant. Too late, Marcellinus realized that this meant he would see Hanska as naked as Takoda. Outside close families, women and men did not normally use the same rooms at the baths, but nobody was about to tell Hanska what she could and couldn't do. By virtue of her skill in battle, she went everywhere a man did. He wondered if anyone would think he had set this up deliberately, and also realized he could never mention it to Tahtay or Kimimela.

For a simple soldier, Marcellinus was wryly amused to realize how complex his social interactions had become.

And so they sat, sweating in one of the caldarium rooms of the Big Warm House, with Hanska and Mikasi cheerfully insulting Takoda about his fertility and Marcellinus looking everywhere except at the voluptuous, muscular, tattooed, and very naked Hanska.

"I don't know how you do it, Takoda," Hanska was saying. "With a little pugio like yours? Most women like a fucking pilum. Take my Mikasi, here . . ."

Takoda cheerfully retorted in even worse taste, and Marcellinus flinched. He was no stranger to ribald humor, but it still knocked him off balance to hear such crassness from women. "So, Takoda. Changing the subject. I'm sure you've noticed that, uh, Kangee hates me."

"We all hate you," Hanska said cheerfully. "You work us too hard."

Marcellinus glared at her, exasperated, then looked away quickly. Mikasi prodded his wife. "Insubordination," he said carefully in Latin, a word Marcellinus had recently taught Mahkah in front of the whole cohort. It was news to Cahokian warriors that excessive familiarity with commanding officers was frowned upon. "Wanageeska does not like it. Remember?"

"Ah," Hanska said. "Sorry. Go on, sir. Kangee hates you?"

Marcellinus turned back to Takoda. "Is there something I can do? I would like to mend the injury between us. And the birth of a new child is sometimes a new beginning. Should I make a gift to her? Or something?"

Takoda was eyeing Hanska. She kicked his shins. "Look up, warrior. Answer the Wanageeska."

"Cahokians died," Takoda said. "Your Roman legion?"

"Yes, but the rest of you don't hate me." Hanska took in a breath to say something, but Marcellinus jabbed a warning finger in her direction without taking his eyes off Takoda, and she desisted.

Takoda shrugged. "Then, you were fighting for your tribe. Now you fight for ours. We adopt warriors from other tribes often."

"The Romans did not kill anyone Kangee knew? Brother, uncle, friend?"

"No."

Mikasi poured water over the hot stones, and more steam flooded the air. "You kill very few of us, really."

"You should tell Kangee that the Wanageeska saved your life at Woshakee," Hanska said to Takoda. "Make her grateful to him. See?"

"But I didn't save his life," Marcellinus objected.

Takoda considered it. "Do you know that you did not?"

"Of course I know!"

"No. If we had fought the Iroqua for Woshakee without you, it would have been a different battle. Maybe in that battle, I not come back."

"All warriors lie about battles anyway," said Hanska.

"Tell no lies," said Marcellinus. "Lies mend nothing. That's not the help I was looking for."

"Give her two more moons, sir," Takoda said. "She will get used to you."

"Ha," said Hanska.

Takoda had told him the same thing long ago. "So, nothing, then."

"She has dreams," said Takoda.

Hanska, suddenly mute, looked from Takoda to Marcellinus and back again.

"Dreams?" Mikasi asked.

Marcellinus's mouth twisted wryly. Cahokians set a lot of store by dreams.

"In her dreams there are more deaths, and it is you. You are there."

"Really?" said Marcellinus.

Takoda shrugged. "You cannot do anything about dreams. So, nothing."

"What kind of deaths?" Hanska asked.

"Battle deaths. More, I did not ask," said Takoda. "Better not to know, because then you think about it too much."

Marcellinus's dreams were full of death, too. But they were dreams of the past, not the future.

The silence had gone on too long. Damn this Cahokian superstition; these people were worse than Scythians. "And you have all had dreams that came true, I suppose."

"No," Mikasi and Takoda said.

"I wish more of mine did," Takoda added, his eyes straying again.

Mikasi laughed, and Hanska kicked Takoda again. "Stop it. Your wife is having a baby. Respect her." To Marcellinus she said, "None of my dreams, either. My sister's friend, though . . ."

"Well, there you are, then."

"Two more moons, Kangee will get over it, sir," said Takoda. "Maybe three."

"Wanageeska?"

Wrapped in a fur cloak, Marcellinus peered at the thawing ice of Cahokia Creek, then back toward the Master Mound and down at the ice again. Now he straightened. "Sisika."

"Call me Sintikala. What do you look at?"

"Distances," he said. "For two reasons. First, we should extend the palisade out this far."

She measured it with her eyes. The current palisade wall ran parallel to the creek, fifty feet behind them. Over it they could see the top of the Longhouse of the Thunderbirds. The sturdy new steel launching rail followed the line of the Master Mound up to its peak and jutted up into the air twenty feet beyond. "Why? We need a bigger longhouse now?"

"No, it's because if we're besieged, we need a source of water inside the fortifications."

"What?"

Marcellinus explained. In Europa, nobody would dream of building a fortification without a source of water *inside*. Yet even with Woshakee as a recent example, Sintikala was reluctant to believe that Cahokia could ever be besieged, guarded as it was with Thunderbirds and Hawks, Eagles and Sky Lanterns, as well as the increasingly competent Cahokian army.

"You might be right," he admitted. "But on principle . . ."

"But Gaius, if we are sieged, even if the palisade comes this far, the Iroqua will just shit in the creek."

Marcellinus frowned.

"And the borrow pits?"

"Ah." There, too, Sintikala was right. The Cahokian bottomlands were basically marshland for many months of the year. Even where they stood now the ground was mostly ice rather than snow. There were plenty of pits within Cahokia where they had dug the soil for their mounds, and the bottoms of those pits often flooded.

"And the second reason is a waterwheel," he said quickly, and explained how the flow of the creek water could be harnessed to provide the power to grind corn. "But mostly I need bellows for the bathhouse and steelworks, and the creek is too far away from them."

"Are you not cold?" she said.

He had to smile at that. "Freezing."

"I think you are not as clever as you think you are. Come on."

Giving it up, he followed her to the left around the palisade. Close by were the three mounds where she, Howahkan, and Kanuna lived. These were really intended to be clan chief houses, but neither Ojinjintka nor the head of the Deer clan, whose name Marcellinus didn't recall, could manage the steps anymore and had moved into town with their families, leaving the mound houses to the more sprightly of the elders.

"I need to show you something," said Sintikala. "Up there."

At the top of her platform mound, smoke drifted out of the smoke hole of her house. Marcellinus hesitated.

"And I have tea of goldenrod. Better than the clover stuff that Nahimana makes."

"I make my own tea now," he said. "Bearberry, dewberry, sassafras."

"Then no tea." She started up the cedar steps, careful of the ice.

Marcellinus stayed at the mound's foot, uncertain. "In your house?"

"Yes, in my house."

"Oh." His mind raced.

"I need to show you all of the land," she said unexpectedly. "And I will not bring it out to you."

"The land?"

"Yes. Great Sun Man told me to show you, and so I will. So, enough talk. Come up now. I have spoken."

As with Great Sun Man's house and all the other houses of clan chiefs or elders on platform mounds, Sintikala's house was surrounded by a low palisade with a gate. Passing inside it felt like entering enemy territory.

Sintikala had no garden. She did not have the time or the need to tend her own corn. Instead, the area inside the palisade held an outdoor fire pit, long unused in the dead of winter; a pile of discarded Hawk struts, pieces of wing material, cords, and straps; and, to his surprise, a low kiln.

He pointed. "What's that for?"

"Pots," she said. "What? Yes, I make pots."

Kicking off her boots, she walked into her house. Marcellinus followed.

The other homes Marcellinus had been in were those of common folk: Nahimana, Akecheta, Mahkah. All those homes had been almost as sparsely furnished as his own. Sintikala's hut was sumptuous by comparison. Its inner walls were lined with shelves, and each shelf bore black and red pots and jars, and baskets decorated in a riot of colors. Against one wall was a swath of cotton fabric and a roll of what looked like deerskin, perhaps wing material. Clothes—everyday tunics, furs, tanned leather flying clothes, and bright ceremonial garb—lined the wall to his right. On her table was another pot, still only half made, with the angular representation of a falcon head and wings etched into it. Beside that was a pile of bark inscribed in charcoal with Kimi's round finger-talk, giving Marcellinus the sudden conviction that Kimimela was teaching it to her mother.

Sintikala's bed was high off the ground, almost head-high to Marcellinus, with a ladder she could use to ascend to it. The blankets were red, the colors and designs of the western folk of the plains.

She knelt in the center of the room and coaxed the fire in the hearth back into life. As the wood and dried corncobs caught, she placed a pot of water over it on a triangular metal stand.

That, at least, he recognized. "My steelworks is good for something, then."

"Yes," she said. "Good for throwing engines and this, uh, fire stand. Not good for Catanwakuwa."

"We have mastered the wire making now. Soon we will strengthen the wings with single thin strands. And wait till you see what I have planned for the Wakinyan."

"No tea?"

It smelled good. "Yes. I want tea. Thank you."

She threw off her fur. Beneath it she wore a short deerskin tunic. Her hair was wet, and she wiped it with a blanket, leaving it endearingly messy.

Marcellinus tried to concentrate. "And so, the land?"

"Soon," she said. "Tea."

Heat filled the room as the fire took off, blazing against the bottom of the water bowl. Marcellinus took off his own furs, aware of how ragged his tunic and Roman leggings were. Busy with casting metal, he had not bathed for two days. It was a good thing the goldenrod tea was so fragrant.

"Many times you have asked about the People of the Hand, and Etowah, many other things about the tribes here in the land. Great Sun Man has often told you to ask me about it. You have not. Why?"

"I don't know," he said.

Sintikala poured tea into wooden beakers, blew on her fingers again, and held them up to the fire. "You need to know things, Gaius. You are no good to Cahokia if you will not learn as well as teach."

"I have learned a lot," he said. "But the truth is that you are often not easy to talk to."

"You are not, either. But still I try. For Cahokia and my daughter."

"Then I will try harder."

She sat by the fire at his feet. For any other woman it would have seemed a subservient position. But Sintikala was sufficiently powerful and unselfconscious that he doubted that it even occurred to her.

She held out a beaker of tea. He took it and sat. "Sisika? I think you are the one person here who has always told me the truth, all the time. Even when it was painful or uncomfortable."

She nodded as if that were obvious. "Great Sun Man knows much and keeps many secrets, as he must. Your warriors and the children want to be admired."

He cleared his throat. "The tea is very good."

"But not as good as your tea?"

He smiled. "Perhaps not."

She shrugged.

"So," he said. "What do I need to know?"

She got to her feet and half grinned. Marcellinus had no idea what to expect, but for some reason he found himself grinning, too. "You are ready?"

"Yes. Show me the land."

And she did.

It was the roll of what he had taken for wing material, but it had been cured and scraped and stretched to almost parchmentlike thinness, and inscribed on it was the outline of a great continent.

Marcellinus was looking at a giant ornate map with the coastline, mountains, lakes, and rivers of Nova Hesperia etched in black ink. "Holy Jove . . . !"

She smiled, happy at his awe.

"Charcoal and bark!" he said to her accusingly. "I have been teaching finger-talk with charcoal and bark, and here you have this?"

Sintikala pointed to the fabric. "This is the ink we use for war tattoos, on skin that is thin like a wing. It is not hard to make. But not so easy that we can give it to children to learn finger-talk."

He understood, of course, but his eyes were already roving the map, devouring the detail. Here was the Mizipi, there the Oyo, and on the other side was the larger tributary of the Wemissori, a great river in itself that drained into the Mizipi after its meandering journey through the western grasslands. Towns and villages were marked with large and small circles, labeled with small pictures, as Sintikala was only now apparently learning to write.

It was not as fine as the maps of Europa and Asia he had seen, but to a man living in the middle of a continent he could scarcely visualize, it seemed miraculous. "How?"

"Many flights. Many traders I have spoken to. I have added much, but it was my father who began it. Others help, chiefs and warriors who have gone far and returned. Kanuna. Ojinjintka."

"This is much better than the shapes you made in the mud."

"Is it?" she said, mocking him.

All right. "Where are the nearest Iroqua? Where is the nearest threat?"

"Here is Chesapica, and all down here by the big water is where the Powhatan live. More speakers of Algon-Quian live far up in the northeast, beyond the Iroqua. But all this, across here . . . this is all Iroqua."

In fact, the area she gestured over was smaller than Marcellinus had supposed. To the north and east of Cahokia were a series of five, maybe six huge lakes. The Iroqua land formed a swath beneath all but the westernmost of them and fell almost entirely above an invisible line that joined Chesapica with Cahokia, the line that marked the trek of the Romans. "But we found Iroqua all along here, too," he objected, gesturing at this middle area.

"Yes, many peoples who speak Iroqua words, peoples related like family to the Iroqua. And below the line are the lands of the Cherokee, and the Delaware and Shawnee, friends to the Iroqua. But the five tribes of the real Iroqua, the Seneca, Caiuga, Onondaga, Onida, and Mohawk who attack us often, they are here in a line in the hills below the Great Lakes."

"And above the lakes?"

"The Hurons. Another people."

He judged distances. "Could we ally with the Hurons against the Iroqua?"

Sintikala shook her head. "They are not Iroqua, but again they speak the same Iroqua tongue. They do not build mounds. They band with the Iroqua and can be their strongest fighters."

"And north of the Huron lands?"

Above the lakes the map had few markings, but Sintikala pointed anyway. "Many Cree here, and then Ojibwa and Cheyenne. Other tribes who like to be cold all the time."

Marcellinus was still awed that they could be dismissing areas the size of whole provinces in Europa in a few sentences. He turned his attention southward again. "Where is Shappa Ta'atan?"

The blob she indicated was halfway between Cahokia and the Market of the Mud, as Great Sun Man had told him. "And Etowah?"

Etowah was farther east of the Mizipi than he would have guessed. "And the People of the Hand?"

Many times farther away to the southwest. "Why are they called by that name? The People of the Hand?"

"Because of the signs they paint on rocks. They are a noble people. They do not build mounds but houses of stone, like you build the Big Warm House. But much bigger even. With, on top . . ." She gestured, hand on hand. "Layers."

"Several floors? Like a hut on top of a hut on top of a hut?"

"Yes."

Tenements. Houses with many floors. Maybe the People of the Hand had independently invented brick. "They are a long way away."

"It is very hot there, sandy and dry. It does not rain, and plants do not grow well."

"Desert," Marcellinus said. "Do they have camels? Large beasts that men can ride, tan beasts with humps?"

"Ride? No. But above it, far up here west of Cahokia, is the big grass where the thousand-thousand buffalo are, and the warriors of the plains. Those are large beasts, but no one can ride one."

"And beyond?" A whole area farther to the west was inscribed onto the skin with a scalloped pattern similar to the markings that indicated Appalachia. "Mountains, there?"

"Yes, the big mountains I have not been to."

"And the People of the Sun? Where are they?"

"Under the floor," she said.

"What?"

She pointed below the bottom edge of the map. "No one has been so far. But their traders come to the Market of the Mud, here, where the Mizipi comes to the big salt water. The People of the Sun are down farther, across that water. They say their mounds are of stone and that they pull men's hearts out of their chests to give to their gods."

Inscribed on this deerskin was a continent equal in size to the entire Roman Imperium. Marcellinus felt very small and at the same time hugely responsible. "What a land," he said in Latin. "What a prize."

"Gaius?"

With an effort, he turned his attention back to the matter at hand. He squinted at the map more closely. "Just a moment. These are not streams, I think." He was pointing at a series of thin lines traced across all the lands east of Cahokia, etched so fine that he had not heeded them earlier. "Streams do not cross and recross like this."

"Those are trails. Paths across the land."

One of the longest led from Cahokia almost to Chesapica; another, deep into the south. And one led straight from Cahokia northeast to the lakes and beyond. "Trails a thousand miles long? No."

"No," she said caustically. "Of course, I am wrong. Every trader makes a new path every time he travels. Every chief who visits another tribe clears his own road. Every warrior makes a new warpath. Why not?"

"Ah."

"They are small paths, but long. Such paths that a Roman might not even notice."

Marcellinus was not encouraged to learn about a system of trails through the wilderness. Again he looked up at the northeast part of the map. "The Haudenosaunee are too near. We must push them back."

"Push?" She laughed.

"Well. Show me again all the mound-builder lands. Point to all the big towns."

She did so: broad swaths of land along the Mizipi and Oyo.

"And the Iroqua, again. The Haudenosaunee League and those tribes that treaty with them."

"I am making this simple, you understand? There are very many tribes, hundreds. Very many ways of making talk. Even the Iroqua have many languages, but closer to each other than to ours. The Algon-Quian are many people. Caddo and Muskogee, then People of the Hand, perhaps also many. And as for the peoples on the Plains . . ."

It was almost a dance, the way her hands moved over the map. Marcellinus tried not to be distracted by her. "Yes, all right. So . . ."

He wondered whether to put into words what he was thinking. Would she be threatened by the idea?

"Speak," she said.

"Sintikala, from this map? The Iroqua see *us* as the big danger."

She shook her head.

"Yes. Cahokia, mound builders, cities that ally with you are all the way down the Mizipi, along the Oyo. And once the Iroqua had lands along the Oyo, too, that they have no longer? And so now the true Haudenosaunee lands are just these, and because of me, and Roman steel . . ." It all made much more sense to him now. Because of Marcellinus, the Iroqua felt under even more threat.

"Still, they kill us," she said. "If they did not, what would we do? Stick your Roman swords into them and force them to build mounds in their villages? No. We would leave them in peace, as they should have left us."

He looked at the map again, uncertain. But Sintikala was right. Marcellinus was still thinking in Roman terms, as if the Cahokians had an Imperium and ruled over all their land. They did not. Their influence was subtle, based solely on language and culture. Great Sun Man won the compliance of nearby villages and towns by providing free hoes and adzes, but his direct influence barely extended beyond Ocatan.

Besides, it hardly mattered. Marcellinus was in a city under attack, and all his friends lived in that city. What the Iroqua thought was irrelevant. They were a brutal people, and the aggression flowed in one direction: from the Iroqua lands toward the Cahokian.

"This area, all of this to the northeast . . . we need a better map. Bigger, so we can see finer details of where the Iroqua live. And we will mark it with words, in writing, so we do not have to remember all the names." He glanced at her sideways. "Or maybe you have a bigger map already?"

"No. In my head I know more of what is there and the high places I can use to get into the air if I come down, but not marked down on a skin. More tea?"

Marcellinus laughed. In the shadow of the huge map, it was a ridiculously domestic question.

But he needed to study the map further. There were levels of detail in it, the smaller features of towns and rivers, that he should try to commit to memory. He still had many more questions.

"Yes, thank you," he said, and held out his wooden cup. "Really, it is very good tea."

PART 3

IROQUA

Chapter 20

Year Three, Flower Moon

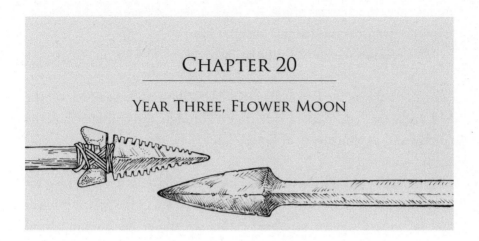

When the massed tribes of the Haudenosaunee fell upon Cahokia and ravaged it, they came by land and water, and with them they brought fire. They came from outside Cahokia and from deep within. And it began long before dawn.

The previous day was midsummer, and Cahokia celebrated long into the night. Many farmers and families had flocked into Cahokia over the past days, bearing their gifts of grain and meat. With their help this was again a year of plenty, with enough food for all. The mound-builder city felt strong and proud.

The granaries exploded in the middle of the night, depleted from the celebration but still full enough to burn. The city came alive to find death in its midst; skulking assassins were at work. In with the villagers had come members of the Mohawk and Caiuga, Seneca and Onida and Onondaga, their distinctive tattoos covered under tunics and animal skins or otherwise disguised, and they had begun to break necks and slit throats long before the incendiaries claimed the first houses of corn. Once the granaries were aflame, armed bands of Iroqua sped through the streets, sparing no Cahokian they came across.

The effrontery of their assault worked in their favor. Never had central Cahokia experienced such an attack: massed warriors by night, under cover of a festival of joy. Racing between the houses, the Haudenosaunee warriors snuffed out life after life.

This was not war. It was murder by night.

Startled awake by the first explosions, Marcellinus rolled and fell off the bed onto the hard-packed dirt floor. Through the chimney hole he could see the orange flare of liquid flame. The screaming began a moment later.

Still feeling the effects of Cahokian beer, Marcellinus scrambled for his tunic, pulled it on, and rolled up onto his feet. His head throbbed, and he winced. As he stumbled across the room, his questing hand found his shrine. He knocked his lares to the floor but grasped the hilt of his gladius.

Trying hard to shake off his befuddlement, Marcellinus swore he would never drink again. Never. Never.

A babble of voices swelled outside the hut like a wave. More screaming, more shouting. There was fighting close by. And for street fighting he would need his pugio. He searched again and found it on the floor under the shrine.

Then Marcellinus dived out of the hut into Cahokian streets already filled with chaos.

A plume of flame reached into the sky from the eastern granary. Aside from that the night was dark, the earlier bonfire and lamps now quenched. Half blind, Marcellinus backed up against the wall of his house and looked away from the flames. Black forms raced between the houses carrying axes and clubs, many of them tall with headdresses. From just thirty feet away came a bellow of agony.

No doubt remained. The streets of the city were swarming with Iroqua.

Marcellinus started forward and tripped over a woman's body. Her throat cut, she had been thrown aside against the wall of the house.

His nose prickled with the twin stenches of liquid flame and burning flesh. His skin crawled.

Just around the next corner a brave crouched over the groveling form of a man. His knife glinted red in the reflected flame light. Marcellinus was on the Iroqua in a moment, hamstringing him with a slash of his gladius and plunging the pugio down into his shoulder, inside the collarbone. The dagger was not long enough to reach the man's heart, but it didn't matter; a third stroke with the gladius severed the Iroqua's windpipe, and he was dead.

Marcellinus ran on, leaving the injured Cahokian where he lay. No time to deal with the wounded. Enemies were running wild, bringing death to the streets of his city. His blood boiled. He needed to kill again.

He did not have to wait long.

Even in the darkness it was easy to tell the Iroqua from the Cahokians. The Cahokians were the ones who staggered out of their huts half naked, some with weapons in hand, gaping foolishly at the clamor and carnage. The Iroqua were the ruthless figures who loped through the streets like deer, methodically clubbing men and women to the ground.

Marcellinus killed four more and then got turned around. He had run out into the thoroughfare to face the influx of Iroqua warriors only to find them bearing down on him from behind. His groggy assumption that the Iroqua were running *into* Cahokia almost got him hacked down with an ax where he stood.

In fact, the enemy was now racing *out* of the city, away from the Master Mound. And there were scores of them, far too many to fight and kill.

Hawk wings were aloft now, fireflies that danced in the skies and shot flaming arrows.

Marcellinus spun, slashing at the legs of an Onondaga who swerved to swing a chert-studded club at his head. He ducked in between houses and ran around to throw himself into the fray again, coming at an enemy war party from the side. Five more warriors shouting "Cahokia!" joined him.

With the Iroqua war band down and screaming, Marcellinus left the Cahokians to saw through the Iroqua scalps and jogged on into the plaza. The Great Mound stood silhouetted against the stars, light at its peak. For a moment he thought the Longhouse of the Wings was aflame, but it was merely lit brightly with torches.

A looming figure ululated and swung at him. Ducking under the ax, Marcellinus slammed his shoulder into the Iroqua's chest and thrust upward into the man's abdomen with his sword.

A Catanwakuwa roared low over their heads, and a nearby hut went up in flames. Marcellinus turned his head from the light, saw Onida tattoos on the shoulder of a nearby warrior, and plunged his pugio into him.

A hundred feet away another house erupted, its thatch burning a vivid orange. Cahokian Hawk wings were deliberately setting fire to their own houses. Marcellinus understood. It was imperative to bring light to this confused battle scene as quickly as possible.

Other Catanwakuwa dipped. Arrows flew, Iroqua fell. Marcellinus whirled right and left. Where should he go? Where was the biggest threat? Where was Great Sun Man? Was anyone taking charge of this mess?

Yes. Ranks of Cahokian warriors lined up in front of the gate to the Great Mound, probably under Wahchintonka's command. They were not fighting but advancing steadily, arrows at the ready in case a greater Iroqua force burst into the plaza. Marcellinus did not expect that to happen—the enemy tide was flowing the other way, and most of the Iroqua were gone from the plaza—but guarding the mound and the longhouses was the right thing to do.

In central Cahokia four of the new brick granaries were aflame, gouts of fire shooting up into the sky from their roofs. To his left he saw a distant plume that could have been the granary that served western Cahokia. But across the plaza and off to the east was a corn house that still looked dark. Safeguarding it seemed imperative; Iroqua warriors could still be sneaking around, and the Cahokian corn reserve was obviously one of their principal targets.

Marcellinus ran, still shouting "Cahokia!" Distinctive though he was, he wanted no one to doubt his allegiance in the flickering light.

He was not the first to think of the granary. A squad of fifteen braves from the First Cahokian stood outside it, shoulder to shoulder, pila at the ready. But by the time he saw them Marcellinus was already distracted.

On top of its platform mound, Sintikala's house was ablaze.

It was the heavy conflagration of liquid flame, not the ordinary oil flames with which other houses of the town had been ignited by the Cahokians themselves. Marcellinus's heart turned over. He hurled himself forward.

It all made terrifying sense. A night attack. A stealthy assault on the Master Mound, though repulsed by the bands of warriors Marcellinus and Great Sun Man had ensured would guard it night and day. The granaries also targets, some now alight. Had the Iroqua also marked out certain houses of key clan chiefs and elders for attack? Or was it coincidence?

He pounded up the mound, but intense heat drove him back. The blazing walls of Sintikala's house collapsed inward, and Marcellinus skidded on the slope and fell forward onto his hands. His gladius slid on the grass, and he snatched it up again and spun as if he expected to find an Iroqua at his back.

No one was there. But if Sintikala had been in that house when the liquid flame had hit it, she was already dead.

And earlier that evening Kimimela had been with her mother. Panic bubbled up into his throat.

Two Iroqua, Onida by their markings, ran toward him. Berserker fury seized Marcellinus. Howling "Roma!" he stormed down the slope and met them head on, slicing the men into bloody wreckage. He stood over their bodies, panting.

A Catanwakuwa looped past him, a hundred feet up. "Gaius! Go to the steelworks!"

It was a woman's voice. Marcellinus saw the flutter of ribbons as Sintikala's Hawk wing continued on, lurching upward into the sky as it passed over her burning house.

"Kimimela!" he screamed up at her. "Where's Kimi?"

"Longhouse! Safe!" Sintikala's voice drifted back to him.

On the mound, then. Indeed, the safest place in Cahokia.

"Gods!" he shouted, and viciously slashed at the already dead Onida corpses at his feet. Adrenaline still overwhelmed him.

"The steelworks," he said, turning.

If he'd thought of it at all, Marcellinus had assumed that the broad glow to the east was the coming of the dawn.

Apparently not.

It would be a long run to the steelworks, out in the darkness away from the city, and perhaps foolhardy to attempt it alone. Marcellinus took a few steps toward the eerie glow, considering it, then saw another house aflame close by him.

It was a simple house no different from those around it except that it was burning and the adjacent houses were not. And it was the house of the chief of the Deer clan, whereas the others were houses of ordinary Deer clan families, brothers and wives and daughters and uncles: good people, mostly pot makers.

"Anapetu," he said, and turned and ran in the other direction.

Not coincidence, then. Sintikala's house was on a platform mound, which indicated rank. But if Iroqua had also burned the house of the Deer clan chief, they definitely knew which houses belonged to leading Cahokians.

A club flew out of the darkness and smacked squarely into his right shoulder. He stumbled and fell, but even as he hit the ground and rolled, the Caiuga who had cast it leaped upon him and kicked him in the head. Marcellinus's sword flipped up into the air, and he let go of it, continuing to roll.

The Caiuga slipped and turned it into a jump. He kicked at Marcellinus's chest just as Marcellinus switched hands with the pugio and drove it upward. Its blade sliced skin, but the gash was only superficial. The warrior leaped past and, regaining his footing, spun to face Marcellinus again.

A stout Cahokian barreled around the corner, spear in hand. Seeing the Caiuga with ax raised, the man bellowed and swung a wild blow at the enemy brave.

The Cahokian was no fighter; a spear was a thrusting weapon, and a fumbled quarterstaff strike could hardly be effective against an Iroqua warrior, but the distraction gave Marcellinus the moments he needed. Gasping, he seized the Iroqua club that lay beside him. Club met ax, and Marcellinus and the Cahokian forced the Caiuga back against the wall of a house. Seconds later the enemy was on his knees with a shattered skull and a deep pugio gash in his gut, and the Cahokian was sawing at the Caiuga's scalp with an unholy glee.

Marcellinus snatched up his gladius and ran on, leaving the man to his spoils.

By the time the sun rose two hours later, a purposeful, bloody-minded calm had descended over the mounds and houses of Cahokia.

By now the Iroqua were gone except for those killed in battle. Bodies littered the streets, both Iroqua and Cahokian, but moving them to charnel pits would have to wait.

It turned out that the Haudenosaunee attack on the steelworks had been rushed or halfhearted; their liquid flame had scorched the outer brick, but the building still stood. The brickworks, however, was a steaming ruin. The entire place would have to be razed and rebuilt.

The Big Warm Houses were intact. The Iroqua had known they were not a strategic target.

On the first plateau of the Great Mound, Marcellinus met with Great Sun Man and the other surviving chiefs and elders in a council of war. Below them whole neighborhoods still smoldered, leaking smoke into the sky. Sintikala was aloft with others of the Hawk clan watching for further attacks, and from a distance Marcellinus had glimpsed the lithe figure of Chumanee hurrying through the plaza with her fellow healers to patch up the Cahokian wounded.

The mood was urgent, and conversation flowed quickly; today there was none of the leisurely discussion of the sweat lodge. The pace was so fast that Marcellinus was glad that Tahtay and Enopay were there to help him understand what was being said.

Three chiefs were dead, those of the Beaver, Wolf, and Deer clans, their houses ignited almost simultaneously with liquid flame. Anapetu had been saved from her own burning house by her son long before Marcellinus had arrived. And Sintikala's house also had been torched, of course, though she had not been in it at the time. Marcellinus shied away from guessing where she might have been. That was not his concern. He was just happy that she and Kimimela were still alive.

"So the Iroqua knew where they all lived," he said.

He had interrupted Great Sun Man. Everyone glared except the war chief himself, who nodded darkly.

"Which means they had spies in the city."

Even now he had to rely on Tahtay to translate the idea of spies, but once the rest of the chiefs understood, they looked angry and frightened, and Marcellinus didn't have the heart to say *I told you so*.

"We invited farmers," Enopay said. "People from far. All were welcome if they brought food."

Enopay's hand rested on top of his head as if he were trying to stop himself from exploding. From the haunted look in his eyes, Marcellinus knew the boy blamed himself.

A ribboned Hawk flew low over the mound top, banked steeply, and swooped down to a running landing beside the group. Sintikala shucked her wings and strode into their midst, her expression bleak. "More Iroqua warriors come."

"What? Where?" Great Sun Man looked out across the plaza, east toward the bluffs, west to the dull gray shadow of the Mizipi.

Sintikala pointed twice, jabbing her finger toward the southeast and southwest. "Armies from there and there. I have signaled the Wakinyan to make ready."

"*Two* Iroqua armies?"

Marcellinus frowned. "Nothing from the north? How do they come from the southwest? Along the river?"

"The creek and the palisade are to the north," Matoshka said impatiently. "Hard to cross and overlooked from this mound. And beyond the creek is the Crescent Lake and the scar."

Great Sun Man moved closer to Sintikala. The two of them had a hurried interchange, their muttered words whipped away by the breeze. Marcellinus glanced around impatiently. Tahtay fidgeted by his side, exuding waves of restless energy. Anapetu raised her hand and patted the air, mutely urging them to be calm.

Great Sun Man turned. "Wanageeska, hear me. The First Cahokian marches south to the edge of the city. You will hold the line there, defend the city, kill Iroqua. Take your war cart in case we need you back quickly. Wahchintonka, hear me. You will defend the Great Mound with the warriors who defended it last night and a hundred more. The Iroqua must not take the Great Mound. You will die before you allow it. Ojinjintka, make the Wakinyan ready to fly. The rest of you, hear me. Gather all the warriors and the strong men and women who can fight and take them to western Cahokia. Many Wolf Warriors are already there. Guard the plazas, guard the mounds, and look to the riverbank, for it is by water that the Iroqua come. We must go."

Marcellinus raised his hand. This was not much of a military briefing, and he needed to say so. "The First Cahokian is but a small number of warriors. How many Iroqua come from the southeast? What if the Iroqua send war parties to flank us?"

Great Sun Man shrugged. "Do not let them."

"The other Iroqua force comes by river? In canoes?"

"Canoes on water and more warriors on land."

"Gaius Wanageeska," Anapetu said.

He ignored her. "How long till the Iroqua armies arrive?"

"Soon." Sintikala pointed at the sky to indicate where the sun would be.

They had an hour or less. "What of the throwing engines? Where should we send them?"

"Four to the river," Sintikala said crisply. "Set them on the Mound of the Flowers or mounds farther downstream if there is time for us to set up a line there. The other four throwing engines stay here on the Great Mound. But the throwing engine that is also the Catanwakuwa launcher: send that one to the river, first and fastest."

Marcellinus blinked and looked at Great Sun Man. "As she says," the war chief said impatiently.

"Yes, sir. Where will you be?"

The war chief pointed upward. "There is wild talk about the Iroqua. I must see for myself, from the air. And then I will go to lead the warriors in western Cahokia."

"Really?" Marcellinus asked skeptically. Sintikala's intelligence could hardly be wild talk. "But in that case—"

Sintikala cut him off. "Gaius. You have your task. Begin it."

"We have spoken," Great Sun Man said.

At their curt tones of command Marcellinus automatically saluted, Roman-style. The Cahokians flinched. "I understand," he said to clarify. "I will begin."

Sintikala and Great Sun Man sprinted along the plateau. They turned the corner and were gone.

Marcellinus again surveyed the city and the lands beyond. He still saw no signs of Iroqua, but his sense of foreboding grew.

The other Cahokian chiefs had not moved either, and Marcellinus realized they were looking to him. They, too, were discomfited by what they had heard from Great Sun Man.

And with such hazy orders, perhaps there was no obligation for Marcellinus to do exactly as he was told.

Marcellinus looked to Anapetu. Now she nodded.

He took a deep breath. "Elders, chiefs, hear me. We already know the trickery and deceit of the Iroqua, and perhaps even Sintikala does not clearly see all there is to be seen. Great Sun Man is wise, but Iroqua warriors from the southeast and southwest in plain sight may distract us from yet more warriors coming in stealth from the east. Such a force could cut off the First Cahokian from the city. Our warriors must not be stretched too thinly. We must stand together. Most of you must go to western Cahokia. But some must help us to establish a battle line across the south *and* east of the city. We must not lose Cahokia."

The chiefs eyed one another as Tahtay crisply clarified some of Marcellinus's more difficult phrases. Several chiefs nodded. Others did not.

"This is not the same as what Great Sun Man said," Howahkan said.

"Of course it is. Great Sun Man told me that I lead the First Cahokian and that I must not let our forces be flanked."

"But we are not First Cahokian, and nor are our warriors," said Kanuna.

Marcellinus eyed him steadily. "Would you like to be?"

Under Akecheta's bellowed commands, the First Cahokian was already falling in as one of the prototype Eagle craft roared off the Great Mound.

Marcellinus glanced up, and his heart leaped into his mouth as the triangular wing unfurled above him. Beneath it hung Sintikala and another woman pilot of her clan, side by side in the lead positions . . . and hanging prone in the third harness, Great Sun Man. Marcellinus had never seen the Cahokian war chief in the air before, had not even known Great Sun Man was a pilot. And perhaps he was not, because the Eagle craft wobbled precariously and slewed sideways in the sky before recovering and banking toward the Mizipi.

Marcellinus shook his head. How terrible would it be if one of his own contributions to Cahokian flight got the Great City's most important chiefs killed just before a critical battle?

No time to worry about it. He had a cohort to lead.

Marcellinus called out quick instructions, and they were off and marching; the central core of his First Cahokian, the men who had trained with him for nearly two years, were leading a much larger and more amorphous group of warriors who now made up his impromptu auxiliary. As they passed, other Cahokian men and women donned armor of wood or steel and either joined them or hurried west to the other battle line in no kind of order. The lack of discipline bothered Marcellinus to distraction: in a crisis everyone should know where he was going and with whom, and who was in charge. With the exception of the four hundred trained warriors who marched in step with him toward the south, the Cahokians were still a rabble, and he had seen just hours earlier that the Iroqua now understood the virtues of careful organization.

Two Hawk wings sprinted by above them, heading south. This morning the skies were almost as busy as the land.

Marcellinus was still thinking it through. A frontal assault, by daylight? Surely the Iroqua knew better than that. Cahokia's defenses were strong, and its Wakinyan were deadly to a large force. So the Iroqua must be taking these things into account. They must have a plan.

At the very least, Marcellinus should expect the Iroqua not to bunch up into ranks as his own First Cahokian would, but remain diffuse. Small nimble groups of warriors with the advantage of mobility to skip and dodge away from the paths of the Thunderbirds to limit their losses. The Wakinyan might not prove decisive in this battle, but their presence would certainly shape the enemy's tactics.

Behind him, by the smoldering brickworks, a Sky Lantern leaped up with two braves clinging precariously to the shallow wooden frame that swayed beneath it. Close to their heads was the deeper framework that carried the fire jar. Even as the lantern rocked at the end of the stout cable that kept it tethered to the ground, one of the braves spared a hand to feed the flames.

Marcellinus shook his head. The risks young Cahokian men would take in search of honor still amazed him.

The lantern continued to rise as the men on the ground paid out the cable from the winch. The wind urged the lantern eastward, pulling the cable into a long draped arc. Well out of earshot at that altitude, its pilots signaled to the men on the ground by using long paddles made of matting.

Marcellinus didn't want to know what the view might be like from up there, out of range of an arrow from the ground, but he hoped the braves had eyes like hawks. Also, he hoped that none of the real Hawk wings flew into the cable. Ribbons had been attached to the cable at intervals to make it more visible, but the Catanwakuwa flew at high speed and their pilots could not look everywhere at once.

A Hawk flew over him, several hundred feet up. From the dexterity of the flight and the compact, powerful body of the pilot Marcellinus knew it was Demothi, Sintikala's second in command. The Hawk swung left, waggled its wings, and then banked back toward Cahokia.

"The Iroqua are to our southeast," Marcellinus called. "Akecheta! Turn them farther left! Stay in formation."

They passed the marks on the ground that indicated where the new palisade would eventually stand. Still being built, the palisade currently protected only the northern and eastern sides of the central city precinct. Marcellinus smiled without humor: too little, too late.

And there were the Iroqua, boiling across the floodplain, thousands of them spread over ten acres or more. As expected, the Haudenosaunee warriors had no formation. Their numbers sent a dark war thrill down Marcellinus's spine.

From the west came the dull thud of an explosion. A hot breeze swept through the city. Far beyond the houses to his right, probably by the Mizipi, a Thunderbird had dropped a load of liquid flame.

This was only one of the two battlefronts. Whoever prevailed today, the Cahokians would need a huge new burial mound to honor their dead.

He looked back, but Demothi had already relayed his message. Half a mile behind him another Thunderbird soared upward, heading their way.

"Halt!" Marcellinus cried, and "Halt!" the message went out through Akecheta to the First Cahokian and via the signalmen to the farthest reaches of the auxiliaries. No sense in engaging the enemy before the Wakinyan had a chance to wreak havoc here as well. He would hold and let the Iroqua come to him.

"First rank, prepare arrows! Third rank, set pila!"

The Cahokians readied for battle in three deep rows, the front rank kneeling with bows in hand and arrows nocked while the line behind stood ready to step past and take its turn at the front. The third rank took several steps back and set pila in open order, each man three feet from the men to his left and right. Their pila were pointed safely at the sky; once the Iroqua warriors approached to within melee distance, the first two ranks of archers would duck back through the third rank and the pila would be lowered.

Marcellinus almost hoped the Wakinyan and the arrows left enough Iroqua alive to fight at close quarters. His bloody soul would sing to see

Mohawks and Onida and Seneca hurling themselves onto the massed spears of the Cahokians.

On the faces of his men he saw the same determination. If the Haudenosaunee night attack had been intended to shatter the Cahokian resolve, it had failed utterly. His warriors boiled with energy. He had never seen an army more primed to maim and slaughter.

"Steady!" he called, walking behind the ranks. At his heels three braves wheeled his war cart, really a chariot pulled by men. He wished he could order them away; the wheeled conveyance seemed ignoble to him. It smacked of cowardice to have a vehicle ready to whisk him away from the front. But this had been one of Great Sun Man's few direct orders, and there was nothing Marcellinus could do about it.

The Wakinyan flew over their right flank and banked for its strafing run across the Iroqua line. An invisible hand squeezed Marcellinus's heart. If he lived to a hundred winters, the traumatic memories would never fade.

The Thunderbird opened up. In their attack on the Romans, the birds had released the liquid flame in large torrents designed to maximize the damage to his tightly packed legion. Here, the fire came out in a steady, broad spray over a wide area.

It was a rolling tide of agony. The Iroqua were so widely spread that only two warriors of every five were doused with the incendiary. Nonetheless, the front of the wave was easy to see. Iroqua fell screaming, and not in the clean drop of men struck by arrows or spears but an untidy flail. Panic-stricken, they tried to wipe the burning oil away, but just as with the 33rd Hesperian, their efforts only spread the incendiary over larger areas of their skin. The Iroqua thrashed like crazy men, and the Wakinyan flew on, still showering horror upon them.

Their fellow Iroqua braves came on, swerving around the fallen. Their blood-chilling battle cries never wavered.

Marcellinus could see the faces of the front-running Iroqua braves now, their eyes wide in fury. His own men shuffled their feet, straining at the leash as they waited for the order. But his First Cahokian would not expend their energy in running across a field. They would stand firm and not be winded, and they would slay their enemies with precision and icy rigor.

"First Cahokian, prepare arms!"

His front rank of archers raised their bows, pulled back the bowstrings.

"First Cahokian, fire!"

A black cloud of arrows hurtled across the narrow space that separated the Cahokians from the howling mob of Iroqua.

"Fire!" came Akecheta's distant call from much farther down the battle line. A second wave of arrows sped across the field.

Marcellinus stepped back a dozen paces. Despite his almost overwhelming urge to kill Iroqua, the melee that was about to break was not for him. In his last major battle it had been different; in fighting with the Romans against Cahokia, his forces had been overwhelmed. Here he must keep a clear head and direct the battle as a commander should in the hope that at least some of his orders might be obeyed.

Half a mile away in the flanks of his army, unrestrained by the cool discipline of the First Cahokian, the auxiliaries were rushing forward to meet the Iroqua charge. Hand-to-hand fighting had begun there, and the dust that they kicked up made it hard to see past them. But in the murk beyond the Cahokian line Marcellinus was sure he could see the shadowy forms of more Iroqua war parties moving eastward.

The First Cahokian would be flanked after all, but whether the Iroqua would attack his forces from the side or run on past to spread death in the city, Marcellinus could not tell. That would have to wait.

A dozen Catanwakuwa flew over him, some firing arrows into the Iroqua horde and others tossing pots of liquid flame to break up the charge. They looped back quickly—no pilot would risk coming to ground behind enemy lines and being carved into bloody meat a moment later—but behind them came another wave of Hawks. High above them all, four Catanwakuwa wheeled and fluttered, sending aerial intelligence down to the Hawk clan members who stood behind Marcellinus, ready to brief him on significant developments. If there was any time for that. At present, there was not.

"Third rank, step forward. Second rank: set pila, fill in!"

The line of men with spears stepped in front of their comrades. A wall of spears dropped into place in close order in front of the rushing Iroqua warriors, many of whom were now hurling spears of their own. Even at a run their aim was sure, and many a Cahokian fell, his place in the rank immediately taken by the man or woman behind. But their Roman breastplates and greaves had mostly kept them safe. So far, Cahokian losses were minimal.

"Well," said Marcellinus, startled. For the Iroqua were not attempting to engage the Cahokian spear wall. Instead, they swung away after flinging their spears and ran back to regroup.

On the edges of his army, auxiliaries were going down. There the Iroqua front line was pushing back the Cahokians. The battle line was bending.

"Merda." His right flank was about to break. Marcellinus signaled to the message keepers behind him. They in turn signaled up to the Hawks wheeling in the air above, one of which broke off and streaked back toward Cahokia. And so the message was sent back: another Wakinyan assault—now—to the right.

The first Thunderbird had reached the farthest extent of its run, off to the east of the battlefield. Marcellinus watched it turn, guessing it had enough height for only a short pass along the Iroqua battle line before it would have to steer back over Cahokian territory. Probably it would not make it even as far as Marcellinus. That would have to be good enough. Perhaps it could still sow enough confusion in the eastern Iroqua flank to Marcellinus's left that the Cahokian auxiliaries could do something about the Iroqua who were now past them and racing into the city.

"Second rank, arrows!"

If the Iroqua would not engage his front line, then his second line should be peppering them with arrows—

Marcellinus had almost looked away when it happened. The flutter of a bizarre movement pulled his eyes back.

The first Thunderbird flipped upward as if it had suddenly transformed into a sparrow. It gave a shudder and skidded violently in the air. As its giant wings folded up altogether, it crashed to the ground.

Time stood still. The deafening howls of the warriors of both sides dipped in shock.

Something hard and fast flew toward Marcellinus, and he instinctively ducked. It slammed into a house fifty feet behind him. Wood, thatch, and soil exploded into the air, but there was no fire: this was a rock, pure and simple, a giant rock that bounced out of the wrecked house and rolled farther into the city.

A rock that could only have been fired from an onager. Either the Iroqua had already captured a Cahokian throwing engine or they had built one of their own after the Cahokian model. But an onager could never have brought down a Wakinyan, especially from such a distance, and could not have been reloaded so quickly.

Somewhere in front of Marcellinus was an Iroqua ballista as well, and unless the shot that had brought down the Wakinyan had been uncanny beginner's luck, they could use it with devastating accuracy.

Once again everything had changed.

Where were they? Where were the Iroqua siege engines?

Marcellinus faced the line of battle again. The Iroqua were falling into a more compact formation, their battle chant swelling. Far to Marcellinus's left the Cahokian auxiliaries had broken and were fleeing into the city, pursued by Iroqua war bands. The shock of seeing the sacred Wakinyan tumble out of the sky had already taken its toll.

The effect on the Hawks was equally dramatic. As one, they banked back toward the Cahokian line as if they, too, could be magically swatted out of the air. In front of Marcellinus, a shiver went through the First Cahokian.

"Stand firm!" he cried. "Stand firm!" But the Iroqua chant was drowning him out.

Another large rock smashed into the Cahokian line not forty yards to his right, bowling men like skittles.

Damn! Whose side were the gods on today?

Not Marcellinus's, obviously. But perhaps that was understandable.

He strode into the ranks of the First Cahokian, still shouting. "Stand firm! Arrows!"

Too late. The massed Iroqua were charging.

"Set spears! Set pila!"

Training paid off. Few of his men could hear him, but the archers were stepping back anyway in an orderly fashion, to be replaced with the pila men. A forest of wood and steel again dropped down in front of the First Cahokian.

This time, the charging Iroqua hit the wall.

Some enemy warriors, unable to control their berserk run, spitted themselves on the Roman spears. Most, nimble and unencumbered with armor, swerved past the waiting spear points and swung their clubs and axes at the Cahokians behind.

The Cahokians had steel on their side, in their discipline as well as their armor. The Iroqua had momentum, numbers, and a species of wild anger that Marcellinus had rarely witnessed. The Iroqua could have been the Huns or Magyars of years gone by. Their ferocity was daunting, and the Cahokian line had been dragged dangerously thin.

"Cahokia!" Marcellinus stepped forward, his height and reach serving him well, and swung his gladius blade into the neck of a Seneca brave. Blood spurted, and the Seneca's head lolled to one side. His ax flew into the air.

A hand grasped Marcellinus's shoulder, and he wheeled, almost lunging again with his gladius. But it was a Cahokian who held him, one of the men tasked with keeping his chariot nearby.

"Back," the warrior said. "You not fight."

"Back be damned!" Marcellinus threw off the warrior's hand and strode behind the Cahokian ranks. The clamor of battle filled his ears. An Iroqua spear flew past his head.

Not fight? Great Sun Man's order, perhaps?

Marcellinus could no longer see Akecheta and could no longer relay his commands along the battle line anyway. His centurion would be in the thick of it by now, as incapable of giving sensible orders as Marcellinus. The melee would play out without further direction.

The second Thunderbird had reached the right flank of the Cahokian army, but battle there had been joined long since. The bird's path seemed tentative to Marcellinus, not penetrating deeply enough into enemy lines. "Farther on!" he shouted at it ineffectually, but it was already retreating back over the Cahokian lines.

On his left flank the Iroqua were still rolling up the Cahokians. The death toll among his auxiliaries must be horrific. The trickle of Iroqua surging past his line and into the city had turned into a flood. Marcellinus's fear had been that they would curl around to attack his army from the rear, but clearly they had other intentions.

A single bolt from a single siege engine had turned the tide of the battle against them. No further rocks came from the unseen onager, nothing from the Iroqua ballista.

At least the Cahokian center was holding. The Haudenosaunee had not yet broken the First Cahokian. But his braves were going down right and left.

From behind him, screams. He risked a glance back over his shoulder—his honor guard was looking, too—and saw a Cahokian woman being dragged by her hair by a man in the headdress of a Mohawk, not fifty yards away. And through the dust and the smoke Marcellinus saw more figures beyond the Mohawk, running through the streets of Cahokia. Great gods, they were still at battle on two fronts and the Iroqua were already sacking the city . . .

The warriors Great Sun Man had left behind to guard the Great Mound, Wahchintonka's men, would not come out to protect the people. They would stay at the palisade of the mound, as they had been ordered.

To Marcellinus's left the Cahokian auxiliaries were in rout, but by some miracle the Cahokians on the right flank had apparently overcome their Iroqua foes, for now they ran in to lend aid against the central Iroqua. Marcellinus could not fathom it. The Iroqua forces had seemed so much denser at that end of the battle line. But a moment later he saw the reason: those right-flank Iroqua had disengaged and were running back toward the trees, firing arrows back over their shoulders.

Not a miracle, then, but a strategy. This was no retreat. The auxiliaries now whooping and pounding into the fray in front of him had not defeated their section of the enemy. This was a planned withdrawal; the Haudenosaunee were ducking away, perhaps called off to fight to the west, where oily clouds still drifted across from the Mizipi.

Marcellinus would not let them all escape. "Forward! March and slay! Hold your line!"

In front of him the arriving Cahokians had turned the tide of battle, and the Iroqua were in genuine trouble. Marcellinus marched his men forward with pilum and sword while the archers in the third rank fired over their heads at the retreating Iroqua.

"Don't chase after them! No run! No run!"

Because that was obviously what the Iroqua wanted: to break the line, have the Cahokians storm after them to mop up, then turn and fight under much more equal terms. Marcellinus would not fall for that, and for the most part his men kept discipline.

Hawks whizzed by overhead. Marcellinus wiped sweat off his face. Was he missing anything? He wasn't. Many men were still locked in hand-to-hand combat, but by and large the action had broken here with startling swiftness.

And as with so many military engagements, it was impossible to tell who had won. In terms of sheer slaughter the edge had to lie with the Cahokians as a result of that first strafing run of liquid flame and their massed fusillades of arrows. But tactically, Marcellinus had a sour feeling that this part of the battle had gone as the Iroqua had planned and that whatever was happening even now to the west was of greater significance.

For all the signaling between the Hawks in the air and the men behind him, Marcellinus had not received a single piece of useful intelligence. Turning on them, he read their expressions in an instant. "Well? What the hell's going on?"

Eyes brimming with fear, they told him.

"Giant canoes on Mizipi. Another Iroqua army, three times this one. A battle. There too, the Iroqua throw stones and big arrows from throwing engines."

Marcellinus tried to control his breathing. "Big arrows" confirmed that the Iroqua had ballistas as well as the onager that had thrown the rocks so close to him. But: "Giant canoes?"

"Like houses that float on water. With broad walls. Ten, perhaps twelve, breathing fire. More fires behind them."

That made no sense. "Speak plainly. What are like houses? The canoes?"

The other warrior was still reading the hand-talk from the latest Catanwakuwa to fly in above them. "Great Sun Man sends his words. You must go to the Mizipi, Wanageeska. We must take you."

Giant canoes? More mighty stone-hurling engines? Marcellinus's mind whirled.

A hundred yards away Akecheta had reappeared and was already reforming the men into lines, glancing his way.

Somewhere in front of them, just a few hundred feet away, were at least two Iroqua throwing engines. It would be impossible for the Iroqua to carry them away at a run. They would have to either defend or abandon them. Marcellinus would rather capture them now than have them firing on Cahokians again later. He made three large, terse warrior-talk signals and pointed, and Akecheta nodded.

His centurion had this in hand. Marcellinus stepped up to the war cart. "All right, take me there. Get me to the Mizipi!"

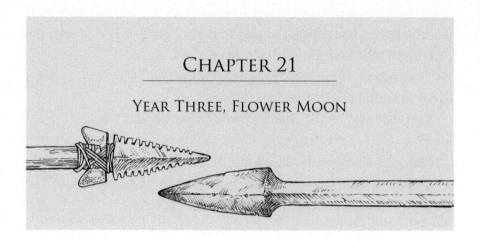

CHAPTER 21

YEAR THREE, FLOWER MOON

The war cart rocked and bounced across the streets of Cahokia. Two more warriors ran alongside the chariot, each carrying a spear in one hand and an ax in the other.

They passed a hut with its thatch ablaze; outside it, two Onida warriors hacked down a Cahokian. Marcellinus nocked an arrow and sent it into the heart of one of the Iroqua. The other yanked the Cahokian's body around to provide a living shield, his flint knife already hewing at the screaming man's forehead. Marcellinus's second arrow flew wide. The Iroqua grinned him a toothy smile as the cart rushed by.

"Go back!" Marcellinus shouted, but his warrior escort surged on grimly. In their wake, the Cahokian perished.

Fires were burning. Men and women ran in all directions. Chaos and panic had claimed the city. It was the same chilling scene that Marcellinus had experienced six hours earlier, except better lit.

Ahead of them a hundred Iroqua attacked the Master Mound, firing arrows at the defenders and shooting upward rather optimistically at the steady succession of Hawks that were being launched from behind it.

They swung around the mound to the right, bringing them under the covering fire of the Cahokian force, and ran through a gauntlet of Cahokian braves to the small protected side gate in the palisade.

Even as they bounced and bumped into the sanctum, the right wheel of the war cart twisted and locked in place. The chariot skidded and fell onto its right side, dumping Marcellinus out onto the ground.

He stood, legs shaking, just as the three warriors who had pulled the cart dropped to their hands and knees. They had run full out for three miles, towing him behind them.

Two men of the Hawk clan hurried to Marcellinus's side and pushed him forward. "What? No, wait . . ."

Again nobody paid him any heed. They hustled Marcellinus toward an Eagle, where another man and woman grabbed him and strapped him in under the right wing.

Terror threatened to consume him. Marcellinus had never flown an Eagle; they were still only half tested. Dangling under a Thunderbird as one of twelve crew members, even one of six or eight, he could do little damage. But aboard one of the much smaller Eagles, however much he tried to help the pilot, any error he made might bring the craft crashing down to the ground.

And besides, the Eagles were not fixed-wing craft like the Thunderbirds. They launched furled, like the Hawks.

But he could have escaped his fate only by doing grievous bodily harm to his fellow pilots, and it was too late now. The man lifted the woman into place while she fastened her own straps, and a warrior of the ground crew did the same for the man. The ground crewman did a quick check of all three of them and then shoved hard to send them over backward. The Eagle wing curled up around them, blocking out the light . . .

"Merda!" Things were moving much too quickly.

He forced himself to think. The woman was the lead pilot, and Marcellinus was under the right wing. So when the Eagle unfurled and when—if—the three of them managed to stabilize the thing, their next action would be an immediate right bank to take them west toward the Mizipi. That meant he would have to push his bar gently but steadily to the left . . .

Was the Sky Lantern still aloft? Which way was the wind blowing now? Where would its cable be? "Shit."

Unseen hands hoisted the Eagle. Marcellinus fought to breathe. The Eagle should be stable enough as long as he kept his wits about him . . . but perhaps it was a mercy that he could not see anything right now.

It felt like a mule had kicked him in the small of the back. His gut dropped away. They were falling free, airborne in an instant. The ball that was the Eagle rolled lightly in the air. Marcellinus heard himself wailing aloud and clamped down on his throat.

He was about to throw up. After that, he had no idea what would happen.

The wings unfurled. He dangled in space a thousand feet above Cahokia. The woman in the lead-pilot position let out a war whoop.

The Eagle's wings spread and locked. The craft swung level. A few inches in front of Marcellinus's chest was a wooden bar. He quickly followed the movements of his copilots, easing the bar to the left and shifting his weight. The wing billowed, and the Eagle jolted and slid sideways in the air. Too much?

No, just enough. The lead pilot straightened up, and Marcellinus did the same.

He could not tell whether the hissing rush in his ears was the air flowing past or the blood pounding in his head. His heart was beating too fast. He exhaled and tried to relax. After all, the idea of the Eagle, a craft midsize between the solo Hawk and the massive Thunderbird, had been his. He had only himself to blame.

The frame of the Eagle creaked alarmingly. In relaxing, Marcellinus had unwittingly pulled the bar closer to his chest and the Eagle's nose had tilted downward. The lead pilot beside him glared.

"Futete," Marcellinus muttered again, correcting his error. These things were so damned sensitive. "Merda, damn . . ."

The Master Mound was already a mile behind. To his left he could see the First Cahokian jogging north in formation; from this height they looked like a wave of silver. He hoped they would maintain discipline and sweep through the city, chasing out the Iroqua and preserving the lives of the Cahokian civilians who were still out in the open, unprotected.

As they flew over the plaza in western Cahokia, he saw the Cahokian siege engines still being hauled laboriously toward the river, the Catanwakuwa thrower out ahead of the others, as ordered. He hoped they would get there before the battle was over.

Then Marcellinus looked ahead to the Mizipi, and his jerk of surprise once again translated itself through the frame of the Eagle.

Nine Viking longships sailed up the river a scant half mile from the southernmost reaches of Cahokia.

Their carved dragon prows reared up over the waters; their square sails billowed. The decks of the longships bristled with warriors.

On the Mizipi's east bank, jogging to keep pace with the longships, was an immense Iroqua force of perhaps two thousand warriors.

Marcellinus blinked. The longships were no mirage. He saw sails, oars, rudders, even the gleam off the copper cauldron used for cooking.

Norse vessels, Viking longships, assisting an Iroqua attack. How was that even possible?

They soared over the massed ranks of the Cahokians. Even from this altitude Marcellinus could pick out Great Sun Man standing on the Mound of the Flowers overlooking his army, arrayed in his chiefly regalia. The Eagle's nose began to dip.

Before they landed, Marcellinus needed a better grasp of what was going on. Where there were Norsemen, there must also be Romans. Mustn't there? If so, as soon as he made it safely to terra firma, Marcellinus had to get out in front of the Cahokian army and try to talk to them.

Even if they just cut him down where he stood.

"Fly on!" he called out. "Fly over the giant canoes!"

The lead pilot grimaced over at him. "Too close!"

"We're high enough! Go fast! I have spoken!"

The Cahokians grunted and swung the Eagle into a shallow dive.

The longships grew in front of Marcellinus with astonishing swiftness. Vertigo gripped him, and he had to force himself not to lock rigid with fear. Racing toward the prow of an enemy ship was terrifying. His order had seemed reasonable when he had given it—they would have only this one chance to see down into the Norse ships—but by the time they swooped across the line of the leading vessels, they were only three hundred feet over the Mizipi.

He had only seconds to survey the Norse line. Leading the fleet upriver from him were three sleek, predatory fifty-oar longships, already using their oarsmen to turn broadside to fire arrows into the Cahokians on the bank. Before him was a drekar with a blood-red sail, one of the huge dragon ships that had struck terror into northern Europan coastlines for a hundred years until the Romans had brought the Norsemen to heel. Behind this drekar came another, then three agile thirty-two-oar Norse river raiders with yellow sails.

Yet another dragon ship sailed behind them to bring up the rear. In its wake came a swarm of tiny boats, genuine Iroqua war canoes.

The longships were stuffed to the gunwales with warriors. Marcellinus looked down into a sea of war paint and grim upturned faces. None were aiming their bows up at him. Rather, the men in the drekar were watching for liquid flame. Of course, the Eagle had none; it was too small to carry cargo as well as people. The enemies eyed each other balefully from their vertical distance.

From their skin color and clothing, the feathers in their hair, even the stance of the man at the rudder, it was clear that the ships were crewed solely by Hesperians.

No Norsemen. No Romans. Just Iroqua in Norse longships. Marcellinus did not know whether to feel relief or even more fear.

Moored in place in the center of the drekar's pine deck sat a siege engine, differently constructed from those of Roma or Cahokia but still easily recognizable as a ballista.

The Eagle looped around into a tight turn. Marcellinus half closed his eyes as his nausea rose. The curve was so steep that it looked for all the world as if they would slide straight into the water.

Marcellinus gulped. How the Iroqua had captured and mastered the Scandinavian vessels and brought them to the Mizipi: that could wait.

For now he just had to figure out how to defeat them.

"Enough," Marcellinus said. "Good. Land."

The order was superfluous. As they shot back across the Mizipi's east bank, the Eagle was dropping rapidly. Marcellinus's heart jumped into his mouth as they swooped over the Cahokian line, seemingly low enough for him to have kicked their feathered headdresses. He cried out in alarm when the pilot put the Eagle into a skidding turn just a few feet up; the ground skewed and leaped up at him. Marcellinus let go of the bar and threw his arms in front of his face.

They landed with a bang that Marcellinus could feel from his waist to his shoulders, transmitted through the frame of the Eagle. His pilot and copilot took the shock of it in their legs, grunting and swearing as they ran.

Belatedly Marcellinus kicked his feet free and helped run the Eagle to a standstill. All three of them dropped onto one knee, gasping, the pilot giving him a reproachful look while the other Cahokian ignored him completely.

Well, let them be as snooty as Roman litter bearers. Marcellinus had other things to concern himself with.

He fumbled with the straps that held him to the wing. The nearest warriors ran forward and helped lift the Eagle off their shoulders. His hands and knees quivered as he stood and got his bearings.

He was behind the Mound of the Flowers. The Cahokian army stood between him and the bank of the Mizipi.

After enduring all that, now he had to run up a mound? Yes. Of course.

Arriving on the flat top of the Mound of the Flowers, Marcellinus was startled by the magnificence of Great Sun Man's war finery. In addition to his woven battle kilt and chest armor, the leather greaves on his legs and arms, and the fine feathered eagle headdress, the war chief wore full face and body paint and the glinting copper earrings of his Long-Nosed God.

Still dizzy from the flight and his run up the mound, Marcellinus was swept by a feeling of unreality. "You didn't dress up like that to fight my army."

Great Sun Man pointed to the Mizipi and the dragon-prowed warships that sailed ever closer. "These are Romans? Your people?"

"No. They are Roman longships—I mean boats, giant war canoes—but they carry no Romans, no Norse, none of my people. The Iroqua captured them and learned how to sail them. And behind them, regular Iroqua war canoes gather like a swarm of bees."

"Just Iroqua?" Great Sun Man nodded in relief. "Then this is a good day."

"What?"

"A good day. A mighty day we will sing of to our children and their children. For today we kill every Iroqua brave among them."

" . . . All right."

"I had feared they were Romans. Iroqua more simple. We will kill and kill, and then we will sing."

"Let's fight first and talk of singing later." Marcellinus looked out toward the Mizipi and up and down the Cahokian ranks and forced himself to concentrate.

At last the fate of the Viking longships had been resolved. The Iroqua must have destroyed the Roman settlement at Chesapica, sunk the giant troop carriers, and stolen the longships. None had escaped to return across the Atlanticus to Roma. The news of the loss of the 33rd Hesperian had never made it back to Hadrianus.

And it was not only the Cahokians who could innovate. In the two years Marcellinus had been in Cahokia the Iroqua had made several giant leaps of their own. Far from foundering in the wake of Cahokian advances, the Iroqua had possessed leaders with the flexibility not only to see the future but to reach out and grasp it. They had spies to steal new ideas—throwing engines, siege tactics, organized military formations—and chiefs and craftsmen with the cunning to put those ideas into practice.

It was no more than the Cahokians had done. The initial ideas had come from Marcellinus, but the Cahokians had raced ahead of him, implementing and improving them. A people who could fly were not about to be bamboozled into superstitious terror by ships or onagers.

Once again Marcellinus had deeply underestimated the mental agility and skills of the Hesperians around him.

And as a result, they now had to face Viking warships on the Mizipi.

He tried to remember everything he knew about longships. It wasn't much. He had only been aboard one briefly, one of the smaller river raiders, when the Norsemen had shuttled him from the giant Roman troop ship to the shores of Nova Hesperia. Never in his career had Marcellinus had any cause to fight a longship. He knew nothing of their weak points and precious little about any sort of naval warfare.

"Great Sun Man, hear me. The Iroqua will shoot from the longships. The first two drekars—largest ships—each have throwing engines, ballistas, on board as well as their arrows and spears. The third ship may also. All of the longships have high sides lined with shields to protect their archers and oarsmen. Like floating palisades. You understand?"

"We can make holes, sink them?"

"Not today. In time we will think of a way, in case more come. But for today, their hulls are too hard."

"We can burn them?"

"The wood of Viking longships is treated against fire. Their hulls will not burn, nor their sails. But the men inside, Great Sun Man, their skins will burn. We should bomb them with the liquid fire anyway."

Soberly, Great Sun Man shook his head. "Already the Iroqua have shot down one of our Thunderbirds, at your battle. We cannot fly low to drop fire on them."

"Great Sun Man, they cannot have expected your Thunderbirds to even make it as far as the Great River. Until this year the Wakinyan did not have such a range. This year they do. In this, the advantage still rests with you."

"Not for long. And spies tell them, perhaps."

"But we should try anyway. For if they beat us back and their warriors land on Cahokian soil . . ."

"Yes, yes, yes. But for every Thunderbird that falls, the fighting heart goes from a thousand of my warriors. The Thunderbirds are more sacred than any man, more than even the memory of Ituha. If I fall, my warriors will just fight harder. But if another Thunderbird falls from the sky, they will panic, fearing that the gods oppose them. You understand?"

"Then let's not lose another bird," said Marcellinus.

"How?"

"Wait. Let me look." With an effort, Marcellinus tore his eyes away from the impossible longships and took in the rest of the battlefield.

To Marcellinus's military eye, from the raised perspective of the Mound of the Flowers, the story so far became clear in moments. The riverbank and the no-man's-land between the two armies was littered with broken bodies, not all of them dead yet. A battle had already taken place here, the battle Marcellinus had heard from a distance while waging his own. In their first assault the Iroqua had fought to capture the east bank or at least occupy the Cahokians while their companion Iroqua war bands on the west side of the Mizipi had stormed and subdued Cahokia-across-the-water. Now, with the far bank secure, the warships could sail up the river with impunity without risking attack from both sides. The next wave of Iroqua would combine bombardment from the floating castles of the longships with the ground assault of the giant Haudenosaunee army on land.

It was a good strategy. Already the Cahokians had been outmaneuvered. They faced an almost impossible battle.

"We must fall back," Marcellinus said.

"Back?" Great Sun Man was incredulous.

"Yes. If we stay here, we must defend against the ships on the river as well as the warriors from the south. If we withdraw to western Cahokia and hold the line there, the Iroqua must disembark the warriors and engines from the longships and form one army against us. A single battlefront. And the closer we can lure the Iroqua to the Great Mound, the better we can attack them from above with the Wakinyan. It will even up the battle."

"No."

"Great Sun Man, hear me. We have already lost the Mizipi."

"No. It is our river."

Marcellinus raised his eyebrows. "Today-now? It does not look like our river."

"The Iroqua shall not have the Mizipi," Great Sun Man said obstinately.

"Withdrawal is not cowardice, Great Sun Man. Why should the Iroqua choose a battleground to their liking? We should decide where we stand and fight!"

"And I have spoken. Wanageeska, I have lost one of Ituha's three Cahokias. I will not lose another. No retreat."

At last Marcellinus understood. Cahokia-across-the-water had fallen. Great Sun Man could not risk western Cahokia as well. And if they were forced back beyond western Cahokia, the sacred Circle of the Cedars would come within range of the Iroqua throwing engines. Any damage to that would be a further blow to Cahokian morale.

Marcellinus looked around, reassessing.

The second of the drekars rocked in the water as the warriors on board fired their siege engine. The bolt flew almost too quickly to be seen, but the swath of destruction it carved in the Cahokian line was clear. The braves on the first drekar were still struggling to load their throwing engine, their oarsmen swinging the boat to bring it to bear on the Cahokians, but Marcellinus knew their position on the Mound of the Flowers could soon come under fire. Nothing he could do about that; a ballista bolt would fly at them too quickly to be dodged.

Meanwhile, half a dozen Cahokian war canoes were racing across the water to engage the first three longships. He pointed. "Great Sun Man, order them back. Longships are too hard a target. We cannot throw away brave warriors like that."

Great Sun Man looked as if he wanted to push Marcellinus off the mound. "What? We must harry them. They are like a palisade. How else? Testudo?"

Suddenly, Marcellinus had the solution.

"No. Not testudo. Something even better. Instead of spending our warriors attacking their palisade, we'll bring Cahokia's palisade to them."

Marcellinus's face cracked into a ferocious grin.

The nine longships sailed upriver, floating forts that dealt death in surge after surge of burning arrows and ballista bolts. The Iroqua archers' bows were able to fire farther and harder than the Cahokian bows, but the Cahokians were partially protected with Roman armor and, for some, Roman shields.

Bolts from both drekars had come winging toward the Mound of the Flowers—one had even flown over it—but the moving, swaying longships proved to be a difficult platform from which to aim. Marcellinus thought it would be a lucky strike indeed if the Iroqua got their range.

Disregarding them, he looked along the ranks of the Cahokian army below him, which seethed and thirsted for battle. He and Great Sun Man had to keep order. If Cahokian discipline crumbled in the face of the Iroqua onslaught, the day was over and Cahokia would fall.

At long last the Cahokian siege engines arrived. The Catanwakuwa launcher remained behind the mound while a mob of Cahokians quickly manhandled an onager and a ballista alongside the Mound of the Flowers and a second ballista toward the Mound of the River. Ideally the throwing engines would have been brought to the crests of the mounds to enable a better view of the battlefield and longer range, but it was too late for that now.

Below Marcellinus, the nearer of the Cahokian throwing engines bucked. Almost without stopping to position it, its crew had fired the first rock. Through sheer luck it plunged into the river only a dozen feet away from the prow of the foremost Iroqua longship, and a cheer went up. Soon afterward, the second siege engine threw its bolt, which sailed high over the lead drekar's mast and plunged into the river a good hundred feet beyond.

Marcellinus ran down to assist them as they hurled rocks and bolts at the parade of longships. But these men were not Akecheta's crew, and the range of the longships proved difficult to get. Missile after missile flew over the Viking vessels or fell short. At least the giant splashes were regularly dousing the Iroqua archers with muddy river water.

Naturally, as soon as the throwing engines were in place, the Iroqua ground forces consolidated into a thrust to assault them. Most were beaten back by the massed Cahokians, but several hundred broke through to threaten their position.

Marcellinus was fighting alongside men he did not know, and the situation was too fluid to wait for instructions from Great Sun Man high on the mound above. He appointed centurions on the spot and divided men into ranks. His voice quickly became hoarse from shouting orders, but soon he had a solid wall of warriors in Roman armor four deep in front of the throwing engines to protect them, drumming their pila against their shields to deter the enemy, and an array of more lightly armored skirmishers with bows and Cahokian spears out to each side in support.

Many more Hawks soared into the air now, launching in quick succession from just a hundred yards behind him. Sintikala sped across the river a few hundred feet up, her Hawk skittering back and forth as she hurled pots of liquid flame into the trio of leading longships. Demothi and other birdmen swirled around her, less adept, firing arrows and throwing bombs and then dropping back to be launched again. Despite their altitude the arrows were coming dangerously close.

At last, there came a pair of Wakinyan, thundering downriver barely two hundred feet above the greasy water. Beneath each swung a full complement of twelve Cahokians and sacks full of incendiary. The leading three longships did their best to scatter, but the third was caught in a deluge of liquid flame from the leading Wakinyan.

The second bird disgorged its stream of liquid torment over the first of the drekars, but in a concerted effort the warriors on board had raised a wide swath of fabric over their heads to protect themselves. Marcellinus swore. More evidence of Iroqua intelligence and innovation: they were using the spare Viking sails, tough and fireproof, to protect themselves.

From the second drekar came a ballista bolt in an almost leisurely arc to punch a ragged hole through the right wing of the rearmost Thunderbird. The wing crumpled, and the Wakinyan went into a spinning cartwheel, plunging into the Mizipi moments later.

The Iroqua had clearly practiced this, their set piece and surely the prime reason for developing their own ballista: negating the Cahokian air advantage by blowing the Wakinyan out of the sky.

Again came that almost supernatural pause in the battle, and then the clamor of Iroqua chants struck up again and the enemy surged over the Cahokians with renewed vigor. In front of Marcellinus, the protective line cracked.

"Back!" His crew was struggling to roll another rock into the cup of the onager, but they would have no time to launch it. "Fall in! To me! To me! Close order!"

Seneca and Onondaga rushed toward them. Marcellinus bellowed and took three steps back onto the lowest slopes of the Mound of the Flowers. Around him, Cahokians nocked quick arrows and let them fly.

"Spears! Pila!"

They were not the First Cahokian, but they were quick enough in their own defense. The warriors formed a close line, shoulder to shoulder, spears and axes at the ready. Several paces backward up the mound gave them the advantage of height. "Second rank! Arrows!" They were doing it already, of course; Marcellinus was surrounded by men who knew how to fight, who had watched the First Cahokian and the Wolf Warriors for years and well knew the advantage of dropping into a tight formation under pressure.

They had lost the siege engines—the Iroqua now clambered over them and hacked at the throwing mechanisms to disable them. But they had not lost their lives. From halfway up the mound the Cahokians hurled spears and shot arrows, and from above them came further covering fire.

An onager ball thudded into the mound not twenty feet from him. Startled, Marcellinus glanced out over the river. The two drekars had turned broadside, and both were rocking back and forth in reaction to the firing of the Iroqua siege engines on their decks.

In the water there was no sign of the crew of the crashed Wakinyan. Marcellinus had no idea whether the other one had retained sufficient height or determination to make it back to the plaza in western Cahokia.

Looking closer, his heart sank. The Mound of the Flowers was almost completely surrounded, and a hundred yards away the Mound of the River had already been overrun by the Iroqua. Downriver, the third drekar was making for the bank unopposed; despite their size, the dragon ships were shallow draft, well capable of beaching.

At the foot of the mound below him, the Iroqua bayed like wolves. Presumably Great Sun Man still stood at the mound's crest.

The Iroqua were within arm's reach of capturing the paramount chief of Cahokia and Marcellinus himself.

Given Akecheta and the First Cahokian, Marcellinus might have consolidated the warriors on the mound into a dense column in close rank and attempted an eruptio, a sudden sortie to break out through the surrounding Iroqua and regroup with the main Cahokian force, which was pinned down several hundred yards away. As it was, all he could think to do was retreat to the highest ground—the mound top—and defend it for as long as possible.

"Stop shooting! No arrows! Don't throw your spears! Save them! No shoot!"

Gathering his wits, alert to every surge and ebb in the Iroqua line, Marcellinus did his best to manage their upward retreat.

As they regained the plateau of the Mound of the Flowers, Great Sun Man's Wolf Warrior general pointed. "Here it comes."

It had taken time, but it was worth waiting for.

From afar it appeared that a giant raft was adrift on the Great River, a floating island of wood several hundred yards wide, like the beard of an ancient god. Branches not yet shorn from the trunks jutted up, pointing toward the sky. A wooden wave sweeping toward the invading ships.

From the natural harbor north of Cahokia a thousand logs floated downriver, herded and guided by some braves in dugouts and others who walked fearlessly from tree to tree with wooden poles in their hands. An almost stately progression of tall oaks, pine, and hemlock swept inexorably toward the Iroqua fleet. The Cahokian palisade had arrived.

From their elevation on the high mound, Marcellinus and the other Cahokians saw it long before the enemy did. Then the Iroqua aboard the leading ships called the alarm, and pandemonium ensued.

The vanguard of the floating forest kissed the prow of the first long-ship. The tree trunks twisted and parted, spreading out on either side of the great Norse vessel as if daunted by the frown of the dragon at its prow. Logs flanked the ship, knocking the vessel askew and interfering with the efforts of the Iroqua oarsmen. The Cahokian log drivers and carpenters steering the trees ran back along the trunks, dived into the river, and swam to shore.

The full force of the barrage hit. Tall trees longer than the longships banged into them. The foremost ship listed to port, the cries of its warrior crew drifting clear across the water.

The Iroqua on the drekars had been slow to see the danger, as their view had been blocked by the ships ahead and their attention devoted to firing on the Cahokians onshore. Now they broke off the attack, their oarsmen jamming their oars desperately into the water to spin their vessels and flee from the incapacitating wood. Snared by the tree trunks, they would be immobilized at best, destroyed at worst. The smaller longships behind them veered toward the far bank of the Mizipi in an attempt to escape the path of the giant trees.

Now the true genius of the riverborne assault became evident: not just the relentless momentum of the wood but the traps hidden within it. For the Cahokians had jury-rigged their palisade with a few surprises for the Iroqua. Dugout canoes and birch-bark war canoes still floated amid the pristine trunks, and all carried cargos of Cahokian liquid fire.

Hawks flew overhead. With a succession of flame-tipped arrows, Sintikala and her clan sprang the trap. Gouts of fire shot up, exploding almost as high as the longships' masts, and quickly spread across the surface of the raft.

The blaze reached the first of the Norse longships. An explosion rocked both the leading longship and the one that came second. Even on the Mound of the Flowers, Marcellinus felt its warmth on his face.

In the time it took the Mizipi to flow a thousand feet, the threat of the Iroqua longships had been neutralized.

Below Marcellinus, the Iroqua land army faltered. Around him, warriors cheered. Great Sun Man stood nodding quietly.

Off in the Cahokian front line the war-party leaders shouted directions and spread orders by warrior-sign. Freed from the pinning fire from the boats, the main Cahokian army surged south toward the Mound of the Flowers. The Iroqua were falling back from the foot of the mound to regroup with their main force. Marcellinus allowed himself a single long exhalation.

"More warriors come."

Great Sun Man was right. Cahokian warriors marched in formation from the east; it was the First Cahokian under Akecheta. Even from here Marcellinus could see the tall figure of Mahkah in the second line, Takoda on the end of the third.

He squinted again at his First Cahokian warriors. Some of them appeared to have shrunk.

Tahtay and Dustu marched in the front line.

"Shit, shit." Marcellinus swallowed. "Sir? Great Sun Man?"

The war chief looked again and became very still.

"Sir. May I go and take command of the First Cahokian?"

"Yes." Great Sun Man's face was ashen as he looked down at the small marching figure of his son. He glanced quickly to the left and right. The Iroqua had dropped back and fallen in quickly, and already were advancing to engage the Cahokians. "Yes, quickly. Go now."

Marcellinus set off down the back of the Mound of the Flowers at a run.

He had misjudged the range of the Iroqua bows. Several arrows flew by his legs or thwocked into the ground at his feet as he danced across the hundred yards that separated him from the First Cahokian. He should have brought a shield. Fortunately, Akecheta saw him coming and commanded a wave of covering fire. Cahokian arrows flew over Marcellinus's head, and for a startling moment he thought he was being attacked from both sides.

As he made it to the First Cahokian, he stumbled and fell. It was Mikasi, Hanska's husband, who grabbed him and stood him upright.

"Thanks," Marcellinus said. "Akecheta!"

Nobody seemed more relieved than Akecheta to have him back in command. His centurion raised his spear to the skies in salute.

Dustu's face was calm, strong, and determined. Tahtay's eyes were wide, but he seemed no more distracted or panic-stricken than anyone else. Neither carried bows; indeed, only half the front rank did. Those who did, however, had arrows nocked.

Marcellinus glanced upward. The sun was a little past the meridian. His men had been fighting for more than half a day already. "Shit," he said again, almost an involuntary tic at this point.

No time to rest now, though. The Iroqua were coming. And Great Sun Man's son was under his protection.

"First Cahokian, fire! First Cahokian, trade!"

His second rank of archers stepped through to take their turn. Mercifully, Tahtay and Dustu passed back into the rear of the cohort, vanishing from Marcellinus's sight.

At last, an army that did exactly what it was told.

"Second rank, fire!"

Another wave of sleek arrows sped across the short distance that separated them from the Iroqua. Dozens of Iroqua warriors fell.

A Wakinyan soared overhead. Turning, it commenced a strafing run along the river.

"First Cahokian, spears!"

From behind, someone pushed a spear into Marcellinus's hand. Fair enough. He was, after all, now standing in the front rank.

The Iroqua advanced not at a charge but at a steady walk, keeping their wind, keeping eye contact with the Cahokians. Outnumbering the

First Cahokian three or four to one, they brandished spears, clubs, and axes and looked absolutely deadly.

It was time to get his gladius bloody again.

"First Cahokian," Gaius Publius Marcellinus roared. "Forward! Take scalps!"

The two lines joined, Iroqua facing Cahokians over a bristling forest of spears. The momentum was with the invaders, and the Cahokian battle line swayed. "Steady!" Marcellinus shouted. "Rear ranks, hold us!"

The men at the back hurled themselves forward to support their comrades. Irresistible forces collided. It became a shoving match. With blades.

Axes flew. The Iroqua were *throwing* them, a move Marcellinus had not seen since the Romans' first incursion onto Nova Hesperian soil, when the Powhatani had tried it. The Powhatani axes—tomahawks—had not deterred the Romans in the slightest, but the Iroqua ax blades were of iron rather than stone and carried a keen edge, and the center of the Cahokian line wavered.

Marcellinus shouted in frustration, dangerously distracting the men closest to him.

The hacking began. Iroqua pulled at the spears of their enemy and hauled themselves up to swing at the Cahokians with swords and clubs. Three braves in the center of the Cahokian line—who were they? who?—had gone down under the Iroqua axes, and the warriors in the Iroqua front line surged forward while their second rank fired arrows from a distance of a few feet, in between their own men, into the Cahokians. It was an insane tactic—the odds were high that they would shoot their own comrades in the back—but it worked. The center line of the Cahokians folded, and the First Cahokian became two halves.

Marcellinus glimpsed this only peripherally. The Iroqua were right up against his own line, and he was yanking and thrusting with his pilum along with the Cahokians on either side of him.

A Huron giant powered himself up onto the spear wall. His face and arms were bright red with war paint, his head bald aside from a roach of porcupine hair, and his eyes looked manic. The vivid scarifications on his flesh were only partially obscured by the wooden matting chest armor he wore. His ax swung down and cleaved the skull of the Cahokian two steps to Marcellinus's right, passing clear through into the man's shoulder.

The Huron's ferocious gaze turned to Marcellinus, and he raised his ax again. Relinquishing his hold on his spear, Marcellinus leaned back and tugged at his gladius, and an Iroqua arrow plinked off the side of his helmet. "Shit!"

The Huron's ax came down, and Marcellinus only just managed to get his sword over his head in time to deflect the killing blow. As best he could, jammed as he was between Cahokian warriors, Marcellinus stabbed at his attacker. The Huron knocked the blade aside with contemptuous ease and was gone, almost falling into a new gap in the line beyond Marcellinus's reach. The Cahokian warrior the Huron had just killed was still standing, held in place by the crush of bodies. Blood sprayed over Marcellinus's breastplate.

Cahokians shoved forward. Marcellinus snatched another glance along the line of melee. Would the line hold? Where the hell was Tahtay?

There he was, forty feet away and still alive, and his gladius was up and stabbing. The crush of the melee eased. But now two more Iroqua sighted Marcellinus and threw themselves at him, screaming their war cries.

"Hotah, left!" came Mahkah's shout from behind him, and Marcellinus gratefully lashed out at the leftmost of his two attackers. Mahkah's spear parried the ax carried by the Iroqua to the right, and then Marcellinus was fighting for his life at close quarters with a Caiuga brave.

Fury swept him, that welcome battle fury that cast all fears from his mind. All distractions melted away. It was time to kill, and kill he did.

The Caiuga fell. Another took his place. Marcellinus hacked and twisted and hacked again. The red haze of battle surrounded him.

Panting, he saw that Mahkah had won his battle, too. "Come!" Marcellinus shouted, but he did not wait to see whether the tall warrior would follow.

He pressed on. His world was axes and limbs and spears. Blood dripped from his arms, none of it yet his own. The gladius had been knocked from his hand long before, and he had grabbed up an ax, then that ax had lodged in an Iroqua rib cage, and he had stumbled forward and plucked another sword from the hand of a dead Cahokian and swept it up and moved to the side again, still facing his foes. The swarm of Iroqua kept coming and coming, but always Marcellinus moved the same way, crabbing leftward across the line of battle with the sun in his face, toward where he had last glimpsed Tahtay.

Then conscious thought returned, because Tahtay was in front of him, now fighting bizarrely with a spear in each hand, using them to stab and shove and hold Iroqua at bay. It would not have worked for a full-grown man, but the Iroqua mostly swerved around and past the boy because of his extreme youth, a mercy even in the desperate heat of battle that Marcellinus understood. The Iroqua had boys fighting in their ranks, too, and mostly the Cahokians were striking them with the flats of their blades.

"Give me your back," Marcellinus gasped; he had been out of breath for an hour, it seemed. Iroqua warriors surrounded them, and Tahtay did not respond, simply dropped one of the pila and seized a sword from the ground, and Marcellinus swung his gladius, and man and boy stood in battle back to back, fighting, panting.

Suddenly the pressure behind Marcellinus vanished as Tahtay was plucked away. Tahtay *leaped* four feet in the air as if he were taking wing, but no; he had been scooped up, swept into the air by a titanic blow to his thigh. It was the giant Huron whom Marcellinus had last seen at the far end of the line, now wielding a heavy club. Through the battle haze and bloodlust Marcellinus realized the Huron had been following him, hunting him down. He had been set the task of killing Marcellinus or had taken it upon himself, and it was this man who had just smashed Tahtay out of the way without a second thought.

Tahtay was down, knocked flying and crashed back down to earth, screaming and writhing. The Huron stepped over him and came for Marcellinus.

Gladius in one hand, ax in the other, Marcellinus lunged. His ax met the Huron's club, and the heavier man prevailed. Marcellinus stumbled back.

Here came Hanska, hacking her way toward them, screaming at the top of her lungs not because she was in pain or distress but because it daunted her foes and gave her an edge. And from behind him Mahkah's cry came again. "Hotah, right!"

He leaped forward and right, and Mahkah came around him to the left, and the two of them fought the Huron with Tahtay lying crumpled at their feet, trying to keep the boy alive for just a few moments more . . .

Marcellinus never saw the blow that felled him.

His feet left the ground, and the weapons flew from his hands. His head filled with the grating shriek of wood and stone against metal; his eyes were seared by an almighty red flash that might have been liquid flame or a granary exploding, and then his mouth was full of bitter earth.

Intense pain gripped him, agony that came from everywhere and nowhere. This was death. He had not saved Tahtay, and death had come for him . . .

He was kneeling with no recollection of how he had raised himself up even that far. Blackness assailed him. He clawed at his face, trying to pull off the helmet that crushed and burned, but his limbs were separate creatures that would not obey. If Marcellinus had been instantly dismembered and crudely shoved back into one piece by the gods, the pain could not have been worse, his disorientation more intense.

He screamed. Someone pushed him back down onto the ground.

Now he could not move at all.

Noise came down around him, a curtain of helpless terror.

All at once he could see again. Above him was the twisted mess of his helmet, and behind it Takoda's face. The warrior had pulled the bent helmet off Marcellinus's head, freeing his skull from the terrible pressure. Blood and torn flesh dripped from the Roman steel.

Another hand waved in front of his face. It was Marcellinus's own. Terrified, he tried to turn from it, afraid his own body was attacking him.

The roaring abated, and the sounds of battle came flooding in. He was still gripped by intense pain, but his body was coming back under his control. Next to him lay Tahtay, now still, his legs oddly twisted. Above him stood three Cahokian warriors in a ring, facing outward: Takoda, Hanska, and Mahkah, fighting for their lives against the swarm of Iroqua that surrounded them.

Mahkah took a brutal blow to the shoulder from the massive Huron and fell onto one knee, half on top of Marcellinus and Tahtay, still fighting. Hanska lunged at the Huron with her gladius, and the warrior jumped back.

At last Marcellinus could move again. He rocked forward, braced himself on Mahkah's shoulder, and shoved himself upright to take Mahkah's place in the circle defending Tahtay.

Blood poured into the Roman's eyes, but he could not even blink. Far above, even the sky was red. Nausea choked him, but he raised his sword to parry an Iroqua mace, then swung at the Caiuga who held it.

His vision blurred. Dancing and hacking and slashing, his Cahokian warriors were moving so quickly that he could no longer tell them apart.

And still, at his feet, Tahtay did not stir.

Rage filled Marcellinus. Where was the Huron? Where had the bastard gone? His head throbbed again in a wave of searing pain.

There. Coming in again from his left. Now that Marcellinus was up and fighting again, the Huron was cutting a swath toward him once more.

Despite his dizziness and pain, Marcellinus stepped forward to meet the Huron's charge. Sword met club, but this time Marcellinus threw himself to the side so that his blade skidded down the club's blood-slickened wooden haft to slice into the Huron's wrist. At the same time, the warrior's shoulder barged him, knocking him backward. Marcellinus stumbled and almost fell, slamming back into Takoda.

The Huron's roar mingled in the air with Hanska's battle scream as she came running in to defend them, gladius whirling. But Marcellinus was quicker as he thrust his sword deep into the Huron's gut, twisted, and shoved again with all his might.

The Huron crashed to the ground, bleeding from his stomach and arm, but still he kicked out at Marcellinus, grabbing for his ax with his other hand. Marcellinus stepped aside, picked up the Huron's club with both hands, and brought it down in a heavy blow on the man's chest armor, crushing his ribs and driving splintered wood and bone deep into his heart. With agony contorting his face, the Huron died.

Marcellinus gulped air into his lungs and swayed. His own blood still flowed down his cheeks like tears. But around him was still the din of battle. He let the Huron's club slip out of his fingers, picked up a gladius, and stepped back to stand over Tahtay and Mahkah, with Hanska to his left and Takoda to his right.

Then more Iroqua warriors surged forward toward them, and once again they were fighting for their lives.

CHAPTER 22

YEAR THREE, FLOWER MOON

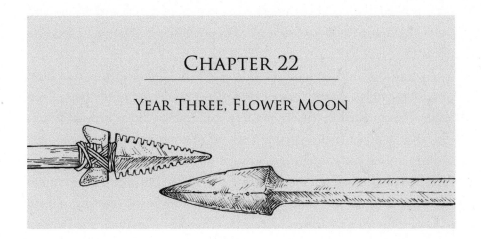

By late afternoon the Cahokians had pushed the Iroqua forces back to the Mizipi, and the enemy retreated before nightfall. They had wrought their damage, dealt their humiliating blow. Fighting on for a second day to try to occupy the Great City and besiege the Master Mound would have been too costly; it was enough to bring the great mound-builder city to its knees and slay the cream of its warriors.

As the Haudenosaunee withdrew, they took with them Cahokian women and children, Roman arms and armor, and many Cahokian scalps. They burned houses and canoes and grain stores, and then their army marched south down the riverbank alongside their five remaining Viking longships. The Cahokian midsummer devastation was over.

Cahokia-across-the-water was a wasteland of destruction and death. Some neighborhoods of western Cahokia were burned to rubble, with few houses left intact. Central Cahokia had suffered significant damage.

Cahokia got little sleep that night. The city was alive with lamps. People moved through the streets to haul away bodies, knock down and quench the smoldering houses. Many mourned their dead; a frail bitter keening lifted on the breeze until the whole city was a single animal, moaning in pain. Healers moved quietly through the streets to help where they could.

Dawn broke, and now it was the older women of the community

who walked the neighborhoods with bowls of gruel and beans and water, bringing food to friends, clan members, strangers, any who needed it.

Marcellinus, too, walked the streets. His head throbbed with a slow, unbearable pulse. At the crest of every wave of pain he nearly passed out again. He coughed up black bile. He could almost hear himself blinking. Overnight he had drifted in and out of consciousness, occasionally dozing, only to be brought awake again by his pain. Now in the early light he could not rest, could barely force himself to sit for longer than a few moments. Even while the First Cahokian was still fighting, a team of Great Sun Man's warriors had rushed from the Mound of the Flowers to claim Tahtay and bear him away. By their haste he knew the boy must be still alive, but where they had taken him, Marcellinus did not know.

Well after dawn, Marcellinus numbly followed the flow of people and found himself once again at the twin mounds on the south edge of the Great Plaza that Great Sun Man had brought him to months before.

The Mound of the Chiefs was open. The charnel house on top of the mound had been wrecked, smashed to splinters with clubs and then set aflame. A trench had been dug into the side of the mound, unearthing old bones that lay strewn on the ground where they had been thrown. An ancient feather cloak that once had lain in state in the tomb of one of Cahokia's venerated rulers had been shredded. Fine black and red pots and other grave goods were smashed. The arrowheads and weapons, of course, had been taken.

The Mound of the Hawks had been similarly desecrated, and beyond it the Mound of the Women. That mound Marcellinus did not even approach out of respect and fear.

The Iroqua had dug up the Cahokians' dead at their most sacred sites. The bones of the Cahokian ancestors had been plundered and defiled. The women the Iroqua had brutalized in life had been desecrated a second time in death.

No one attempted to tidy up the mess. The Cahokians preserved a respectful cordon around their mounds. Picking up the bones of their ancestors, purifying and reburying them, and reconsecrating the site would be tasks for another day and a most solemn ceremony.

Marcellinus turned away. These were not his ancestors. This was not for him.

In the East Plaza stood a corral of wood, hastily erected, surrounded by a contingent of Cahokian Wolf Warriors. Within the corral were several dozen Iroqua prisoners, many wounded and bloody, enemies who had not managed to escape from Cahokia and had been captured at the end of the day. They had started out defiant, but their resistance was shriveling from lack of food and water, their untreated wounds, and the grim inevitability of their fate.

They met his eyes, though. All these men knew of Marcellinus and recognized him. To the Iroqua, he was a strange and alien creature, his skin bizarrely tinted, his clothing freakish.

Marcellinus stepped up to the corral. He still had the sick headache, but he had no doubt that once he got over the corral fence he could slay many of these vicious barbarians with his bare hands before the Wolf Warriors could stop him.

"Gaius? Come away from the prisoners."

He turned. She was dirty and battered, the Hawk war paint around her eyes smeared, but she was alive. "Sisika."

She shook her head reprovingly, but when she reached up to his temple, her hand came away bloody. "You are hurt."

Marcellinus almost laughed but swayed dangerously instead. "A little."

"You should find a healer."

"It doesn't matter," he said. "Kimimela?"

"Kimimela and Enopay are not harmed."

He started to nod, but the pain and the ever-present blackness that lurked at his shoulder warned him to keep his head still.

"Tahtay . . ." he began, and then the lump that rose in his throat muted him.

Gently, she took his arm. "Come," she said.

In his fragility it took Marcellinus an age to climb the Mound of the Sun. Often he staggered and would have fallen if Sintikala had not held him up.

"Stop. Come no farther."

Great Sun Man stood at the brow of the mound. He wore his full regalia of office: the kilt in its blocky geometric patterns, the sash and feather cape, a necklace of wolf's teeth, heavy copper ear spools in the image of the Long-Nosed God.

Sintikala released him. Marcellinus swayed. "We . . . came to see Tahtay."

"The shaman is here. You will stay away."

"Shaman?" Marcellinus took another step or two up the long cedar stairs. "But Tahtay lives? He gets better?"

"He lives. Whether he gets better is in the hands of—" Great Sun Man made the hand-talk gesture that meant "gods" or "medicine." Fortunately, it was a one-handed gesture, since he held his heavy chert mace in the other.

Marcellinus eyed the mace warily. Perhaps he should find out more about Great Sun Man's gods, after all. It might help him understand the man, for surely he did not today.

"Have . . ." Emotion almost unmanned him, and he swallowed and tried again. "Have other healers seen Tahtay? Healers who are not shamans?"

"You may not ask."

"Great Sun Man . . ." Marcellinus spread his arms. "Let me come up and talk to you as a friend and as a man."

"No."

"Why not?"

"Because you came here leading an army against Cahokia."

Hardly the response Marcellinus had expected. "Uh . . . You knew of that before today."

"Because, after that battle between Romans and Cahokians, it was only my word that kept you from being bled and burned. Or strangled where you knelt, like your common warriors."

Marcellinus's fists clenched. "I had no common warriors. And this is old history, Great Sun Man, of many winters past."

"Left alive, you changed us. Instead of bringing warriors and death, you brought your Roman ideas. And gained the same result. Death."

"Great Sun Man—"

"I will tell you when you can speak again."

After a moment's pause, Marcellinus nodded.

Pitiless, Great Sun Man continued. "The steel you bring, the brick and the iron, the way of making war. All of those things. And so, a Mourning War with the Iroqua becomes a big war. A mound becomes a mountain. And today the ashes of Cahokia float down the Mizipi."

Marcellinus stared, unblinking.

"All on my word. I did not listen to my elders, or to my shamans, or to Ituha. I was blinded, my eyes filled with the things you brought to Cahokia."

"I will speak now," Marcellinus said tightly.

"You will not. Because Cahokia is ruined, and my son is crippled, and you? Even you are broken and useless and no longer worthy. So hear me, Wanageeska: your warriors are no longer your warriors. You will not lead, and you will not give training. You will live, but only because your death would bring sorrow to some of my people. They are foolish, but I will not wound their hearts further. But you will stay away from the First Cahokian, and from me, and from Tahtay."

If Marcellinus was exiled from all that he knew, he was as good as dead.

But Great Sun Man spoke the truth. Marcellinus had brought this upon them. The deaths of thousands of Cahokians and Iroqua. The sack and desecration of Cahokia. The maiming of Tahtay. All his improvements—bathing, steelmaking, teaching—paled into insignificance next to the evil he had wrought.

Besides, Marcellinus would not have argued back against an Imperator, and so he did not argue back against the war chief. Instead, he bowed.

He thought that that would be the end of it, that Great Sun Man would stalk away, but the chieftain said more. "Your longships that brought death to Cahokia. Your throwing engines that were used against us and brought our sacred Wakinyan tumbling out of the sky, your steel that brought the Iroqua here. That first night, when the war parties came and you fought them, I should have known that you had brought them, too. Before you, the Iroqua would never come so near. Our nations have fought before, many raids, but we were matched, we were equal. It is you who changed everything." Great Sun Man laughed, a spiteful sound. "But when Ituha speaks, I do not listen, because I think I know better. I think I am wise for walking among my people. I think I am wise, keeping an enemy of Cahokia alive. I think I am wise, but I am not wise."

Marcellinus broke his silence. "You are wise, and what you say is right. But I can—"

His head still bowed, he heard Great Sun Man step off the top of the mound and walk down toward him. Fear stopped his mouth then. Not fear of death, for Marcellinus did not fear death and never had. Rather, the callow fear that Great Sun Man would strike him on the head with the chert mace and that such a blow would drive him even further into pain and disgrace. Another blow to his skull might make a beggar of him, lying on a bed having to be fed and bathed, a burden to those around him. In comparison, death would be a blessing.

"Sorry," he said.

Great Sun Man stopped on the step above Marcellinus, looming over him. Marcellinus waited for the blow or the dismissal, or to be picked up bodily and thrown down the mound.

"Tahtay's skin no longer burns to the touch," Great Sun Man said. "He will live in shame, for his leg is still smashed and twisted. Tahtay will never be a warrior, never be a man. Now go down and do not come back."

"Thank you, sir," said Marcellinus. He wanted to say, *You are wrong, a twisted walk be damned, your son will always be a man*, but he had used up every fragment of his goodwill.

Instead he said, "I commend Akecheta and Mahkah to you. Akecheta, you have already seen as a bold leader. Mahkah is quick and canny in battle and thinks well on his feet. He fights nobly and selflessly. And he is a good judge of men; although young, he would have been my next centurion. Use both warriors well, I beg you. Use their bravery and skill. Do not neglect or waste them merely because they were friends of mine."

Dry-lipped and dry-eyed, Marcellinus turned to begin the long walk back down the Mound of the Sun.

"Stop," Sintikala told him.

Marcellinus stopped. In the intensity of his words with Great Sun Man, he had forgotten she still stood a few steps below.

Now she spoke past him to Great Sun Man. "Let the Wanageeska see Tahtay."

"Go away," the war chief said. "I have spoken."

"Please," said Sintikala. "Please, Mapiya."

The breath caught in Marcellinus's throat.

She had continued to speak after she had been dismissed. Mapiya must be Great Sun Man's true name, which Marcellinus had never heard.

He also had never heard Sintikala plead with anyone before.

Great Sun Man turned and walked up the steps. Marcellinus closed his eyes, overwhelmed. The moment expanded. The breeze blew cool on his neck.

From above, Great Sun Man said, "He may come up."

Taking his arm, Sintikala helped Marcellinus up the remaining stairs. Great Sun Man did not wait but strode on.

On the first terrace Tahtay lay on a mattress of twigs and straw out in the cool open air where the gods could look down upon him. He whimpered softly in delirium. The blankets that swathed his right thigh were dark and bloody.

Two women held Tahtay still and stopped him from dislodging his bandages. One was Chumanee, the healer. The other, from her features and the way she cried gently, could only be Tahtay's mother, Nipekala. Behind the rough bed the shaman, Youtin, murmured and shook a turtle-shell rattle.

Huyana, Great Sun Man's first wife, sat on the steps that led up to the peak of the mound with her head in her hands. Marcellinus remembered that Huyana was childless, perhaps making Tahtay the closest thing she had to a son.

Marcellinus hung back. He could do nothing for Tahtay, and he did not wish to disturb a mother's sorrow or a shaman's ritual. His presence could only distress Nipekala, who surely had to know how he had failed to protect her son.

"He will live," Sintikala said quietly. "He is calmer now."

Marcellinus knew of no legionary medicus who could assess a wounded man's chance of survival from twenty paces. She was guessing, and he tried not to hate her for the desperate hope her words gave him. "You'd better be right."

Sintikala placed her hand on his breast and tried to look up into his face. "You will not lose him."

Marcellinus could not meet her eye. "Take me away from here."

He had raised his voice, and both Chumanee and Youtin glanced around. The shaman made the whisking motion with his hand that he often made on seeing the Roman; whether it was a gesture of dismissal or some attempt to avert the evil eye, Marcellinus had never bothered to find out. But surges of anger and nausea rocked him, and Sintikala grabbed him again. "Come."

In holding Marcellinus up she had jolted him, and the pain in his head and spine was excruciating. He sagged onto her and managed not to cry out only by biting his tongue.

Sintikala pushed back. "Gaius? Stand up."

"Let me die."

"Do not be stupid. Come. You must rest."

He stood upright, his hand on her shoulder. Once again Chumanee, Youtin, and Nipekala had their attention focused on Tahtay. Only Huyana watched Marcellinus and Sintikala as they stepped back off the plateau onto the endless stairs.

CHAPTER 23

YEAR THREE, FLOWER MOON

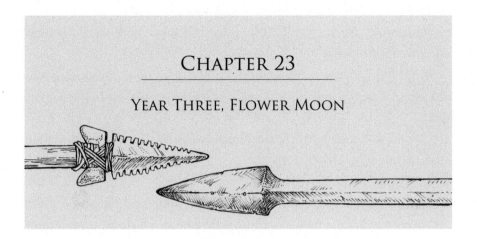

In the morning light, Enopay walked in the wreckage with his bark and his charcoal, a child amid devastation.

Not so long ago Tahtay had held his hands over Enopay's eyes to shield him from the horrors of war. Now Tahtay lay on the Mound of the Sun, struggling to live, while Enopay walked the battlefield and wrote down the names of the dead.

This time no one had come to bring Marcellinus food in the dawn, but once again he had felt compelled to return to the killing fields. He had not known what to expect. He certainly had not expected a small boy to be performing a census of the slain.

He made a forlorn figure, walking alone among the fallen. Marcellinus's heart came a little closer to breaking. "Enopay."

The boy turned away and made another note on his bark.

"Enopay. Who said you must do this?"

"Nobody," Enopay said. "Leave me alone."

Within arm's reach, Marcellinus stopped, his hands by his sides. "I will help you, Enopay. Or I will do this instead. You should—"

"Do not tell me. Do not speak at all. Why are you still here?"

"I want to help," Marcellinus said. "I want to make this right."

"Giving orders, you are a big man. When there is work to be done burying the dead, where are you? Nowhere. Always you fall down."

The breeze felt cool on Marcellinus's forehead and neck.

"Go away," Enopay said. "Go away and make another clever new thing we do not need in Cahokia, so more of us can die."

Bitter phlegm rose in Marcellinus's throat. He could not speak, could not move. Enopay walked on, looking about him and scribbling on his bark.

"I will make this right," Marcellinus said again, more to himself than to the boy.

As the sun set the next day, Great Sun Man addressed his people from the top of the Master Mound. From where he stood alone, several hundred yards away on the edge of the Great Plaza, Marcellinus could barely see the paramount chief, but through luck or good design he could hear the man's words clearly.

Understanding was harder to come by. In his polemic, Great Sun Man invoked gods and mythologies with which Marcellinus had only a glancing familiarity. The chief told his people how boldly they had fought against the Iroqua, and drew parallels with a story about the folk hero, Red Horn, that Marcellinus did not know, at which point everyone cheered so loudly that he had to look off to the side to watch the hand-talkers who were relaying the chief's words back through the crowd. He supposed it was the equivalent of a Roman Imperator giving a speech to the legions assembled in the Campus Martius before a campaign, invoking the battles of Julius Caesar and Trajan.

Great Sun Man came back to reality, and Marcellinus paid attention again. He knew enough about oration to know that the climax of the speech was coming. Besides, the rays of the sun were falling obliquely across the sand of the Great Plaza, the shadows enormous, and Marcellinus knew that Great Sun Man's speech would end exactly at sunset.

"The Iroqua have gone home for the winter to eat their corn and get fat and rest. The Iroqua think they have dealt us a heavy blow, but we will rise to our feet again. The Iroqua think they have won, but they have not won. Because after the winter, in the Grass Moon or the Planting Moon, Cahokia will take the Mourning War back to the Iroqua, and this time their rivers will run with blood and their mountains will wail. This time the Iroqua will be the people who mourn."

Marcellinus had barely slept the previous night, and his headaches continued unabated. If he slept as poorly tonight, he might as well volunteer to serve as a sentry. At least that way he would put his wakefulness to good use.

"Our Hawks patrol the lands to the north and east, mapping the land, learning where the Iroqua gather. We will send the stealthiest of our scouts deep into Iroqua territory. Soon I will send some of our great warriors down the Mizipi to demand that other mound-builder towns and villages ready their warriors in the springtime, in our time of need, to help us wipe away the stain of the Haudenosaunee from our lands and let us live in peace forever."

The small figure of Enopay stood on the Master Mound with Great Sun Man's shamans and battle chiefs. Akecheta was there, and Wahchintonka, and other strong men of the Wolf Warriors.

Sintikala was not there. She was leading the air patrols.

The shadows lengthened, and the golden rays of the setting sun sparkled like fire off the thatched roofs that remained unburned. Great Sun Man's rhetoric was coming to an end, and spread out before him the Cahokians rallied and cheered.

"We will take the Mourning War back to the Iroqua, and we will destroy them. We will come upon them from the air, and the rivers, and the land. We will burn them and scalp them; we will place our feet on their necks and drown them in their own Great Lakes. Once before, long ago, we pushed the Iroqua back from the Oyo. Now we must push them farther yet. This wide land cannot hold Cahokia and also the snakes of the Iroqua. I have spoken."

This was not the Great Sun Man Marcellinus had come to know. The battle had changed the chieftain. They were in new territory now.

"By the bones of my dead fathers and the broken bones of my living son, I promise to do this."

Marcellinus wondered how Tahtay felt about such a pledge.

But perhaps it was not so different from the speech he had made himself to the Fighting 33rd the evening they had discovered the burned and mutilated body of Thorkell Sigurdsson. In that speech Marcellinus had promised to "grind the redskins' bones to powder," and he might have invoked the memory of a long-ago Germanic slaughter or two to make his words resonate.

Great Sun Man would do what he must to save his people. As Marcellinus had tried to do for his legion and then for Cahokia, only to fail both times.

But while Marcellinus still breathed, he would keep fighting. For Enopay. For Kimimela and Tahtay, and all the Cahokians who had just died trying to protect their city, and those who wept for them.

It would not be easy. Marcellinus was no longer a leader. He was once again a man without a job, a foreign interloper in a giant metropolis, potentially as invisible as any cobbler or tanner or message runner on the streets of Subura. But he would think of something. He would do whatever it took.

Great Sun Man was a worthy chief, a man of immense strength and power. Marcellinus was sure Great Sun Man would work night and day to lead the Cahokians to victory the next year. He just hoped it would be enough.

EPILOGUE

YEAR THREE, HEAT MOON

The afternoon Great Sun Man and Enopay returned from Ocatan, Marcellinus was helping a party of Wolf Warriors raze a fire-gutted granary in Cahokia-across-the-water.

Oddly, in all the time Marcellinus had lived in the Great City he had never paddled across the Mizipi to visit the third Cahokia. By all accounts it had been a pleasant little township, a quiet colony of the larger and more rambunctious city. It had its own mounds, its own more human-scaled central plaza, even its own Big Warm House.

Cahokia-across-the-water had possessed a calm rhythm and an air of quiet contentment. People from central Cahokia had poked good-natured fun at their country cousins on the far bank in the same way they joked about the bumpkins of the upland villages. But nobody was laughing now.

Now Cahokia-across-the-water was a ghost town, wrecked and burned. Carrying away the bodies of the dead to the base of a new mound, pulling down the charred huts, destroying what remained of the town in order to rebuild it: this was hard, dirty, and thankless work, and it was where Marcellinus needed to be. Cahokia proper was regaining its spirit and determination; people had begun to smile again, if a little grimly. Humanity was returning. Hope and confidence were building. But Cahokia-across-the-water was a mortuary.

The canoes that had escorted the war chief home from Ocatan had peeled off for the east bank, but Great Sun Man, Wahchintonka and six other warriors, and Enopay had already pulled their canoe ashore and were striding toward them, Enopay as usual having to take an additional skipping step to keep up.

Marcellinus stood in silence. Great Sun Man passed him with a curt nod and went to clap the other men on the back, thanking them for their efforts. Enopay stopped and looked up at Marcellinus unblinking.

Tahtay still could not travel, could barely stand. Marcellinus wondered what he thought of his father taking Enopay on a weeklong journey downriver. "Hello, Enopay."

"Eyanosa. Why are you here?"

"There is work to be done, burying the dead," Marcellinus said with a straight face.

Enopay grimaced. "I am sorry for what I said."

"But you were right."

"You should rest your head. It is bleeding again."

Marcellinus did not reach up to touch his wound. His hands were filthy and blistered, caked in charcoal and ash. "I know."

The silence grew. To fill it, Marcellinus asked, "And how was Ocatan?"

"Hot. Even hotter than here." Enopay paused. "But not damaged. Not burned. Their women do not weep. In Ocatan, we could pretend this had not happened."

The massive army of the Iroqua had shot a few waves of arrows into Ocatan from their longships, lobbed liquid flame at its gate, and then passed it by. Cahokia had been their target, and they had barely broken step to swat at the smaller town.

So much for the fortress the Cahokians had designed to guard their southern reaches, where the rivers met.

"They will send us food, and wood, and strong men and women to help us rebuild. To feel less guilty."

Marcellinus grunted. He hoped that worked out better for the Ocatani than it was working for him.

"And when we avenge ourselves on the Iroqua, they will march by our side."

Great Sun Man had completed his tour of the workers, had cast an unhappy eye over the silent blackened remains of the town, and was heading back toward his canoe. Enopay shuffled his feet. "Also, I have something you wanted."

All Marcellinus wanted was peace and an end to his infernal headaches. "Oh?"

The boy dug into his pouch and held out a small copper figurine. It was a birdman amulet of a type sometimes worn by shamans, a flat plate the size of Marcellinus's thumb bearing the incised image of a winged Hawk warrior, complete with sharp-beaked mask.

"What of it?" Marcellinus rarely associated with shamans. He took it from Enopay and almost dropped it.

The amulet was not copper. Its weight left no doubt.

Marcellinus blinked and felt an emptiness yawn beneath his feet. Today was a day determined to roll back the calendar, strip away the years, and send his thoughts back to their roots.

Gold. The main reason he'd been sent to Nova Hesperia in the first place.

For gold, Marcellinus had marched a legion over a thousand miles into one of the deadliest wildernesses on earth. His first conversation with Sintikala had been about gold. In a way, Marcellinus had given his life for gold. His old life, anyway.

He had never found any. But Enopay had.

"Where?"

"I traded a sword and two shields for it in Ocatan. But it came up from the south, not long ago. From Shappa Ta'atan, maybe, or farther down the Mizipi."

Marcellinus had a sudden urge to throw it as hard as he could and watch it sink into the muddy waters of the Mizipi.

Enopay looked disappointed. "You are not happy?"

"There is gold in Nova Hesperia, after all," he said.

Shivers radiated up his spine. Somehow this golden amulet's very existence convinced Marcellinus that the Romans would return in force to pillage Nova Hesperia again, and soon.

The Romans would die for gold. And they would kill for it. They would stop at nothing to possess it.

He wondered how long he would have to wait.

ACKNOWLEDGMENTS

I'm sure all readers and writers of alternate history are aware of how key events in their own lives could have gone very, very differently. And so . . .

Huge, world-spanning gratitude to Dario Ciriello, who took a chance on my original novella, *A Clash of Eagles*, and published it in the *Panverse Two* anthology, which led to its winning the 2010 Sidewise Award for Alternate History. Sincere thanks to the Sidewise Award panel of Stephen Baxter, Evelyn Leeper, Kurt Sidaway, Jim Rittenhouse, Stuart Shiffman, and Steven H Silver, who paid me the awesome compliment of that award and helped to enable the next steps.

Sincere and devout thanks to the beta readers who soldiered heroically through the novel-length *Clash of Eagles* manuscript in its various incarnations and provided detailed and perceptive critiques. Karen Smale, Chris Cevasco, Peter Charron, Fiona Lehn, Galen Dara, Wendy Wagner, Darrin McGraw, Duncan Kuehn, Lisa May, Stephen Blount, Ed Rosick, Jim Strickland, and Carole Ann Moleti: you all went above and beyond the call of duty. I was lucky to have each and every one of you.

For feedback on the opening chapters I'd like to thank the members of Taos Toolbox 2011 not already named above: Christie Yant, Jeff Petersen, Jeff Duntemann, Sean Eret, Scott Hawkins, Lisa Morton, and instructors Walter Jon Williams and Nancy Kress. Go Dieselbears!

I am forever indebted to my agent, Caitlin Blasdell of Liza Dawson

Associates, for taking me on in the first place, for astute editing suggestions and business acumen, and for continuing sane guidance as I march forward on this epic trek.

My deepest gratitude also goes to my editor Mike Braff at Del Rey/Penguin Random House for his enthusiasm and good cheer, dedication, and keen story instincts.

Finally, my wife, Karen Smale, has served as first reader, proofreader, travel companion, angst wrangler, and my most essential cheerleader, and I can't thank her enough.

Of course, despite the earnest efforts of everyone named above to keep me flying straight, the responsibility for any errors or outright peculiarities that remain in *Clash of Eagles* rests solely with me.

Appendixes

APPENDIX I:
CAHOKIA AND THE MISSISSIPPIAN CULTURE

Many people are familiar with the Aztecs and the Maya and the other great civilizations of Mesoamerica. Far fewer seem to know of the thriving and extensive cultures of North America in the centuries before the arrival of European ships.

For over five hundred years the Mississippian civilization dominated the river valleys of eastern North America, building thousands of towns and villages along the Mississippi, the Ohio, and many other rivers. Like the Adena and Hopewell cultures before them, they built mounds by the tens of thousands: conical mounds, ridge mounds, and the distinctive square-sided, flat-topped platform mounds. In all likelihood the founding events of Mississippian culture took place in Cahokia and then radiated out across the continent.

In its heyday Cahokia was a huge city covering over five square miles, occupied by about 20,000 people and containing at least 120 mounds of packed earth and silty clay, many of them colossal. In the twelfth and early thirteenth centuries Cahokia was larger than London, and no city in northern America would be larger until the 1800s. Cahokia's skyline was dominated by the gigantic mound known today as Monks Mound, a thousand feet square at the base and a hundred feet high. Monks Mound had four terraces, and archeological data reveal that it was topped with a large wooden structure 105 feet long and 48 feet wide. This great earthwork and longhouse overlooked a Grand Plaza nearly fifty acres in area, meticulously positioned and leveled with sandy loam fill a foot deep. Cahokia's central 205 acres were protected by a bastioned palisade two miles long and constructed of some 20,000 logs, enclosing the Great Mound and Great Plaza and eighteen other mounds. The downtown area was surrounded by perhaps a dozen residential neighborhoods, some of which had their own plazas. Cahokia was bounded several miles to the west by the Mississippi and to the east by river bluffs of limestone and sandstone, and was surrounded by the floodplains of the American Bottom that allowed the cultivation of maize in vast fields to feed its population.

Much of Cahokia was built in a flurry of dedicated activity around A.D. 1050, but to this day nobody knows why or by whom. The city and its immense mounds are not claimed by any existing tribe or tradition, and no tales about the city's foundation or dissolution have been passed down through oral history. The Illini who lived in the area when white settlers arrived appeared to know little about the mounds and did not claim them or show much interest in them. However, archeologists and ethnographers are reasonably confident that the ancient Cahokians were Siouan-speaking, and I have gone along with that assumption in the Hesperian Trilogy.

We can, however, be certain that the original residents of the Great City did not call it Cahokia. "Cahokia" is actually the name of an Algonquian-speaking tribe that probably did not come to the area until several hundred years after the fall of the city. Nor did the Iroquois call themselves by that name. "Iroquois" is probably a French transliteration of an insulting Huron word for the Haudenosaunee. However, in this case and some others I have used familiar terms to avoid needless obscurity. For the river names, I may be on firmer ground (so to speak). The Mississippi and Missouri rivers are named from the French renderings of the original Algonquian or Siouan words, and the Ohio River was indeed "Oyo" to the Iroquois. "Chesapeake" and "Appalachia" have their roots in Algonquian words.

Even for names that are unambiguously Native American, it is sometimes not clear when those names started to be used. The individual names of the Five Nations of the Iroquois may not have been in wide use before A.D. 1500, although the ancestral Iroquois certainly had a strong cultural tradition by the 1200s and were building longhouses long before that. I also may have anticipated the foundation of the Haudenosaunee League by a few hundred years. Other aspects of the longhouse culture, along with their clothing and weaponry styles, are taken from the historical and archeological record. As far as the "hand-talk" is concerned, the Plains Sign Language did indeed become something of a lingua franca, though perhaps not as early or universally as I have postulated.

Otherwise, in writing *Clash of Eagles* I have tried my best to remain accurate to geographical and archeological ground truth. The size and layout of Cahokia are accurate for the period to the extent that the geography of the city and its environs has often not so subtly driven the plot. Every mound featured in the book exists, and I placed the Big Warm House and the brickworks and steelworks in open areas where there were no known mounds or buildings. The Circle of the Cedars corresponds to a monumental circle of up to sixty tall cedar marker posts designed as an early calendar, based on seasonal celestial alignments. The established large-scale agriculture and fishing, available natural resources, food types and weaponry, pottery and basketry, and so forth, are as accurate as I can make them. Granaries, houses, hearths, storage pits, and so on, all match current archeological findings. Chunkey was a real game. The clothing depicted is true to the times, including details of Great Sun Man's regalia and his copper ear spools of the Long-Nosed God; much of what later would become stereotypical Native American clothing, including large feather war bonnets and extensive beadwork, probably originated centuries after Cahokia.

We have much less detailed knowledge of the social structure of ancient Cahokia, and extrapolation can be dangerous. Although Hernando de Soto found strongly hierarchical chiefdoms with a complex caste system in his 1539–1543 expedition to southeastern areas at the tail end of the Mississippian era, it does not follow that those social systems were universal. In fact, in Cahokia's case the evidence may point the other way—to a heterarchy of diverse organizations within the city.

I have assumed a pragmatic, rather nonhierarchical structure for Cahokia rather than the superstitious and ritual-bound structures that some postulate for such societies.

Clearly, I have given the Hesperians credit for a few additional technological achievements. Native flying machines are unsupported by the archeological record, although because they are made of sticks, skins, and sinew and wrecked Catanwakuwa and Wakinyan are ceremonially dismantled and often burned, we might not find their remains even if they had existed. However, birds and flying were highly revered in the cultures of the Americas before the European invasion. Hawks, falcons, and thunderbirds were venerated and are central motifs observed throughout ancient American cultures. There is evidence for a falcon warrior ideology in Cahokia and also strong suggestions that the birdman cult originated in Cahokia before spreading across the Mississippian world. Feathered capes, birdmen, and falconoid symbolism abounded. Bird eyes, wings, and tails are extremely common iconography on pots, chunkey stones, and other items. In many Native American traditional stories, key figures are able to fly.

Catanwakuwa and Wakinyan may be a stretch, but oddly, I may be on slightly safer ground with the Sky Lanterns. Although this is speculative, it has been suggested that balloons may have been feasible for peoples of a Mississippian technology level. Julian Nott, a prominent figure in the modern ballooning movement, has pointed out that the people who created the Nazca lines in pre-Inca Peru had all the necessary technologies and materials to create balloons. To prove his point he has constructed and flown a hot air balloon with a bag consisting of 600 pounds of cotton fabric made in the pre-Columbian style, launched and powered by burning logs, with a gondola constructed of wood and reeds. For the Cahokians, the cotton would have been the key. Cotton grows only weakly in Illinois north of the Ohio River and can be wiped out easily by frost, so realistically their cotton would have to be imported from the south. But since the Cahokian trading network extended to the Gulf of Mexico, this would have been at least possible.

The Mourning War is an authentic idea, with many historical examples of long-standing feuds and territorial disputes between native peoples of North America. Although there is no direct evidence of such a large-scale and pervasive feud between the Mississippian and Haudenosaunee nations, there is archeological support for an increase in the palisading of towns and villages from A.D. 1200 on in those cultures and also in Algonquian territory. Clearly, these peoples were not establishing such vigorous defenses just for fun. And although people nowadays tend to associate the practice of scalping with the colonial wars, it was in fact a form of violence frequently perpetrated long before the arrival of Europeans.

The Iroquois were noted for their competence in the lethal arts. However, there are no grounds for believing them responsible for the deaths of the Cahokian women buried in Mound 72 (the Mound of the Women), as Great Sun Man tells Marcellinus. In our world, those women probably perished as part of a home-grown ritualized killing. In reality the women may not even have been from Cahokia; their teeth and bones are more typical of people originating from the satellite towns and eating poorer diets.

Just in case there is any doubt, the People of the Hand include the ancestral Pueblo peoples at the tail end of the Great House culture centered in Chaco Canyon, and the People of the Sun are the postclassic Mayan culture. Both of these peoples—and others indigenous to the ancient Americas—will appear in future books.

Many of Cahokia's mounds still remain, and walking among them inspires awe. The Cahokia Mounds State Historic Site is just across the Mississippi from modern St. Louis, Missouri. It is well worth a visit and, failing that, can be investigated on the Web at www.cahokiamounds.org.

Appendix II: The Cahokian Year

The approximate correspondence between the Julian calendar and the Cahokian moons and festivals is as follows:

Januarius	Snow Moon
Februarius	Hunger Moon
Martius	Crow Moon
Liberalia	Spring Planting Festival
Aprilis	Grass Moon
Maius	Planting Moon
Junius	Flower Moon
Vestalia	Midsummer Feast
Julius	Heat Moon
Augustus	Thunder Moon
September	Hunting Moon
Sol Sistere	Harvest Festival
October	Falling Leaf Moon
November	Beaver Moon
December	Long Night Moon
Bruma	Midwinter Feast

In Cahokia, the exact dates of spring, midsummer, harvest, and midwinter are determined by the position of the sun on the horizon at sunrise and sunset, as measured from the Circle of the Cedars.

In order to maintain the alignment of the lunar cycles with the annual solar cycle, a thirteenth month is added into the Cahokian calendar every three years. This is the *Dancing Moon*. As its name implies, the Dancing Moon can be inserted into the Cahokian calendar at the most convenient time, as chosen by the shamans.

Other ceremonies and celebrations occur during the Cahokian year but are scheduled when the signs, time, and weather are right, at times that may appear arbitrary to the uninitiated.

APPENDIX III:
NOTES ON THE MILITARY OF THE ROMAN IMPERIUM IN A.D. 1218

After the death of Septimius Severus in A.D. 211, the bloody civil war between his sons Caracalla and Geta nearly destroyed the Imperium. No one then alive could have foreseen that that decadelong firestorm would forge a new, stronger Roma that would last another thousand years.

Once the turbulence subsided and the rebuilding began, Roma's new Imperator and Senate did their utmost to prevent such a calamity from ever happening again. A thoughtful and intelligent Imperator, Geta proposed a number of civil reforms designed to limit his own powers and those of his successors, and having lived in terror of the vicious and predatory Caracalla for the previous ten years, the Senate was only too happy to pass those reforms into law. By and large Geta succeeded in stabilizing the Imperium and returning it to its former greatness, but further military reforms were needed in the centuries that followed to prevent the Roman army from growing too strong and again playing a political role. Key to the successful preservation of the Pax Romana was deterring individual legions from aligning themselves with pretenders to the Imperial throne. This had the useful secondary effect of strengthening Roma's borders against the threats of barbarian invasion.

And so by A.D. 1218 the army has been reformed and streamlined while maintaining those elements which enabled Roma to establish a mighty Imperium in the first place. The legionary structure is largely intact, but mobility between ranks and the assignation of commanding officers is now almost entirely merit-based, reducing the opportunities for ambitious young consuls or governors to seize control of their local legions and mount a bid for the Imperial purple. Rather than being kept separate, legionaries and auxiliaries are combined within their cohorts and considered equal members of their units, reducing the risk of mutiny. Finally, officers and soldiers are now permitted to marry and to take leave between campaigns, and they receive sizable bonuses in money and land upon honorable retirement from the army.

APPENDIX IV:
GLOSSARY OF MILITARY TERMS FROM THE ROMAN IMPERIUM

A glossary of Roman terms, Latin translations, and military terminology appears below. Many aspects of Roman warfare have remained unchanged since classical times, but language does evolve, and in a few cases the meanings of words have migrated from their original usage in the Republic and the early Empire.

Aquila: The Eagle, the standard of a Roman legion. Often golden or gilded and carried proudly into battle; the loss of an Eagle is one of the greatest shames that can befall a legion.

Aquilifer: Eagle bearer; the legionary tasked with carrying the legion's standard into battle (plural: aquiliferi).

Auxiliaries: Noncitizen troops in the Roman army, drawn from peoples in the provinces of the Imperium. Career soldiers trained to the same standards as legionaries, they can expect to receive citizenship at the end of their twenty-five-year service. Originally kept in their own separate units, auxiliaries have now been integrated into the regular legionary cohorts.

Ballista: Siege engine; a tension- or spring-powered catapult that fires bolts, arrows, or other pointy missiles of wood and metal. Resembles a giant crossbow and often is mounted in a wooden frame or carried in a cart.

Basilica: Public building or hall used for business and legal matters, generally situated in or near the Forum.

Braccae: Celtic woolen trousers, held up with a drawstring.

Camp Prefect: Also known as praefectus castrorum. Third in command of a Roman legion, after the legate (Praetor) and the First Tribune. Often an enlisted man who has worked his way up through the ranks from centurion.

Campus Martius: Field of Mars; an area originally situated outside the walls of Roma and used for military training, parades, and triumphs, later absorbed into the city.

Cardo: Colloquial term for the wide main street oriented north-south in Roman cities, military fortresses, and marching camps (more formally known as the Via Praetoria/Via Decumana).

Castra: Military marching camp; temporary accommodation for a legion, often rebuilt each night on the march.

Centurion: Professional army officer in command of a century.

Century: Army company, ideally eighty to a hundred men.

Close order: Infantry formation, with men massed at a separation often as small as eighteen inches, making a phalanx or another close formation difficult to penetrate or break up.

Cohort: Tactical unit of a Roman legion; each cohort consists of six centuries. Sometimes the First Cohort in a legion is double-strength.

Consul: High-ranking civil official, annually elected during the times of the Roman Republic, appointed during the early Empire, and, after the civil reforms of Geta, now once again elected into office, but for a two-year term.

Contubernium: Squad of eight legionaries who serve together, bunk together in a single tent (in a castra) or building (in a fortress barracks), and often are disciplined together for infractions (plural: contubernia).

Cuneus: Literally, "wedge" or "pig's head"; dense military formation used to smash through an enemy's battle line or break through a gap.

Curia: Roman Senate House, assembly hall.

Dignitas: Dignity.

Eruptio: Literally "eruption"; sudden sally or sortie, unexpected military breakout.

Forum: Public square or plaza, often a marketplace.

Gens: Family; often used in a larger sense akin to a clan or tribe.

Gladius: Roman sword (plural: gladii).

Greek fire: Liquid incendiary, probably based on naphtha and/or sulfur, although the recipe was lost in Europa and is a closely guarded secret in Nova Hesperia.

Imperator: Emperor; Roman commander in chief.

Imperium: Empire; executive power, the sovereignty of the state.

Intervallum: Walkway or area just inside the exterior fortifications of a castra; in other words, the space between the ramparts and the blocks of tents.

Lares: Roman household gods, domestic deities, guardians of the hearth.

Legate: Senior commander of a legion, more completely known as legatus legionis. By the thirteenth century, "legate" and "Praetor" are synonymous.

Legion: Army unit of several thousand men consisting of ten cohorts, each of six centuries.

Legionary: Professional soldier in the Roman army. A Roman citizen, highly trained, who serves for twenty-five years.

Mare: Sea.

Medicus: Military doctor, field surgeon, or orderly.

Onager: Siege engine; torsion-powered, single-armed catapult that launches rocks or other nonpointy missiles. Literally translates to "wild ass" because of its bucking motion when fired. Often mounted in a square wooden frame.

Open order: Infantry formation, with soldiers in battle lines separated by up to six feet and often staggered, providing room to maneuver, shoot arrows, throw pila, or swing gladii and switch or change ranks.

Orbis: Literally, "circle"; a defensive military formation in the shape of a circle or square, adopted when under attack from a numerically superior force.

Patrician: Aristocratic, upper-class, or ruling-class Roman citizen.

Phalanx: Tight mass of heavy infantry in close order, moving and fighting as one.

Pilum: Roman heavy spear or javelin (plural: pila).

Pleb: Plebeian; ordinary Roman citizen, as distinct from patrician.

Praetor: Roman general, commander of a legion or of an entire army. In the Republic and early Empire the term was also used for some senior magistrates and consuls; the latter usage has died out by the time of Hadrianus III, and only legionary commanders are referred to as Praetors.

Praetorium: Praetor's tent within a castra or residence within a fortress, situated at the center of the encampment.

Pugio: Dagger carried by legionaries; Roman stabbing weapon.

Roma: The city of Roma, capital of the Roman Imperium, although often used as shorthand to mean the Imperium as a whole.

Senior Centurion: Also known as the primus pilus. The most experienced and highly valued centurion in the legion, he commands the first century within the First Cohort.

Sesterces: Silver coins, Roman currency.

Signifer: Standard-bearer; the legionary tasked with carrying a signum for a century (plural: signiferi).

Signum: A century's standard, usually consisting of a number of metal disks and other insignia mounted on a pole (plural: signa).

Subura: Notorious slum and red-light district within the Urbs Roma.

Testudo: Literally, "tortoise"; Roman infantry formation in which soldiers in close order protect themselves by holding shields over their heads and around them, enclosing them within a protective roof and wall of metal.

Tribune: Roman officer, midway in rank between the legion commander and his centurions. Originally a more generalized military staff officer; by A.D. 1218 the tribunes have administrative and operational responsibilities for specific cohorts within their legion.

Urbs: City.

Appendix V: Further Reading

If there are two books that have changed my life, they are Jared Diamond's *Guns, Germs, and Steel* and Charles C. Mann's *1491: New Revelations of the Americas before Columbus.* Although the genesis of all the ideas in *Clash of Eagles* is now hazy, these two books certainly primed my obsession with the pre-Columbian civilizations of North (and South) America. Then I read Timothy Pauketat's astonishing book *Ancient Cahokia and the Mississippians,* and I was well on my way. A partial list of books I have found useful in researching and writing the Cahokian and Native American aspects of *Clash of Eagles* would include the following:

Colin G. Calloway, *One Vast Winter Count: The Native American West before Lewis and Clark*, 2003.
W. P. Clark, *The Indian Sign Language*, 1885.
Thomas E. Emerson and R. Barry Lewis, *Cahokia and the Hinterlands: Middle Mississippian Cultures of the Midwest*, 1999.
Melvin L. Fowler, *The Cahokia Atlas: A Historical Atlas of Cahokia Archeology,* 1997.
Robert Hall, *An Archaeology of the Soul: North American Belief and Ritual*, 1997.
Michael Johnson and Richard Hook, *American Woodland Indians*, 1992.
Michael Johnson and Jonathan Smith, *Tribes of the Sioux Nation,* 2000.
Michael Johnson and Jonathan Smith, *Tribes of the Iroquois Confederacy,* 2003.
Barrie E. Kavasch, *Native Harvests: American Indian Wild Foods and Recipes*, 2005.
George R. Milner, *The Moundbuilders*, 2005.
Claudia Gellman Mink, *Cahokia, City of the Sun*, 1992.
Timothy R. Pauketat, *Ancient Cahokia and the Mississippians*, 2004.
Timothy R. Pauketat, *Chieftains and Other Archaeological Delusions*, 2007.
Timothy R. Pauketat, *Cahokia: Ancient America's Great City on the Mississippi*, 2009.
Timothy R. Pauketat, *An Archeology of the Cosmos: Rethinking Agency and Religion in Ancient America*, 2012.

Timothy R. Pauketat and Thomas E. Emerson, *Cahokia: Domination and Ideology in the Mississippian World*, 2000.

Daniel K. Richter, *Facing East from Indian Country*, 2001.

Robert Silverberg, *The Mound Builders*, 1968.

Dean Snow, *The Iroquois*, 1996.

David Hurst Thomas, *Exploring Ancient Native America: An Archeological Guide*, 1994.

W. Tomkins, *Indian Sign Language*, 1931.

Carl Waldman, *The Atlas of the North American Indian*, revised edition, 2000.

C. Keith Wilbur, *Indian Handicrafts*, 1990.

C. Keith Wilbur, *Woodland Indians*, 1995.

Ray A. Williamson, *Living the Sky: The Cosmos of the American Indian*, 1987.

The books I've read about ancient Rome and its personalities, military campaigns, artillery, and so forth, must number in the hundreds, but the ones I referred to most while writing *Clash of Eagles* include the following:

Alberto Angela, *A Day in the Life of Ancient Rome*, 2009.

Anthony R. Birley, *Septimius Severus: The African Emperor*, 1988.

Duncan B. Campbell and Brian Delf, *Greek and Roman Artillery 399 BC–AD 363*, 2003.

Lionel Casson, *Ships and Seamanship in the Ancient World*, 1971 and 1995.

Lionel Casson, *Travel in the Ancient World*, 1974.

Lionel Casson, *Everyday Life in Ancient Rome*, 1998.

Ross Cowan and Adam Hook, *Roman Battle Tactics 109 BC–AD 313*, 2007.

Ross Cowan and Sean O'Brogain, *Roman Legionary AD 69–161*, 2013.

F. R. Cowell, *Life in Ancient Rome*, 1961.

Keith Durham and Steve Noon, *Viking Longship*, 2002.

Nic Fields, Gerry Embleton, and Sam Embleton, *Roman Battle Tactics 390 BC–110 BC*, 2010.

Adrian Goldsworthy, *The Complete Roman Army*, 2003.

Adrian Goldsworthy, *How Rome Fell*, 2009.

John Keegan, *The Face of Battle*, 1976.

Kevin F. Kiley, *An Illustrated Encyclopedia of the Uniforms of the Roman World*, 2013.

Konstantin Nossov, *Ancient and Medieval Siege Weapons*, 2005.

Graham Sumner, *Roman Military Dress*, 2009.

John Warry, *Warfare in the Classical World*, 1995.

About the Author

Alan Smale grew up in Yorkshire, England, but now lives in the Washington, D.C., area. By day he works as a professional astronomer, studying black holes, neutron stars, and other bizarre celestial objects. However, too many family vacations at Hadrian's Wall in his formative years plus a couple of degrees from Oxford took their toll, steering his writing toward alternate, secret, and generally twisted history. He has sold numerous short stories to magazines, including *Asimov's* and *Realms of Fantasy*, and won the 2010 Sidewise Award for Best Short-Form Alternate History.

About the Type

This book was set in Garamond, a typeface originally designed by the Parisian type cutter Claude Garamond (c. 1500–61). This version of Garamond was modeled on a 1592 specimen sheet from the Egenolff-Berner foundry, which was produced from types assumed to have been brought to Frankfurt by the punch cutter Jacques Sabon (c. 1520–80).

Claude Garamond's distinguished romans and italics first appeared in *Opera Ciceronis* in 1543–44. The Garamond types are clear, open, and elegant.